RESOUNDING PRAISE FOR
NEW YORK TIMES BESTSELLING AUTHOR

SUSAN ELIZABETH PHILLIPS

"[HER] TRADEMARK . . . [IS] FUN ROMANCE WITH WITTY
BANTER AND CHARACTERS WHO WILL HAVE YOU
LAUGHING, CHEERING, AND PERHAPS EVEN CRYING A
BIT . . . [A] FABULOUS ROMANTIC STORY [IS] SOMETHING
YOU CAN COUNT ON WHEN PHILLIPS'S NAME IS ON IT."
COLUMBIA STATE

"PHILLIPS IS A MASTER OF HER CRAFT . . . FUNNY, SMART,
SATISFYING."
CONTRA COSTA TIMES

"SUSAN ELIZABETH PHILLIPS'S BESTSELLING NOVELS HAVE
HELPED TO GIVE ROMANCE FICTION SOMETHING IT
LONG DESERVED—RESPECTABILITY."
CHICAGO SUN-TIMES

"IF YOU THINK YOU CAN STOP READING PHILLIPS'S BOOKS
AT ONE, YOU PROBABLY THINK YOU CAN EAT ONLY TWO
BITES OF TRIPLE CHOCOLATE CHEESECAKE, TOO."
TORONTO STAR

"SHE MAKES YOU LAUGH, MAKES YOU CRY, MAKES YOU
FEEL GOOD."
JAYNE ANN KRENTZ

SUSAN ELIZABETH PHILLIPS

Nobody's Baby But Mine

AVON BOOKS
An Imprint of HarperCollinsPublishers

This is a work of fiction. Names, characters, places, and incidents are products of the author's imagination or are used fictitiously and are not to be construed as real. Any resemblance to actual events, locales, organizations, or persons, living or dead, is entirely coincidental.

AVON BOOKS
An Imprint of HarperCollins *Publishers*
10 East 53rd Street
New York, New York 10022-5299

Copyright © 1997 by Susan Elizabeth Phillips
Inside cover author photo by Ron Stewart Portraiture
Library of Congress Catalog Card Number: 96-96877
ISBN: 0-380-78234-0
www.avonromance.com

First Avon Books printing: February 1997

Avon Trademark Reg. U.S. Pat. Off. and in Other Countries, Marca Registrada, Hecho en U.S.A.
HarperCollins® is a trademark of HarperCollins Publishers Inc.

Printed in the U.S.A.

40 39 38 37 36 35 34 33

To my mother

1

"Let me get this straight," Jodie Pulanski said. "You want to give Cal Bonner a *woman* for a birthday present."

The three offensive linemen, who were spending the November evening sitting in the back booth at Zebras, the DuPage County sports bar favored by the Chicago Stars football players, all nodded at once.

Junior Duncan gestured toward the waitress for another round. "He's going to be thirty-six, so we wanted to make this extra special."

"Bull," Jodie said. Everybody who knew anything about football knew that Cal Bonner, the Stars' brilliant quarterback, had been demanding, temperamental, and generally impossible to get along with ever since the season started. Bonner, popularly known as the "Bomber" because of his fondness for throwing explosive passes, was the top-ranked quarterback in the AFC and a legend.

Jodie crossed her arms over the form-fitting white tank top that was part of her hostess uniform. It didn't occur to either her or any of the three men at the table to consider the moral dimensions of their discussion, let alone notions of political correctness. This was, after all, the NFL. "You

think if you get him a woman, he'll ease up on all of you,''
she said.

Willie Jarrell gazed down into his beer through a pair of
thickly-lashed dark brown eyes. ''Sonovabitch been kickin'
so much ass lately, nobody can stand being around him.''

Junior shook his head. ''Yesterday, he called Germaine
Clark a *debutante*. Germaine!''

Jodie lifted one eyebrow, which was penciled several
shades darker than her brassy blond hair. Germaine Clark
was All-Pro and one of the meanest defensive tackles in
the NFL. ''From what I've seen, the Bomber already has
more women than he knows what to do with.''

Junior nodded. ''Yeah, but, the thing of it is, he doesn't
seem to be sleepin' with any of them?''

''What?''

''It's true.'' Chris Plummer, the Stars' left guard spoke
up. ''We just found it out. His girlfriends have been talking
to some of the wives, and it seems Cal's not using them
for anything more than window dressing.''

Willie Jarrell spoke up. ''Maybe if he waited until they
were out of diapers, he could get turned on.''

Junior chose to take his remark seriously. ''Don't say
things like that, Willie. You know Cal won't date 'em till
they're twenty.''

Cal Bonner might be getting older, but the females in his
life weren't. No one could remember him dating anyone
over the age of twenty-two.

''Far as anybody knows,'' Willie said, ''the Bomber
hasn't slept with anybody since he broke up with Kelly,
and that was last February. It's not natural.''

Kelly Berkley had been Cal's beautiful twenty-one-year-
old companion until she'd gotten tired of waiting for a wedding ring that wasn't ever going to come and run off with
a twenty-three-year-old guitarist for a heavy metal band.
Since then, Cal Bonner had been concentrating on winning

football games, dating a new woman every week, and kicking his teammates' asses.

Jodie Pulanski was the Stars' favorite groupie, but although she hadn't yet turned twenty-three, none of the men suggested that she offer her own body as Cal Bonner's birthday present. It was a well-known fact he'd already rejected her at least a dozen times. That made the Bomber Public Enemy Number One on Jodie's personal hate list, even though she kept a collection of blue-and-gold Stars' jerseys in her bedroom closet, one jersey for every Stars player she'd slept with, and was always eager to add more.

"What we need is somebody who won't remind him of Kelly," Chris said.

"That means she needs to be real classy," Willie added. "And older. We think it would be good for the Bomber to try someone maybe twenty-five."

"Sort of dignified." Junior took a sip of beer. "One of those society types."

Jodie wasn't known for her brains, but even she could see the problem with that one. "I don't think too many society types are going to volunteer to be a man's birthday present. Not even Cal Bonner's."

"Yeah, that's what we was thinking, too, so we might have to use a hooker."

"But a real classy one," Willie said hastily, since everyone knew Cal didn't go for hookers.

Junior gazed glumly into his beer. "Problem is, we haven't been able to find one."

Jodie knew some hookers, but none of them were what she'd call classy. Neither were her friends. She ran with a group of hard-drinking, party-loving women, whose single goal in life was to sleep with as many professional athletes as they could. "What do you want from me?"

"We want you to use your connections and find somebody for him," Junior said. "His birthday's coming up in ten days, and we got to have a woman for him before then.''

''What's in it for me?''

Since all three of their jerseys already hung in her closet, they knew they'd have to go out on a limb. Chris spoke cautiously. ''You got a particular number you're interested in adding to your collection?''

''Other than number eighteen,'' Willie quickly interjected, eighteen being the Bomber's number.

Jodie thought about it. She'd rather screw over the Bomber than find him a woman. On the other hand, there was one particular number that she wanted real bad. ''As a matter of fact, I do. If I find your birthday present, number twelve's mine.''

The men groaned. ''Shit, Jodie, Kevin Tucker's got too many women as it is.''

''That's your problem.''

Tucker was the Stars' backup quarterback. Young, aggressive, and sublimely talented, he had been handpicked by the Stars to take over the starting position when age or injury prevented Cal from getting the job done. Although the two men were polite in public, both were fierce competitors, and they hated each other's guts, which made Kevin Tucker all the more desirable to Jodie.

The men grumbled, but eventually agreed that they'd make sure Tucker did his part if she found the right woman for Cal's birthday present.

Two new customers entered Zebras, and since Jodie was the bar's hostess, she got up to greet them. As she made her way to the door, she mentally sorted through her female acquaintances, trying to come up with one of them who would qualify, but she drew a blank. She had a lot of female friends, but not a single one of them was classy.

Two days later, Jodie was still mulling over the problem as she dragged her hangover into the kitchen of her parents' home in suburban Glen Ellyn, Illinois, where she was temporarily living until she got her Visa paid off. It was almost noon on Saturday, her parents were gone for the weekend, and she didn't have to be at work until five, which was a good thing because she needed time to recover from last night's partying.

She opened the cupboard door and saw nothing but a can of decaf. *Shit.* It was sleeting outside, and her head hurt too much to drive, but if she didn't have a quart of caffeine inside her by kickoff time, she wouldn't be able to enjoy the game.

Nothing was going right. The Stars were playing in Buffalo that afternoon, so she couldn't look forward to the players coming into Zebras after the game. And when she finally did see them, how was she going to break the news that she hadn't been able to find the birthday present? One of the reasons the Stars paid so much attention to her was because she could always get them women.

She gazed out the kitchen window and saw a light on at the geek's house next door. The geek was Jodie's private name for Dr. Jane Darlington, her parents' neighbor. She was a Ph.D. doctor, not a medical one, and Jodie's mom was always going on about what a wonderful person she was because she'd been helping the Pulanskis with mail and shit ever since they'd moved in a couple of years ago. Maybe she'd help Jodie out with some coffee.

She did a quick fix on her makeup and, without bothering to put on underwear, slipped into a pair of tight black jeans, Willie Jarrell's jersey, and her Frye boots. After grabbing one of her mother's Tupperware containers, she headed next door.

Despite the sleet, she hadn't bothered with a jacket, and by the time Dr. Jane got around to answering the bell, she was shivering. "Hi."

Dr. Jane stood on the other side of the storm door staring

at her through geeky, oversize glasses with tortoiseshell frames.

"I'm the Pulanskis' daughter Jodie. From next door."

Dr. Jane made no move to invite her inside.

"Listen, it's cold as hell out here. Can I come in?"

The geek finally pushed open the storm door and let her in. "I'm sorry. I didn't recognize you."

Jodie stepped inside, and it didn't take her more than two seconds to figure out why Dr. Jane hadn't been in any big hurry to admit her. The eyes behind the lenses were teary and her nose red. Unless Jodie was more hungover than she thought, Dr. Jane had been crying her nerdy little heart out.

The geek was tall, maybe five-eight, and Jodie had to look up as she extended the pink Tupperware container. "Can I bum a couple of scoops of coffee? There's nothing but decaf in the house, and I need something stronger."

Dr. Jane took the container, but she seemed to do it reluctantly. She didn't strike Jodie as the stingy type, so her reaction probably meant she wasn't in the mood for company. "Yes, I'll—uh—get you some." She turned away and headed for the kitchen, obviously expecting Jodie to wait where she was, but Jodie had a half hour to kill before the pregame show started, and she was curious enough to follow.

They passed through a living room that, at first glance, seemed pretty boring: off-white walls, comfortable furniture, boring-looking books everywhere. Jodie was getting ready to pass right through when the framed museum posters on the walls caught her attention. They all seemed to have been done by some lady named Georgia O'Keeffe, and Jodie knew she had a dirty mind, but she didn't think that explained why every one of the flowers looked like female sex organs.

She saw flowers with deep, dark hearts. Flowers with petals flopping over moist, secret centers. She saw—jeez.

It was a clamshell with this little wet pearl, and even somebody with the cleanest mind in the world would have to look twice at that one. She wondered if maybe the geek was a dike. Why else would she want to look at flower pussies every time she went into her living room?

Jodie wandered into the kitchen, which was pale lavender with pretty floral curtains hanging at the window, although these flowers were regular ones, not the X-rateds in the living-room paintings. Everything in the kitchen was cheery and cute except for the owner, who looked more dignified than God.

Dr. Jane was one of those neat, tweedy women. Her tailored slacks had small, tidy brown-and-black checks, and her soft, oatmeal-colored sweater looked like cashmere. Despite her height, she was small-boned, with well-proportioned legs and a slender waist. Jodie might have felt envious of her figure except for the fact that she had no boobs, or at least none to speak of.

Her hair was jaw-length—pale blond with streaks of flax, platinum, and gold that couldn't have come from a bottle. It was arranged in one of those conservative hairstyles that Jodie wouldn't have been caught dead in—brushed loosely back from her face and held in place with a narrow brown velvet clip-on headband.

She turned slightly so that Jodie got a better look. Too bad about those big, geeky glasses. They hid a nice set of green eyes. She had a good forehead and a decent nose, neither too big nor too small. Her mouth was sort of interesting, with a thin upper lip and a plump bottom one. And she had great skin. But she didn't seem to do much with herself. Jodie would have added a lot more makeup. All in all, the geek was a good-looking woman, but sort of intimidating, even with those red-rimmed eyes.

She put the lid on the Tupperware and held it out toward Jodie, who was just about to take it when she spotted the crumpled wrapping paper on the kitchen table and the small pile of gifts lying next to it.

"What's the occasion?"

"Nothing, really. It's my birthday." Her voice had an interesting huskiness to it, and for the first time Jodie noticed the tissues crumpled in her hand.

"Hey, no kidding. Happy birthday."

"Thank you."

Ignoring the Tupperware container in Dr. Jane's outstretched hand, Jodie walked over to the table and looked down at the assortment of presents: a puny little box of plain white stationary, an electric toothbrush, a pen, and a gift certificate for Jiffy Lube. Pathetic. Not a pair of crotchless panties or a sexy nightie in sight.

"Bummer."

To her surprise, Dr. Jane gave a short laugh. "You're right about that. My friend Caroline always comes through with the perfect gift, but she's on a dig in Ethiopia." And then, to Jodie's surprise, a tear skidded out from under her glasses and slipped down her cheek.

Dr. Jane stiffened, as if it hadn't happened, but the presents really were pathetic, and Jodie couldn't help but feel sorry for her. "Hey, it's not so bad. At least you don't have to worry about the sizes being wrong."

"I'm sorry. I shouldn't . . ." She stiffened her bottom lip, but another tear slid out from beneath her glasses.

"It's okay. Sit down, and I'll make us some coffee." She pushed Dr. Jane down into one of the kitchen chairs, then took the Tupperware container over to the counter where the coffeemaker sat. She started to ask Dr. J. where the filters were, but her forehead was all crumpled, and she seemed to be taking deep breaths, so Jodie opened a couple of cupboards until she found what she wanted and began making a fresh pot.

"So what birthday is it?"

"Thirty-four."

Jodie was surprised. She wouldn't have taken Dr. J. for any more than her late twenties. "Double bummer."

"I'm sorry to be carrying on like this." She dabbed her nose with a tissue. "I'm not usually so emotional."

A couple of tears was hardly Jodie's idea of "carrying on," but for such an uptight chick, this was probably big-time hysterical. "I said it's okay. You got any doughnuts or anything?"

"There are some whole wheat bran muffins in the freezer."

Jodie made a face and headed back to the table. It was small and round with a glass top and metal chairs that looked like they belonged in a garden. She sat across from Dr. Jane.

"Who gave you the presents?"

She tried to manage one of those smiles that held people at a distance. "My colleagues."

"You mean the people you work with?"

"Yes. My associates at Newberry, and one of my friends at Preeze Laboratories."

Jodie didn't know about Preeze Laboratories, but New-berry was one of the most la-de-da colleges in the United States, and everybody was always bragging about the fact that it was located right here in DuPage County.

"That's right. Don't you teach science or something?"

"I'm a physicist. I teach graduate classes in relativistic quantum field theory. I also have special funding through Preeze Labs that lets me investigate top quarks with other physicists."

"No shit. You must have been a real brain in high school."

"I didn't spend much time in high school. I started college when I was fourteen." One more tear trickled down her cheeks, but, if anything, she sat even straighter.

"Fourteen? Get out of here."

"By the time I was twenty, I had my Ph.D." Something

inside her seemed to give way. She set her elbows on the table, balled her hands into fists, and propped her forehead on top of them. Her shoulders trembled, but she made no noise, and the sight of this dignified woman coming all unraveled was so pathetic that Jodie couldn't help feeling sorry for her. She was also curious.

"You got troubles with your boyfriend?"

She kept her head ducked and shook her head. "I don't have a boyfriend. I did. Dr. Craig Elkhart. We were together for six years."

So the geek wasn't a dike. "Long time."

She lifted her head, and although her cheeks were wet, her jaw had a stubborn set to it. "He just married a twenty-year-old data-entry clerk named Pamela. When he left me, he said, 'I'm sorry, Jane, but you don't excite me anymore.' "

Considering Dr. J's, basic uptight personality, Jodie couldn't exactly blame him, but it had still been a shitty thing to say. "Men are basically assholes."

"That's not the worst part." She clasped her hands together. "The worst part is that we were together for six years, and I don't miss him."

"Then what are you so broke up about?" The coffee was done, and she got up to fill their mugs.

"It's not Craig. I'm just . . . It's nothing, really. I shouldn't be going on like this. I don't know what's wrong with me."

"You're thirty-four years old and somebody gave you a Jiffy Lube gift certificate for your birthday. Anybody would be bummed."

She shuddered. "This is the same house I grew up in; did you know that? After Dad died, I was going to sell it, but I never got around to it." Her voice developed a faraway sound, as if she'd forgotten Jodie was there. "I was doing research on ultrarelativistic heavy-ion collisions, and I didn't want any distractions. Work has always been the center of my life. Until I was thirty, it was enough. But then one birthday followed another.''

''And you finally figured out all that physics stuff isn't giving you any thrills in bed at night, right?''

She started, almost as if she'd forgotten Jodie was there. Then she shrugged. ''It's not just that. Frankly, I believe sex is overrated.'' Uncomfortable, she looked down at her hands. ''It's more a sense of connection.''

''You don't get much more connected than when you're burning up the mattress.''

''Yes, well, that's assuming one burns it up. Personally . . .'' She sniffed and stood, slipping the tissues into the pocket of her trousers where they didn't presume to leave a bump. ''When I speak of connection, I'm thinking of something more lasting than sex.''

''Religious stuff?''

''Not exactly, although that's important to me. Family. Children. Things like that.'' Once again she drew her shoulders back and gave Jodie a brush-off smile. ''I've gone on long enough. I shouldn't be imposing on you like this. I'm afraid you caught me at a bad time.''

''I get it! You want a kid!''

Dr. J. delved into her pocket and yanked out the tissues. Her bottom lip trembled, and her entire face crumpled as she dropped back into the chair. ''Yesterday Craig told me that Pamela is pregnant. It's not . . . I'm not jealous. To be honest, I don't care enough about him anymore to be jealous. I didn't really want to marry him; I don't want to marry anybody. It's just that . . .'' Her voice faded. ''It's just . . .''

''It's just that you want a kid of your own.''

She gave a jerky nod and bit her lip. ''I've wanted a child for so long. And now I'm thirty-four, and my eggs are getting older by the minute, but it doesn't seem as if it's going to happen.''

Jodie glanced at the kitchen clock. She wanted to hear

the rest of this, but pregame was starting. "Do you mind if I turn on your TV while we finish this?"

Dr. J. looked confused, as if she weren't exactly sure what a TV was. "No, I suppose not."

"Cool." Jodie picked up her mug and headed for the living room. She sat down on the couch, put her mug on the coffee table, and fished the remote out from under some kind of brainy journal. A beer commercial was playing, so she hit the mute button.

"Are you serious about wanting a baby? Even though you're single."

Dr. Jane had her glasses on again. She sat in an over-stuffed chair with a ruffle around the bottom and the clam-shell painting hanging right behind her head, the one with that fat, wet pearl. She pressed her legs together, her feet side by side, anklebones touching. She had great ankles, Jodie noticed, slender and well shaped.

Once again that back stiffened, as if somebody had strapped a board to it. "I've been thinking about it for a long time. I don't ever plan to marry—my work is too important to me—but I want a child more than anything. And I think I'd be a good mother. I guess today I realized I have no way to make it happen, and that's hit me hard."

"I got a couple of friends who are single moms. It's not easy. Still, you've got a lot better paying job than they do, so it shouldn't be so tough for you."

"The economics aren't a problem. My problem is that I can't seem to come up with a way to go about it."

Jodie stared at her. For a smart woman, she sure was dumb. "Are you talking about the guy?"

She nodded stiffly.

"There've got to be a lot of them hanging around that college. It's no big deal. Invite one of them over, put on some music, give him a couple of beers, and nail him."

"Oh, it couldn't be anyone I know."

"So pick up somebody in a bar or something."

"I could never do that. I'd have to know his health history." Her voice dropped. "Besides, I wouldn't know how to pick someone up."

Jodie couldn't imagine anything easier, but she guessed she had a lot more going for her than Dr. J. "What about one of those, you know, sperm banks?"

"Absolutely not. Too many sperm donors are medical students."

"So?"

"I don't want anyone who's intelligent fathering my child."

Jodie was so surprised, she neglected to turn up the volume on the pregame show, even though the beer commercial had ended and they'd begun to interview the Stars' head coach, Chester "Duke" Raskin.

"You want somebody stupid to be the father of your kid?"

Dr. J. smiled. "I know that seems strange, but it's very difficult for a child to grow up being smarter than everyone else. It makes it impossible to fit in, which is why I could never have had a child with someone as brilliant as Craig or even chance a sperm bank. I have to take into account my own genetic makeup and find a man who'll compensate for it. But the men I meet are all brilliant."

Dr. J. was one weird chick, Jodie decided. "You think because you're so smart and everything that you've got to find somebody stupid?"

"I know I do. I can't bear the idea that my child would have to go through what I did when I was growing up. Even now . . . Well, that's neither here nor there. The point is, as much as I want a child, I can't just think about myself."

A new face on the screen caught Jodie's attention. "Oh, jeez, wait a minute; I got to hear this." She snatched the remote and hit the volume button.

Paul Fenneman, a network sportscaster, was doing a

taped interview with Cal Bonner. Jodie knew for a fact that
the Bomber hated Fenneman's guts. The sportscaster had a
reputation for asking stupid questions, and the Bomber
didn't have any patience with fools.

The interview had been pretaped in the parking lot of
the Stars Compound, which was located on the outskirts of
Naperville, the largest town in DuPage County. Fenneman
spoke into the camera, looking real serious, like he was
getting ready to cover a major war or something. "I'm
speaking with Cal Bonner, the Stars' All-Pro quarterback."

The camera focused on Cal, and Jodie's skin went
clammy from a combination of lust and resentment. Damn,
he was hot, even if he was getting old.

He stood in front of this big Harley hog wearing jeans
and a tight black T-shirt that outlined one of the best sets
of pecs on the team. Some of the guys were so pumped up
they looked like they were getting ready to explode, but
Cal was perfect. He had a great neck, too, muscular, but
not one of those tree trunks like a lot of the players had.
His brown hair had a little curl to it, and he wore it short
so he didn't have to bother with it. The Bomber was like
that. He didn't have any patience with stuff he thought was
unimportant.

At a little over six feet, he was taller than some of the
other quarterbacks. He was also quick, smart, and he had
a telepathic ability to read defenses that only the finest players share. His legend had grown nearly as big as the great
Joe Montana's, and the fact that it didn't look like Jodie
would ever have number eighteen hanging in her closet was
something she could never forgive.

"Cal, your team had four turnovers against the Patriots
last week. What are you going to do against the Bills so
that doesn't happen again?"

Even for Paul Fenneman, that was a stupid question, and
Jodie waited to see how the Bomber would handle it.

He scratched the side of his head as if the question was

so complicated he had to think it over. The Bomber didn't have any patience with people he didn't respect, and he had a habit of emphasizing his hillbilly roots in situations like this.

He propped one boot up on the footpeg of the Harley and looked thoughtful. "Well, Paul, what we're gonna have to do is hang on to the ball. Now, not having played the game yourself, you might not know this, but every time we let the other team take the ball away from us, it means we don't have it ourselves. And that ain't no way to put points on the board."

Jodie chuckled. She had to hand it to the Bomber. He'd gotten old Paul right in the numbers with that one.

Paul didn't appreciate being made to look like a fool. "I hear Coach Raskin's been real happy with the way Kevin Tucker's been looking in practice. You're going to be thirty-six soon, which makes you an old man in a young man's game. Any worries Kevin'll be taking over as starter?"

For a fraction of a second, the Bomber's face stiffened up like a big old poker, then he shrugged. "Shoot, Paul, this ol' boy ain't ready for the grave yet."

"If only I could find somebody like him," Dr. Jane whispered. "He'd be perfect."

Jodie glanced over and saw her studying the television. "What are you talking about?"

Dr. J. gestured toward the screen. "That man. That football player. He's healthy, physically attractive, and not very bright. Exactly what I'm looking for."

"Are you talking about the *Bomber*?"

"Is that his name? I don't know anything about football."

"That's Cal Bonner. He's the starting quarterback for the Chicago Stars."

"That's right. I've seen his picture in the paper. Why

can't I meet a man like that? Someone who's a bit of a dim bulb.''

"Dim bulb?"

"Not very intelligent. Slow."

"Slow? The Bomber?" Jodie opened her mouth to tell Dr. Jane that the Bomber was the smartest, trickiest, most talented—not to mention meanest—sonovabitchen quarterback in the whole freakin' NFL when this big dizzy rush hit her smack in the middle of her head, an idea so wild she couldn't believe it had even come into her brain.

She sank back into the couch cushions. *Holy shit.* She fumbled for the remote and pushed the mute button. "Are you serious? You'd choose somebody like Cal Bonner to be the father of your baby?"

"Of course I would—assuming I could see his medical records. A simple man like that would be perfect: strength, endurance, and a low IQ. His good looks are an added bonus."

Jodie's mind ran in three different directions all at once. "What if . . ." She swallowed and tried not to get distracted by an image of Kevin Tucker standing naked right in front of her. "What if I could arrange it?"

"What are you talking about?"

"What if I could set it up so you could get Cal Bonner in bed?"

"Are you joking?"

Jodie swallowed again and shook her head.

"But I don't know him."

"You wouldn't have to."

"I'm afraid I don't understand."

Slowly, Jodie told her story, leaving out a part here and there—like what a badass the Bomber was—but pretty much being honest about the rest. She explained about the birthday present and the kind of woman the guys wanted. Then she said that with a little cosmetic enhancement, she thought Dr. J. herself could fit the bill.

Dr. J. got so pale she started looking like the little girl in that old Brad Pitt vampire flick. "Are you— Are you saying you think I should pretend to be a prostitute?"

"A real high-class one because the Bomber doesn't go for hookers."

She rose from her chair and began pacing around the room. Jodie could almost see her nerd brain working away like a calculator, adding up this and that, pushing plus buttons and minus buttons, getting a look of hope around her eyes and then sagging back against the fireplace mantel.

"The health records..." She gave a deep, unhappy sigh. "Just for a moment I thought it might actually be possible, but I'd have to know his health history. Football players use steroids, don't they? And what about STDs and AIDS?"

"The Bomber doesn't touch drugs, and he's never been too much for sleepin' around, which is why the guys are setting this up. He broke up with his old girlfriend last winter and doesn't seem to have been with anybody since."

"I'd still have to know his medical history."

Jodie figured between Junior and Willie, one of them could sweet-talk a secretary into giving her what she needed. "I'll have a copy of his medical records by Tuesday, Wednesday at the latest."

"I don't know what to say."

"His birthday is in ten days," Jodie pointed out. "I guess what it all comes down to is whether or not you've got the guts to go for it."

2

What had she done? Jane Darlington's stomach took a turn for the worse as she made her way into the ladies' room at Zebras, where Jodie Pulanski had brought her to meet the football player who was driving her to Cal Bonner's condominium that very night. Ignoring the women chatting at the basins, she headed into the nearest stall, latched it, and leaned her cheek against the cold metal divider.

Was it only ten days since Jodie had shown up at her door and turned her life inside out? What insanity had possessed her to agree to this? After years of orderly thinking, what had convinced her to do something so reckless. Now that it was too late, she realized she'd made a high-school student's mistake and forgotten the second law of thermodynamics: order inevitably leads to disorder.

Maybe it was a regression. As a youngster, she was always getting herself into scrapes. Her mother had died several months after her birth, and she'd been raised by a cold, withdrawn father who only seemed to pay attention to her when she misbehaved. His attitude, combined with the fact that she was bored in school, had led to a series of pranks that had culminated in her elementary-school principal's house being painted a bright shade of pink by a local contractor.

The memory still gave her satisfaction. The man had been a sadistic child-hater, and he'd deserved it. Luckily, the incident had also forced the school authorities to see the light, and they began to accelerate her through the system so that she had no more time for mischief. She'd buried herself in her increasingly challenging studies while she shut herself off from a peer group that regarded her as a freak, and if she sometimes thought she liked the rebellious child she had been better than the intense, scholarly woman she had become, she'd simply regarded it as one more price she'd had to pay for the sin of being born different.

Now it seemed that rebellious child still lived. Or maybe it was simply fate. Although she had never placed any credence in mystical signs, discovering that Cal Bonner's birthday fell exactly at her most fertile time of the month had been too portentous for her to ignore. Before she'd lost her courage, she'd picked up the telephone and called Jodie Pulanski to tell her that she was going to go through with it.

By this time tomorrow, she might be pregnant. A distant possibility, it was true, but her menstrual cycle had always been as orderly as the rest of her life, and she wanted this so badly. Some people might think she was being selfish, but her longing for a baby didn't feel selfish. It felt right. People saw Jane as a person to be respected, to be held in awe. They wanted her intellect, but no one seemed to want the part of her that she most needed to share, her capacity to love. Her father hadn't wanted that, and neither had Craig.

Lately she had imagined herself sitting at the desk in her study lost in the data being displayed on the computer screen before her—the intricate calculations that might someday unlock the secrets of the universe. And then in her vision a noise would disturb her concentration, the sound of an imaginary child coming into her study.

She would lift her head. Cup her hand over a soft cheek. "Mama, can we fly my kite today?"

In her vision she would laugh and turn from her computer, abandoning her search for the secrets of the universe to explore the heavens in a more important way.

The flush of the toilet in the next booth brought her out of her reverie. Before she could fly any kites, she had to get through tonight. That meant she had to seduce a stranger, a man who would know far more about seduction than someone who'd only had one lover.

In her mind she saw Craig's pale, thin body, naked except for the black socks he wore because he had poor circulation. Unless she had her period or he had one of his migraines, they'd made love nearly every Saturday night, but it was over quickly and not very exciting. Now she felt ashamed of having spent so long in such an unsatisfactory relationship, and she knew loneliness had driven her to it.

Male companionship had always been a problem for her. When she'd been in school, her classmates were too old for her, a problem that had persisted even after she had her degree. She wasn't an unattractive woman, and a number of her colleagues had asked her out, but they were twenty years her senior, and she'd been vaguely repulsed. The men who had attracted her, the ones her own age, were the graduate students taking her seminars, and dating them violated her sense of ethics. As a result, she'd earned the reputation of being aloof, and they'd stopped asking.

That had finally changed when she'd received the Preeze fellowship. She was investigating top quarks as part of the ultimate quest for every physicist, the search for the Grand Unification Theory, that simple equation, much like Einstein's $E=mc^2$, that would describe all the parts of the universe. One of the scientists she had met at a University of Chicago seminar had been Craig.

At first she'd thought she'd found the man of her dreams. But, although they could rethink Einstein's Gedanken experiment without ever growing bored, they never laughed, and they never exchanged the sort of confidences she'd always imagined lovers should share. Gradually, she accepted the fact that their physical relationship was little more than a convenience for both of them.

If only her relationship with Craig had better prepared her to seduce Mr. Bonner. She knew men didn't consider her sexy, and she could only hope he was one of those awful creatures who didn't care very much with whom he was sexually engaged as long as he was physically satisfied. She feared he would recognize her for the fraud she was, but at least she would have tried, at least she would have a chance. And she had no alternative. She'd never use a sperm bank and risk having a brilliant child who would grow up as she had, a lonely freak of nature who felt disconnected from those around her.

The sound of chatter faded as the women left the rest room. She knew she couldn't hide out forever, and she hated the image of herself cowering, so she finally opened the door. As she slipped out of the stall, she caught her reflection in the wall of mirrors and, for a fraction of a moment, thought it belonged to someone else.

Jodie had insisted she wear her hair down and had even brought over hot rollers to set it so that it now fell in a soft tousle around her face. Jane found the style a bit untidy, and she hoped Jodie was right when she insisted that a man would consider it sexy. She'd also permitted Jodie to do her makeup, which the young woman had applied with a heavy hand. Jane hadn't protested, however. Her ordinary application of antique rose lipstick and a dab of light brown mascara was hardly appropriate for a hooker, even a high-class one.

Her gaze finally dropped to the outfit she and Jodie had shopped for together. In the past ten days, Jane had grown to know Jodie Pulanski better than she wanted to. The younger woman was shallow and self-centered, interested only in clothes, going to bed with football players, and getting drunk. But she was also wily, and for reasons that Jane still didn't understand, she was determined to pull off this sordid encounter.

Jane had steered her away from black leather and studs toward a slimly cut ecru silk suit with a short skirt that molded to her body in a way that left few mysteries. The wrapped jacket was fastened at one side with a single snap, and the neckline dipped nearly to the waist, its soft draping camouflaging Jane's unimpressive bust line. A lacy white garter belt, pair of sheer stockings, and stiletto heels completed the outfit. When Jane had mentioned underpants, Jodie had scoffed.

"Hookers don't wear them. Besides, they'll only get in your way."

Jane's stomach pitched and the swell of panic she'd been suppressing all day rose up to suffocate her. What had she been thinking of? This whole idea was insane. She must have been deluded to believe she could go through with this bizarre plan. It had been one thing to map it out intellectually, but it was quite another to carry it through.

Jodie burst into the rest room. "What the hell's keeping you? Junior's here to pick you up."

Jane's stomach pitched. "I—I've changed my mind."

"Like hell. You're not going to chicken out on me now. Damn, I knew this would happen. Stay right here."

Jodie rushed out the door before Jane could protest. She felt flushed and cold at the same time. How had she gotten herself into this mess? She was a respectable professional woman, an authority in her field. This was madness.

She darted toward the door only to have it nearly hit her in the face as Jodie rushed back in carrying a bottle of beer. She opened her palm. "Swallow these."

"What are they?"

"What do you mean? They're pills. Can't you see that?"

"I told you I was farsighted. I can't see anything close without my glasses."

"Just swallow them. They'll relax you."

"I don't know . . ."

"Trust me. They'll take the edge off."

"I don't think it's a good idea to take strange medication."

"Yeah, yeah. Do you want a kid or not?"

Misery swelled inside her. "You know I do."

"Then swallow the fucking pills!"

Jane swallowed them, using the beer to wash them down, then shuddering because she hated beer. She protested again as Jodie dragged her out of the rest room and the cool fingers of air trickling under her skirt reminded her she wasn't wearing panties. "I can't do this."

"Look, it's no big deal. The guys are getting Cal drunk. They'll clear out as soon as you arrive, and all you have to do is keep your mouth shut and jump on him. It'll be over before you know it."

"It's not going to be quite that easy."

"Sure it is."

Jane noticed some of the men staring at her. For a moment she thought something was wrong—that she had a streamer of toilet paper dragging from her shoe or something—and then she realized they weren't looking at her critically, but sexually, and her panic mounted.

Jodie pulled her toward a dark-haired, no-neck monster standing at the bar wearing an olive green trench coat. He had heavy black eyebrows that had grown together until they looked like one giant caterpillar crawling over his brow.

"Here she is, Junior. Don't let anybody say Jodie Pulanski can't deliver."

The monster ran his eyes over Jane and grinned. "You

done all right, Jodie. She's real classy. Hey, what's your name, sweetheart?''

Jane was so rattled she couldn't think. Why hadn't she planned for this? Her eyes fell on one of the neon signs that she could read without her glasses. ''Bud.''

''Your name's Bud?''

''Yes.'' She coughed, stalling. Her adult life had been dedicated to the search for truth, and lying didn't come easily. ''Rose. Rose Bud.''

Jodie rolled her eyes.

''Sounds like a effin' stripper,'' Junior said.

Jane regarded him nervously. ''It's a family name. There were Buds who came over on the *Mayflower*.''

''Is that right.''

She began to elaborate in an attempt to be more convincing, but she was so anxious she could hardly think. ''Buds fought in all the major wars. They were at Lexington, Gettysburg, the Battle of the Bulge. One of my female Bud ancestors helped establish the Underground Railway.''

''No kidding. My uncle used to work for the Santa Fe.'' He tilted his head and regarded her suspiciously. ''How old are you, anyway?''

''Twenty-six,'' Jodie interjected.

Jane shot her a startled glance.

''She looks a little older than that,'' Junior said.

''She's not.''

''I got to hand it to you, Jodie. This one ain't nothin' like Kelly. Maybe she'll be just what the Bomber needs. I sure hope he doesn't get turned off by the fact that she's so old.''

Old! What kind of twisted value system did this man have that he regarded a woman in her late twenties as old? If he knew she was thirty-four, he'd dismiss her as ancient.

Junior cinched the belt on his trench coat. ''Come on, Rose; let's get you out of here. Follow me in your car.''

He started toward the door only to stop so suddenly she

nearly bumped into him. "Damn, I almost forgot. Willie said to put this on you."

He reached into his pocket. She stiffened as she saw what he withdrew. "Oh, no. I don't think—"

"Got to, babe. It's part of the job."

He encircled her neck with a fat pink bow. She lifted her hand to her throat, and her stomach pitched as she touched the loops of satin ribbon.

"I'd rather not wear this."

"Too bad." He finished tying it. "You're a gift, Rose Bud. A birthday present from the guys."

Melvin Thompson, Willie Jarrell, and Chris Plummer— three members of the Stars offensive line—watched Cal Bonner line up his last putt. They'd set a course across the carpet of the Bomber's spacious, but sparsely furnished, living room, where he and Willie were playing for a hundred bucks a hole. The Bomber was up four hundred.

"So who'd you rather bonk?" Willie asked Chris as Cal tapped his putt straight into the oversize Dunkin' Donuts commuter mug that marked the fifth hole. "Mrs. Brady or Mrs. Partridge?"

"That's easy." Chris was also a big fan of *Nick at Night*. "I'd do Mrs. Brady."

"Yeah, me, too. Man, was she hot."

It was Willie's turn to putt, and, as Cal moved out of the way, his right guard lined up for the same mug. "Somebody said her and Greg got it on in real life." Willie's putt rolled past on the right.

"No shit. Did you know that, Cal?"

Cal took a sip of scotch and watched Willie miss his second putt. "I don't even know what the hell you boys are talking about."

"Mrs. Brady on *The Brady Bunch*," Melvin explained, "and Mrs. Partridge on *The Partridge Family*. If you had the chance to fu—" He stopped himself just in time. "If you got to bonk one of them, which one would it be?''

The linemen had a side bet going on who could last the longest before uttering their favorite obscenity. Cal wasn't part of that bet because he'd refused to give up his freedom of expression, which was just fine with the rest of them since they knew he'd probably win. Although Cal could turn the field blue during a game, once he was out of uniform, he seemed to lose interest.

"I guess I'd have to give it some thought." Cal drained his glass and took the putter back after Willie finally tapped it in for a three. He eyed his next putt, a sharp dogleg left into a KFC bucket. He didn't play any game, not even a living-room putting contest, without the intention of winning. The urge to compete had taken him from Salvation, North Carolina, to the University of Michigan, where he'd led the Wolverines to two consecutive Big Ten Championships before he'd gone on to the National Football League and become one of its best quarterbacks.

Chris finished off his beer. "Here's one for you. Would you rather bonk that *Beauty and the Beast* chick or Pocahontas?''

"Pocahontas," Melvin replied.

"Yeah, Poc, for sure," Willie concurred.

"You know who I'd like to f—uh, bonk," Chris said. "Brenda Starr. Damn, she's hot.''

Cal couldn't hold back a grin at that one. God, he loved these jerks. Week after week they put their asses on the line to protect him. He'd been riding them hard lately, and he knew they didn't like it, but the Stars had a chance of going all the way to the Super Bowl this year, and he wanted it bad.

It had been the worst year of his life. His brother Gabriel had lost his wife Cherry and only child Jamie, two people Cal had deeply loved, in a car accident. Since then, he couldn't muster the enthusiasm to do anything except play ball.

He banked his next putt off the TV cabinet, combining his touch on the golf greens with his skill at the pool table, and put the ball within inches of the KFC bucket.

"Hey, that's not fair," Willie protested. "You didn't say we could bank the shots."

"I didn't say we couldn't."

Melvin checked his watch and refilled Cal's glass from a bottle of very old, very expensive scotch. Unlike his teammates, Cal seldom got drunk, but this was his birthday, he had the blues, and he was trying to make an exception. Unfortunately, he had a cast-iron stomach, and it wasn't all that easy.

He smiled as he remembered his last birthday. Kelly, his former girlfriend, had planned a big surprise party for him, but she wasn't good with details, and he'd shown up before any of the guests. He thought maybe he should miss Kelly more, but what he mostly felt when he thought about her was embarrassment that she'd dumped him for a twenty-three-year-old guitarist who'd offered her a wedding ring. Still, he hoped she was happy. She'd been a sweet girl, even though she used to irritate the hell out of him.

He was a yeller, by nature. He'd didn't mean anything by it; it was just the way he communicated. But whenever he'd yelled at Kelly, she'd burst into tears instead of standing up to him. She made him feel like a bully, which meant he couldn't ever completely relax and just be himself around her.

It was a problem he'd always had with the girls he dated. He was naturally attracted to the nice ones, the ones who cared about other people and weren't just out for themselves. Unfortunately, girls like that tended to be wimps, and they'd let him run right over them.

A lot of the more aggressive women, the ones who might have been able to stand up to him, turned out to be money-grubbers. Not that he blamed a woman for looking out for herself, as long as she was up front about it.

Phoebe Calebow, the Stars' owner and his nominee for best woman in the world when she wasn't being a pain in the ass, said he wouldn't have so much trouble with females if he'd stop dating such young ones, but she didn't understand. Football was a young man's game. *He* was young, dammit! And since he could pick and choose when it came to women, why should he choose a desperate thirty-year-old who was starting to turn brown around the edges when he could have a beautiful young woman with some dew-sparkle still left on her? He refused to think of himself as anything but in his prime, especially now that he had Kevin Tucker breathing down his neck. Cal swore he'd burn in hell before he'd let that cocky sonovabitch take over his job.

He finished the last of his scotch and felt the beginnings of the faint buzz that told him he was finally getting to the place he wanted to be, the place where he'd forget about the deaths of two people he loved, where he'd forget about Kevin Tucker and getting older and the fact that it seemed like forever since he'd felt the inclination to take one of those eager little dew-sparklers he'd been dating to bed. At the same time he noticed Chris checking his watch for the third time in fifteen minutes. "Going somewhere, Chris?"

"What? Uh, no." He exchanged glances with Melvin. "Naw, I just wondered what time it was."

"Three minutes later than when you last looked." Cal picked up the putter and headed into the dining room, which had some kind of limestone floor and a pricey crystal chandelier, but no furniture. What was the point? He liked to keep things loose and easy, and he sure wasn't planning any fancy dinner parties. When he entertained his friends, he chartered a plane and flew everybody to Scottsdale.

Besides, he didn't believe in accumulating a lot of unnecessary possessions since living in the same place too long made him antsy, and the less he had, the easier it was to move. He was a great player because there was no clutter in his life. No permanent houses, no permanent women, nothing that could make him feel old and used up. Nothing that could cause him to lose his edge.

The doorbell rang, and Willie's head shot up. "That must be the pizzas I ordered."

All three of them charged toward the door.

Cal regarded them with amusement. All night, there had been something going on between them. Now it seemed he was about to find out what.

Jane stood in the spacious entry of Cal Bonner's luxury condominium. With the fat pink bow tied around her neck, she was gift-wrapped and special-delivered.

Her heart beat so rapidly she was surprised the men couldn't see the skin moving beneath the plunging neckline of her suit. She was also feeling a little muzzy, not at all like herself, and she suspected those pills Jodie had given her had kicked in.

Junior of the caterpillar eyebrow took her coat and whispered brief introductions to three men who could only be football players. The one named Chris was white with a prematurely receding hairline and the most massive neck she'd ever seen on a human being. Melvin was black, and his wire-rimmed glasses gave him a faintly scholarly look that was at odds with his enormous frame. Willie had warm coffee-colored skin that accented a pair of huge lady-killer eyes.

Junior finished his introductions and shoved his thumb in her direction. "Jodie done great, didn't she? I told you she'd come through."

The men assessed her, and Willie nodded. "Real classy. But how old is she?"

"Twenty-five," Junior replied, cutting another year off her mythical age.

"Nice legs," Chris said as he circled her. "Great ass,

too.'' He curved his hand over her right buttock and squeezed.

She whirled around and kicked him hard in the shin.

"Hey!"

Too late, she realized she'd made a big mistake. A woman who traded in lust would hardly react so violently to being fondled. She recovered quickly and regarded him with all the haughtiness of an upper-class call girl. "I don't give free samples. If you're interested in buying the merchandise, make an appointment."

Far from being offended, they started to laugh, and Willie nodded his approval. "You're just what the ol' Bomber needs."

"He's gonna be smilin' tomorrow," Melvin chuckled.

"Come on, boys. It's party time!"

Junior pushed her forward, and as she tottered across the limestone floor on her ridiculously high heels, they all started to sing. *Happy birthday to you, Happy birthday to you . . .*

Dry-mouthed and terrified, she reached the end of the foyer. On her next step, her heels sank into the white carpet. She turned, spotted Cal Bonner, and froze. Even through her narcotic-induced haze, one agonizing fact became completely clear. The television screen had lied.

He stood silhouetted against a wall of windows with nothing behind him but the cold November night. On television she'd seen a country hick with a good body and bad grammar, but the man staring at her from the other side of the room had nothing of the hick about him. She had chosen a warrior.

He cocked his head to the side and studied her. His gaze was cold and grim, and it sent frightening impressions running through her head.

Gray eyes so pale they were almost silver. Eyes that knew no mercy.

Crisp brown hair whose tendency to curl hadn't quite

been tamed by a no-nonsense cut. A man who made his own rules and answered to no one.

Hard muscle and sinewy strength. A physical animal.

Brutal cheekbones and a ruthless jaw. No softness there. Not even a speck of the gentler emotions. This man was a conqueror, designed by nature to make war.

A chill traveled along her spine. She knew without question that he would be ruthless with anyone he decided was his enemy. Except she wasn't his enemy, she reminded herself. He'd never know what she had planned for him. Besides, warriors didn't care about things like illegitimate offspring. Babies were a natural consequence of rape and pillage and not to be given a second thought.

Rough hands, accompanied by raucous male laughter, pushed her toward the man she had chosen to be the father of her child.

"Here's your birthday present, Cal."

"From us to you."

"Happy birthday, buddy. We cared enough to send the very best."

One final shove pitched her against him. She bumped into a muscular chest. A strong arm encircled her before she could fall, and she caught a faint whiff of scotch. She tried to pull away, but he hadn't yet made up his mind to release her, so that proved impossible.

Her sudden helplessness was frightening. He stood nearly a head taller than she, and there wasn't an ounce of fat on his lean, conditioned body. She had to force herself not to struggle to get free because she knew he would crush her if he sensed her weakness.

An image flashed through her mind, of her body naked beneath his, and she immediately pushed it away. If she thought about that part of it, she wouldn't have a prayer of pulling this off.

His cupped hand slid up her arm. "Well, now, I don't think I ever got a birthday present quite like this one. You guys got more tricks up your sleeve than a deer's got ticks.''

The sound of that deep, country drawl immediately steadied her. He might have the body of a warrior, but he was only a football player, and not a very intelligent one at that. The knowledge of her own superior brainpower gave her enough confidence to look up into those pale eyes as he slowly released the grip that held her captive.

"Happy birthday, Mr. Bonner.'' She had intended her voice to sound sultry, but instead it sounded professorial, as if she were greeting a student who'd slipped into class late.

"He's Cal,'' Junior said. "It's short for Calvin, but I'd advise you not to call him that because it pisses him off big time, and making the Bomber mad isn't something I'd recommend. Cal, this is Rose. Rose Bud.''

He lifted one eyebrow. "You guys brought me a stripper?''

"That's exactly what I thought, but she's not. She's a hooker.''

Distaste flickered across his expression, then disappeared. "Well, now, I thank y'all a whole lot for thinkin' about me, but I'm gonna have to pass.''

"You can't do that, Cal,'' Junior protested. "We all know how you feel about hookers, but Rose, here, ain't your ordinary street corner whore. Hell, no. She's a real *classy* whore. Her family came over on the *Mayflower* or something. Tell him, Rose.''

She was so busy trying to absorb the fact that she—Dr. Jane Darlington, a respected physicist with only one lover in her past—was being called a whore that it took her a moment to muster a haughty response. "A Bud served with Miles Standish.''

Chris glanced toward Melvin. "I know him. Didn't he play for the Bears back in the eighties?''

Melvin laughed. "Damn, Chris, did you spend any time

in the classroom while you were in college?''

"I was playing ball. I didn't have time for that shit. Besides, we're not talking about that now. We're talking about the fact that it's the Bomber's birthday, we got him the best freakin' present money could buy, and he wants to freakin' pass!''

"It's because she's too old,'' Willie exclaimed. "I told you we should have gone for somebody younger, but y'all kept sayin' how she wasn't supposed to remind him of Kelly. She's only twenty-four, Cal. Honest.''

Just like that, she'd lost another year.

"You can't pass.'' Chris stepped forward, a belligerent look in his eyes. "She's your birthday present. You got to fu—er—bonk her.''

Her skin grew hot, and since she couldn't be caught blushing, she turned away and pretended to study the living room. Its low-pile white carpet, gray sectional sofa, stereo equipment, and large-screen television were expensive but uninteresting. She noticed various containers tossed down on the carpet: a plastic cup, a KFC bucket, an empty cereal box. In addition to being a hayseed, Mr. Bonner was a slob, but since messiness wasn't genetic, it didn't concern her.

He flipped the golf putter he'd been holding from one hand to the other. "Tell you what, guys. People exchange presents all the time. How about I trade her in for a steak dinner?''

He couldn't do that! She would never find anyone more perfect to father her child.

"Shit, Bomber, she cost a hell of a lot more than a steak dinner!''

She wondered how much. Junior had handed her the money, which she'd tucked into her purse without looking, then slid under the front seat of her car. First thing tomorrow, she'd donate every dollar to the college scholarship fund.

He drained the liquor in his glass. "I appreciate the

thought, guys, but I guess I just don't feel like having a whore tonight.''

Anger hit her like a molecular collision. How dare he talk about her like that! Her emotions sometimes betrayed her, but her mind seldom did, and now it was shouting at her to do something. She couldn't give up this easily. He was ideal, and somehow she had to find a way to make him change his mind. Yes, he was physically terrifying, and she didn't believe he would be a gentle lover, but a few minutes rough handling wouldn't kill her, and hadn't she chosen him because he was her opposite in every way?

"Aw, come on, Bomber," Willie said. "She's hot. I'm getting hard just looking at her."

"Then take her." Bonner jerked his head toward the hallway. "You know where the spare bedroom is."

"*No!*"

They all turned to stare at her.

She thought of his cornpone accent and reminded herself that he wasn't anything more than a simpleminded football player. The pills gave her courage. All she had to do was outwit him. "I'm not a piece of meat that gets passed around. I work under exclusive contract, and my contract calls for me to practice my craft only with Mr. Bonner." Avoiding his eyes, she looked toward the other men. "Why don't you gentlemen leave now so he and I can discuss this privately?"

"Yeah, why don't we do that," Melvin said. "Come on, guys."

He didn't have to convince them. They rushed toward the foyer with a speed that was at odds with their size.

Melvin turned back to her at the last minute. "We expect our money's worth, Rose. You give Bomber the works, you hear? Anything he wants."

She gulped and nodded. A moment later, the front door slammed shut.

She and the man they called the Bomber were alone.

3

Jane watched the Stars' quarterback refill his glass from a bottle sitting on the coffee table. As he raised the tumbler to his lips, he studied her with pale piercing eyes that looked as if they could carry out a scorched-earth campaign all by themselves.

She had to come up with some way to seduce him before he threw her out, but what? She could simply strip off her clothes, but since her small-breasted body wasn't exactly pinup quality, that might be the quickest way to get thrown out. Besides, it was hard to get enthusiastic about undressing in front of a stranger who was standing in a fully lit room that had a wall of curtainless windows. When she'd envisioned the nudity part of this, she'd imagined someplace very dark.

"You might as well go on with 'em, Rosebud. I believe I told you I ain't much for hookers."

His atrocious grammar renewed her commitment. With every one of his linguistic mistakes, her unborn child's IQ dropped another few points.

She stalled for time. "I've always found it inadvisable to stereotype any group of people."

"You don't say."

"Condemning a person solely on the basis of ethnicity,

35

religion, or even that person's professional activities is illogical.''

"Is that so? What about murderers?"

"Murderers aren't, strictly speaking, a cohesive group, so it's hardly the same thing." She knew that engaging him in a debate probably wasn't the best method of turning him on, but she was a much better debater than seducer, and she couldn't resist driving her point home. "America was founded on principles of ethnic diversity and religious freedom, yet blind prejudice has caused most of the evils in our society. Don't you find that ironic?"

"Are you trying to tell me it's my patriotic duty as a loyal son of Uncle Sam to show you the cracks in my bedroom ceiling?"

She started to smile until she saw by his expression that he was serious. In the face of such blessed brainlessness, her unborn child's IQ took another welcome tumble downward.

For a moment, she weighed the morality of deliberately manipulating someone so dull-witted, not to mention deficient in humor, but her need for the services of his warrior's body won out over her principles. "Yes, I suppose in a way it is."

He upended his tumbler. "All right, Rosebud. I guess I'm drunk enough to give you a chance before I throw you out. G'wan and show me what you got."

"I beg your pardon."

"Let's see the goods."

"The goods?"

"Your body. Your bag of tricks. How long you been a hooker, anyway?"

"It's— Uh . . . Actually, you're my first client."

"Your first client?"

"Please don't let that alarm you. I've been very well trained."

His face tightened and she remembered his distaste for

prostitutes, a fact that made this particular charade all the more difficult to carry off. When she'd pointed this out, Jodie had brushed it aside by saying that his teammates were going to get him drunk, and he wouldn't be as particular. But although Jane could see that he was imbibing, he didn't look very drunk.

Once again, she would have to lie. Maybe it was the pills, but she seemed to be getting a better grip on the whole process. It was simply a matter of inventing a new reality, embellishing it with a few pertinent details, and doing her best to retain eye contact throughout the process. "You're probably from the old school, Mr. Bonner, that still believes women in my profession can only get their training in one way, but that's not true any longer. I, for example, am not promiscuous."

His glass stalled in midair. "You're a hooker."

"True. But I think I mentioned that you're my first client. Up until now I've only been intimate with one man. My late husband. I happen to be a widow. A very *young* widow."

He didn't look as if he were buying any of this, so she began to embellish. "My husband's death left me in terrible debt, and I needed something that paid better than minimum wage. Unfortunately, with no marketable skills, I didn't have many choices. Then I remembered that my husband had always complimented me on the intimate aspects of our marriage. But please don't think that just because I've only had one partner, I'm not highly qualified."

"Maybe I'm missin' something, but I don't rightly see how somebody who claims to have had—What'd you say? One partner?—can be well trained."

He had a point. Her brain clicked away. "I was referring to the instructional videotapes my agency has all its new employees watch."

"They train you by watching videos?" His eyes nar-

rowed, reminding her of a hunter looking down a gun sight.
"Now, ain't that interesting."

She felt a little surge of pleasure as her child lost another
few points on the Iowa Test of Basic Skills. Even a computer couldn't have picked a more perfect match.

"They're not ordinary videos. Nothing you'd want an
impressionable child to see. But the old methods of on-the-
job training aren't practical in our current era of safe sex,
at least not for the more discriminating agencies."

"Agencies? Are you talking about whorehouses?"

Each time she heard that repellent word it stung a bit
more. "The politically correct term is 'pleasure agency.' "
She paused. Her head felt as if it were floating off her
shoulders. "Just as prostitutes are better referred to as sexual pleasure providers or SPPs."

"SPPs? You sure are a reg'lar encyclopedia."

It was curious, but his accent seemed to be growing
thicker by the minute. It must be the liquor. Thank goodness he was too dull-witted to realize how outlandish this
conversation had become. "We have slide shows and guest
lecturers who discuss their various specialties with us."

"Like what?"

Her mind raced. "Uh . . . Role playing, for example."

"What kind of role playing?"

What kind, indeed? Her mind shuffled through various
scenarios, searching for one that didn't involve physical
pain or degradation. "Well, we have something we call
Prince Charming and Cinderella."

"What's that like?"

"It involves . . . roses. Making love on a bed of rose petals."

"Sounds a little too girly to appeal to me. You got anything spicier to offer?"

Why had she mentioned role playing? "Of course, but
since you're my first customer, I think I can give you more
value if we stick to the basics."

"Missionary stuff?"

She gulped. "My current specialty." He didn't look too excited by the prospect, although his face showed so little expression, it was hard to tell. "That, or—I think I might have a talent for being the—uh—the partner on top."

"Well, I guess you've just about overcome my prejudice against hookers."

"Sexual pleasure providers."

"Whatever. But the thing of it is, you're a little old for me."

Old! That *really* frosted her. He was thirty-six, but he had the nerve to regard a woman of twenty-four as old! Maybe it was her floating head, but the fact that she wasn't really twenty-four no longer made a difference. It was the principle that counted.

She mustered a look of sympathy. "I'm sorry, I must have misunderstood. I assumed you were able to handle a grown woman."

Whatever he was swallowing went down the wrong pipe and he choked.

Feeling decidedly malicious, she gestured toward his telephone. "Would you like me to call the office and have them send out Punkin'? If she has her homework done, she should be available."

He stopped coughing long enough to level her with a sonic blast from those eyes. "You're not twenty-four. Both of us know you're not a day under twenty-eight. Now go ahead and show me what you learned from those training films about warm-up activities. If you catch my interest, maybe I'll reconsider."

More than anything, she wanted to tell him to go to hell, but she wouldn't let her indignation, no matter how justified it might be, keep her from her goal. How could she entice him? She hadn't given any consideration to foreplay, assuming he would simply get on top of her, perform the deed, and roll off the way Craig had done it.

"What kind of warm-up activities have you preferred in the past?"

"Did you bring any Reddi Whip with you?"

She could feel herself blushing. "No, I didn't."

"How 'bout handcuffs?"

"No!"

"Dang. I guess it really don't matter then. I'm open-minded." He lowered himself into the room's largest armchair and waved a hand vaguely in her direction. "You go on there, Rosebud, and—whadyacall—improvise. I'll prob'ly like whatever you come up with."

Maybe she could do a seductive dance for him. She was a good dancer in private, but in public she tended to be awkward and self-conscious. Perhaps she could do a routine from one of her aerobics classes, although between her demanding work schedule and the fact that she preferred brisk walking as an exercise form, she usually dropped out before the session was over. "If you'd like to put on some of your favorite music . . ."

"Sure." He got up and walked over to the stereo cabinet. "I think I might have some highbrow stuff. I bet a SPS such as yourself loves longhair music."

"SPP."

"Isn't that what I said?" He slipped a compact disc into the machine, and as he resumed his seat, the living room was filled with the lively music of Rimsky-Korsakov's "Flight of the Bumblebee." A piece with such a frenzied tempo was hardly her idea of seductive music, but what did she know?

She performed a few shoulder rolls from the warm-up part of her aerobics class and tried to look sultry, but the quick pace of the music made it difficult. Still, the chemicals surging through her bloodstream spurred her on. She added some side stretches, ten on the right and then ten on the left so she wouldn't get lopsided.

Her hair brushed her cheeks as she moved in a manner

that she could only hope was alluring, but as he watched her with those scorched-earth eyes, she couldn't see any evidence that he was getting swept away with lust. She thought about touching her toes, but that didn't seem like a very graceful dance movement. Besides, she couldn't reach them without bending her knees. Inspiration struck.

One. Two. Three. Kick!
One. Two. Three. Kick!

He crossed his legs and yawned.

She experimented with a small hula routine.

He glanced at his watch.

It was hopeless. She stopped and let the bumblebee fly on without her.

"And here I was waitin' for you to get to the jumpin' jacks part."

"I don't dance well with people watching."

"Guess you should have spent a little more time with them training videos. Or a couple of old John Travolta movies." He got up and walked over to lower the volume on the music. "Can I be honest with you here, Rosebud?"

"Please."

"You're not turnin' me on." He reached into his back pocket and pulled out his wallet. "Let me give you a little extra for your time."

She could barely resist the urge to cry, despite the fact that she wasn't a crier by nature. He was going to kick her out, and she would have lost her best chance to have the child of her dreams. Desperation made her voice husky. "Please, Mr. Bonner. You can't dismiss me."

"I sure can."

"You'll . . . You'll get me fired. The Stars' account is a very important one to my agency."

"If it's so damned important, why did they send you? Anybody can see you don't know diddly about being a hooker."

"There's a—a convention in town. They were short-handed."

"So what you're sayin' is . . . I ended up with you by default."

She nodded. "And if they find out you weren't satisfied with my services, they'll fire me. Please, Mr. Bonner, I need this job. If they dismiss me, I'll lose my benefits."

"You get benefits?"

If prostitutes didn't get benefits, they certainly should. "They have an excellent dental plan, and I'm scheduled for a root canal. Couldn't we . . . Couldn't we just go into the bedroom?"

"I don't know, Rosebud . . ."

"Please!" With a sense of desperation, she snatched up his hands. Squeezing her eyes shut, she pulled them to her breasts and held them there, palms flat.

"Rosebud?"

"Yes?"

"What are you doing?"

"Letting you . . . feel my breasts."

"Uh-huh." His hands remained still. "Did any of those training videos suggest you take off your clothes first?"

"The jacket's very thin, so I'm sure it doesn't make any difference. As I'm certain you can tell, I don't have anything on under it."

The heat from his palms burned through the fragile silk into her skin. She didn't let herself imagine what those hands would feel like without the tissue-thin barrier. "You may move your hands on them if you like."

"I appreciate the offer, but— You plannin' on openin' your eyes anytime soon?"

She'd forgotten they were shut, and she quickly raised her lids.

It was a mistake. He was standing so near that she had to tilt her neck to gaze at him. From such close range, his features had blurred, but not quite enough to hide the fact

that his mouth looked even harder than she'd first thought.
She saw a small scar on the side of his chin, another near
his hairline. He was all muscle and steel. There wasn't a
playground bully on this planet who'd have the nerve to
torment this man's child.

That's my swing, geek face! Get off it or I'll punch you.
Brainy Janie's got cooties . . . Brainy Janie's got coo-
ties . . .

"Please. Couldn't we just go to your bedroom?"

She loosened her hands, and he slowly released her
breasts. "You really want this bad, don't you, Rosebud?"

She nodded.

He gazed at her, and his warrior's eyes revealed none of
his thoughts.

"I'm bought and paid for," she reminded him.

"That's right. You are." He seemed to be mulling it
over. She waited patiently, giving his sluggish brain all the
time it needed to work.

"Why don't you just go back to your employer and say
we did the dirty."

"I have a very transparent face. It would immediately be
apparent that I was lying."

"There doesn't seem to be any other way out of this,
then, does there?"

Her hopes began to soar. "I'm afraid not."

"All right, Rosebud; you win. I guess we'd better head
on upstairs." He slipped his index finger under the pink
ribbon. "You sure you didn't bring any handcuffs with
you?"

She felt her throat move against his finger as she swallowed. "I'm sure."

"Let's get it over with, then."

He tugged on the ribbon as if it were a dog collar. Her
heart thudded as he led her out into the foyer and up the
carpeted steps without releasing her. The side of her body

brushed against his. She tried to move away, but he held her captive.

As they climbed the stairs, she regarded him through the corners of her eyes with apprehension. She knew it was only her imagination, but he seemed to have grown taller and bigger. Her gaze swept from his chest to his hips, and her eyes widened. Unless she was mistaken, he wasn't quite as detached as he seemed. Beneath those jeans he seemed to be fully aroused.

"In here, Rosebud."

She stumbled as he drew her through the doorway into the master bedroom, still trying to figure out how someone as inept as she had managed to excite him. She reminded herself that she was female, and he had a caveman mentality. In his drunken state, he must have decided that any woman would do. She should be grateful he was dragging her into his cave by the ribbon instead of her hair.

He flipped a switch. Recessed lighting illuminated a king-size bed made up with blankets, but no comforter. It sat opposite a wall that held a row of windows covered with plantation shutters. There was a chest of drawers, a comfortable chair, a set of bedside tables, but very little clutter.

He released her ribbon and turned away to shut the door. She gulped as he twisted the lock. "What are you doing?"

"Some of my buddies have the key to this place. I'm guessin' you'd just as soon we didn't have any company. 'Course if I'm wrong . . ."

"No, no. You're not wrong."

"You sure? Some PSSs specialize in groups."

"SPPs. And those are level threes. I'm only a level one. Could we turn out the lights, please?"

"How am I going to see you if we do that?"

"There's quite a bit of moonlight coming in through those shutters. I'm certain you'll be able to see just fine. And it'll be more mysterious that way."

Without waiting for permission, she made a dash for the light switch and flicked it off. The room was immediately bathed in the wide bars of moonlight slipping through the shutters.

He walked over to the bed and turned his back to her. She watched him draw his knit polo shirt over his head. The muscles of his shoulders rippled as he tossed it aside. "You can put your clothes on that chair there."

Her knees trembled as she walked toward the chair he had indicated. Now that the moment of reckoning had come, she was nearly paralyzed with a fear that even narcotics couldn't quite overcome. It had been one thing to plan this encounter in the abstract, but it was quite another to face the reality of having sex with a stranger. "Maybe you'd like to talk a bit first. Get to know each other a little better."

"I lost interest in talking when we walked through that bedroom door."

"I see."

His shoes hit the floor. "Rosebud?"

"Yes?"

"Leave the bow on."

She clutched the back of the chair for support.

He turned to her and, with a flick of his fingers, opened the button on his jeans. Bars of moonlight fell across his naked chest and down over his hips. His arousal was so pronounced she couldn't tear her eyes away from it. Had she done that?

He spoiled her view by sitting on the edge of the bed to pull off his socks. His bare feet were straight and narrow, much longer than Craig's had been. So far everything about him was larger than Craig. She took a long, steadying breath and slipped out of her heels.

Wearing only his unbuttoned jeans, he lay down on the bed and leaned against the pillows. She reached for the snap at the side of her jacket. He crossed his arms behind his head and watched.

As her fingers touched the snap, ripples of panic turned her skin to gooseflesh, and she fought to reassure herself. What difference did it make if he saw her naked? It wasn't as if she had anything unusual beneath her clothes, and she needed him so desperately. Now that she had seen him, she couldn't imagine anyone else siring her child.

But her hand felt as if it were paralyzed. She noticed that his zipper had crept down, revealing a narrow blade of hair bisecting a flat abdomen.

Do it! her brain screamed. *Let him see you*! But her fingers wouldn't move.

He watched her, saying nothing. There was no kindness in that hard-eyed gaze. No gentleness. Nothing to reassure her.

As she tried to shake off her paralysis, she remembered that Craig hadn't liked sexual foreplay. He'd told her that with men, the end result was all that mattered. Cal would probably appreciate it if she simply let him get to it. She began walking toward the bed.

"I got some rubbers in the top drawer in the bathroom, Rosebud. Go get 'em."

Even though his request made everything more complicated, she was pleased with this evidence of his survival skills. He might not be book smart, but he had street smarts, a valuable asset to pass on to a child.

"No need," she said softly. "I came prepared."

She extended her leg slightly, then tugged on her skirt with her left hand. The white silk crept up to her thigh. She reached underneath, and as she withdrew the condom she had tucked in the top of her stocking, she was hit full force by the moral implications of what she was doing. She had deliberately sabotaged the condom, and this was thievery.

Studying particle physics either distanced people from God or brought them closer. For her, the latter had happened, and she was defying everything she believed in. At the same time, she began to rationalize. He had no use for what she wanted, and she wasn't harming him in any way by taking it. He was merely a device. This would have absolutely no negative effect on him.

Setting aside her qualms, she peeled apart the package and handed the condom to him. Even in the dim light, she wasn't taking any chances that he would notice the package had been tampered with.

"Well, now, aren't you an efficient little thing."

"Very efficient." Drawing a steadying breath, she tugged her skirt just high enough so that she could kneel on the edge of the mattress. Then she straddled his thighs, determined to get this over with as quickly as she could.

He gazed up at her, his arms crossed behind his head, the condom between his fingers. Staying on her knees, she garnered her courage and reached for the open waistband of his jeans. Her fingertips brushed the taut skin of his abdomen, and the next thing she knew, she was flat on her back.

With a hiss of alarm, she gazed up at him. His weight pressed her into the mattress, and the heels of his hands pinioned her shoulders so she couldn't move. "Wh-what are you doing?"

His mouth tightened into a hard, thin line. "The game's over, lady. Who the hell are you?"

She gasped for breath. She didn't know whether it was his weight or her own fear, but her lungs felt as if they'd collapsed. "I—I don't know what you mean."

"I want the truth, and I want it now. Who are you?"

She'd underestimated his street smarts, and she knew she couldn't afford another convoluted explanation. Her only chance to salvage this situation lay in simplicity. She thought of Jodie Pulanski and forced herself to look directly into his eyes.

"I'm a big fan."

He regarded her with disgust. "That's what I figured. A bored society bimbo with a hankerin' for football jerseys."

Bimbo! He thought she was a *bimbo!* The novelty of it distracted her, and it took a moment to recover. "Not all jerseys," she said hastily. "Just yours."

She hoped he wouldn't ask her the number because she had no idea. The personal research she'd done had centered on his medical records: low cholesterol, twenty-twenty vision, no family history of chronic disease, only a variety of orthopedic injuries that were of no concern to her.

"I should kick your ass out of here."

Despite his words, he didn't move, and as she felt him pressed hard against her thigh, she knew why. "But you won't."

For a long moment, he said nothing. Then he reared back, releasing her shoulders. "You're right. I guess I'm drunk enough to forget that I gave up groupies years ago."

He moved to the side of the bed and shucked his jeans. With the bars of moonlight falling across his body, there was something primitive about him and elementally male. She looked away as he tugged on the sabotaged condom. This was it, then.

Her mouth went dry as he turned back and reached for the snap that held her jacket together. She flinched and made an instinctive grab for his hand.

He clenched his teeth in something that resembled a snarl. "Make up your mind, Rosebud, and do it fast."

"I want to . . . I want to keep my clothes on." Before he could respond, she gripped his wrist and shoved his hand under her skirt. Once she'd done that, she released him, because if he couldn't take it from there by himself, she was doomed.

She needn't have worried.

"You sure are full of surprises, Rosebud." He stroked up the length of her stocking, then moved higher, tracing the path of the garter to the point where it met the lacy belt. Now he knew exactly how little she had on beneath her skirt.

"You don't believe in wasting any time, do you?"

She could barely force the words through the constriction in her throat. "I want you. Now."

She willed herself to open her legs, but the muscles in her thighs were so rigid, she could barely force them apart. He stroked them, soothing her as if she were a cat with an arched back.

"Relax, Rosebud. For somebody who wants it so bad, you sure are tense."

"An—anticipation." *Please give me my baby. Just give me my baby and let me out of here.*

His fingers brushed the soft hair at the juncture of her thighs, and she wanted to die from the embarrassment of it. She winced as his touch grew more intimate, then tried to turn the sound into a moan of passion. She had to relax. How could she possibly conceive when she was so tense?

"Am I hurting you?"

"No. Of course not. I've never been more aroused."

He gave a snort of disbelief and began to push her skirt to her waist, only to have her grab it at the top of her thighs. "Please don't do that."

"I'm startin' to feel like a sixteen-year-old again, makin' out in the alley behind Delafield's Drugstore." His voice had a husky sound to it she hadn't heard before, giving her the impression that he didn't find that particular fantasy entirely unpleasant.

What would it have been like, she wondered, to be the teenage girl making out with the town football hero in the alley behind the drugstore? When she had been sixteen, she was in college. At best, her male classmates had treated her as a kid sister; at worst, they had made snide remarks about "the little bitch who broke the grade curve."

He trailed his mouth over the bodice of her jacket. She felt the moist heat of his breath on her breast, and she nearly leaped off the bed as his lips found the bump of her nipple.

A hot rush of desire, as unexpected as it was overwhelming, rushed through her. He closed his mouth over her nipple and teased it through the silk with the tip of his tongue. Sensation flooded through her body, waves of it, crashing in on her.

She fought against what was happening. If she permitted herself to derive even a moment's pleasure from his caress, she would be no better than the prostitute she was impersonating. This had to be a sacrifice, or she could never live with herself.

But Craig had always ignored her breasts, and the sensations were so sweet.

"Oh, please . . . Please don't do that." Desperately, she reached out for him and tried to draw him on top of her.

"You're mighty hard to please, Rosebud."

"Just do it. Do it, will you!"

She heard something that sounded like anger in his voice. "Whatever the lady wants."

His fingers opened her. And then she felt an awful pressure as he pushed himself inside. She turned her cheek into the pillow and tried not to cry.

He cursed and began to pull away.

"No!" She clutched at his hips and dug her fingernails into those hard buttocks. "No, please don't!"

He went still. "Then wrap your legs around me."

She did as he said.

"Tighter, dammit!"

She tightened her grip, then squeezed her eyes shut as he began to move slowly inside her.

The stretch hurt, but she had expected his brutal warrior's strength to inflict pain. What she hadn't expected was how quickly the pain changed to warmth. His movements were unhurried—deep, slow thrusts of silk and steel that unfurled ribbons of pleasure inside her.

Sweat from his body dampened the fragile barrier of her clothing. He reached under her and caught her hips in his hands. He tilted them up, angling his own body in such a way that hot spasms licked at her. Her excitement grew even as she fought to suppress it. Why couldn't Craig have loved her like this just once?

The fact that she was finding pleasure in having sex with a stranger shamed her, and as the sensations intensified, she tried to concentrate on her research by conjuring up thoughts of the top quark that obsessed her. But her mind refused to focus on subatomic particles, and she knew she had to act or he would push her to orgasm, something that would be unforgivable. She steeled herself, even as her brain warned her of the danger of inciting a warrior.

"Are you . . . going to take all day?"

He went absolutely still. "What did you say?"

She gulped, and her voice held a soft croak. "You heard me. I thought you were supposed to be a great lover? Why is it taking you so long?"

"So long?" He drew back far enough to glare down at her. "You know something, lady? You're crazy!" And then he lunged.

She bit her lip to keep from crying out as he drove deep. Again and again.

She clung to him with her thighs and her arms, meeting his fierce thrusts with a grim determination. She would stay with him, and she would feel nothing.

But her body rebelled. Those intolerable pleasure waves grew strong. She gasped. Climbed.

And then his muscles stiffened. Every part of him went rigid, and she felt the moment when he spilled himself inside her.

She clutched her hands into fists, her own pleasure forgotten. *Swim! Swim, all you warrior babymakers! Swim, all you sweet little brainless babymakers!* With a rush of tenderness for the gift he was giving her, she turned her lips to his damp shoulder and gave him a soft kiss of gratitude.

He slumped forward, his weight heavy on her.

She kept her thighs clutched around his hips, not letting him go even as she felt him begin to withdraw. Just a little longer. Not yet.

The power of her will was no match for his strength. He pulled away and sat up on the edge of the bed. Bracing his elbows on his knees, he stayed there, staring into space and breathing deeply. The bow that had been fastened around her neck had come untied, and, as she moved, it slipped onto the pillow.

Bars of moonlight slashed across his back, and she thought she had never seen anyone who looked so lonely. She wanted to reach out and touch him, but she couldn't intrude on his privacy. The wrongness of what she had done struck her like a blow. She was a liar and a thief.

He rose and headed for the bathroom. "I want you gone when I come out."

4

As Cal stood under the locker-room shower, he found himself thinking about Rosebud instead of the grueling practice he had just completed or the fact that his shoulder ached, his ankle throbbed, and nothing on him seemed to be recovering as quickly as it used to. It wasn't the first time he'd thought about Rosebud since his birthday night two weeks ago, but he couldn't explain why she kept popping into his mind or why he'd been so immediately attracted to her. He only knew that the instant she had walked into his living room with that fat pink bow around her neck, he'd wanted her.

Her appeal confounded him because she wasn't his type. Although she was attractive with her blond hair and those light green eyes, she wasn't in the same league with the beautiful girls he'd been dating. Her skin was outstanding, he'd give her that, sort of like French vanilla ice cream, but she was too tall, too flat-chested, and too damned old.

He ducked his head and let the shower water splash over him. Maybe he'd been drawn in by all her contradictions: the intelligence in those green eyes that fought the cocka-mamie story she'd told him, a funny aloofness in her manner that kept running headlong into her clumsy attempts to seduce him.

He'd quickly figured out that she was an upper-crust groupie looking for a cheap thrill by pretending to be a hooker, and he hadn't liked the idea that he was attracted to a woman like that, so he'd told her to leave. But he hadn't put any real energy behind it. Instead of being irritated by her lies, he'd mainly been amused by her desperate earnestness as she'd spun out one story after another.

But it was what had happened in his bedroom that he couldn't forget. Something had been very wrong. Why had she refused to take off her clothes? Even when they were going at it, she wouldn't let him undress her. It had been strange, and so damned erotic he couldn't quit thinking about it.

He frowned, remembering that she hadn't let him make her come. That bothered him. He could read people pretty well, and although he'd known she was a liar, he'd figured she was essentially harmless. Now he wasn't so sure. It was almost as if she had some hidden agenda, but he couldn't imagine what it was beyond putting a check mark in front of his name before she moved on to her next celebrity jock.

Just as Cal was rinsing the shampoo out of his hair, Junior yelled into the shower room. "Hey, Bomber, Bobby Tom's on the phone. He wants to talk to you."

Cal slapped a towel around his hips and hurried to the telephone. If it had been anybody else in the football world from the NFL commissioner to John Madden, he'd have told Junior he'd call back. But not Bobby Tom Denton. They hadn't played together until the last few years of B.T.'s career, but that made no difference. If B.T. wanted his right arm, Cal figured he'd probably give it to him. That's how much respect he had for the former Stars' player who, in his opinion, had been the best wide receiver in NFL history.

Cal smiled as that familiar Texas drawl came over the phone lines. "Hey, Cal, you comin' down to Telarosa for my charity golf tournament in May? Consider this your personal engraved invitation. Got a big barbeque in the works and more beautiful women than even you're gonna know what to do with. 'Course, with Gracie lookin' on, I'll have to leave it up to you to entertain them. That wife of mine keeps me on a real tight leash.''

Since injuries had prevented Cal from playing in B.T.'s last few tournaments, he hadn't met Gracie Denton, but he knew Bobby Tom well enough to realize there was no woman in the world who could keep him on a leash.

"I promise to do my part, B.T."

"That'll make Gracie real happy. Did you know she got herself elected mayor of Telarosa right before Wendy was born?''

"I'd heard.''

Bobby Tom went on to talk about his wife and new baby girl. Cal wasn't too interested in either, but he pretended to be because he knew it was important to B.T. to act as if his family was the center of his life now that he was retired, and that he didn't miss football at all. Bobby Tom never complained about being forced from the game by blowing out his knee, but Cal knew it still had to be ripping his guts apart. Football had been B.T.'s life, just like it was Cal's, and without those games to look forward to, Cal knew his former teammate's existence was as empty as a Tuesday night stadium.

Poor B.T. Cal gave the former wide-out high marks for not whining about the injustice of being forced out of the game, even as he promised himself he wouldn't let anything in the world push him into retirement until he was ready. Football was his life, and nothing would ever change that. Not age. Not injuries. Nothing.

He finished his conversation, then went to his locker to dress. As he pulled on his clothes, his thoughts drifted away from Bobby Tom Denton and back to his birthday night. Who was she, damn it? And why couldn't he get her off his mind?

*   *   *

"You made me come all the way over here today just so you could ask me about my transportation expenses to the Denver conference?" Jane never lost control in professional situations, but as she looked at the man who governed her day-to-day activities at Preeze Laboratories, she wanted to scream.

Dr. Jerry Miles lifted his head from the papers he'd been studying on his desk. "You may regard these kinds of details as minor annoyances, Jane, but as the director of Preeze Laboratories, I assure you they're not minor to me."

He thrust his hand back through his limp, too-long graying hair as if she'd frustrated him beyond bearing. The gesture seemed as studied as his appearance. Today Jerry's uniform consisted of a snagged, yellow polyester turtleneck sweater, threadbare navy jacket with a dandruff-flecked collar, and rusty corduroy slacks now mercifully concealed by the desk.

It wasn't Jane's habit to judge people by their clothing—most of the time she was too preoccupied even to notice—but she suspected Jerry's unkempt appearance was deliberately cultivated to conform to the image of the eccentric physicist, a stereotype that had died out a good decade earlier, but which Jerry must believe would camouflage the fact that he could no longer keep up with the exploding body of knowledge that made up modern physics.

String theories mystified him, supersymmetry left him baffled, and, unlike Jane, he couldn't handle the complex new mathematics that scientists such as she were practically inventing on a daily basis. But despite his shortcomings, Jerry had been appointed director of Preeze two years ago, a maneuver engineered by the older and more conservative members of the scientific establishment, who wanted one of their own to head such a prestigious institution. Jane's association with Preeze had been a hellish snarl of bureaucracy ever since. By contrast, her position on the Newberry College faculty seemed remarkably uncomplicated.

"In the future," Jerry said, "we're going to need more documentation from you to justify this sort of expense. Your cab fare from the airport, for example. Outrageous."

She found it mind-boggling that a man in his position could find nothing better to do than harrass her about something so inconsequential. "The Denver airport is quite far from the city."

"In that case, you should have used the hotel shuttle."

She could barely swallow her frustration. Not only was Jerry scientifically incompetent, but he was a sexist, since her male colleagues didn't have to undergo this kind of scrutiny. Of course, they hadn't made Jerry look like a fool either.

When Jane had been in her early twenties and still operating in a fog of idealistic zeal, she had written a paper that had patently disproved one of Jerry's pet theories, which had been a slapdash piece of work that had nonetheless garnered him accolades. His stock within the scientific community had never been the same, and he'd neither forgotten nor forgiven her.

Now, his brow furrowed, and he launched into an assault on her work, not a simple thing since he comprehended so little of it. As he pontificated, the depression that had dogged her ever since her failed attempt to get pregnant two months earlier, settled in deeper. If only she were carrying a child now, everything might not seem so bleak.

As a fierce seeker of the truth, she knew what she had done that night was morally wrong, but she was confused by the fact that something about it had seemed so right, maybe the fact that she could not have chosen a better candidate to be her baby's father. Cal Bonner was warrior, a man of aggression and brute strength, all qualities she lacked. But there was something more, something she couldn't entirely explain, that spoke of his absolute suitability. An internal female voice, ancient and wise, told her what logic couldn't explain. It would be Cal Bonner or no one.

Unfortunately that internal voice didn't tell her how she was to find the courage to approach him again. Christmas had come and gone, but as desperately as she wanted a baby, she couldn't imagine arranging another sexual coupling.

The sight of Jerry Miles's lips thinning into a cat-that-ate-the-canary smile yanked her back to the present. "... tried to avoid this, Jane, but in view of the difficulties we've been having over the past few years, I don't seem to have a choice. As of now, I'm requiring that you submit a report to me by the last day of each and every month detailing your activities and bringing me up to date on your work."

"A report? I don't understand."

As he began to elaborate on what he wanted from her, she couldn't hide her shock. No one else was required to do anything like this. It was bureaucratic busywork, and the very idea went against the essense of everything Preeze stood for.

"I won't do it. This is blatantly unfair."

He regarded her with a faintly pitying look. "I'm sure the Board will be unhappy to hear that, especially since your fellowship is up for review this year."

She was so outraged, she could barely speak. "I've been doing excellent work, Jerry."

"Then you shouldn't mind preparing these reports for me each month so I can share your enthusiasm."

"No one else has to do this."

"You're quite young, Jane, and not as well established as the others."

She was also a woman, and he was a sexist jerk. Years of self-discipline prevented her from saying any of this out loud, especially since she would end up hurting herself more than him. Instead, she rose to her feet, and, without a word, marched from his office.

She fumed as she rode down to the main floor in the elevator and stalked across the lobby. How much longer was she going to have to put up with this? Once again, she regretted the fact that her friend Caroline was out of the country. She very much needed a sympathetic ear.

The gray January afternoon held that ugly hint of permanence that always seemed to hang over northern Illinois at this time of year. She shivered as she climbed into her Saturn and sped toward the elementary school in Aurora where she was scheduled to do a science program for the third graders.

Some of her colleagues teased her about her volunteer work there. They said that having a world-renowned theoretical physicist teaching elementary-school children, especially disadvantaged ones, was like having Itzhak Perlman teaching beginning violin. But the state of science education in the elementary schools disturbed her, and she was doing her small part to change it.

As she hurried into the assembly room where the third graders were waiting and set down the supplies she'd brought with her for the experiments, she forced herself to put aside thoughts of Jerry's newest act of bureacratic sadism.

"Dr. Darling! Dr. Darling!"

She smiled at the way the third graders had corrupted her last name. It had happened during her first visit two years ago, and since she hadn't bothered to set them straight, the appellation had stuck. As she returned their greetings and gazed into their eager, mischievous faces, her heart twisted. How she wanted a child of her own.

She felt an unexpected rush of disgust directed entirely at herself. Was she going to spend the rest of her life filled with self-pity because she didn't have a child, but not doing anything to correct the situation? It was no wonder she hadn't been able to conceive a warrior's baby. She didn't have a backbone!

As she began her first experiment, using a candle and an empty oatmeal box, she made up her mind. From the beginning she'd known her chances of conceiving after only one attempt were slight, and now it was time to try again—this weekend, when her fertility was at its peak.

She knew from her dedicated perusal of the newspaper's sports' section that the Stars would be in Indianapolis for the AFC Championship quarterfinals this weekend. According to Jodie, Cal was going to his family home in North Carolina shortly after the season was over, so if she put this off any longer, he might be gone.

Her conscience chose that moment to remind her that what she was doing was immoral, but she firmly silenced that nagging voice. On Saturday, she would put her misgivings behind her and head for Indianapolis. Maybe this time the legendary quarterback could score a touchdown just for her.

It had rained all day in Indianapolis, delaying the Stars' Saturday morning flight out of Chicago and backing up the schedule. By the time Cal left the hotel bar on Saturday night and headed for the elevator, it was nearly midnight, an hour past the team's normal game-night curfew. He passed Kevin Tucker, but neither man spoke. They'd already said everything they had to at a press conference a few hours earlier. They both hated the public ass-kissing they were forced to do, but it was part of the job.

At every one of these conferences, Cal was forced to look the reporters straight in the eye and go on and on about Kevin's talent and how much he appreciated his support and how both of them only wanted what was best for the team. Then Kevin would start in about all the respect he had for Cal and how privileged he was just to be part of the Stars. It was all bull. The reporters knew it. The fans knew it. Cal and Kevin sure knew it, but, still, they had to go through the motions.

When Cal got to his room, he loaded a videocassette of the Colts' last game into the VCR that the hotel had provided and kicked off his shoes. As he lay back on the bed to watch, he pushed thoughts of Kevin Tucker aside to concentrate on the Colts' defensive line. He fast-forwarded to the second quarter and pushed the play button, then watched until he found what he wanted. He hit the rewind button and watched again.

With his gaze firmly fixed on the screen, he unwrapped his pillow mint and ate it. Unless his eyes were playing tricks, their safety had a bad habit of signaling a blitz by looking twice toward the sideline. Cal smiled and tucked the information away.

Jane stood in front of Cal Bonner's hotel-room door dressed in the ecru silk suit and taking deep breaths. If tonight didn't work, she would have to learn to live with self-pity because she couldn't go through this again.

She realized she'd forgotten to take off her glasses, and she quickly stuck them into her purse, then hitched the gold-chain strap higher on her shoulder. If only she had some of Jodie's little relaxation pills, this might be easier, but tonight she was on her own. Summoning all her willpower, she raised her hand and knocked.

The door swung open. She saw a bare chest. Blond chest hair. A pair of green eyes.

"I—I'm sorry. I seem to have the wrong room."

"I guess that depends on who you're looking for, buttercup."

He was young, perhaps twenty-four or twenty-five, and arrogant. "I was looking for Mr. Bonner."

"Aren't you lucky, then, because you found something better. I'm Kevin Tucker."

She finally recognized him from the televised games

she'd been watching, although he looked younger without his helmet. "I was told Mr. Bonner was in 542." Why had she trusted Jodie to get the correct information?

"You were told wrong." His mouth grew faintly sullen, and she gathered that she'd insulted him by not recognizing him.

"Do you happen to know where he might be?"

"Oh, I know, all right. What kind of business do you have with the old man?"

What kind of business, indeed? "It's private."

"I'll just bet it is."

His leer annoyed her. This young man definitely needed to be put in his place. "I happen to be his spiritual advisor."

Tucker threw back his head and laughed. "Is that what they call it? Well, I sure hope you can help him deal with all his problems about getting old."

"I keep the conversations I have with my clients confidential. Could you please tell me his room number?"

"I'll do you one better. I'll take you there."

She saw wily intelligence in his eyes and knew that even with his good looks and glow of health, he was far too bright ever to be a candidate to father her child. "You don't have to do that."

"Oh, I wouldn't miss it for the world. Just let me get my key."

He got his key, but he didn't bother with either a shirt or shoes, and he padded barefoot down the hallway. They rounded a corner and went down another corridor before they stopped in front of 501.

It was difficult enough facing Cal without having an on-looker, so she quickly extended her hand and shook his. "Thank you very much, Mr. Tucker. I appreciate your help."

"No problem." He withdrew his hand and banged his knuckles twice against the door.

"I believe I can take it from here. Thank you again."

"You're welcome." He made no move to leave.

The door swung open, and Jane caught her breath as she once again found herself face-to-face with Cal Bonner. Next to the youthful glory of Kevin Tucker, he looked more battleworn than she remembered, and, if anything, more formidable: a case-hardened King Arthur to Tucker's callow Lancelot. She hadn't remembered quite how powerful his presence was, and she fought an instinctive urge to step back.

Tucker's drawl seemed deliberately insolent. "Look what I found wandering around, Calvin. Your personal spiritual advisor."

"My what?"

"I was given Mr. Tucker's room number by mistake," she said hastily. "He graciously offered to escort me here."

Tucker smiled at her. "Did anybody ever tell you that you talk funny? Like you should be narrating wildlife films on public television."

"Or be somebody's damn butler," Cal muttered. His pale eyes raked her. "What are you doing here?"

Tucker crossed his arms and leaned back against the doorjamb to watch. Jane had no idea what had transpired between these two men, but she knew they weren't friends.

"She came here to give you spiritual advice on dealing with the problems of old age, Calvin."

A small muscle twitched at the corner of Cal's jaw. "Don't you have some training films to watch, Tucker?"

"Nope. I already know everything God does about the Colts' defense."

"Is that so?" He regarded him with those seasoned campaigner's eyes. "Did you happen to notice their safety signals whenever they're about to blitz?"

Tucker stiffened.

"I didn't think so. Go do your homework, kid. That

golden arm of yours ain't worth a damn 'til you learn how to read a defense.''

Jane wasn't entirely certain what they were talking about, but she understood that Cal had somehow put Kevin in his place.

Tucker pulled away from the doorjamb and winked at Jane. "You'd better not stay too long. Old guys like Calvin need their beauty sleep. Now you feel free to stop by my room when you're done. I'm sure he won't have worn you out."

Although the young man's gall was amusing, he still needed to be put in his place. "Do you require spiritual advice, Mr. Tucker?"

"More than you can imagine."

"Then I'll pray for you."

He laughed and took off down the hall, all youthful strut and blatant disrespect. She smiled in spite of herself.

"Why don't you go right along with him, Rosebud, since you think he's so damn funny?"

She turned her attention back to Cal. "Were you that cocky when you were young?"

"I wish everybody'd quit talkin' about me like I've got one foot in the damn grave!"

Two women rounded the corner and came to a stop as they caught sight of him. He grabbed her arm and pulled her inside. "Get in here."

As he shut the door behind her, she glanced around the room. The pillows were bunched up against the headboard of the king-size bed, and the spread was rumpled. Static flickered on the silent screen of the television.

"What are you doin' in Indianapolis?"

She swallowed. "I think you know the answer to that." With a boldness she couldn't believe she possessed, she slid the palm of her hand down over the light switch by the door.

The room plunged into a darkness that was relieved only

by the flickering silver light from the television screen.

"You don't believe in messin' around, do you, Rose-bud?"

Her courage was rapidly flagging. This second time was going to be even more difficult than the first. She dropped her purse to the floor. "What's the point? We both know where this is headed."

With a thudding heart, she looped her fingers over the waistband of his slacks and pulled him toward her. As his hips pressed against hers, she felt him grow hard, and it was as if every cell in her body came alive.

For someone who had always been timid with the opposite sex, playing the femme fatale was a powerful experience. She sank her fingers into his buttocks and pressed her breasts to his chest. Running her hands up along his sides, she curled her body against him, moving seductively.

But her sense of power was short-lived. He pinioned her to the wall and caught her chin in a rough grasp. "Is there a Mr. Rosebud?"

"No."

His grip tightened. "Don't mess with me, lady. I want the truth."

She met his eyes without flinching. In this, at least, she didn't have to lie. "I'm not married. I swear."

He must have believed her because he released her chin. Before he could question her further, she pushed her hands between them and released the snap on his slacks.

As she struggled with the zipper, she felt his hands on the bodice of her jacket. She opened her mouth to protest just as he pulled it apart.

"No!" She snatched at the gaping silk, ripping a seam in the process as she covered herself.

He immediately stepped away from her. "Get out of here."

She clutched the jacket together. He looked furious, and she knew she'd made a mistake, but the only way she could keep this from becoming unbearably sordid was to preserve her modesty.

She forced herself to smile. "It's more exciting this way. Please don't spoil it."

"You're making me feel like a rapist, and I don't like it. You're the one who's after me, lady."

"It's my fantasy. I came all the way to Indianapolis so I could feel ravaged. With my clothes on."

"Ravaged, huh."

She clutched the jacket tighter over her bare breasts. "With my clothes on."

He thought for a moment. If only she could read his mind.

"You ever done it against a wall?" he asked.

The prospect excited her, and that was the last thing she wanted. This was about procreation, not lust. Besides, it might be harder to get pregnant that way. "I prefer the bed."

"I guess the person doing the ravaging gets to decide that, doesn't he?"

The next thing she knew, he had shoved her against the wall and pushed her skirt up far enough to catch the back of her thighs. He splayed them, lifted her off the floor, and stepped into the nakedness between.

The hard strength of his body should have frightened her, but it didn't. Instead, she looped her arms around his shoulders and held on.

"Put your legs around me." His voice was a low, husky command, and she instinctively obeyed.

She felt him free himself, and she expected him to enter her roughly, but he didn't. Instead, he touched her with one gentle fingertip.

She buried her face in the side of his neck and sank her teeth into her bottom lip to keep from crying out. She concentrated on the intrusion instead of the pleasure, on the embarrassment of opening herself like this to a stranger's touch. She had made herself his whore. That was all she meant to him, a slut to be used for a few moments of sexual pleasure and then discarded. She nurtured her humiliation so she wouldn't experience desire.

His finger traced the entry to her body. She shuddered and focused on the strain in her splayed thighs, the uncomfortable pull of her muscles, anything except that silken stroking. But it was impossible. The sensations were too sweet, so she dug her fingernails into his back and bucked against him.

"Ravage me, damn it!"

He cursed, and the sound was so savage, she flinched. "What the hell's wrong with you?"

"Just do it! Now!"

With a low growl, he caught her hips. "Damn you!"

She bit her lip as he thrust inside her, then gripped his shoulders tighter so she wouldn't lose him. All she had to do was hang on.

The heat from his body burned through his shirt into her breasts. The wall bruised her spine, and he had spread her legs so far apart the muscles ached. She no longer had to worry about suppressing her pleasure. She wanted only for him to finish.

He thrust so deeply inside her that she winced. He would have made love to her if she had given him any sign at all, but she hadn't wanted that. She had been determined to take no pleasure, and he'd granted her wish.

His shirt grew damp beneath her palms, and he used her so that he made her feel as if he were punishing them both. She barely held on to him through his orgasm. When it happened, she tried to will her body to absorb the essence of his, but her badly bruised soul wanted only to escape.

Seconds ticked by before he finally withdrew. He slowly stepped away from her and lowered her to the floor.

Her legs were so rubbery, she could barely stand. She

refused to look at him. She couldn't bear this thing she had done, not once, but twice.

"Rosebud . . ."

"I'm sorry." She bent down to snatch up her purse and grabbed the doorknob. With her jacket clutched together in one hand and her thighs wet, she ran out into the hallway.

He called her name. That silly name she had taken from a beer sign. She couldn't tolerate his coming after her and watching her fall apart, so she lifted her hand and waved without looking back. It was a jaunty wave, one that said, *So long, sucker. Don't call me. I'll call you.*

The door slammed behind her.

He'd gotten the message.

5

The following evening Cal sat in his accustomed place toward the back of the chartered plane that was returning the Stars to Chicago from Indianapolis. The lights were out in the cabin, and most of the players either slept or listened to music through headsets. Cal brooded.

His ankle ached from an injury he'd received in the fourth quarter. Afterward, Kevin had gone in to replace him, been sacked three times, fumbled twice, and still thrown the ball fifty-three yards for the winning touchdown.

His injuries were coming faster now: a shoulder separation at training camp, a deep thigh bruise last month, and now this. The team physician had diagnosed a high ankle sprain, which meant Cal wouldn't be able to practice this week. He was thirty-six years old, and he tried not to remember that even Montana had retired at thirty-eight. He also wasn't dwelling on the fact that he didn't recover as quickly as he used to. In addition to his ankle injury, his knees throbbed, a couple of his ribs hurt, and his hip felt as if it had a hot poker shoved right through it. He knew he'd spend a good part of the night in his whirlpool.

Between the ankle injury and the disastrous incident with Rosebud, he was more than glad to have this weekend behind him. He still couldn't believe that he hadn't used a rubber. Even when he was a teenager, he'd never been that careless. What really galled him was the fact that he hadn't even thought about it until after she'd left. It was as if the minute he'd set eyes on her, his brain had gone into hibernation, and lust had taken over.

Maybe he'd taken one too many blows to the head because he sure as hell felt like he was losing his mind. If it had been any groupie other than Rosebud, he would never have let her into his room. The first time he'd had an excuse since he'd been half-drunk, but this time there weren't any excuses. He'd wanted her, and he'd taken her; it had been as simple as that.

He couldn't even figure out what her appeal was. One of the perks of being an athlete was picking and choosing, and he'd always chosen the youngest and the most beautiful women. Despite what she'd said, she was at least twenty-eight, and he had no interest in women that old. He liked them fresh and dewy, with high, full breasts, pouty mouths, and the smell of newness about them.

Rosebud smelled like old-fashioned vanilla. Then there were those green eyes of hers. Even when she was lying, she'd looked at him dead on. He wasn't used to that. He liked flirty, fluttery eyes on women, but Rosebud had no-nonsense eyes, which was ironic considering the fact that nothing about her was honest.

He brooded all the way back to Chicago and kept at it right on into the next week. The fact that he was held out from practice made him even more bad-tempered than usual, and it wasn't until Friday that his rigid self-discipline finally kicked in, and he blocked out everything except the Denver Broncos.

The Stars were playing in the semifinals for the AFC Championship, and despite his sore shoulder, he managed to perform. Injuries, however, hampered their defense, and they weren't able to stop the Broncos' passing attack. Denver won, twenty-two to eighteen.

Cal Bonner's fifteenth season in the NFL came to an end.

*   *   *

Marie, the secretary Jane shared with two other members of Newberry's Physics Department, held out several pink message slips as Jane walked into the office. "Dr. Nguyen at Fermi called; he needs to speak with you before four o'clock, and Dr. Davenport has scheduled a departmental meeting for Wednesday."

"Thanks, Marie."

Despite the secretary's sour face, Jane could barely resist giving her a hug. She wanted to dance, sing, jitterbug on the ceiling, then race through the corridors of Stramingler Hall and tell all her colleagues that she was pregnant.

"I need your DOE reports by five."

"You'll have them," Jane replied. The temptation to share the news was nearly irresistible, but she was only a month along, Marie was a judgmental sourpuss, and it was too early to tell anyone.

One person knew, however, and as Jane collected her mail and walked into her office, a nagging worry burrowed through her happiness. Two nights ago Jodie had dropped by the house and spotted the books on pregnancy that Jane had unthinkingly left stacked on the coffee table. Jane could hardly hide her condition from Jodie forever, and she didn't try to deny it, but she was uneasy about trusting someone so self-centered to keep quiet regarding the circumstances surrounding her child's conception.

Although Jodie had promised that she'd carry Jane's secret to the grave, Jane didn't have quite that much faith in her integrity. Still, she had seemed genuinely happy and sincere in her desire to keep the secret, so, as Jane closed herself in her office and flipped on her computer, she decided not to waste any more energy worrying about it.

She logged on to the electronic preprint library at Los Alamos to see what new papers on string theory and duality had been posted since yesterday. It was an automatic act, the same one performed daily by every top-level physicist in the world. The general public opened a newspaper first thing in the morning. Physicists connected with the library at Los Alamos.

But this morning, instead of concentrating on the list of new papers, she found herself thinking about Cal Bonner. According to Jodie, he was spending most of February traveling around the country fulfilling his commercial endorsement obligations before he left for North Carolina in early March. At least she wouldn't have to worry about bumping into him at the corner grocery store.

The knowledge should have been comforting, but she couldn't quite shake off her uneasiness. She determinedly turned her attention back to her computer screen, but the words wouldn't come into focus. Instead, she found herself envisioning the nursery she wanted to decorate.

She'd already decided it would be yellow, and she would paint a rainbow running up the walls and across the ceiling. Her mouth curved in a dreamy smile. This precious child of hers was going to grow up surrounded by everything beautiful.

Jodie was pissed. The guys had promised her a night with Kevin Tucker if she came up with the Bomber's birthday present, but it was the end of February, more than three months later, and they still hadn't delivered. Watching Kevin flirt with one of her girlfriends didn't sweeten her mood.

Melvin Thompson had rented Zebras for a party, and all the players who were still in town were there. Although Jodie was officially working, she'd been sipping from everybody's drinks all night so she was finally ready to confront Junior Duncan when she found him in the back room shooting pool with Germaine Clark shortly after midnight.

"I need to talk to you, Junior."

"Later, Jodie. Can't you see me and Germaine have a game going?"

She wanted to pull the cue right out of his hands and bash him over the head with it, but she wasn't quite that drunk. "You guys made me a promise, but I still don't have number twelve hanging anywhere near my closet. You might have forgot about Kevin, but I sure haven't."

"I told you we're working on it." He aimed for the center pocket and missed. "Shit."

"That's what you've been saying for three months, and I'm not buying it anymore. Every time I try to talk to him, he looks at me like I'm invisible."

Junior stepped aside so Germaine could take his turn, and she was happy to see that he looked a little uncomfortable. "The thing of it is, Jodie, Kevin's been givin' us a few problems."

"Are you sayin' he doesn't want to sleep with me?"

"It's not that. It's just that he's been seeing a couple other women, and it's gotten sort of complicated. Tell you what? How 'bout I fix you up with Roy Rawlins and Matt Truate?"

"Get real. If I'd wanted those two benchwarmers, I could have screwed them months ago." She crossed her arms. "We had a deal. If I found you a hooker for the Bomber's birthday present, I got a night with Kevin. I lived up to my part of the bargain."

"Not exactly."

The sound of that Carolina drawl coming from directly behind her sent a shiver down her spine, just like somebody'd stomped right over her grave. She turned and looked into the Bomber's pale gray eyes.

Where had he come from? The last time she'd seen him, a couple of blondes had been trying to make time with him at the bar. What was he doing back here?

"You didn't come up with a *hooker*, did you, Jodie?"

She licked her lips. "I don't know what you're talking about."

"I think you do." She jumped as he curled his long fingers around her arm. "Excuse us, guys. Jodie and me are going to step outside and have ourselves a little chat."

"You're crazy! It's freezing out there."

"We won't stay long." Without giving her a chance to argue, he pulled her away from the pool table and toward the back door.

All day the radio had been warning that temperatures would be dipping into the single digits that night, and as they hit the alley, their breath made vapor clouds in the air. Jodie shivered, and Cal regarded her with grim satisfaction. He was finally going to have his questions answered.

Mysteries had always made him edgy, both on the football field and in real life. In his experience a mystery generally meant somebody was getting ready to run a play that wasn't in the book, and he didn't like those kinds of surprises.

He knew he could have pressed the guys for some answers, but he didn't want them to suspect how much time he'd spent thinking about Rosebud. Until he'd overheard Jodie's conversation with Junior, it hadn't occurred to him to talk to her.

No matter how hard he tried, he couldn't seem to put the matter of Rosebud to rest. He found himself worrying about her at the strangest times. Who could predict how many hotel rooms she'd stumbled into recently, with her story about SPPs and spiritual advisors? For all he knew, she'd moved on to the Bears by now, and he couldn't help wondering which one of them she wasn't undressing for.

"Who is she, Jodie?"

She wore only her hostess uniform, a clingy scooped-neck top with a zebra-striped short skirt, and her teeth were already chattering. "A hooker I found out about."

Part of his brain whispered a warning that maybe he

should let it go at that. How did he know he wasn't poking into things he was better off not knowing? But one of the factors that made him a great quarterback was his ability to sense danger, and for some reason he didn't understand, the hairs on the back of his neck had begun standing up.

"You're bullshitting me, Jodie, and I don't like it when people do that." He let go of her arm, but, at the same time, he moved a few inches closer, trapping her between himself and the brick wall.

Her eyes darted to the side. "She's somebody I met, okay?"

"I want a name."

"I can't— Look, I can't do that. I promised."

"You shouldn't have."

She started rubbing her arms, and her teeth began to chatter. "Jesus, Cal, it's colder than hell out here."

"I don't even feel it."

"She's . . . Her name is Jane. That's all I know."

"I don't believe you."

"This is bullshit!" She jerked to the side, trying to push past him, but he shifted his weight, blocking her way. He knew he was scaring her, and that was just fine with him. He wanted to get this over with as quickly as possible.

"Jane what?"

"I forget." She clutched her arms tighter and hunched her shoulders.

Her defiance annoyed him. "Hanging around the guys means a lot to you, doesn't it?"

She regarded him warily. "It's okay."

"I think it's a lot more than okay. I think it's the most important thing in your sad little life. And I know you'd be real upset if none of the players came in to Zebras anymore. If none of them wanted to hang out with you, not even the backups."

He knew he had her, but she made one last stab at defying him. "She's a nice lady having a hard time, and I'm not going to hurt her."

"Name!"

She hesitated, then gave in. "Jane Darlington."

"Keep talking."

"That's all I know," she said sullenly.

He lowered his voice until it was barely more than a whisper. "This is your last warning. Tell me what I want to know, or I'll make you off-limits to every player on the team."

"You're a real shit."

He didn't say a thing. He just stood there and waited.

She rubbed her arms for warmth and regarded him with belligerence. "She's a physics professor at Newberry."

Of all the things he had expected to hear, that one wasn't even on the list. "A *professor?*"

"Yeah. And she works at one of those labs, too. I don't know which one. She's a geek—real smart—but she doesn't have a lot of guys, and . . . She didn't mean any harm."

The more answers he got, the more the skin on the back of his neck tightened. "Why me? And don't try to tell me she's a Stars' groupie because I know that's not true."

She was shaking with the cold. "I promised her, okay. This is like her whole life and everything."

"I've just run out of patience."

He could see her trying to figure out whether she was going to protect her own hide or rat on her friend. He knew the answer even before she spoke.

"She wanted to have a kid, all right! And she doesn't want you to know about it."

A chill shot through him that had nothing to do with the temperature.

She regarded him uneasily. "It's not like she's going to show up when the kid's born and ask for money. She's got a good job, and she's smart, so why don't you just forget about the whole thing.''

He was having a hard time dragging enough air into his lungs. ''Are you telling me she's pregnant? That she used me to get herself pregnant?''

''Yeah, but it's not like it's really your kid. It's like you're just a sperm donor. That's the way she thinks about it.''

''A sperm donor?'' He felt as if he were going to explode—as if the top of his head was about to blow right off. He hated any kind of permanence—he wouldn't even live in the same place for very long—yet now he'd fathered a child. He had to fight to stay in control. ''Why me? Tell me why she choose me?''

A thread of fear reappeared beneath her hostility. ''You're not going to like this part.''

''I'll just bet you're right.''

''She's this genius. And being so much smarter than everybody else made her feel like a freak when she was growing up. Naturally she didn't want that for her kid, so it was important for her to find somebody who wasn't like her to be the sperm donor.''

''Wasn't like her? What do you mean?''

''Somebody who . . . Well, who wasn't exactly a genius.''

He wanted to shake her until every one of her chattering teeth hit the ground. ''What the hell are you trying to say? Why did she choose me?''

Jodie eyed him warily. ''Because she thinks you're stupid.''

''The isotope's three protons and seven neutrons are unbound.'' Turning her back on the eight students in her graduate seminar, six males and two females, Jane continued sketching on the board. ''Take one neutron away from Li-11, and a second one will also leave. Li-9 stays behind, binding it and the two remaining neutrons as a three-body system.''

She was so intent on explaining the complexity of neutron halos in isotopes of lithium that she paid no attention to the slight disturbance that was arising behind her.

''Li-11 is called a Borromean nucleus along with . . .'' A chair squeaked. She heard whispers. ''Along with . . .'' Papers rustled. More whispers. Puzzled, she turned to investigate the source of the disturbance.

And saw Cal Bonner leaning against the sidewall, his arms crossed, fingers tucked under his armpits.

All the blood rushed from her head, and for the first time in her life, she thought she was going to faint. How had he found her? What was he doing here? For a moment she let herself pretend that he wouldn't recognize her in her professional attire. She wore a conservative double-breasted woolen dress, and her hair was pulled into the French twist that kept it out of her way when she worked. She had her glasses on—he'd never seen her with glasses. But he wasn't fooled for a moment.

A thick silence fell over the room. Everyone in her class seemed to recognize him, but he paid no attention to their reactions. He only looked at her.

She had never been the target of such undisguised hatred. His eyes were narrowed and deadly, hard lines bracketed his mouth, and, as she watched him, she felt as unbound as the nucleus of the isotope she had just been describing.

With so many curious eyes looking on, she had to pull herself together. There were ten minutes left in the class. She needed to get him out of here so she could finish. ''Would you wait for me in my office until I'm done here, Mr. Bonner? It's just down the hall.''

''I'm not going anywhere.'' For the first time he turned to stare at her eight graduate students. ''Class is over. Get out.''

The students scrambled to their feet, closing their notebooks and grabbing their coats. Since she couldn't engage in a public battle with him, she addressed them as calmly as possible. "I was nearly done anyway. We'll pick up here on Wednesday."

They filed out of the room within seconds, darting curious glances at the two of them as they left. Cal uncoiled from the wall, shut the door, and punched the lock.

"Open the door," she said immediately, filled with alarm at being confined with him in this small windowless classroom. "We can talk in my office."

He resumed his earlier position. Leaning against the doorjamb, he crossed his arms and tucked the fingers in his armpits. His forearms were tan and muscular. A strong blue vein throbbed there.

"I'd like to take you apart."

She sucked in air as panic raced through her. His posture suddenly seemed full of significance, the sign of a man forcibly restraining himself.

"Nothing to say? What's the matter, Dr. Darlington? You sure were full of words when we met before."

She fought to calm herself, hoping against hope that he had simply discovered she wasn't who she'd said she was and had come here to redeem his warrior's pride. *Please don't let it be anything else,* she prayed.

He walked slowly toward her, and she took an involuntary step backward.

"How are you living with yourself?" he sneered. "Or is that genius brain of yours so big it's taken over the place where your heart should be? Did you think I wouldn't care, or were you just counting on me never finding out?"

"Finding out?" Her voice was barely a whisper. She bumped into the chalkboard as dread slithered down her spine.

"I care, Professor. I care a lot."

Her skin felt hot and clammy at the same time. "I don't know what you're talking about."

"Bull. You're a liar."

He purposefully advanced on her, and she felt as if she were trying to swallow great lumps of cotton. "I want you to leave."

"I'll just bet you do." He drew so close his arm brushed her own. She caught the scent of soap, wool, and fury. "I'm talking about the baby, Professor. The fact that you set out to get yourself pregnant with my kid. And I hear you hit the jackpot."

All the strength left her body. She sagged against the chalk tray. *Not this. Please, God, not this.* Her body felt as if it were closing down, and she wanted to curl in on herself.

He didn't say anything; he simply waited.

She drew a deep, shuddering breath. She knew it was useless to deny the truth, but she could barely form her words. "It doesn't have anything to do with you now. Please. Just forget about it."

He was on her in a second. She gave a guttural scream as he gripped her by the shoulders and jerked her away from the board. His lips were pale with suppressed rage, and a vein pulsed at his temple. "Forget about it? You want me to forget?"

"I didn't think you'd care! I didn't think it would matter to you!"

His lips barely moved. "It matters."

"Please . . . I wanted a baby so badly." She winced as his fingers dug into her arms. "I didn't mean to involve you. You weren't ever supposed to know. I've never—I've never done anything like this before. It was an . . . an ache inside me, and I couldn't come up with another way."

"You had no right."

"I knew—I knew what I was doing was wrong. But it didn't seem wrong. All I could think about was having a baby."

He slowly released her, and she sensed he was barely

holding onto his self-control. "There were other ways. Ways that didn't involve me."

"Sperm banks weren't a viable option for me."

His eyes raked her with contempt, and the menace in his soft Carolina drawl made her want to cringe. "Viable? I don't like it when you use big words. See, I ain't a hotshot scientist like you. I'm just a dumb jock, so you'd better keep everything real simple."

"It wasn't *practical* for me to use a sperm bank."

"Now why's that?"

"My IQ is over 180."

"Congratulations."

"I didn't have anything to do with it, so it's not something I'm proud of. I was born that way, but it can be more of a curse than a blessing, and I wanted a normal child. That's why I had to be very careful in my selection." She twisted her hands in front of her, trying to think how she could say this without angering him even more. "I needed a male with—uh—average intelligence. Sperm bank donors tend to be medical students, men like that."

"Not Carolina hillbillies who make their living throwing a football."

"I know I've wronged you," she said quietly, her fingers twisting one of the brass buttons on the front of her dress, "but there's nothing I can do at this point except apologize."

"You could have an abortion."

"No! I love this baby with all my heart, and I would never do that!"

She waited for him to argue with her, but he said nothing. She spun away, hugging herself with her arms and moving to the side of the classroom so she could put as much distance between them as possible, protecting herself, protecting her baby.

She heard him coming toward her, and she felt as if she were being regarded through the crosshairs of a high-powered rifle. His voice was whispery and strangely disembodied. "This is the way it's going to be, Professor. In a few days, the two of us are taking a trip across the state line into Wisconsin, where the press won't be likely to sniff us out. And once we're there, we're getting married."

She caught her breath at the venom in his expression.

"Don't plan any rose-covered cottage because this is going to be a marriage made in hell. As soon as the ceremony's over, we're each going our own way until after the baby's born. Then we'll get a divorce."

"What are you talking about? I'm not marrying you. You don't understand. I'm not after your money. I don't want anything from you."

"I don't much care what you want."

"But why? Why are you doing this?"

"Because I don't believe in stray kids."

"This child won't be a stray. It's not—"

"Shut up! I've got a whole ton of rights, and I'm going to make sure every one of them is spelled out, all the way down to a joint custody agreement if I decide that's what I want."

She felt as if all the air had been sucked from her lungs. "Joint custody? You can't have it. This baby is mine!"

"I wouldn't bet on that."

"I won't let you do this!"

"You lost any say in the matter when you came up with your nasty little scheme."

"I won't marry you."

"Yeah, you will. And you know why? Because I'll destroy you before I let a kid of mine be raised as a bastard."

"It's not like that anymore. There are millions of single mothers. People don't think anything of it."

"I think something of it. Listen to me. You put up a fight, and I'll demand *full* custody of that baby. I can keep you in court until I bankrupt you."

"Please don't do this. This is my baby! Nobody's baby but mine!"

"Tell it to the judge."

She couldn't say anything. She had moved into a bitter, pain-filled place where speech was impossible.

"I'm used to rolling around in the mud, Professor, and to tell you the truth, it doesn't bother me all that much. I even kind of like it. So we can either do this in private and keep it clean, or we can go public and make it nasty, not to mention real expensive. One way or another, I'm calling the shots."

She tried to absorb what he was saying. "This isn't right. You don't want a child."

"A kid is the last thing I want, and I'll curse you to hell until the day I die. But it's not his fault that his mother is a lying bitch. It's like I said; I don't believe in strays."

"I can't do this. It's not what I want."

"Tough. My lawyer'll get in touch with you tomorrow, and he'll have a big fat prenuptial for you to sign. The way it's written, both of us will come out of the marriage with exactly what we took in. I can't touch your assets, and you sure as hell can't touch mine. My financial responsibility is to the kid."

"I don't want your money! Why won't you listen? I happen to be able to take care of this child all by myself. I don't want anything from you."

He ignored her. "I have to be back in North Carolina soon, so we're getting this over with right away. By this time next week, the two of us are going to be married, and after that, we'll use my lawyer to communicate about the kid and set up transfers back and forth."

He was destroying all her wondrous plans. What a mess she'd made of everything. How could she hand her child over to this barbarian, even for short visits?

She was going to fight him. He had no right to stake a claim to her baby! She didn't care how many millions of dollars he had or how expensive a court fight would be—this child was hers. She wouldn't let him barge in and take over. He had no right—

Her indignation slammed headlong into her conscience. He did have a right. He had every right. Thanks to her deviousness, he was the child's father, and whether she liked it or not, that gave him a say about the future.

She made herself face the truth. Even if she could afford a lengthy court battle with him, she wouldn't do it. She had gotten into this situation by turning her back on her principles, convincing herself that the end justified the means, and look where that had led her. She couldn't do it any longer. From this point on, she must base every decision on only one criterion: what was best for this child?

She grabbed her notes from the lectern and made her way to the door. "I'll think about it."

"You do that. You've got until four o'clock Friday afternoon."

"Dr. Darlington barely made the deadline." Brian Delgado, Cal's lawyer, tapped the prenuptial agreement that lay in the center of his desk. "She didn't get here until nearly four, and she was very upset."

"Good." Even after a week, Cal couldn't contain his rage over what she'd done to him. He could still see her standing in the classroom wearing that dark orange dress with a double row of gold buttons fastening her up tight. For a moment he hadn't recognized her. Her hair had been swept back into one of those efficient hairdos, and big glasses covered up her green eyes. She'd looked more like the CEO of a company than any woman he'd ever had in his life.

He stalked over to the windows, where he stared blindly down at the parking lot. In two more days he'd be a married man. *Son of a bitch.* Everything inside him rebelled, everything except the moral code he'd been raised with that told him a man didn't abandon his kid, even a kid he didn't want.

The idea of this kind of permanence made him feel as if he were strangling. Permanence was for after his career, for the time when was too damned old to throw a ball, not for now, while he was still in his prime. He'd do his duty by this kid, but Dr. Jane Darlington was going to pay the price for manipulating his life. He didn't let anybody push him around. Never had and never would.

He ground out the words. "I want her punished for this, Brian. Find out everything you can about her."

"What exactly are you looking for?"

"I want to know where she's vulnerable."

Delgado was still young, but he had the eyes of a shark, and Cal knew he was the right man for the job. Delgado had been representing Cal for the past five years. He was smart, aggressive, and no leaks had ever come out of his office. Sometimes Delgado could be overeager in his desire to please his most valuable client—a few times he'd gone off half-cocked—but Cal figured there were worse faults. So far he'd handled this mess with speed and efficiency, and Cal didn't doubt that he'd handle the rest of it equally well.

"She's not going to get away with this, Brian. I'm marrying her because I have to, but that's not the end of it. She's going to discover she picked the wrong man to push around."

Delgado looked thoughtful as he tapped the prenup with the top of his pen. "She seems to lead a quiet life. I don't imagine I'll find too many skeletons."

"Then find out what's important to her and bring her down that way. Put your best people on it. Investigate her work life and her professional life. Find out what matters most to her. Once we know that, we'll know exactly what we're going to take away."

Cal could almost see the wheels turning in Delgado's

mind as he sifted through the challenges of the job he'd been given. Another less aggressive attorney might have balked at an assignment like this, but not Brian. He was the sort who enjoyed feasting on a kill.

As Cal left the office, he made up his mind to protect the people he most cared about from what Jane Darlington had done. His family still mourned the deaths of Cherry and Jamie, and he wouldn't add to their wounds. As for the baby . . . People'd been calling him a tough son of a bitch for as long as he could remember, but he was also fair, and he wouldn't let the kid be punished for its mother's sins.

He shied away from thinking any more about the baby. He'd deal with those responsibilities later. For now, all he cared about was revenge. It might take a while, but he was going to hurt her, and he'd do it in a way she'd never forget.

The night before the wedding, Jane was so full of dread she couldn't eat or sleep, but, as it turned out, the actual ceremony proved to be anticlimactic. It took place at the office of a Wisconsin judge and lasted less than ten minutes. There were no flowers, no friends, and no kiss.

At the end of the ceremony, Brian Delgado, Cal's attorney, told her that Cal would be returning to North Carolina in another week and that Delgado would handle any necessary communications. Other than his brusquely delivered wedding vows, Cal didn't speak to her at all.

They left the ceremony in separate cars just as they had arrived, and by the time she got home, Jane was lightheaded with relief. It was over. She wouldn't have to face him again for months.

Unfortunately, she hadn't counted on the *Chicago Tribune*. Two days after the ceremony, a *Tribune* sports writer, acting on a tip he received from an anonymous Wisconsin county clerk, broke the story of the secret marriage of the city's most famous quarterback to Dr. Jane Darlington, a distinguished professor of physics at Newberry College.

The media circus began.

6

"I'll never forgive you for this," Jane hissed as she snatched up the two halves of her seat belt and shoved them together.

"Just remember who showed up with a bow around her neck." Cal jabbed the stubs from their boarding passes into the pocket of his sport coat and settled into the seat beside her. He bristled with hostility, and she couldn't remember ever being in the presence of such naked hatred.

It was Monday, only five days since their makeshift wedding ceremony, but everything had changed. The flight attendant serving the first-class passengers stopped beside their seats, calling a temporary halt to the bitter verbal battle that had been going on between them in one form or another since the *Trib* story had been published three days earlier. She held out a tray with two glasses of champagne.

"Congratulations! The crew's so excited about having both of you on board today. We're all big Stars' fans, and we're thrilled about your marriage."

Jane forced a smile as she took the champagne. "Thank you."

Cal said nothing.

The flight attendant's gaze slipped over Jane, assessing the woman who had managed to snag the city's most prominent bachelor. Jane was beginning to grow accustomed to the flicker of surprise on people's faces when they saw her for the first time. They undoubtedly expected Cal Bonner's wife to look and dress like a Victoria's Secret model, but Jane's well-cut tweed jacket, camel trousers, and bronze silk shell fell short of the mark. All of her clothes were of good quality, but conservative. The classic styles suited her, and she had no desire to make herself over into a fashion butterfly.

She'd arranged her hair in a loose French twist, a style she had always liked because it was neat and timeless. Her friend Caroline said it was too stuffy, but she'd also admitted it did a good job of setting off Jane's rather delicate bone structure. Her jewelry was minimal, small gold knots in her ears and the plain gold wedding band Cal's attorney had purchased for the ceremony. It looked strange on her finger, and she pretended it wasn't there.

As she resettled her glasses, she considered Cal's well-known partiality for very young women. He would undoubtedly have been much happier if she'd shown up in a miniskirt and rhinestone bra. She wondered what would happen when he discovered how old she really was.

Just looking at the belligerent thrust of that hard, square jaw unnerved her. If the man had ever held an elevated thought in his head, he concealed it. Sitting next to him, she felt like a detonated smart bomb.

"Drink this." She passed her champagne glass over to him as the flight attendant moved away.

"Why should I?"

"Because I'm pregnant, and I can't. Or do you want everybody to know about that, too?"

He glared at her, downed the contents, and thrust the empty glass back at her. "Next thing, you'll turn me into a damned alcoholic."

"Since you've had a drink in your hand most of the times I've been with you, I doubt you have far to go."

"You don't know crap."

"Charming vocabulary. Pungent."

"At least I don't sound like I swallowed a dictionary. How much longer do you figure it'll take you to finish burpin' up all them big words?"

"I'm not certain. But if I do it slowly enough, maybe you'll be able to understand a few of them."

She knew that sparring with him like this was infantile, but it was better than the hostile silences that left her nerves ragged and her eyes searching for the nearest exit. Instead of reassuring her, the fact that he had been making an obvious effort to avoid the slightest physical contact between them left her feeling as if he didn't trust himself to hold back if he ever got his hands on her. She didn't like being frightened, especially when she knew she was so very much in the wrong, and she'd made up her mind to meet his belligerence aggressively. No matter what, she wouldn't let him suspect she was afraid.

Her emotional upheaval was only one of the changes that the catastrophic events of the past few days had produced. She'd arrived at Newberry on Friday morning, two days after their wedding, to find an army of reporters shouting questions at her and shoving microphones in her face. She'd pushed through the crowd and made a mad dash for her office, where Marie had met her with an awestruck look and an enormous stack of phone messages, including one from Cal.

She'd reached him at his home, but he cut off her questions with a snarl, then read her the press release his attorney had written. It stated that the two of them had been introduced by mutual friends several months ago, and that their decision to marry had been sudden. It listed her academic credentials and described his pride in her professional accomplishments, a sentiment he'd accompanied with a derisive snort. Then it announced that the couple would be spending the next few months honeymooning in

Cal's hometown of Salvation, North Carolina.

Jane had erupted. "That's impossible! I have classes to teach, and I'm not going anywhere."

His sneer carried over the phone line. "As of five o'clock today, you're taking one of them—what do you call 'em?—a temporary leave of absence."

"I certainly will not be."

"Your college says different."

"What are you talking about?"

"Ask your boss." He slammed the phone down.

She'd immediately marched into the office of Dr. William Davenport, head of Newberry's Physics Department, where she discovered Cal was giving the college a major endowment as a token of his appreciation for their flexibility regarding her work schedule in the upcoming months. She'd felt impotent and humiliated. With nothing more than the stroke of a pen over his checkbook, he'd taken control of her life.

The flight attendant stopped to pick up their glasses. As soon as the woman disappeared, she vented her smoldering resentment on Cal. "You had no right to interfere in my career."

"Get off it, Professor. I bought you a few extra months vacation. You should be thanking me. If it wasn't for me, you wouldn't have all this free time to do research for that lab you work for."

He knew far too much about her, and she didn't like it. It was true that being temporarily relieved of her teaching schedule would benefit her research for Preeze, although she wasn't going to admit that to him. Her computer equipment was already en route to North Carolina, and with the aid of a modem, the change in location wouldn't affect her work. Under other circumstances, she would have been delighted with three months free time, but not when she hadn't arranged for it herself, and not when she had to spend any part of it with Calvin Bonner.

"I could do my research a lot better in my office at home."

"Not with a whole army of reporters camped out on your doorstep asking why the city's most famous newlyweds are livin' in two different states." His eyes flicked over her as if she were debris. "I go to Salvation this time every year and stay until training camp starts in July. Maybe that giant brain of yours can come up with a convincing excuse for not bringing my brand-new bride along, but I can't seem to think of anything."

"I don't understand how you can perpetrate a fraud like this on your family. Why don't you just tell them the truth?"

"Because, unlike you, nobody in my family's a good liar. It'd be all over town before long, and then the whole world would have the details. Do you really want the kid to grow up knowing how we met?"

She sighed. "No. And stop calling her 'the kid.' " Once again she wondered if the baby would be a boy or a girl. She hadn't made up her mind whether she'd let them tell her after she'd had her ultrasound.

"Besides, my family's been through enough in the past year, and I'm not puttin' them through any more."

She remembered Jodie mentioning the death of Cal's sister-in-law and nephew. "I'm truly sorry about that. But whenever they see us together, they'll know something's wrong."

"That's not going to be a problem because you won't be spending a lot of time with them. They'll meet you, they'll know who you are, but don't plan on getting chummy. And one more thing. If anybody asks how old you are, don't tell 'em you're twenty-eight. If you get pressed, admit to twenty-five, but no older."

What was going to happen when he found out she was thirty-four, not twenty-eight? "I'm not going to lie about my age."

"I don't see why not. You lied about everything else."

She fought back another wave of guilt. "Nobody's going to believe I'm twenty-five. I won't do it."

"Professor, I'd seriously advise you not to piss me off any more than you already have. And don't you have contact lenses or something so you don't have to wear those damned egghead glasses all the time?"

"They're actually bifocals." She took a certain pleasure in pointing that out.

"Bifocals!"

"The kind with an invisible line. There's no correction at the top, but magnification at the bottom. A lot of *middle-aged* people wear them."

Whatever unpleasant response Cal was about to make was cut off as a burly passenger struggling toward the coach section with two large carry-on bags banged one of them into his arm. She stared at the man in fascination. It was fifteen degrees outside, but he was wearing a nylon tank top, presumably so he could show off his muscles.

Cal noticed her interest in the man's attire and gave her a calculated look. "Where I come from, we call those muscle tops wife-beater shirts."

He'd obviously forgotten he wasn't messing with one of his little love bunnies. She smiled sweetly. "And here I thought hillbillies never hit their sisters."

His eyebrows slammed together. "You don't have any idea what hillbillies do, Professor, but I suspect you'll be finding out soon."

"Hey, sorry to interrupt, Cal, but I was wondering if you'd autograph this for my kid." A middle-aged businessman thrust a pen at Cal, along with a memo pad that bore the name of a pharmaceutical company. Cal complied, and before long another man appeared. The requests continued until the flight attendants ordered everyone to their seats. Cal was polite to the fans and surprisingly patient.

She took advantage of the interruption to begin reading

a journal article written by one of her former colleagues on
the decay products of the six-quark H particle, but it was
difficult to focus on nonlinear physics with her own world
so far out of kilter. She could have refused to go with him
to Salvation, but the press would have hounded her and
cast a shadow over her child's future. She simply couldn't
risk it.

No matter what, she had to keep their tawdry story from
becoming public knowledge. The humiliation she'd face, as
gruesome as that would be, wasn't nearly as bad as what
that information would do to her child growing up. She had
promised herself she would base all her decisions on what
was best for this baby, and that was why she had finally
agreed to go with him.

She pushed her glasses more firmly on her nose and once
again began to read. Out of the corner of her eye, she saw
Cal glaring at her, and she decided it was a good thing she
didn't have psychic ability because the last thing she
wanted to do was read his mind.

Bifocals! Cal thought. God, how he hated those glasses.
He mentally cataloged all that he disliked about the woman
sitting next to him and concluded that, even if he set aside
the issue of her character, there was a lot to choose from.

Everything about her was too serious. She even had serious hair. Why didn't she loosen it up from that damned
thingamabob? It was a great color, he'd give her that. He'd
had a couple of girlfriends with hair that color, but theirs
had come out of a bottle, and Jane Darlington's could only
have come from God.

With the exception of that small lock of hair that had
escaped its confines to make a silky S behind her ear, this
was one serious woman. Serious hair and serious clothes.
Pretty skin, though. But he sure as hell didn't like those
big nerdy *bifocals*. They made her look every one of her
twenty-eight years.

He still couldn't believe he'd married her. But what else

could he have done and still been able to live with himself? Let his kid grow up without a father? With the way he'd been raised, that wasn't even a possibility.

He tried to feel good about the fact that he'd done the right thing, but all he felt was rage. He didn't want to be married, damn it! Not to anybody. But especially not to this uptight prig with her liar's heart.

For days he'd been telling himself she was no more permanent than a temporary live-in girlfriend, but every time he spotted that wedding band on her finger, he felt a sickening premonition. It was as if he were watching the scoreboard clock tick off the final days of his career.

"I can't imagine buying a car without seeing it first." Jane gazed around at the interior of the new hunter green Jeep Grand Cherokee that had been waiting for them in the parking lot at the Asheville airport with the key hidden in a magnetic case under the front bumper.

"I hire people to do this kind of thing for me."

His nonchalance about his wealth made her waspish. "How pretentious."

"Watch your language, Professor."

"It means wise," she lied. "You might try working it into a sentence sometime with a person you really admire. Tell them you think they're pretentious, and they'll feel warm and fuzzy all day."

"Thanks for the suggestions. Maybe I'll use it next time I'm on TV."

She regarded him suspiciously, but couldn't see even a trace of mistrust in his expression. It occurred to her that these last few days were turning her into a bitch.

She stared glumly out the window. Despite the gloom of the chilly, overcast March day, she had to admit the country was beautiful. The mountainous contours of western North Carolina formed a stark contrast to the flat Illinois landscape where she'd grown up.

They crossed the French Broad River, a name that would have made her smile under other circumstances, and headed west on Interstate 40 toward Salvation. Ever since she'd first heard the name of Cal's hometown, something about it had struck a chord in the back of her mind, but she couldn't remember what.

"Is there some reason I should recognize the name Salvation."

"It was in the news a while back, but most of the locals don't like to talk about it."

She waited for more information and wasn't too surprised when none was forthcoming. Next to the Bomber, she was a magpie. "Do you think you could let me in on the secret?"

He took so long responding that she thought he was ignoring her, but he finally spoke. "Salvation was where G. Dwayne Snopes settled. The televangelist."

"Wasn't he killed in some kind of small plane crash a few years ago?"

"Yeah. While he was on his way out of the country with a few million dollars that didn't belong to him. Even at the height of his career, the town's leaders never thought much of him, and they don't like having Salvation's name associated with him now that he's dead."

"Did you know him?"

"We met."

"What sort of man was he?"

"He was a crook! Any fool could figure that out."

The nuances of polite conversation were obviously beyond his mental capabilities. She turned away and tried to enjoy the scenery, but being plunged into a new life with a dangerous stranger who hated everything about her made it tough.

They eventually left the highway for a winding two-lane road. The gears of the Jeep ground as they headed up one side of a mountain and then curved down the other. Rusty double-wide mobile homes sitting in weedy lots at the side of the road provided a sharp contrast to the gated entrances of posh residential developments built for retirees around lush golf courses. Her stomach was beginning to get queasy from the switchbacks when Cal turned off the highway onto a gravel road that seemed to go straight up.

"This is Heartache Mountain. I need to stop and see my grandmother before we get settled. The rest of my family's out of town now, but she'll kick up a fuss if I don't bring you to see her right away. And don't go out of your way to be nice. Remember that you won't be around for long."

"You want me to be rude?"

"Let's just say I don't want you winning any popularity contests with my family. And keep the fact that you're pregnant to yourself."

"I wasn't planning on announcing it."

He swung into a deeply rutted lane that led to a tin-roofed house badly in need of paint. One of the shutters hung crookedly, and the front step that led up to the porch sagged. In view of his wealth, she was shocked by its condition. If he cared about his grandmother, he could surely have spared a little money to fix up this place.

He turned off the engine, climbed out of the car, and came around the front to open her door. The courtesy surprised her. She remembered that he'd done the same when she'd gotten into the car at the airport.

"Her name's Annie Glide," he said as she got out, "and she'll be eighty next birthday. She's got a bad heart and emphysema, but she's not ready to give up yet. Watch that step. Damn. This place is going to fall down right around her ears."

"Surely you can afford to move her out of here."

He looked at her as if she'd lost her mind, then walked to the door and slammed his fist against it. "Open up, you old bat, and tell me why this step isn't fixed!"

Jane gaped at him. This was the way he treated his dear old granny?

The door squeaked open, and Jane found herself staring at a stoop-shouldered woman with bleached blond hair sticking out in tufts all over her head, bright red lipstick, and a cigarette hanging out of the corner of her mouth. "You watch the way you talk to me, Calvin James Bonner. I can still whup you, and don't you forget it."

"Have to catch me first." He plucked the cigarette out of her mouth, ground it beneath the toe of his shoe, and folded her in his arms.

She gave a wheezy cackle and patted his back. "Wild as the devil and twice as bad." She peered around his back to scowl at Jane, who was standing at the top of the steps. "Who's that?"

"Annie, this is Jane." His voice developed a steely note. "My wife. Remember I called to tell you about her. We got married last Wednesday."

"Looks like a city gal. You ever skinned a squirrel, city gal?"

"I—uh—can't say as I have."

She gave a dismissive snort and turned back to Cal. "What done took you so long to come see your granny?"

"I was afraid you'd bite me, and I had to get my rabies shots up to date."

This sent her into a gale of witchy laughter, culminating in a coughing spasm. Cal looped his arm around her and steered her into the house, cussing her out for her smoking the entire time.

Jane pushed her hands into the pockets of her jacket and thought about how there weren't going to be any easy successes for her the next few months. Now she'd failed the squirrel-skinning test.

She wasn't anxious to go inside, so she walked across the porch to the place where a brightly colored wind sock whipped from the corner of the roof. The cabin was tucked into the side of the mountain and surrounded by woods, with the exception of a clearing to the side and back for a garden. The way the mist clung to the distant mountain peaks made her understand why this part of the Appalachian chain was called the Smokies.

It was so quiet she could hear a single squirrel rustling through the bare branches of an oak tree. Until that moment, she hadn't realized how noisy a town, even a peaceful suburban one, could be. She heard the crack of a twig, the caw of a crow, and breathed in the damp, chill scent of March woodlands not yet ready to leave winter behind. With a sigh, she crossed the porch to the door. She already knew enough about Annie Glide to realize the old woman would take any retreat as a sign of weakness.

She stepped directly into a small, cluttered living room that was a curious amalgam of the old and gaudy with the new and tasteful. A rich, thick-piled smoky blue carpet held an assortment of worn furniture upholstered in everything from faded brocade to threadbare velvet. The gilded coffee table had a broken leg crudely repaired with silver duct tape, and faded red tassels held fragile lace curtains back from the windows.

There was an obviously expensive stereo cabinet complete with a compact disc player sitting on a wall perpendicular to an old stone fireplace. The rough-hewn mantel held an assortment of clutter including a guitar-shaped ceramic vase filled with peacock feathers, a football, a stuffed pheasant, and a framed photograph of a man who looked familiar, although Jane couldn't quite place him.

Through a small archway off to the left she could see part of a kitchen with a peeling linoleum floor and a state-of-the-art cooking range. Another doorway presumably led to bedrooms in the back.

Annie Glide lowered herself with a great deal of effort into an upholstered rocker while Cal paced in front of her, glowering. ". . . then Roy said you pulled your shotgun on him, and now he tells me he won't come out here again without a five-hundred-dollar deposit. Nonrefundable!''

"Roy Potts don't know the difference between a hammer and his colon.''

"Roy is the best damn handyman in these parts.''

"Did you bring me my new Harry Connick, Jr. CD? Now that's what I really want, not some fool handyman nibbin' into my business.''

He sighed. "Yeah, I brought it. It's out in the car.''

"Well, go on and get it for me.'' She waved him toward the door. "And move that speaker when you get back. It's too close to my TV.''

As soon as he disappeared, she speared Jane with her blue eyes. Jane felt a curious desire to throw herself on her knees and confess her sins, but she suspected the cantankerous woman would simply smack her in the head.

"How old are you, gal?''

"I'm thirty-four.''

She thought that one over. "How old does he think you are?''

"Twenty-eight. But I didn't tell him that.''

"You never told him different, either, did you?''

"No.'' Although she hadn't been invited to sit, she found a place at the end of an old velvet couch. "He wants me to tell everyone I'm twenty-five.''

Annie rocked for a while. "You gonna do it?''

Jane shook her head.

"Cal told me you're a college professor. That must mean you're a real smart lady.''

"Smart about some things. Dumb about others, I guess.''

She nodded. "Calvin, he don't put up with much foolishness.''

"I know.''

"He needs a little foolishness in his life.''

"I'm afraid I'm not too good at that sort of thing. I used to be when I was a child, but not much anymore.''

Annie looked up at Cal as he came in the door. "When I heard how fast you two got married, I thought she might have done you bad like your mama done your daddy."

"The situations aren't the same at all," he said tonelessly.

Annie tilted her head toward Jane. "My daughter Amber wasn't nothin' more than a little white-trash gal spendin' all her time runnin' after boys. Laid her a trap for the richest one in town." Annie cackled. "She caught him, too. Cal here was the bait."

Jane felt sick. So Cal was the second generation of Bonner male trapped into marriage by a pregnant female.

"My Amber Lynn likes to forget she growed up dirt-poor. Isn't that so, Calvin?"

"I don't know why you're always giving her such a hard time." He walked over to the CD player, and a few moments later, the sounds of Harry Connick, Jr. singing "Stardust" filled the cabin.

Jane realized Connick was the man in the photograph on the mantel. What a strange old woman.

Annie leaned back in the chair. "That Connick boy has got him one beautiful voice. I always wished you could sing, Calvin, but you never could manage it."

"No, ma'am. Can't do much but throw a football." He sat down on the couch next to Jane but not touching her.

Annie closed her eyes, and the three of them sat quietly listening to the honey-sweet voice. Maybe it was the gray day, the deep quiet of the woods, but Jane felt herself begin to relax. Time ticked away, and a curious alertness came over her. Here in this ramshackle house lying in the shadows of the Great Smoky Mountains, she began to feel as if she were on the verge of finding some missing part of herself. Right here in this room that smelled of pine and must and chimney smoke.

"Janie Bonner, I want you to promise me something."

The feeling faded as she heard herself being addressed

for the first time by her married name, but she didn't get a chance to tell Annie she'd be using her maiden name.

"Janie Bonner, I want you to promise me right now that you'll look out for Calvin like a wife should, and that you'll think about his welfare before you think about your own."

She didn't want to do any such thing, and she struggled to hide her dismay. "Life's complicated. That's a hard thing to promise."

" 'Course it's hard," she snapped. "You didn't think bein' married to this man was gonna be easy, did you?"

"No, but . . ."

"Do what I say. You promise me right now, gal."

Under the force of those sharp blue eyes, Jane's own will dissolved, and she found she couldn't deny this old woman. "I promise that I'll do my best."

"That's good enough." Once again, her lids closed. The creak of her rocker and her wheezy breathing underscored the smooth molasses voice coming from the speakers. "Calvin, promise me you're gonna look after Janie Bonner like a husband should and that you'll think about her welfare before you think about your own."

"Aw, Annie, after all these years of waitin' for the right girl to come along, you think I wouldn't take care of her once I found her?"

Annie opened her eyes and nodded, having failed to notice either the malevolent gaze Cal shot at Jane or the fact that he hadn't promised a single thing.

"If I'd of made your mama and daddy do this, Calvin, maybe things would of been easier for them, but I wasn't smart enough, then."

"It didn't have anything to do with being smart, you old hypocrite. You were so happy to see your daughter catch a Bonner that you didn't care about anything else."

Her mouth pursed and Jane saw where her crimson lipstick had bled into the age lines around her lips. "Bonners always thought they was too good for Glides, but I guess we showed them. Glide blood runnin' true and strong in all three of my grandsons. At least it is in you and Gabriel. Ethan's always been a sissy boy, more Bonner than Glide.''

"Just because Ethan's a preacher doesn't make him a sissy." He rose from the couch. "We have to go now, but don't you think I've forgotten about that front step. Now where are you hiding those damn cigarettes?"

"Somewhere you won't find them.''

"That's what you think." He headed for an old bureau next to the kitchen door where he dug into the bottom drawer and pulled out a carton of Camels. "I'll be taking these with me.''

"You just want to smoke 'em yourself." She rose from the rocker with great difficulty. "When Calvin comes back, you come with him, Janie Bonner. You got a lot to learn 'bout bein' married to a country boy.''

"She's working on a real important research project," Cal said, "so she's not going to have much time for visiting.''

"Is that true?" Jane thought she saw a flash of hurt in the old woman's eyes.

"I'll come visit whenever you like.''

"Good.''

Cal's jaw clenched, and she realized she'd displeased him.

"Now go away." Annie shooed them toward the door. "I want to listen to my Harry without all this talk.''

Cal opened the door for Jane to slip through. They had just reached the car when Annie's voice stopped them.

"Janie Bonner!''

She turned to see the old woman regarding them through the screen door.

"Don't you wear nothin' to bed, not even in the winter, you hear me, gal? You go to your husband the way your Maker made you. Stark naked. Keeps a man from strayin'.''

Jane couldn't summon an appropriate response, so she waved and got in the car.

"That'll be the day," Cal muttered as they drove away from the house. "I'll bet you wear clothes in the shower."

"It really galls you, doesn't it, that I didn't strip for you?"

"The list of what you've done that galls me, Professor, is so long I don't know where to start. And why did you tell her you'd come back whenever she likes? I brought you here because I had to, but that's it. You're not spending any more time with her."

"I already told her I'd come back. How do you suggest I get out of it?"

"You're the genius. I'm sure you can figure something out."

7

As they drove down off the mountain, Jane saw an old drive-in movie theater on the right. The screen still stood, although it was damaged, and a deeply rutted gravel lane led to a ticket booth that had once been painted yellow, but had faded to a dirty mustard. The overgrown entrance was marked with an enormous starburst-shaped sign outlined in broken bulbs with the words, *Pride of Carolina*, written inside in flaking purple-and-yellow script.

Jane couldn't tolerate the thick silence that had fallen between them any longer. "I haven't seen a drive-in in years. Did you used to come here?"

Somewhat to her surprise, he answered her. "This is where all the high-school kids got together in the summer. We'd park in the back row, drink beer, and make out."

"I'll bet it was fun."

Jane didn't realize how wistful she'd sounded until he shot her a curious glance. "You never did anything like that?"

"I was in college when I was sixteen. I spent my Saturday nights in the science library."

"No boyfriends."

"Who was going to ask me out? I was too young for

my classmates, and the few boys I knew who were my own age thought I was a freak.''

She realized too late that she'd just given him a golden opportunity to take another verbal swipe at her, but he didn't do it. Instead he turned his attention back to the road as if he regretted having even such a short conversation with her. She noticed that the hard edges of his profile made him seem very much a part of these mountains.

They'd approached the outskirts of Salvation before he spoke again. ''I've always stayed at my parents when I visit, but since I couldn't do that this year, I bought a house.''

''Oh?'' She waited for him to offer a few details, but he said nothing more.

The town of Salvation was small and compact, nestled in a narrow valley. The quaint downtown section held an assortment of stores, including a charmingly rustic restaurant, a shop that featured twig furniture, and the pink-and-blue caboose-shaped Petticoat Junction Cafe. They passed an Ingles grocery store, then crossed a bridge. Cal turned onto another winding, climbing road, then pulled into a lane paved with fresh gravel and came to a stop.

Jane stared at the two wrought-iron gates directly in front of them. Each held a pair of gold praying hands at its center. She swallowed, barely repressing a moan. ''Please tell me this isn't yours.''

''Home sweet home.'' He got out of the car, pulled a key from his pocket, and fiddled with a control box on a stone pillar to the left. Within seconds, the gates with their praying hands swung open.

He climbed back in the car, put it into gear, and drove forward. ''The gate operates electronically. The realtor left the controls inside.''

''What is this place?'' she said weakly.

''My new house. It's also the only piece of real estate in

Salvation that'll give us enough privacy to hide our nasty little secret from the world.''

He rounded a small curve, and Jane caught her first glimpse of the house. "It looks like Tara on steroids.''

The gravel drive ended in a motor court that formed a crescent in front of a white, colonial plantation house. Six massive columns stretched across the front, along with a balcony of elaborate gold grillwork. A fanlight of jewel-toned colored glass topped the double-wide front door, while three marble steps led to the veranda.

"G. Dwayne liked to do things in a big way," Cal said.

"This was his house?" Of course it was. She'd known it the moment she'd seen the praying hands on the gates. "I can't believe you bought the house of a crooked tele-vangelist.''

"He's dead, and I need privacy.'' He stopped the Jeep in front, then craned his neck to look up at the ornate fa-cade. "The realtor guaranteed I'd like it.''

"Are you saying this is the first time you've seen it?"

"G. Dwayne and I weren't close, so he never put me on his guest list.''

"You bought a house without looking at it?" She thought about the car she was riding in and didn't know why she was even surprised.

He climbed out without replying and began to unload. She got out, too, and stooped down to pick up one of her suitcases, only to have him brush her aside. "You're in my way. Get inside. It's unlocked.''

With that gracious invitation, she mounted the marble stairs and opened the front door. As she stepped inside and caught her first glimpse of the interior, she saw that it was even worse than the outside. The open foyer had at its cen-ter an overly grandiose fountain with a marble sculpture of a Grecian maiden pouring water from an urn balanced on her shoulder. The fountain was running, thanks, no doubt, to the realtor who had unloaded this monstrosity on Cal, and the multicolored lights hidden beneath the water gave the whole thing a certain Las Vegas look. Hanging above the foyer like an inverted wedding cake was an enormous crystal chandelier made up of hundreds of prisms and teardrops held together with gold swags and filigree.

Turning to the right, she entered a sunken living room that was furnished with fake French rococo furniture, elaborately fringed draperies, and an Italian marble fireplace complete with cavorting cupids. Perhaps the room's most vulgar piece was the coffee table. Its round glass top was supported by a center column shaped like a kneeling blackamoor, naked except for a crimson-and-gold loincloth.

She moved on to the dining room where a pair of crystal chandeliers topped a table that could easily seat twenty. But the most oppressive of the downstairs rooms was the study, which was outfitted with Gothic arches, thick, olive green velvet drapes, and dark, heavy furniture including a massive desk and a chair that looked as if it could have belonged to Henry VIII.

She reentered the foyer just as Cal was bringing in his golf clubs. As he leaned them against the side of the fountain, she looked up toward the second floor, which was surrounded by a balcony of grillwork that was even more ornate than the balcony outside. "I'm afraid to see the upstairs."

He straightened and regarded her with cold eyes. "You don't like it? I'm hurt. Hillbillies like me spend our whole lives dreaming of owning a beautiful place like this."

She barely repressed a shudder as she turned away and headed upstairs, where she wasn't surprised to find more swags, fringe, velvet, and gilt. She opened a door at one end and stepped into the master bedroom, which was a nightmare of red, black, and gold. It held still another chandelier along with a king-size bed resting on a platform. A red-brocade canopy decorated with heavy gold-and-black tassels topped the bed. Something caught her eye, and as she walked closer, she saw that the underside of the canopy held an enormous mirror. She quickly backed away, only to realize that Cal had entered the room behind her.

He went over to the bed and looked under the canopy to see what had caught her attention. "Well, what do you know? I always wanted me one of these. This house is even better than I thought it'd be."

"It's awful. Nothing more than a monument to greed."

"Doesn't bother me none. I wasn't the one who cheated the God-fearing."

His narrow-mindedness maddened her. "Think of all those people sending Snopes money they squeezed out of their food budget and social security checks. I wonder how many malnourished children went into that ceiling mirror?"

"A couple dozen for sure."

She shot him a quick look to see if he was joking, but he had wandered over to explore an elaborate ebony cabinet that held electronic equipment.

"I can't believe how callous you're being about this." She didn't even know why she was trying to make someone so self-involved and intellectually impaired see beyond his limits.

"You'd better not say that in front of G. Dwayne's creditors. More than a few of them are finally getting paid because I bought this place." He slid out a deep drawer in the cabinet. "He sure did have a taste for porn. There must be a couple dozen X-rated videos in here."

"Perfect."

"You ever see *Slumber Party Panty Pranks*?

"That does it!" She stomped over to the cabinet, dug into the drawer, and filled her arms with the cassettes. The pile was so large, she had to brace it under her chin as she headed out the door to find a garbage can. "Starting now, this house is G-rated."

"That's right," he called after her. "The only use you've got for sex is to get yourself knocked up."

She felt as if she'd been kicked in the stomach. She stopped at the top of the stairs and turned to face him.

He glared at her with those damn-the-torpedo eyes, his hands splayed on his hips, chin jutted forward, and she wouldn't have been surprised if he'd told her to meet him outside so they could settle this with their fists. Once again, she realized how woefully ill equipped she was to handle this man. Surely there had to be a better way than sniping.

"Is this how we want to live for the next three months?" she asked quietly. "With the two of us attacking each other?"

"Works for me."

"But we'll both be miserable. Please. Let's call a truce."

"You want a truce?"

"Yes. Let's stop all these personal attacks and try to get along."

"No dice, Professor." He stared at her for a long moment, then walked forward, his steps unhurried, but still threatening. "You're the one who started this dirty little war, and now you're going to live with the consequences." He brushed past her and headed down the stairs.

She stood there with her heart pounding as he disappeared out the front door. Moments later, she heard the sound of the Jeep driving away. Deeply depressed, she dragged herself to the kitchen, where she deposited the videotapes in the trash.

The requisite Snopes's family crystal chandelier hung over an island workspace topped with black granite that made it look like a crypt, an effect that was enhanced by the shiny black marble floor. The connecting breakfast nook had a charming bay window and a beautiful view. Unfortunately, the view had to fight a built-in banquette upholstered in blood red velvet and wallpaper printed with metallic red roses so full-blown they seemed on the verge of decay. The entire area looked as if it had been decorated by Dracula, but at least the view was pleasant, so she decided to settle in there until she felt more able to cope.

For the next few hours, she alternated between putting away the groceries that had been delivered, making phone calls to tie up loose ends in Chicago, writing a quick note to Caroline, and brooding. As evening approached, the quiet in the house grew thick and oppressive. She realized her last meal had been a very early breakfast, and though she had little appetite, she began putting together a small meal from the badly stocked pantry.

The groceries that had been delivered included multiple boxes of Lucky Charms, cream-filled chocolate cupcakes, white bread, and bologna. It was either hillbilly gourmet or the dream diet of a nine-year-old boy—either way, it didn't appeal to her. She preferred her food fresh and as close to its natural state as possible. Deciding on a grilled cheese sandwich made from Styrofoam white bread and rubbery slices of artificial cheese, she settled on the red velvet banquette to eat.

By the time she'd finished, the events of the day had caught up with her, and she wanted nothing more than to stumble into bed and sleep, but her suitcases weren't in the foyer. She realized Cal must have put them away while she'd been exploring the house. For a moment, she remembered that awful master bedroom and wondered if he thought she was going to share it with him. She immediately dismissed the idea. He'd been avoiding even the slightest physical contact with her; she certainly didn't have to worry about him being sexually aggressive.

The knowledge should have comforted her, but it didn't. There was something so overwhelmingly male about him that she couldn't help feeling threatened. She simply hoped her superior intelligence would win over his physical strength.

The colored lights of the fountain in the foyer below threw grotesque fun-house shadows on the walls as she made her way upstairs to find a bedroom for herself. With a shudder, she headed toward the door at the end of the hallway, choosing it only because it was farthest from the master bedroom.

The charming little nursery she found surprised her. Simply decorated with blue-and-white-striped wallpaper, it held a comfortable rocker, white enameled bureau, and matching crib. Above it hung a needlework prayer mounted in a simple frame, and she realized this was the only religious object she'd seen inside the house. Someone had designed this little boy's nursery with love, and she didn't believe it had been G. Dwayne Snopes.

She sank down in the wooden rocker that sat by a window with tieback curtains and thought about her own child. How could it ever grow strong and happy with two parents constantly at war? She remembered the promise she'd made Annie Glide to put Cal's welfare before her own and wondered how she had let the old lady trap her into agreeing to something so impossible. It seemed even more ironic in view of the fact that he had promised nothing in return.

Why hadn't she been wilier and ducked the old lady's prodding as he'd done? Still, in light of the wedding vows she'd spoken, what difference did one more broken promise make?

As she rested her head against the back of the rocker she searched for a way to make peace with him. Somehow she had to accomplish it, not because of what she'd said to Annie, but because it was best for the baby.

A little after midnight, Cal sealed himself in the study to call Brian Delgado at home. While he waited for his attorney to answer the phone, he viewed the room's Gothic furnishings with distaste, including the trophy heads mounted on the walls. He liked his blood sport to involve able-bodied men, not animals, and he made up his mind to get rid of them as soon as possible.

When Brian answered, Cal was in no mood to chitchat, so he got right to the point. "What have you found out?"

"Nothing yet. Dr. Darlington doesn't seem to have any skeletons in her closet—you were right about that—maybe because her personal life has been almost nonexistent."

"What does she do with her spare time?"

"She works. That seems to be her life."

"Any blots on her professional record?"

"Problems with her boss at Preeze Labs, but that looks more like professional jealousy on his part. High-level particle physics still seems to be pretty much a boys' club, especially with the older scientists."

Cal frowned. "I hoped you'd have more by now."

"Cal, I know you want this handled yesterday, but it's going to take a while unless you want to attract all kinds of attention."

He shoved his hand through his hair. "You're right. Take the time you need, but handle it. I'm giving you complete authority to act. I don't want this pushed aside."

"Understood."

They talked for a few minutes about the terms Cal was being offered to renew his contract with a fast-food chain, and then they discussed a proposed endorsement for an athletic clothing manufacturer. Cal was just ready to hang up when a thought occurred to him.

"Send one of your people out tomorrow to buy up a batch of comic books. Soldier of fortune stuff, action heroes—have them throw in a couple of Bugs Bunny. I'll need four or five dozen."

"Comic books?"

"Yeah."

Brian asked no more questions, even though Cal knew he wanted to. Their conversation ended, and he headed upstairs in search of the woman who had so deviously altered his life.

He didn't feel even a pang of guilt for wanting revenge. The gridiron had taught him a lot of survival lessons, and one of them was fundamental. If somebody laid a dirty hit

on you, you had to strike back twice as hard or pay for it
in the future, and that was something he wouldn't risk. He
had no intention of living the rest of his life looking over
his shoulder trying to figure out what she might be up to
next. She needed to understand exactly who she'd tangled
with and exactly what the consequences would be if she
ever tried to deceive him again.

He found her in the nursery curled up in a rocker with
her glasses resting in her lap. In her sleep she appeared
vulnerable, but he knew what a lie that was. From the beginning, she'd been cold-blooded and calculating as she'd
gone about getting what she wanted, and in the process
she'd altered the course of his life in a way he'd never
forgive. And not only his life, he reminded himself, but the
life of an innocent child.

He'd always liked kids. For over ten years he'd spent a
lot of his time working with underprivileged ones, although
he'd done his best to keep that information from the press
because he didn't want anybody trying to make him over
into Saint Cal. When he finally got around to getting married, he'd always figured he'd stay that way. He'd grown
up in a stable family, and it bothered him to watch his
buddies and their ex-wives shuffle their kids back and forth.
He'd sworn he'd never do that to a child, but Dr. Jane
Darlington had taken the choice away from him.

He walked farther into the room and watched the blade
of moonlight caught in her hair turn it into silver. One stray
lock curled softly over her cheek. She'd taken off her
jacket, and her silk top clung to her breasts so that he could
watch their gentle rise and fall.

Asleep, she looked younger than the formidable physics
professor who'd instructed her class on Borromean nuclei.
That day there had been something parched about her, as
if she'd been closed up inside so long that all her juices
had dried up, but asleep and bathed in moonlight she was

different—dewy, renewed, plumped up—and he felt the stirrings of desire.

His physical reaction bothered him. The first two times he'd been with her he hadn't known what she was like. Now he knew, but his body didn't seem to have gotten the message.

He decided it was time for the next scene in their unpleasant melodrama, and he pressed the toe of his shoe down on the front of the rocker. The chair tilted, and she startled awake.

"Bedtime, Rosebud."

Her green eyes flew open and immediately darkened with wariness. "I—I must have fallen asleep."

"Big day."

"I was looking for a bedroom." She slipped on her glasses, then pushed her hands through her hair, where it had fallen forward over her face. He watched silvery blond drizzles trickle through her fingers.

"You can take the Widow Snopes's room. Come on."

He could see that she didn't want to follow him, but she wanted another argument even less. It was a mistake for her to telegraph her emotions the way she did. It made the game too easy.

He led her down the hallway, and as they came closer to the master bedroom, her nervousness grew. He felt a grim satisfaction watching it happen. What would she do if he touched her? So far, he'd avoided any physical contact, not quite trusting himself to stay in control. He'd never hit a woman—could never even have imagined doing such a thing—but the urge to damage her was primal. As he observed her nervousness, he knew he had to test her.

They reached the door just before his own. He extended his hand toward the knob and deliberately brushed her arm.

Jane jumped as she felt his touch and spun to face him. His eyes were full of mockery, and she realized he knew exactly how nervous he was making her. There was something dangerous about him tonight. She had no idea what he was thinking; she only knew that they were alone in this big, ugly house, and she felt defenseless.

He pushed open the door. "We've got connecting bedrooms, just like those old-time houses used to have. I guess G. Dwayne and his wife didn't get along real well."

"I don't want a connecting bedroom. I'll sleep in one of the rooms at the other end of the hall."

"You'll sleep wherever I tell you."

Prickles of alarm skidded up her spine, but she lifted her head and met his gaze. "Stop bullying me."

"This isn't bullying. Bullies can't back up their threats. I can."

His lazy drawl held an edge of menace, and her stomach twisted. "Exactly what are you threatening?"

His gaze slid over her, lingering at the hollow of her neck, her breasts, passing down to her hips, then returning to her eyes. "You cost me my peace of mind, not to mention a wad of cash. To my way of thinking, that means you've got some big debts to pay off. Maybe I just want you close by while I decide when I'm going to start collecting."

The sexual threat was unmistakable, and she should have been enraged—certainly frightened—but instead, a curious jolt passed through her, as if her nerve endings had received an electrical shock. She found her reaction deeply disturbing, and she tried to move away from him, only to back into the doorjamb.

He lifted his arm and splayed one hand on the edge of the frame, just next to her head. His leg brushed the side of hers, and all of her senses grew alert. She saw the hollows beneath his cheekbones, the rim of black that surrounded the irises of his pale gray eyes. She caught the faint scent of laundry detergent on his knit shirt and something else, something that shouldn't have a smell, but did. The scent of danger.

His voice was a husky whisper. "The first time I strip you naked, Rosebud, it's going to be in broad daylight because I don't want to miss a thing."

Her palms grew damp, and an awful wildness rose inside her. She felt a suicidal desire to peel her silk shell over her head, unfasten her slacks, to strip herself naked for him right here in the hallway of this sinner's house. She wanted to answer his warrior's challenge with one of her own, a challenge as ancient and powerful as the first woman's.

He moved. It was almost nothing. A slight shift of his weight, but it brought the chaos of her thoughts back in order. She was a middle-aged physics professor whose only lover wore socks to bed. What kind of opponent was she for this seasoned sexual warrior who seemed to have chosen sex as a weapon to subjugate her?

She was deeply shaken and just as determined not to let him use her weakness to his advantage. She lifted her gaze to his. "You do what you have to, Cal. I'll do the same."

Did she imagine a flicker of surprise on his face? She couldn't be certain as she turned into the room and shut the door.

The sun streaming through the windows awakened her the next morning. She propped herself up on the pillows and admired the Widow Snopes's bedroom, which was painted a pale blue with chalk white trim and soft iris accents. Its simple cherry furniture and braided rugs gave the room the same homey feel as the nursery.

Jane glanced uneasily toward the door that led to a master bath linking her bedroom with Cal's. She vaguely remembered hearing a shower running earlier, and she could only hope he'd already left the house. Last night she had placed her own toiletries in a smaller bathroom down the hall.

The Jeep was gone by the time she had finished dressing, gotten unpacked, and made her way to the kitchen. She found a note from Cal on the counter with the number of a grocery store that delivered and instructions to order whatever she wanted. She ate a piece of toast, then phoned in a list of items more suitable to her taste buds than foam-filled chocolate cupcakes.

Not long after the groceries arrived, another deliveryman showed up with her computer equipment. She had him carry it to her bedroom, where she spent the next few hours setting up a workspace for herself on a table she moved in front of the window, so she could gaze at the mountains whenever she remembered to look up from her computer screen. For the rest of the day, she worked, stopping only long enough to take a walk outside.

The grounds around the house nearly made up for the interior. Shadowed by the surrounding mountains, they were a bit overgrown, and it was too early for anything to be in bloom, but she loved their feeling of isolation and slightly abandoned look. She saw a rough path leading up the side of the nearest mountain and began to follow it, but after less than ten minutes, she found herself gasping for breath from the effects of the altitude. As she turned back, she decided she'd make herself go a bit farther each day until she reached the notch at the top.

By the time she went to bed that night, she still hadn't seen Cal, and he was gone when she awakened the next morning. Late that afternoon, however, he walked into the foyer as she came downstairs.

He gave her that familiar contemptuous look, as if she'd crawled out from under a rock. "The realtor hired a couple of women to keep the house clean while it was on the market. She said they did a good job, so I told them to stay on. They'll be coming a couple times a week starting to-morrow."

"All right."

"They don't speak much English, but they seemed to know what they're doing. Stay out of their way."

She nodded and thought about asking him where he had been until two o'clock in the morning, the time she'd heard the toilet flush in the adjoining bathroom, but he had already turned to leave. As the door shut, she wondered if he was going off to be with another woman.

The thought depressed her. Even though their marriage was a sham, and he didn't owe her fidelity, she wished he'd give it to her, just for the next three months. A premonition of disaster settled over her, a sense of impending doom that made her so uncomfortable, she hurried back to her computer and buried herself in work.

Her days settled into a routine, but the uneasiness never quite went away. To keep it at bay, she worked most of the time, although she managed a walk each day. She barely saw Cal, something that should have eased her mind, but didn't, since she realized he had virtually imprisoned her. She had no car, he didn't offer to lend her his, and the only people she saw were deliverymen and the two Korean cleaning women. Like a feudal lord with a moated castle, he had deliberately cut her off from the town and its people. She wondered what he planned to do when his family returned.

Unlike a medieval noblewoman, she could have put an end to her imprisonment anytime she wanted. A phone call to a taxi company would have done the job, but she didn't have any real desire to go out. With the exception of the prickly Annie Glide, she knew no one here, and although she would have enjoyed seeing something of the area, she couldn't resist the luxury of uninterrupted time.

Never in her life had she been able to devote herself so completely to pure science. There were no classes to teach, no faculty meetings to attend, no errands to run, nothing to distract her from her research. With her computer, modem, and telephone, she was linked to everything she needed, from the Los Alamos electronic library to the data coming in from crucial experiments being conducted in the world's billion-dollar supercolliders. And work kept her uneasy thoughts at bay.

She began to lose track of time as she absorbed herself in the mathematics of duality, applying theoretical physics to unravel mathematical puzzles. Using a free-flowing mathematics of intuition, she pondered convoluted curves and mirror symmetry. She applied quantum field theory to count holes in four-dimensional space, and wherever she went, she left scribbled notes to herself—ideas scratched on the backs of pizza coupons that came in the mail, formulas written with a stubby golf pencil over the margins of the morning newspaper. One afternoon she walked into her bathroom only to see that she'd unthinkingly used her antique rose lipstick to draw a doughnut shape that was remodeling into a sphere on the bathroom mirror. With that, she knew she had to get out.

She grabbed her white Windbreaker, emptied the notes she'd stuffed into the pockets on previous walks, and left through the French doors at the rear of the house. As she made her way across the yard toward the path up the side of the mountain that she'd been climbing a little higher each day, her thoughts returned to the problems of convoluted curves. Would it be possible . . .

The shrill call of a bird blasted through her conjecture and made her aware of her surroundings. What was she doing pondering quantum geometry in the middle of all this beauty? If she weren't careful, she'd become so strange that no child would want her as a mother.

As she climbed higher, she forced herself to observe the world around her. She drew in the rich scents of pine and leaf mold and felt the sun shining with new warmth. The trees had a fragile green lacework on them. Spring was arriving, and before long these mountain slopes would be alive with blooms.

But instead of being buoyed by the beauty, her spirits drooped, and the premonition of disaster that had been nagging at the edges of her consciousness for days grew stronger. By immersing herself so completely in her work, she had kept herself from thinking, but with the quiet of the damp woods around her, that was no longer possible.

As her breathing grew labored, she made her way to a rocky area off to the side of the path where she could rest. She was so tired of living with guilt. Cal would never forgive her for what she had done, and she could only pray that he wouldn't take his hostility out on their child.

She remembered his veiled sexual threat the night they had arrived and realized she had no idea if he'd really try to force himself on her. She shivered and looked down on the valley, where she saw the house with its dark-shingled roof and crescent-shaped motor court. She watched a car turn into the gated lane. Cal's Jeep. Had he come back to grab a fresh comic book from his collection?

They were scattered all over the house: *X-Men, The Avengers, The Vault of Horror*, even *Bugs Bunny*. Every time she saw a new comic book, she sent up a silent prayer of thanksgiving that at least this one thing had gone right. Intelligence tended toward the norm. Surely his mental slowness would balance her own genius and keep her child from being a freak. She silently expressed her gratitude by making certain his comics were never disturbed, not even by the cleaning women.

But that gratitude didn't extend to her imprisonment. As much as the isolation helped her work, she realized she was giving him too much power by tolerating it. What would he do, she wondered, if she didn't return? He knew she went for walks, but how would he react if she didn't come back? What if she made her way beyond the gates, found a telephone, and took a taxi to the airport?

The idea of upsetting him elevated her spirits a few small notches. Leaning back on her elbows, she tilted her face and enjoyed the sunshine until she felt the chill of the rocky ledge through her wool slacks. Then she rose and gazed back down into the valley.

The house and its owner lay beneath her; the mountains rose above. She began to climb.

8

Cal stalked into the family room with Jane's purse clutched in his hand and strode over to the French doors that led to the deck, but he still couldn't see any sign of her. That meant only one thing. She'd taken off up the mountain.

He knew she walked most days, but when he'd asked her about it, she'd told him she never went far. Well, she'd obviously gone far today, so far she'd gotten lost! For someone with an IQ of 180, she was the stupidest woman he'd ever met.

"Damn!" He flung the purse down on the couch. The latch flew open and the contents spilled.

"Something wrong, C-Man?"

"What? Uh, no." Cal had forgotten about his youngest brother Ethan. When Ethan had shown up at the gate twenty minutes earlier, Cal had made up an excuse about having to return a phone call and stuck him in here while he'd tried to find a clue to his missing wife's whereabouts.

Buying himself a few days' extra time before he introduced Jane to his family was proving to be even tougher than he'd thought. Ethan had been back from his ski trip for three days, his parents from their vacation for two, and all of them had been hounding him.

"I was looking for my wallet," he lied. "I thought Jane might have put it in her purse."

Ethan rose from an easy chair near the fireplace, which was large enough to roast a Honda, and walked over to peer out the patio doors. Cal's anger softened a bit as he gazed at his brother. While he and Gabe had shone on the playing fields, Ethan had made his mark in school theatrical productions. Although he was a decent athlete, organized sports held no appeal for him simply because he'd never been able to grasp the importance of winning.

Blond, more slightly built than either Cal or Gabe, and heartbreakingly handsome, he was the only one of the three Bonner brothers who took after their mother, and his male-model good looks had caused him to endure an endless amount of ribbing from Cal and Gabe. He had thickly lashed light brown eyes and a nose that had never been broken. His dark blond hair was conservatively cut and always combed. Normally he favored oxford shirts, neatly pressed Dockers, and penny loafers, but today he wore an ancient Grateful Dead T-shirt and jeans. On Ethan, the outfit looked like Brooks Brothers.

Cal frowned at him. "Did you iron that T-shirt?"

"Just a little touch-up."

"Jesus, Eth, you've got to stop doin' crap like that."

Ethan smiled his Christ smile solely because he knew how much it irritated his big brother. "Some of us take pride in our appearance." He regarded Cal's muddy boots with distaste. "Others of us don't care how we look."

"Can it, asshole." Cal's language always deteriorated when he was around Ethan. There was just something about the kid's unflappability that made him want to cuss. Not that it bothered Ethan one bit. As the youngest of three boys, his brothers had toughened him up at an early age. Even as children, Cal and Gabe had sensed that Ethan was more vulnerable than they were, so they'd made sure he could take care of himself. Although no one in the Bonner family ever admitted it, all of them secretly loved Ethan best.

Cal also respected him. Ethan had gone through a wild period, during college and into his early twenties, where he'd drunk too much and slept with too many women, but when he'd received the call, he'd made up his mind to live as he preached.

"Visiting the sick's part of my job," Ethan said. "Why don't I just look in on your new wife?"

"She wouldn't like it. You know how women are. She wants to be all fixed up before she meets the family, so she can make a good first impression."

"When do you think that's going to be? Now that Mom and Dad are back in town, they're champing at the bit to meet her. And Annie's really rubbing it in because she's seen her and we haven't."

"It's not my fault all of you chose now to go gallivanting around the country."

"I've been back from my ski trip for three days."

"Yeah, well, it's like I told everybody when I came over for dinner last night, Jane got sick right before you got back. Damned flu. She should be feeling better in a few days—next week at the latest—and then I'll bring her over to the house. But don't expect to see much of her. Her work's real important to her, and she can't spend too much time away from her computer right now."

Ethan was only thirty, but he regarded him through old, wise eyes. "If you need to talk, C-Man, I'm willing to listen."

"There's nothing for me to talk about except the way everybody in this family wants to stick their noses in my business."

"Not Gabe."

"No, not Gabe." Cal jammed his hands into the back pockets of his jeans. "I wish he would."

They each fell silent, preoccupied with thoughts of their

wounded middle brother. He was down in Mexico, on the run from himself.

"I wish he'd come home," Ethan said.

"He left Salvation years ago. It's not home to him anymore."

"I guess no place is home without Cherry and Jamie."

Ethan's voice tightened, and Cal looked away. Anxious to break the mood, he began picking up the contents of Jane's purse. Where was she? These past two weeks he'd forced himself to stay away and let his temper cool.

He also wanted her to feel her isolation and understand that he was the one holding the key to her prison. Unfortunately she didn't seem affected.

Ethan came over to help. "If Jane's flu is this bad, maybe she should be in the hospital."

"No." Cal reached for a small calculator and pen so he didn't have to look at his brother. "She's been pushing herself pretty hard, but she'll feel better as soon as she gets some rest."

"She sure doesn't look like one of your bimbos."

"How do you know what she looks—?" He lifted his head and saw Ethan studying her photo on the driver's license that had fallen out of her wallet. "None of the women I dated were bimbos."

"They weren't exactly rocket scientists." He laughed. "This one practically is. I still can't believe you married a physicist. The way I remember it, the only thing that got you through high-school physics was the fact that Coach Gill taught the class."

"You're a damned liar. I got an A in that class."

"Deserved a C."

"B minus."

Ethan grinned and waved the driver's license. "I can't wait to tell Dad I won my bet."

"What bet?"

"The age of the woman you married. He said we'd have

to schedule the wedding ceremony around her Girl Scout meetings, but I said you'd come to your senses. I believed in you, bro, and looks like I was right.''

Cal was irritated. He hadn't wanted everybody to know that Jane was twenty-eight, but with Ethan staring at the date of birth on her driver's license, he couldn't deny it. ''She doesn't look a day over twenty-five.''

''I don't know why you're so sensitive. There's nothing wrong with marrying someone your own age.''

''She's not exactly my age.''

''Two years younger. That's not a big difference.''

''Two years? What the hell you talkin' about?'' He snatched the license away. ''She's not two years younger than me! She's—''

''Uh-oh.'' Ethan backed away. ''I think I'd better go.''

Cal was too stunned by what he saw on the license to hear the amusement in his brother's voice, nor did he notice the sound of the front door closing a few moments later. He couldn't take in anything except the date on the driver's license he held in his hand.

He scrubbed the laminate with his thumb. Maybe it was just a smear on the plastic that made the year of her birth look like that. Or maybe it was a misprint. Damned DMV couldn't get anything right.

But he knew it wasn't a misprint. There was no mistaking those grim, condemning numbers. His wife was thirty-four years old, and he'd just taken the sack of a lifetime.

''Calvin, he'll be comin' to fetch you before long,'' Annie Glide said.

Jane set down the tea she'd been sipping from an ancient white ceramic mug that bore the remains of an American flag decal and gazed at Annie across the cluttered living room. Despite its unorthodox decor, this house felt like a home, a place where a person could belong. ''Oh, I don't think so. He doesn't know where I am.''

"He'll figure it out soon enough. Boy's been roamin' these mountains ever since he was in diapers."

She couldn't imagine Cal ever wearing diapers. Surely he'd been born with a belligerent attitude and a full set of chest hair. "I can't believe how close your house is to his. The day I met you it seemed as if we drove several miles before we got to those awful gates."

"You did. Road winds all the way 'round Heartache Mountain goin' through town. This morning, you just took the shortcut."

Jane had been surprised when she'd reached the notch in the mountain and looked down the other side to see the tin roof of Annie Glide's cabin. At first she hadn't recognized it, but then she'd spotted the colorful wind sock flying at the corner of the porch. Even though it had been nearly two weeks since they'd met, Annie had greeted her as if she'd been expected.

"You know how to make corn bread, Janie Bonner?"

"I've made it a few times."

"It's no good lest you fold in a little buttermilk."

"I'll remember that."

"Before I took so sick, I used to make my own apple butter. Nothin' as good as cold apple butter on warm corn bread. You got to find you real soft apples when you make it, and watch yourself peelin' 'em 'cause ain't nobody on earth likes to bite into a big tough ol' piece of peel when they're expectin' good smooth apple butter."

"If I ever make any, I'll be careful."

Annie had been doing this ever since Jane had arrived, tossing out recipes and bits of folk wisdom: ginger tea for colds, nine sips of water for hiccups, beets to be planted on the twenty-sixth, twenty-seventh, or twenty-eighth of March, but no later or they'd be puny.

Despite the improbability of her ever using any of this information, she'd found herself taking it all in. Annie's advice represented the continuity between one generation and the next. Roots went deep in these mountains, and as someone who had always felt so very rootless, each tidbit seemed like a solid link with a family that had a history and traditions, everything she craved.

". . . and if you're gonna make you some dumplin's, put a egg in that dough and a pinch of sage." She started to cough, and Jane regarded her with concern. When she recovered, she waved her hand displaying fingernails painted a bright cherry red. "Listen to me goin' on. It's a wonder you haven't just said, 'Annie, shut your yap; you done wore out my ears.'"

"I love listening to you."

"You're a good girl, Janie Bonner. I'm surprised Calvin married you."

Jane laughed. Annie Glide was the most unexpected person. The only one of her grandparents Jane had ever known had been her father's self-centered and narrow-minded mother.

"I miss my garden. Had that worthless Joey Neeson plow for me a couple weeks ago, even though it goes against my grain to have strangers 'round here. Calvin, he's always sending strangers up here to fix things, but I won't have it. Don't even like family nibbin' in my business, let alone strangers." She shook her head. "I was hopin' I'd be strong enough to get my garden put in this spring, but I was foolin' myself. Ethan said he'd come by to help me, but that poor boy has so much work with his church, I didn't have the heart to do nothin' but tell him weren't no sissy boy plantin' my garden." She gave Jane a sideways glance from her crafty blue eyes. "Sure am gonna miss my garden, but I won't have strangers plantin' for me."

Jane saw right through the old woman's wiles, but it didn't occur to her to be annoyed. Instead, she felt curiously flattered. "I'll be happy to help you if you show me what to do."

Annie pressed her hand to her chest. "You'd do that for me?"

Jane laughed at her feigned amazement. "I'll enjoy it. I've never had a garden."

"Well, now, that's just fine. You make Calvin bring you over here first thing tomorrow, and we'll get those 'taters in right away. It's real late—I like to do it at the end of February, during the dark of the moon—but they still might turn out if we get 'em in right away. Then we plant onions, and after that some beets."

"It sounds great." She suspected the old woman wasn't eating as well as she should, and she stood. "Why don't I fix us a little lunch? I'm getting hungry."

"Now that's a real good idea. Amber Lynn's back from her trip, and she done brung over some of her bean soup yesterday. You can heat that up. 'Course she don't make it like I taught her, but, then, that's Amber Lynn for you."

So Cal's parents had returned. As she headed to the kitchen, she wondered how he was explaining not bringing her to meet them.

Jane served their soup in one china bowl and one plastic. She accompanied it with squares of corn bread from a pan on the counter. As they ate at the kitchen table, she couldn't remember enjoying a meal more. After two weeks of isolation, it was wonderful just being around another person, especially one who did more than bark out orders and glare at her.

She cleaned up the dishes and was bringing a mug of tea to Annie in the living room when she noticed three diplomas among the clutter of paintings, ceramic ballerinas, and wall clocks hanging next to the doorway.

"Those belong to my grandsons," Annie said, "but they give 'em to me. They knowed it always bothered me the fact I had to quit school after sixth grade, so each of 'em give me their college diplomas the same day they graduated. That there's Calvin's hangin' at the top."

Jane fetched her glasses from the kitchen table and gazed at the top diploma. It was from the University of Michigan, and it stated that Calvin E. Bonner had received a Bachelor of Science degree . . . with highest distinction.

Summa Cum Laude.

Jane's hand flew to her throat. She whirled around. "Cal graduated *summa cum laude?*"

"That's what they call it when a body's real smart. I thought you, bein' a professor, would of knowed that. My Calvin, he was always smart as a whip."

"He—" She swallowed and fought to go on as a roaring sounded in her ears. "What did he get his degree in?"

"Now didn't he tell you that? Lot of athletes, they take real easy classes, but my Calvin, he wasn't like that. He got hisself a degree in biology. Always liked roamin' in the woods, pickin' up this 'n' that."

"Biology?" Jane felt as if she'd just taken a punch in the stomach.

Annie narrowed her eyes. "Strikes me strange you don't know any of this, Janie Bonner."

"I guess the subject never came up." The room began to sway, and she felt as if she were going to faint. She turned awkwardly, sloshing hot tea over her hand, and stumbled back into the kitchen.

"Janie? Somethin' wrong?"

She couldn't speak. The handle broke off the mug as she dropped it into the sink. She pressed her fingers to her mouth and fought a rising tide of horror. How could she have been so stupid? Despite all her conniving, she'd brought about the very disaster she'd tried so hard to avoid, and now her child wasn't going to be ordinary at all.

She clutched the edge of the sink as hard reality overcame her rosy daydreams. She'd known Cal had attended the University of Michigan, but she hadn't believed he'd been serious about it. Didn't athletes take the minimum number of courses to get by and then leave before they graduated? The fact that he'd majored in biology and graduated with honors from one of the most prestigious universities in the country had such brutal ramifications she could barely take them in.

Intelligence tended toward the mean. That fact screamed at her. The one quality she prized in him—his stupidity—was nothing more than an illusion, an illusion he had deliberately perpetuated. By not seeing through it, she'd condemned her child to the same life of isolation and loneliness she'd lived herself.

Panic clawed at her. Her precious child was going to be a freak, just like her.

She couldn't let that happen. She'd die before she'd permit her child to suffer as she'd suffered. She'd move away! She'd take the baby to Africa, some remote and primitive part of the continent. She'd educate the child herself so that her precious little one would never know the cruelty of other children.

Her eyes stung with tears. What had she done? How could God have let something so cruel happen?

Annie's voice penetrated her misery. "That'll be Calvin now. I told you he'd come after you."

She heard the slam of a car door, the pounding of footsteps on the front porch.

"*Jane!* Where is she, dammit?"

Jane charged into the living room. "You *bastard*!"

He stalked forward, his face twisted. "Lady, you've got some *explaining* to do!"

"God, I *hate* you!"

"Not any more than what I think of *you*!" Cal's eyes blazed with anger and something else that was now so clear Jane couldn't believe she hadn't seen it all along—a keen, biting intelligence.

She wanted to throw herself at him and scratch that intelligence from his eyes, chop open his cranium and pluck it from his brain. He was supposed to be stupid! He read comic books! How could he betray her like this?

The last of her self-control shredded, and she knew she had to get away before she fell apart. With an exclamation of fury, she whirled around and dashed back into the kitchen, where she flew out the rickety back door.

As she began to run, she heard a roar of rage coming from behind her. "You get back here! Don't make me run after you, or you'll be sorry!"

She wanted to hit something. She wanted to throw herself in a deep hole and let the earth close in on top of her, anything to stop the awful pain raging inside her body. This baby that she already loved more than she'd ever loved anything was going to be a freak.

She didn't hear him come up behind her, and she gasped when he spun her around. "I told you to *stop*!" he shouted.

"You've ruined *everything*!" she screamed back.

"Me?" His face was pale with rage. "You damned *liar*! You're an old lady! A goddamn old lady!"

"I'll *never* forgive you for this!" She balled her hand into a fist and hit him in the chest so hard the pain shot into her arm.

He was spitting fury. He began to grab her by both arms, but she had been transported into a place of vengeance and she wouldn't be restrained. This man had harmed her unborn child, and she, who had never hit another person, wanted his blood.

She went wild. Her glasses flew off, but she didn't care. She kicked and clawed and tried to damage him in any way she could.

"You stop this right now! *Stop it*!" His bellow shook the very treetops. Once again he tried to restrain her, but she sank her teeth into his upper arm.

"Ouch!" His eyes widened with outrage. "That hurt, dammit!"

The violence felt good. She lifted her knee to slam it into his groin and found her feet swept out from under her.

"Oh, no, you don't . . ."

He went down with her, breaking her fall with his own body, then twisting to pinion her against the ground.

The fight had taken everything out of her, but he was a man who took hits for a living, and he wasn't even winded. He was, however, enraged, and he let her have it.

"You settle down right now, you hear me? You're acting like a crazy woman! You *are* crazy! You lied to me, cheated me, and now you're trying to *kill* me, not to mention the fact that you can't be doing that baby any good with your carryin' on. I swear to God I'm going to have you locked up in a mental ward and shot full of Thorazine."

Her eyes stung with tears that she didn't want him to see, but couldn't hold back. "You've ruined everything."

"Me?" He bristled with outrage. "I'm not the one who's acting like a lunatic. And I'm not the one who told everybody I was twenty-eight fucking years old!"

"I never told you that, and don't you curse at me!"

"You're thirty-four! *Thirty-four!* Were you ever planning on mentioning that to me?"

"When was I supposed to mention it? Should I have told you when you were stalking me in my classroom, or when you were screaming at me over the telephone? How about when you pushed me on the airplane? Or maybe I should have let you know after you locked me up in your house? Is that when I should have told you?"

"Don't try to weasel out of it. You knew it was important to me, and you deliberately misled me."

"Deliberately? Now there's a big word for a dumb jock. Do you think it's cute putting on that asinine hillbilly act and making everyone think you're a moron? Is that your idea of a good time?"

"What are you talking about?"

She spit the words at him. "University of Michigan. *Summa cum laude.*"

"Oh, that." Some of the tension left his body, and his weight eased on her.

"God, I hate you," she whispered. "I would have had a better chance at a sperm bank."

"Exactly where you should have gone in the first place."

Despite his words, he no longer sounded quite so angry, but acid churned in her stomach. She knew she had to ask him, even though she dreaded hearing the answer, and she forced out the words. "What's your IQ?"

"I have no idea. Unlike you, I don't keep it tattooed on my forehead." He rolled to the side, which allowed her to struggle to her feet.

"Then your SATs. What were they?"

"I don't remember."

She regarded him bitterly. "You're a liar. Everybody remembers their SATs."

He swiped at some wet leaves on his jeans as he rose.

"Tell me, dammit!"

"I don't have to tell you anything." He sounded annoyed, but not particularly dangerous.

That didn't calm her. Instead, she once again felt a swell of hysteria. "You tell me right now, or, I swear to God, I'll find some way to murder you! I'll put ground glass in your food! I'll stab you with a butcher knife while you're sleeping! I'll wait until you're in the shower and throw in an electrical appliance! I'll—I'll club you in the head with a baseball bat some night when you walk in the door!"

He stopped brushing his jeans and gazed at her with what looked more like curiosity than apprehension. The fact that she knew she was only making herself appear more irrational further inflamed her. "Tell me!"

"You are some bloodthirsty woman." Looking faintly bemused, he shook his head. "That electrical appliance thing . . . You'd need an extension cord or something to reach all the way into the shower. Or maybe you weren't planning to plug it in."

She gritted her teeth, feeling prodigiously foolish. "If it wasn't plugged in, it wouldn't electrocute you, now would it?"

"Good point."

She took a deep breath and tried to regain her sanity. "Tell me your SATs. You owe me that much."

He shrugged and bent over to pick up her glasses. "Maybe fourteen hundred, or somethin' like that. Mighta been a little lower."

"*Fourteen hundred*!" She punched him as hard as she could, then stomped away from him into the woods. He was a hypocrite and a fraud, and she felt sick down to the very depth of her soul. Even Craig wasn't as smart as this man.

"That's dumb compared to you," he called after her.

"Don't ever speak to me again."

He came up next to her, but didn't touch her. "Come on, Rosebud, you've got to settle down enough so I can take you apart for what you've done to me, which is a whole lot worse than my damned SATs."

She whirled on him. "You didn't do anything to *me*! You've done it to my child, don't you see that? Because of you, an innocent child is going to grow up to be a freak."

"I never told you I was stupid. You just assumed."

"You said *ain't*! That first night we were together, you said *ain't* twice!"

A muscle twitched at the corner of his mouth. "A little local color. I'm not apologizin'."

"There are comic books all over the house!"

"I was just livin' up to your expectations."

She collapsed then. She turned her back to him, crossed her arms against the nearest tree trunk, and rested her forehead against her wrist. All the humiliations of her childhood returned to her: the taunts and cruelties, the awful isolation. She had never fit in, and now, neither would her child.

"I'm going to take the baby to Africa," she whispered.
"Away from civilization. I'll teach her myself, so she
doesn't have to grow up with other children taunting her."

A surprisingly gentle hand settled over the small of her
back and began to rub. "I'm not going to let you do that
to him, Rosebud."

"You will once you see what a freak she is."

"He's not going to be a freak. Is that how your father
felt about you?"

Everything within her went still. She pulled away from
him and fumbled in the pocket of her Windbreaker for a
tissue. She took her time blowing her nose, wiping her eyes,
regaining her self-control. How could she have let herself
fall apart like this? It was no wonder he thought she was
crazy.

She gave her nose a final blow. He held out her glasses,
and she put them on, ignoring the strands of moss caught
in one hinge. "I'm sorry for causing such a dreadful scene.
I don't know what came over me. I've never hit anyone in
my life."

"Feels good, doesn't it?" He grinned, and to her amazement, a dimple popped into the hard plane of his cheek.
Stunned, she gazed at it for several long moments before
she was able to pick up her train of thought.

"Violence doesn't solve anything, and I could have hurt
you quite badly."

"I'm not trying to get you cranked up again, Rosebud,
but you don't have a whole lot going for you when it comes
to packin' a punch." He took her arm and began steering
her back toward the house.

"This is my fault. Everything's been my fault from the
beginning. If I hadn't let myself buy into every conceivable
stereotype about athletes and Southerners, I would have
been a more astute judge of your mental abilities."

"Uh-huh. Tell me about your father."

She nearly stumbled, but his hand on her elbow steadied

her. "There's nothing to tell. He was an accountant for a company that manufactured paper punches."

"Smart man?"

"An intelligent man. Not brilliant."

"I think I'm getting the picture here."

"I don't have any idea what you're talking about."

"He didn't have a clue what to do with you, did he?"

She picked up her pace. "He did his best. I really don't want to discuss it."

"Did it occur to you that your problems as a kid might have had more to do with your old man's attitude than with the size of your brain?"

"You don't know anything."

"That's not what my diploma says."

She couldn't respond because they had reached the back of the house, and Annie waited for them at the screen door. She glared at her grandson. "What's wrong with you? You get a pregnant woman upset like that, it'll put a mark on the baby, for sure."

"What do you mean?" He bristled with belligerence. "Who told you she's pregnant?"

"You wouldn't have married her otherwise. You don't have that much sense."

Jane was touched. "Thank you, Annie."

"And you!" Annie turned on her. "What was in your head carryin' on like that? If you go berserk every time Calvin upsets you, that baby's gonna strangle on the cord long before it has a chance to catch its first breath."

Jane thought about addressing the physiological improbability of that happening, but decided to save her breath. "I'll be more careful."

"Next time he makes you mad, just take a shotgun to him."

"Mind your own business, you old bat," Cal growled. "She's got enough ideas of her own for doin' me in."

Annie tilted her head toward Jane, and a sadness seemed

to come over her. "You listen to me, Janie Bonner. I don't know what happened between you and Calvin so he ended up marryin' you, but from what I saw a few minutes ago, the two of you don't have no love match goin'. He's married you, and I'm glad about that, but I'm tellin' you right now that if you did anything havey cavey to bring him around, you'd better make sure Amber Lynn and Jim Bonner never find out about it. They're not as broad-minded as me, and if they even suspect you've hurt their boy, they'll cut you off at the knees, you understand what I'm sayin'?"

Jane swallowed hard and nodded.

"Good." She turned to Cal. The sadness faded, and her old eyes grew sly. "I'm surprised somebody with such a bad case of the flu as Janie here had enough strength to walk over the mountain."

Cal cursed softly under his breath. Jane stared at Annie. "What do you mean? I don't have the flu?"

Cal grabbed her arm and began to pull her away. "Come on, Jane, you're going home."

"Wait a minute! I want to know what she meant by that."

Cal drew her round the side of the house, but not before she heard Annie's cackle. "You remember what I told you about that cord gettin' twisted, Janie Bonner, 'cause I think Calvin's about to upset you again."

9

"**Y**ou told everybody in your family I had the flu?" Jane said as they drove down off the mountain. It was easier talking about this small deception than the larger one.

"You got a problem with that?"

"I expected to meet your parents. I thought that's why you brought me here."

"You'll meet 'em. When I decide to introduce you."

His arrogance was like setting a spark to tinder. This was the result of letting him spend the last few weeks calling all the shots, and it was time she put a stop to it. "You'd better decide soon because I'm not going to let you keep me cooped up any longer."

"What are you talkin' about, cooped up? Here I've gone out of my way to make sure you can work without a lot of people bothering you, and you're complaining."

"Don't you dare act like you're doing me a favor!"

"I don't know what else you'd call it."

"How about *imprisonment? Incarceration? Solitary confinement?* And just so you don't accuse me of going behind your back, I'm breaking out of the joint tomorrow to help Annie plant her garden."

"You're *what?*"

Think about Annie and her garden, she told herself, instead of the fact that her child would be another misfit. She snatched off her glasses and began cleaning the dirt from them with a tissue, concentrating on the job as if it were a complicated equation. "Annie wants to get her garden in. If the potatoes aren't planted in the next few days, they'll be puny. We're also planting onions and beets."

"You are *not* putting in a garden for her. If she wants a garden, I'll hire Joey Neeson to help her."

"He's worthless."

"You don't even *know* Joey."

"I'm just repeating what I heard. The reason nothing's getting done is because she doesn't want strangers around her place."

"Well, that's just too bad because you're not doing it for her."

She opened her mouth to launch another attack, but before she could get the first word out, he cupped her head and pushed her down on the seat so that her cheek squashed against his thigh.

"What are you doing?" She tried to sit up, but he held her down.

"My mom. She's coming out of the shoestore."

"I'm not the only one who's gone crazy! You have completely lost your mind!"

"You're not meeting my family until I decide you're meeting them!" While he held her fast, he steered with his opposite knee and waved. Damn! Why couldn't his parents have stayed away longer, like another two months or so? He knew he had to let them meet the Professor, but he'd hoped to postpone it as long as he could. Now his elderly wife had ruined everything with her morning's trek over the mountain.

He glanced down. Her cheek lay mashed against his thigh, and her hair felt soft under his fingers. She was always so tidy, but now her French braid had pretty much given up the ghost. Silky blond tendrils tumbled over his hand and across the faded denim of his jeans. She sure did have pretty hair, even decorated with twigs and bits of dried leaves. The elastic band holding the braid together was barely hanging on, and he had to resist the urge to pull it off and loosen the rest with his fingers.

He knew he had to let her up soon, since she was madder than a wet hen and starting to sputter, but he kind of liked the idea of her head in his lap, even if she was spitting nails. He noticed that she didn't have more than a speck of makeup left on her face. Still, without those glasses, she looked kind of cute. Sort of like seventeen going on twenty-five. Maybe he could still pass her off as—

As if she'd let him. Damn, but she was one hardheaded woman. He remembered how many times he'd wished Kelly hadn't been quite so sweet. Kelly was a beautiful girl, but he'd never been able to have a decent fight with her, which meant he couldn't ever entirely relax. One thing he had to say about the Professor—she sure knew how to have a good fight.

He frowned. Were his feelings toward her softening? *Hell, no.* He had a long memory, and he wouldn't ever forget how she'd tricked him. It was just that he seemed to have lost the white-hot rage that had carried him through the first couple of weeks. Maybe it had finally burned itself out when she'd leaned her head against that tree trunk and told him she was taking the baby to Africa.

Except for what she'd done to him, he was beginning to realize that she was probably a decent person. Too damn serious and uptight as hell. Still, she worked hard—he'd seen lots of evidence of that from those equations she left like mouse droppings all over the house—and she'd made her way in a man's world. The fact that she wanted to help Annie spoke well of her, even though it made things twice as tough for him. Maybe his feelings *had* softened a little. She'd been so upset today when she found out he wasn't the dummy she'd counted on that he'd actually felt guilty. Her old man sure had done a number on her.

Once again he looked down at her and saw that a blond lock had escaped from her French braid and now curled in a figure eight over his zipper. He nearly groaned aloud. He'd been hard ever since he pushed her into his lap. Even earlier, if he counted that skirmish they'd had when they were lying on the ground at Annie's. But instead of easing up, it was getting worse, and if she turned her head even a little bit, she'd see that his zipper wasn't close to lying flat. No question about it. Fighting with the Professor had turned him on, and he was beginning to think it was time he did something about it. So far he'd had nothing but inconvenience from this marriage; it was about time he took advantage of its one convenience.

"Ouch! Damn it!" He snatched his hand away from her head and rubbed his thigh. "That's twice now you bit me! Don't you know that human saliva is a hundred times more dangerous than an animal's?"

"I supposed you learned that while you were getting your *summa cum laude* degree in biology!" She struggled to sit back up and shoved her glasses on. "I hope you get gangrene and they do the amputation without anesthetic. And they use a chain saw!"

"I'm going to see if my house has an attic where I can lock you up, just like men used to do in the old days when they found out they were stuck with a crazy wife."

"I'll bet if I were eighteen instead of thirty-four, you wouldn't be thinking about locking me up. You'd be stuffing me full of bubble gum and showing me off all over town! Now that I know you're an intelligent man, your attraction to infants seems even more peculiar."

"I am *not* attracted to infants!" He turned into the lane that led to the house.

"You certainly don't seem very confident of your ability to handle a grown woman."

"I swear, Jane— Damn!" He slammed on the brakes and reached over to push her back down on the seat, but he was too late. His father had already spotted her.

He cursed and reluctantly lowered the window. As he stopped his car well behind the muddy red Blazer, he called out, "What's up, Dad?"

"What do you think is up? Open this damn gate and let me in!"

Great, he thought with disgust. This was just great, a perfect addition to a miserable day. He punched the button that controlled the gate, nodded at his father, and hit the accelerator, shooting past the Blazer too quickly for the old man to get a good look at Jane.

Those softer feelings he'd been experiencing toward her only moments earlier vanished. He didn't want her meeting his parents. Period. He hoped it wouldn't occur to his father to mention any of the activities that had been taking up so much of his time. The less Jane knew about his private life, the better he liked it.

"You follow my lead," he said. "And whatever you do, don't let him know you're pregnant."

"He'll find out eventually."

"We're going to make it later. A lot later. And take off those damned *bifocals*!" They reached the house, and Cal hustled her inside before he went back out to greet his father.

Jane heard the door slam and knew he was upset. Good! Mr. Summa cum laude deserved to be upset. Biting her lip, she made her way to the kitchen. When she got there, she pressed her hand over her waist. *I'm sorry, little one. I didn't know. I'm so sorry.*

She plucked a few shreds of dried leaves out of her messy hair. She should try to straighten herself up before Cal's father came in, but she couldn't summon the energy to do more than push her glasses up on her nose while she tried to figure out how she was going to raise a genius.

She heard Cal's voice. ". . . and since Jane was feeling a lot better today, we went over to see Annie."

"Seems if she was feelin' better, you might have driven her into town to meet your parents."

She dropped her Windbreaker on one of the counter stools and turned to face the men coming into the kitchen.

"Dad, I went over this with you and Mom last night at dinner. I explained . . ."

"Never mind." Cal's father stopped as he caught sight of her.

Her mental image of him as a jolly old man with a round belly and fringe of white hair had dissolved the instant she'd caught sight of him at the gate. Now she felt as if she were staring at an older version of Cal.

He was equally imposing—big, handsome, rugged—and he looked exactly right in his red flannel shirt, rumpled slacks, and scuffed leather boots. His thick dark hair, worn longer and shaggier than his son's, had a few strands of silver, but he appeared to be no older than his early to mid-fifties, much too young and too good-looking to have a thirty-six-year-old son.

He took his time assessing her, and she didn't have any difficulty recognizing that straight-on, no-holds-barred gaze as a mirror of his son's. As she returned his scrutiny, she knew she would have to prove herself worthy. Still, he gave her a warm smile and extended his hand.

"I'm Jim Bonner. Glad we're finally getting to meet."

"Jane Darlington."

His smile disappeared as his eyebrows slammed together. He released her hand. "Most women around here take their husband's name when they get married."

"I'm not from around here, and the name is Darlington. I'm also thirty-four years old."

Behind her back, she heard a choking sound. Jim Bonner laughed. "You don't say."

"I certainly do. Thirty-four and getting older by the second."

"That's enough, Jane." The warning note in Cal's voice advised her not to reveal any more secrets, but he might not have spoken.

"You don't look sick."

"I'm not." She felt something brush her back and realized she'd lost the elastic holding her French braid.

"She started feeling better a couple of hours ago," Cal interjected. "Must not have been the flu after all."

Jane turned far enough to give him a faintly pitying look—she wasn't going to support him in his lies—but he pretended not to see.

Jim picked up an X-Man comic from the counter and regarded it quizzically. "Book-Of-The-Month-Club?"

"Jane reads them for relaxation. You want a beer, Dad?"

"No. I'm on my way to the hospital."

Concern drove away the caustic remark Jane had been about to make regarding the comic. "Is something wrong?"

"How about a sandwich?" Cal said too quickly. "Jane, make Dad and me a couple of sandwiches."

"I'll be happy to make your father a sandwich. You can fix your own."

Jim raised one eyebrow at his son in an expression Jane suspected meant something like, *After all these years, is this the best you could do for a wife?*

She refused to be cowed. "Are you having some tests done? I hope you're not ill."

Cal shot forward. "You've got some dirt on your face, sweetheart, from that walk you took at Annie's. Maybe you'd better go upstairs and get cleaned up."

"There's no big mystery about it," Jim said. "I'm a doctor, and I have patients to visit."

For a moment she couldn't move as the magnitude of the mistake she'd made once again drove its way home.

She whirled on Cal. "Your father's a *doctor*? How many more family skeletons do you have locked up?"

Her own heart might be breaking, but he seemed amused. "I know you were hopin' for a moonshiner, sweetheart, but I guess this just isn't your lucky day. Although, come to think of it—Dad, didn't you tell me your great-grampa had a still someplace up in the mountains?"

"That's what my father told me." Jim studied Jane. "Why do you care?"

Cal didn't let her reply, which was a good thing, because the lump in her throat had grown too large to permit speech. "Jane's sort of a hillbilly groupie. She's a city girl herself, but she likes all that backwoods stuff, and she's been real disappointed to find out we wear shoes."

Jim smiled. "I guess I could take mine off."

A woman's voice, soft and Southern, sounded from the foyer. "Cal, where are you?"

He sighed. "In the kitchen, Mom."

"I was passing by, and I saw the gate open." Like Cal's father, the woman who appeared in the doorway looked too young to have a thirty-six-year-old son, and she also seemed much too sophisticated to be the daughter of Annie Glide. Pretty, trim, and stylish, she wore her light brown hair in a short, trendy cut that curved behind her ears and emphasized a pair of clear blue eyes. Discreet frosting camouflaged whatever strands of gray had emerged. Her tall figure set off slim black trousers topped by a loosely cut fleece jacket in grape-colored wool with an abstract silver pin on the lapel. In comparison, Jane felt like a street urchin with her dirty face and leaf-flecked hair falling willy-nilly.

"You must be Jane." She walked forward, one hand extended in welcome. "I'm Lynn Bonner." Her greeting was warm, but as Jane took her hand, she received the impression of a deep reserve. "I hope you're feeling better. Cal said you were under the weather."

"I'm fine, thank you."

"She's thirty-four," Jim announced from his spot next to the counter.

Lynn looked startled, and then she smiled. "I'm delighted."

Jane found herself warming to Lynn Bonner. Jim sat down on one of the counter stools and stretched out his legs. "Cal said she's a hillbilly groupie. She sure is gonna love you, Amber."

Jane saw Cal shoot his father a puzzled look. She noted a faint trace of insolence in Jim Bonner's tone that hadn't been there before, but his wife showed no reaction. "I'm sure Cal told you we just got back from a combined vacation and medical conference. I was so sorry you weren't feeling well enough to join us for dinner last night. We'll make it up on Saturday. Jim, if it doesn't rain, you can grill."

Jim crossed his ankles. "Shoot, Amber, since Jane here likes hillbilly ways so much, why don't you forget grilling and make her some of those Glide family specials. We could have beans and fatback, or how 'bout some of that souse like your mama used to fix. You ever eat souse, Jane?"

"No, I don't believe I have."

"I can't imagine Jane wanting that," Lynn said coolly. "Nobody eats souse anymore."

"Maybe you could bring it back in fashion, Amber. You could tell all your ritzy friends about it next time you go to one of those big charity affairs in Asheville."

Cal had been staring at his parents as if he'd never seen them before. "When did you start calling Mom Amber?"

"It's her name," Jim replied.

"Annie uses it, but I've never heard you do it."

"Who says people have to keep doing things the same way?"

Cal glanced toward his mother, but she made no comment. Clearly uncomfortable, he turned away and once again opened the refrigerator door. "Are you sure nobody wants a sandwich? How about you, Mom?"

"No, thanks."

"Souse is part of the Glide family heritage," Jim said, unwilling to give up that particular avenue of conversation. "You haven't forgotten about that, have you, Amber?" He stabbed his wife with eyes so remote that Jane experienced a surge of sympathy for Cal's mother. She knew exactly how it felt to be on the receiving end of a gaze like that. Without waiting for an answer, he turned to Jane. "Souse is like sausage, Jane, but it's made from a hog's head, minus the eyeballs."

Lynn smiled a bit stiffly. "It's disgusting. I don't know why my mother ever made it. I just talked to her on the cell phone; that's how I knew you were feeling better. She seems to have taken to you, Jane."

"I like her." Jane was as anxious to change the subject as her new mother-in-law. Not only were the undercurrents of tension between Cal's parents disconcerting, but her stomach hadn't been entirely predictable lately, and she didn't want to take any chances with a discussion of eyeballs and a hog's head.

"Cal told us you're a physicist," Lynn said. "I'm so impressed."

Jim rose from the stool. "My wife didn't graduate from high school, so she sometimes gets intimidated when she meets people with advanced degrees."

Lynn didn't seem at all intimidated, and Jane found herself beginning to dislike Jim Bonner for his not-so-subtle put-downs. His wife might be willing to ignore his behavior, but she wasn't. "There certainly isn't any reason to be intimidated," she said evenly. "Some of the most foolish people I know have advanced degrees. But why am I telling you this, Dr. Bonner? I'm sure you've observed the same thing firsthand."

To her surprise, he smiled. Then he slipped his hand

inside the back of his wife's coat collar and rubbed her
neck with the familiarity of someone who'd been doing
exactly that for nearly four decades. The intimacy of the
gesture made Jane realize she'd stepped into water far too
deep for her, and she wished she'd kept her mouth shut.
Whatever marital disharmony was going on between them
had undoubtedly been going on for years, and it was none
of her business. She had enough of her own marital disharmony to worry about.

Jim stepped away from his wife. "I've got to get going,
or I'll be late for my rounds." He turned to Jane and gave
her arm a friendly squeeze, then smiled at his son. "It was
nice meeting you, Jane. See you tomorrow, Cal." His affection for Cal was obvious, but as Jim left the kitchen, she
noticed that he didn't so much as glance at his wife.

Cal set a package of sandwich meat and cheese on the
counter. As they heard the sound of the front door closing,
he gazed at his mother.

She regarded him with perfect equanimity, and Jane noticed the invisible "No Trespassing" sign she had been
wearing disappeared now that her husband had gone.

He looked troubled. "Why's Dad calling you Amber? I
don't like it."

"Then you'll have to speak with him about it, won't
you?" She smiled at Jane. "Knowing Cal, he won't think
to take you any place but the Mountaineer. If you'd like to
see some of the local shops, I'd be happy to show you
around. We could have lunch afterward."

"Oh, I'd love that."

Cal stepped forward. "Now, Jane, you don't have to be
polite. Mom's understanding." He slipped his arm around
his mother's shoulders. "Jane can't spare any time from
her research right now, but she doesn't want to hurt your
feelings. She's saying yes when she really wants to say
no."

"I understand completely." Lynn's expression said she

didn't understand at all. "Of course, your work is more important than socializing. Forget I said anything."

Jane was appalled. "No, really—"

"Please. You don't need to say another word." Turning her back on Jane, she hugged Cal. "I have to get to a meeting at church. Being the minister's mother is becoming a full-time job; I wish Ethan would get married." She glanced over at Jane, her eyes cool. "I hope you can spare some time for us on Saturday night."

Jane felt the rebuke. "I wouldn't miss it."

Cal escorted his mother to the door, where they spoke for a few moments. Afterward, he returned to the kitchen.

"How could you do that?" she said. "You made me seem like a snob to your mother?"

"What difference does it make?" He straightened his leg to pull his car keys from the right pocket of his jeans.

"Difference? It was a direct insult to her."

"So?"

"I can't believe you're being so obtuse."

"Now I get it." He set his keys on the counter. "You want to be the dearly beloved daughter-in-law. That's it, isn't it?"

"I simply want to be courteous."

"Why? So they can start to like you, and then have their guts ripped out when they find out we're getting a divorce?"

Uneasiness settled in the pit of her stomach. "Exactly what are you saying?"

"They've already mourned one daughter-in-law," he replied quietly. "I'm not going to have them mourn another. When they find out about our divorce, I want them cracking a bottle of champagne and celebrating their oldest son's narrow escape from a bad marriage."

"I don't understand." Even though she did.

"Then let me spell it out. I'd appreciate it very much if

you made sure that my parents can't stand the sight of you.''

Her hands began to tremble, and she clasped them together in front of her. Until that moment, she hadn't realized that she'd been entertaining a subtle, but nonetheless powerful, fantasy of being made to feel part of Cal's family. For someone who had always wanted to belong, this was the final irony. "I'm the designated bad guy."

"Don't look at me like that. You came into my life uninvited and turned everything upside down. I don't want to be a father right now; I sure as hell don't want to be a husband. But you took away my choice, and now you have to make some of that up to me. If you've got an ounce of compassion in that heart of yours, you won't hurt my parents.''

She turned away and blinked her eyes. He couldn't have asked anything that would disturb her more. Once again she would be the outsider, and she wondered if this was always to be her role in life? Would she always stand on the fringes gazing in at other people's families, at the bonds that seemed to come so easily to everyone else? But this time, if Cal had his way, she would be more than an oddity. This time she was to be loathed.

"A big chunk of my life is here in Salvation," he said. "My friends. My family. You'll just be around for a couple of months and then disappear."

"Leaving behind nothing but bad memories."

"You owe me," he said softly.

There was a sense of justice in what he was asking that was almost eerie in its perfection. What she had done to Cal was immoral, which was why she'd been dogged by guilt for months, and now she had a chance to serve penance. He was right. She hadn't done anything to deserve a place in his family. And she owed him.

He fiddled with his keys on the counter, and she realized he was uncomfortable. It was rare to see him looking anything but self-confident, and it took her a moment to understand. He was afraid she wouldn't go along with his wishes, and he wanted a way to convince her.

"You might have noticed my parents are a little tense with each other right now. That weren't like this before Cherry and Jamie died."

"I know they married when they were teenagers, but they're even younger than I expected."

"I was my dad's high school graduation present. Mom was fifteen when she got pregnant, sixteen when I was born."

"Oh."

"They kicked her out of school, but Annie told us that mom stood under the stadium during his graduation ceremony, wearing her best dress even though nobody could see her, just so she could hear him give the valedictory address."

Jane considered the thirty-year-old injustice. Amber Lynn Glide, the poor mountain girl, had been kicked out of school for being pregnant while the rich boy who'd gotten her that way stood at the podium and received the community's accolades.

"I know what you're thinking," Cal said, "but he didn't get off scot-free. He had it plenty rough. Nobody expected him to marry her, but he did, and he had to support a family while he went through college and med school."

"With help from his parents, I'll bet."

"Not at first. They hated my mom, and they told him if he married her, they wouldn't give him a penny. They kept their word for the first year or so, but then Gabe came along, and they finally kicked in for tuition."

"Your parents seem very troubled."

He immediately grew defensive. She realized it was one thing for him to comment on the problem, but quite another for her to. "They're just upset, that's all. They've never been very demonstrative, but there's nothing wrong with their marriage, if that's what you're getting at.''

"I'm not getting at anything.''

He snatched up his keys from the counter and made his way toward the door that led to the garage. She stopped him before he got there.

"Cal, I'll do what you want with your parents—I'll be as obnoxious to them as I can—but not with Annie. She's halfway to the truth, anyway.'' Jane felt a kinship with the old woman, and she had to have at least one friend or she'd go crazy.

He turned to look at her.

She squared her shoulders and lifted her head. "That's the deal. Take it or leave it.''

He slowly nodded. "All right. I'll take it.''

10

Jane groaned as she rose to turn off her computer, then slipped out of her clothes to prepare for bed. For the past three days, she'd spent her mornings helping Annie plant her garden, and every muscle ached.

She smiled as she folded her jeans and put them away in the closet, then pulled out her nightshirt. Usually she bristled around dictatorial people, but she loved having Annie boss her around.

Annie had bossed Cal, too. On Wednesday morning he'd insisted on driving Jane to Heartache Mountain. When they'd gotten there, Jane had pointed out the front step and suggested he stop hiring other people to do what he should do himself. He'd set to work with a great deal of grumbling, but it wasn't long before she'd heard him whistling. He'd done a good job on the step and then made some other needed repairs. Today he'd bought several gallons of paint at the hardware store and begun scraping the exterior of the house.

She slipped into a short-sleeved gray nightshirt with an appliqué of Goofy on the pocket. Tomorrow night she would be dining with Cal's parents. He hadn't mentioned her promise to distance them, but she knew he hadn't forgotten.

Although she was tired, it was barely eleven o'clock, and she felt too restless to go to bed. She began to tidy her work area and found herself once again wondering where Cal went at night. She suspected he was seeing other women, and she remembered the reference Lynn had made to the Mountaineer. She'd asked Annie about it today and learned that it was a private club of some sort. Was that where he met his women?

Even though this wasn't a real marriage, the idea hurt. She didn't want him sleeping with anyone else. She wanted him sleeping with her!

Her hands stilled on the stack of printouts she'd been straightening. What was she thinking of? Sex would only make an already complex situation impossible. But even as she told herself that, she remembered the way Cal had looked today with his shirt off while he'd stood on the ladder and scraped the side of Annie's house. Watching those muscles bunch and flex every time he moved had made her so crazy she'd finally grabbed his shirt, thrown it at him, and delivered a stern lecture on the depletion of the ozone layer and skin cancer.

Lust. That's what she was dealing with. Pure, unadulterated lust. And she wasn't going to give in to it.

She needed something to do that would distract her, so she carried her overflowing trash can downstairs and emptied it in the garage. Afterward, she gazed out the kitchen bay window at the moon and found herself contemplating the ancient scientists—Ptolemy, Copernicus, Galileo—who'd tried to unravel the mysteries of the universe with only the most primitive of instruments. Even Newton couldn't have envisioned the tools she used, from the powerful computer on her desk to the world's giant particle accelerators.

She jumped as the door behind her opened, and Cal walked in from the garage. As he moved across the kitchen, it occurred to her that she had never seen a man so at home in his body. Along with his jeans, he wore a wine red henley, the kind made out of waffle-knit underwear fabric, and a black nylon parka. Tiny needle-points of sensation prickled at her skin.

"I thought you'd be in bed," he said, and she wondered if she imagined the slight huskiness she heard in his voice.

"Just thinking."

"Dreaming about all those potatoes you planted?"

She smiled. "As a matter of fact, I was thinking about Newton. Isaac," she added.

"I've heard the name," he said dryly. The hem of his parka flopped over his wrists as he pushed his hands into his jeans pockets. "I thought you modern-day physicists had forgotten all about old Isaac in your passion for the Big Guy."

Hearing Einstein referred to in that way amused her. "Believe me, the Big Guy had a lot of respect for his predecessor. He just didn't let Newton's laws limit his thinking."

"I still think that's disrespectful. Isaac did all that work, then old Albert had to come along and upset it."

She smiled again. "The best scientists have always been rebels. Thank God they still don't execute us for our theories."

He tossed his parka over one of the counter stools. "How's the search for the top quark coming?"

"We found it in 1995. And how do you know what kind of work I'm doing?"

He shrugged. "I make it my business to know things."

"I'm investigating the *characteristics* of the top quark, not looking for it."

"So how many top quarks fit on the head of a pin?"

"More than you can imagine." She was still surprised that he knew anything about her research.

"I'm asking you about your work, Professor. I promise

you that I can at least grasp the concept, if not the particulars.''

Once again she'd let herself forget how bright he was. Easy to do with that muscular jock's body standing in front of her. She pulled her thoughts up short before they could move any farther in *that* direction. "What do you know about quarks?"

"Not much. They're a basic subatomic particle, and all matter is made up of them. There are—what?—six kinds of quarks?"

It was more than most people knew, and she nodded. "Top and bottom quarks, up and down, strange and charm. They got their names from a song that's in James Joyce's *Finnegans Wake*."

"See, that's part of the problem with you scientific types. If you'd take your names from Tom Clancy books—things people actually read—then the general public would understand what you do better."

She laughed. "I promise if I discover something important, I'll name it Red October."

"You do that." He looped his leg over a stool, then regarded her expectantly. She realized he was waiting for her to tell him more about her work.

She walked to the corner of the counter and rested one hand on the granite top. "What we know about the top quark is quite surprising. For example, it's forty times heavier than the bottom quark, but we don't know why. The more we understand about the top quark's characteristics, the closer we come to exposing the cracks in the standard model of particle physics. Ultimately, of course, we're looking for the final theory that will lead us to a new physics.''

"The Theory of Everything?"

"The name is facetious. It's more accurately called the Grand Unification Theory, but, yes, the Theory of Everything. Some of us think the top quark will unlock a small part of it.''

"And you want to be the Einstein of this new physics."

She busied herself wiping a speck from the granite with the tip of her finger. "There are brilliant physicists all over the world doing the same work."

"And you're not intimidated by any one of them, are you?"

She grinned. "Not a bit."

He laughed. "Good luck, Professor. I wish you well."

"Thank you." She waited for him to change the subject—most people's eyes began to glaze over when she talked about her work—but instead, he got up, grabbed a bag of taco chips from the pantry, and slouched down into the red velvet banquette in the alcove, where he began questioning her about the way the supercolliders worked.

Before long, she found herself sitting across from him munching on taco chips as she described the Tevatron collider at Fermilab as well as the new collider being built by CERN in Geneva, Switzerland. Her explanations merely induced more of his questions.

At first she answered eagerly, thrilled to find a layman who was genuinely interested in particle physics. It was cozy sitting in this warm kitchen late at night, munching on junk food and discussing her work. It almost felt as if they had a real relationship. But the fantasy evaporated when she realized she was explaining the components of the lepton family to him, and, much worse, that he was taking it in.

Her stomach twisted as she absorbed how easily he grasped these difficult concepts. What if her baby turned out to be even more brilliant than she feared? The idea made her dizzy, so she jumped into a complicated explanation of the Higgs boson that soon left him behind.

"Afraid you lost me, Professor."

If only she could scream at him that she'd lost him because he was too dumb to understand, but all she could say was, "It gets pretty hairy." She rose from the table. "I'm tired. I think I'll turn in for the night."

"All right."

She decided this would be as good a time as any to put an end to her imprisonment. He was in a fairly good mood, so maybe he'd handle the news better. "By the way, Cal, I need to do something about getting a car. Nothing fancy, just basic transportation. Who should I see?"

"No one. If you have to go some place, I'll take you."

As quickly at that, his affability vanished. He rose from the table and walked out of the kitchen, putting an end to the discussion.

But she wasn't nearly done, and she followed him across the cavernous family room toward the study. "I'm used to my independence. I need my own car." And then, waspishly, "I promise I won't wave at your friends when I drive through town."

"No car, Professor. That's the way it's going to be." Once again, he walked away from her, this time disappearing into the study. She compressed her lips and marched forward. This was ridiculous. Cal seemed to have forgotten they lived in the twentieth century. And that she had her own money.

She stopped in the doorway. "Unlike your girlfriends, I'm old enough to have my driver's license."

"The joke's wearing thin."

"Except it's not exactly a joke, is it?" She regarded him thoughtfully. "Are you sure all this has to do with protecting your parents? Are you sure it isn't more about keeping me locked up so my advanced age and general lack of bimbo qualities don't embarrass you in front of your friends?"

"You have no idea what you're talking about." He sprawled down behind the massive wooden desk.

She regarded him dispassionately. "I'm not even close

to being the kind of woman all your buddies expected you to marry, am I? I'm not pretty enough to be your wife, my breasts aren't big enough, and I'm too old. Big time embarrassment for the Bomber.''

He crossed his ankles and propped his boots on the desk. ''If you say so.''

''I don't need your permission to buy a car, Cal. I intend to do it whether you like it or not.''

He hit her dead on with those scorched-earth eyes. ''Like hell.''

Completely exasperated and in no mood to enter into a full-fledged battle, she turned toward the door. Tomorrow she'd do as she liked, and he could just live with it. ''I've had all of you I can take for right now. Good night.''

''Don't you walk away from me!'' He moved so quickly that she didn't see him coming, and before she could get through the doorway, he'd blocked it. ''Did you hear me?''

She splayed her hands on her hips and glared up at him. ''Back off, buster!''

Seconds ticked away, each one crackling with tension. His forehead wrinkled and his lips tightened, but at the same time, she detected something that seemed almost like anticipation in his eyes, as if he wanted to fight with her. It was the most astonishing thing. She was used to people who avoided conflict, but Cal seemed to enjoy it, and, to her surprise, she was more than willing to join in.

Before she got a chance, however, he dropped his gaze and the corner of his mouth curled. ''Goofy.''

She'd been called many things, but never that, and her temper flared. ''*What* did you say?''

''Your nightshirt.'' He reached down and, with the tip of his finger, traced the cartoon appliqué that lay on the upper slope of her breast. ''Goofy.''

''Oh.'' Her anger deflated.

He smiled and began using his fingernail, running it back and forth over the outline of the figure. The skin of her breast tightened, and her nipple hardened in response. She hated reacting to something that was obviously a calculated move on his part. No wonder he had a big ego; he could probably turn women on in his sleep.

"I hope you're arousing yourself because you're not doing a thing to me."

"Is that so?" He glanced down at the front of her nightshirt where the evidence clearly pointed to the contrary.

He was so arrogant; so sure of himself. She needed some small measure of revenge, so she shook her head and regarded him sadly. "You haven't figured it out yet, have you, Cal?"

"Figured what out?"

"Never mind." She sighed. "I guess you're probably a fairly nice guy underneath all that bluster, and I don't want to hurt your feelings."

An edge of belligerence crept into his voice. "Don't you worry about my feelings. What haven't I figured out yet?"

She made a helpless, fluttery gesture that was surprisingly effective considering the fact that she'd never done anything like that before. "This is silly. I really don't want to talk about it."

"Talk!"

"All right, then. To be blunt, the thing you don't seem to be able to grasp is the fact that you're not my type. You just don't turn me on." *Liar, Liar, pants on fire.*

He dropped his hand. "I don't turn you on?"

"Now I've made you angry, haven't I?"

"Angry? Why the hell should I be angry?"

"You look angry."

"Well, that just goes to show that you're not as perceptive as you think."

"Good. Besides, I'm sure my lack of response to you is simply a problem with my perception. It probably doesn't have anything to do with you."

"Damn right."

A little shrug. "I've just always preferred a different type of man."

"What type is that?"

"Oh, men who aren't quite as large. Not quite as loud. Gentle men. Scholarly men."

"Like Dr. Craig Elkhart?" He spit out the name.

"What do you know about Craig?"

"I know he dumped you for a twenty-year-old secretary."

"She wasn't a secretary. She was a data-entry clerk. And he didn't dump me."

"That's not the way I heard it. The guy dumped you like a load of wet cement."

"He most certainly did not. We parted by mutual agreement."

"Mutual, my ass."

"You're just throwing up a smoke screen because I wounded your pride when I said I wasn't attracted to you."

"I've met a lot of women who were liars, but you take the cake. Admit it, Professor. I turn you on so much you can hardly stand it. If I put my mind to it, I could have you naked and begging in thirty seconds flat."

"There's nothing more pathetic than an aging man boasting of his flagging sexual prowess."

"Flagging!"

She watched a slow flush spread across his cheekbones and knew she'd really done it. She'd pushed him past his limit, and now she absolutely had to shut up. "Don't worry, Cal. Somewhere there's a woman who'll care enough to take her time with you."

The flush spread to his ears.

She patted his chest. "And if that doesn't work, I've heard they're doing wonders with implants."

Those pale eyes widened, almost as if he couldn't believe what he was hearing.

"I think there are also some nonsurgical devices based

on air pressure and vacuum. I could probably even design something for you, if it came to that.''

''That's it!'' The flush receded, and before she knew what was happening, he'd dropped his shoulder, pushed it not ungently against her stomach, and upended her.

''Upsey-daisy, sweetheart.''

She found herself staring at the seat of his jeans. Faded denim stretched tight over slim, hard-muscled hips. She began to feel dizzy and wasn't certain she could entirely blame it on the blood rushing to her head. ''Cal?''

''Uh-huh?''

''Please put me down.''

''In a minute.'' He headed out into the foyer, moving carefully in deference to her pregnancy. He'd hooked one of his arms behind her knees to hold her in place, and he patted the back of one bare thigh as he mounted the stairs. ''Just stay real still, now, and everything'll be fine.''

''Where are we going?''

''We're paying the Evil Queen a visit.''

''Evil queen? What are you talking about? Put me down!''

They reached the top of the stairs. ''Quiet, now. I have to concentrate real hard so I don't turn too fast and slam that head of yours right into the wall, givin' you a nasty concussion that would lower your IQ to somewhere in the vicinity of human and make you behave like a reasonable human being.''

''My bedroom's over there.''

''The Evil Queen's this way.'' He marched toward his own bedroom.

''*What* evil queen? What are you talking about? And put me down right this minute or I'll scream bloody murder, then do the job for real!''

''I already hid all the electrical appliances, and I'm not taking a shower without locking you in the closet first.'' He dropped his shoulder, and she found herself being lowered onto something soft. She looked up into her own reflection.

Her hair was tousled, her nightshirt twisted around her thighs, and her skin rosy. Cal stood next to the bed. He leaned forward and gazed up at the mirror mounted above the bed.

"Mirror, mirror, on the wall, who's gonna be the most naked lady of all?"

The Evil Queen! She snatched a pillow and threw it at him. "Oh, no, you don't." She vaulted toward the other side of the bed, only to have him grab her nightshirt and pull her back down.

"Time for good ol' Goofy to make himself scarce so the grown-ups can play."

"I don't want to play with you, and don't you dare try to pull off my nightshirt, you arrogant ass!"

The mattress sagged as he straddled her thighs. "And you've got a very nice one yourself, I couldn't help but notice. What say we take a closer look?" He reached for the hem of the nightshirt.

"Don't, Cal." She slapped her hands down, but even as she pressed the garment to her thighs, she knew she wanted to let him take it off her. Why couldn't she? They were married, weren't they?

Still straddling her, he leaned back on his right calf. "You don't seriously think we're going to live here for three months without getting intimate."

Her heart pounded, her body pulsed with need, and her brain cried out the truth. He didn't have the slightest bit of affection for her. She was nothing more than a sexual convenience. She gritted her teeth. "Have you forgotten that you don't like me?"

"True, but one thing doesn't necessarily have anything to do with the other. You don't like me, either."

"That's not exactly so."

"You do like me?"

"I don't *dislike* you. You're probably a decent person. In your own twisted way, I know you think you're doing the right thing about all this, but I just wish you were different."

"Dumber."

"That. And not so big. Everything about you is too big for me—not just your body, but your personality, your bank account, your temper, and, definitely, your ego."

"Don't you talk to me about temper! I'm not the one going around trying to electrocute people. And if we're throwing out things that are too big, what about that gargantuan brain of yours?" He drew his leg over her and resettled himself at the end of the bed, where he leaned against the bedpost.

She knew she'd done the right thing, but it was still painful. She pointed out the obvious. "To you, I'm just an available body."

"You're my wife."

"A technicality." She sat up so she was leaning against the headboard. "You want me to be unpleasant to your parents and stay away from your friends but, at the same time, you expect me to make love with you. Can't you understand how I might find that a little demeaning?"

"No." He gazed at her, and his flared nostrils and tight lips dared her to argue with him. He was going to take his stand, even though he knew it was indefensible.

"I guess I shouldn't be surprised you feel like that since it's typical of the way celebrity athletes traditionally treat their groupies. Women are good enough for a quick romp in bed, but not good enough to be part of a big shot's life."

"Are you saying you want to be part of my life? That's pretty hard to believe, Professor, considering the fact that you don't seem to like anything about me."

"You're deliberately misinterpreting. I'm merely saying that I refuse to sleep with you at night knowing you don't like me, especially when you want to keep me locked up during the day. Don't deny that you'd behave differently if one of your bimbos had done what I did."

"None of my bimbos is smart enough to plan what you did! And I don't have any bimbos!"

She lifted one eyebrow. "A man like you wants his wife to be a reflection of himself. You want youth and beauty standing next to you because that's how you want everyone to see you, as young and healthy, a perfect physical specimen who doesn't have a worry about anything, certainly not about Kevin Tucker taking away your job."

He threw his leg over the side of the bed and stood. "This is the most boring conversation I ever had."

"Just another sign of how incompatible we are because I think the conversation's pretty fascinating. What are you going to do when your playing days are over, Cal?"

"I don't have to worry about that for a long time."

"I've seen you limp when you get out of the car after you've been sitting for a long time, and I have a feeling those thirty-minute showers I hear you take in the morning aren't about personal cleanliness. Your body has taken a beating, and it's not going to do it much longer."

"Now you're an expert on orthopedics."

"I know what I see."

"I'm not buying you a car." He headed for the door.

"I didn't ask you to," she called after him. "I intend to buy my own."

"No, you're not." He poked his head back in the door. "And I *am* taking you to bed."

She untangled herself from the covers and pushed her nightshirt down as she stood up. "I'm not going to bed with a man who dislikes me."

"We'll work on that part of it."

"We've never had a date."

"We've already *done it* twice!"

"That was nothing more than a medical procedure."

His eyes narrowed.

"We've never even kissed," she went on, driving her point home.

"Now that's something we can fix real easy." He advanced on her, a sense of purpose glittering in his eyes.

"Cal, I didn't mean . . ." She couldn't go on. She wanted to kiss him.

He encircled her wrists with his hands. The bedpost bumped against her spine. "Consider this a scientific experiment, Professor."

He leaned forward, drawing her hands behind her back and around the bedpost at the same time. She felt as if she'd been tied to a stake, except his gentle fingers were the only bonds holding her in place.

As he gazed down, her heart gave a nervous kick against her ribs. "Let's see how you taste."

His head dipped and his lips brushed hers. They were soft and warm, slightly parted, barely touching. Her eyes drifted shut. She felt as if she were being grazed by a feather and wondered how someone so strong could have such a tender touch.

He continued to tease her with his mouth. The barest brush, the slightest touch. Her senses swirled. She wanted more and she went up on tiptoe, slanting her mouth across his and deepening the kiss.

He drew back. Another graze. A glance.

She leaned into him again, and he nipped her bottom lip. Was that a warning that only the quarterback called the play? Her body throbbed with frustration.

He rewarded her obedience by closing his lips over hers and lightly tracing the bow with the tip of his tongue. She moaned. If he gave this much attention to a simple kiss, what would he do if she let him get to the rest of her?

She couldn't stand it any longer, and once again she reared up on her tiptoes. This time he didn't object. The gentle tantalizer disappeared, and he took full possession of what she offered. With his hands occupied shackling hers behind the bedpost, he could only use his mouth on her, and he used it well, filling her with his tongue and leaning into her so she could feel his passion.

She pressed her own body against his and lost herself in a new way of kissing, a mating that was more erotic than any sex act she'd ever experienced. She could be male and female, the possessor and the possessed. She moved her body against him, using it as if she were a snake, rubbing breasts and belly, thighs and hips. Her body burned with the thrill of everything that had been missing for her, and in her passion, she had a brief glimpse of how it might be if they were more to each other than bodies.

She heard a moan, but this time it didn't come from her. It was hoarse, muffled, urgent. Her hands were suddenly free, while his were on her thighs, sliding beneath her nightshirt.

Oh, yes. She wanted him there. *Hurry. Touch my softest place. My sweetest place.* Her body urged him to boldness while her mind and heart cried out not to give herself so cheaply. She wanted to be courted, to be wooed and won, even if only for her body. Just once in her life, she wanted to feel what other women felt when men pursued them.

His fingers touched the soft curls. "Stop!" Her exclamation sounded as if it were part command, part howl.

"No."

"I mean it, Cal." She gasped for breath, struggled for control. "Get your hands out from under my nightshirt."

"You want me here. You know you do."

He was still pressed hard against her, and she wished she'd touched him there first, before she'd told him to stop. Just one quick touch so she could see how he felt against her hand. "I want you to stop."

He jerked away from her. "This is stupid! This is so damn stupid I can't believe it! The two of us are trapped together in this stinking marriage. We can't stand each other, and the only consolation we're going to find is in bed, but you're too damn stubborn to cooperate!''

He'd proven her point in spades, and she swallowed her hurt so she could let him know it. "I *knew* you didn't like me.''

"What are you talking about?''

"You just said it. You just said that *we* can't stand each other, even though I already said *I* didn't dislike you. So that leaves you. You just admitted how you felt about me.''

"I did *not* say that.''

"You most assuredly did.''

"Well, I didn't mean it.''

"Ha!''

"Rosebud . . .''

"Don't you call me that, you jerk! Sex is just another form of sport to you, isn't it? Something to do when you're not on the football field or drinking beer with your buddies. Well, I don't feel that way about it. You want to have sex with me, fine! You can have sex with me! But on my terms.''

"And exactly what terms are those?''

"You're going to have to *like* me first! A lot!''

"I already like you a lot!'' he roared.

"You are pathetic!'' With an exclamation made up of equal parts fury and frustration, she snatched a pillow from the bed, threw it at his head, and flounced back to her bedroom.

Moments later, she heard a loud thud, as if somebody's fist might very well have connected with a wall.

11

Cal's parents lived on a hilly residential street shaded by mature trees and lined with older homes. Vines that would soon bloom with clematis and morning glory clung to the mailboxes, and empty white latticework planters waiting to be filled with colorful blooms perched on front porches.

The Bonner house sat at the top of a steep slope carpeted with ivy and rhododendron. It was a graceful two-story cream stucco topped by a roof of curving pale green Spanish tiles, with the shutters and trim painted the same light green. Cal pulled the Jeep under the porte cochère off to the side, then came around the front to open the door for her.

For a moment his eyes lingered on her legs. He hadn't commented on her soft, taffy-colored skirt and sweater ensemble, even though she'd rolled the skirt twice at the waistband so that a good three inches of thigh showed through her pale hose. She thought he hadn't noticed and figured her thirty-four-year-old thighs weren't any match for all those long-stemmed aerobicized legs he was used to, but now the flicker of admiration in his eyes made her wonder if she'd misjudged.

She couldn't remember ever being so confused. Last

171

night she'd felt as if she'd run through an entire gamut of emotions with him. When they'd talked in the kitchen, there had been a sense of companionship she'd never expected. There had also been laughter, anger, and lust. Right now, the lust disturbed her most.

"I like your hair," he said.

She'd left it down, along with abandoning her glasses and taking twice her normal time to apply her makeup. The way his gaze slid over her made her think it was more than just her hair he liked. Then he frowned.

"No funny business tonight, you hear me?"

"Loud and clear." She deliberately stuck a burr under his saddle so she'd stop thinking about last night. "Don't you want to throw your coat over my head to make sure none of the neighbors get a good look at me? Now what am I saying? If any of them spot me, you can just tell them I'm the mother of one of your girlfriends."

He grabbed her arm and steered her toward the front door. "One of these days I'm going to slap a piece of duct tape right over that smart mouth of yours."

"Impossible. You'll already be dead. I spotted an electric hedge trimmer in the garage."

"Then I'm going to tie you up, toss you in a closet, throw in a dozen rats crazed from hunger, and lock the door."

She lifted her eyebrow. "Very good."

He grunted and opened the front door.

"We're in here," Lynn called out.

Cal led her into a beautifully decorated living room done almost entirely in white, with accent pieces in peach and soft mint green. Jane barely had a chance to take it in before her attention was caught by one of the most beautiful men she had ever seen.

"Jane, this is my brother Ethan."

He walked forward, took her hand, and looked down at

her through kind blue eyes. "Hello, Jane. We finally meet."

She could feel herself melting, and she was so surprised by her reaction to him that she barely managed to acknowledge his greeting. Could this blond-haired, finely chiseled, soft-spoken man really be Cal's brother? Gazing into his eyes, she felt the same swell of emotion she sometimes experienced when she saw a newborn baby or a photograph of Mother Teresa. She found herself sneaking a glance at Cal, just to see if she'd missed something.

He shrugged. "Don't look at me. None of us can figure it out."

"We think he might be a changeling." Lynn rose from the couch. "He's the family embarrassment. Goodness knows, the rest of us have a list of sins a mile long, but he makes us look even worse in comparison."

"For very good reason." Ethan regarded Jane with absolute sincerity. "They're all the spawn of Satan."

By now Jane had more than a passing acquaintance with the Bonner sense of humor. "And you probably mug old ladies in your spare time."

Ethan laughed and turned to his brother. "You finally caught yourself a live one."

Cal muttered something inaudible, then glared at her with a silent reminder that she was supposed to be alienating everybody, not buddying up. She hadn't forgotten, but neither had she let herself think too much about that part of it.

"Your father had a delivery," Lynn said, "but he should be back any minute now. Betsy Woods's third. You remember; she was your first prom date. I think your father has delivered the babies of every old girlfriend any of you boys ever had."

"Dad took over the practice from his own father," Ethan explained. "For a long time Dad was the only doctor around here. He's got help now, but he still works too hard."

The discussion reminded her that she needed to find a doctor soon. And it wouldn't be Jim Bonner.

As if she'd conjured him, he appeared in the archway. He looked rumpled and tired, and Jane saw an expression of concern flicker across Lynn's features.

As Jim came into the room, his big voice boomed. "How come nobody has a drink?"

"I have a pitcher of margaritas waiting in the kitchen." Lynn's forehead smoothed, and she moved toward the door.

"We'll come with you," Jim said. "I can't stand this room, not since you and that fancy decorator ruined it. All this white makes me feel as if I can't sit down."

Jane thought the room was lovely and found Jim's remark uncalled-for. The four of them followed Lynn into the kitchen, whose warm pine and tasteful accessories gave it a cozy country charm. Jane wondered how Cal could stand their own garish house after being raised in such a comfortable place.

Jim shoved a beer at his son, then turned to Jane. "Would you like a margarita?"

"I'd rather have a soft drink."

"Baptist?"

"Pardon?"

"Are you a teetotaler?"

"No."

"We have some nice white wine in the house. Amber's made herself over into something of a wine expert, haven't you, honey?" His words sounded like those of a proud husband, but their bite told a different story.

"That's enough, Dad." Cal's voice held a touch of steel. "I don't know what's going on here, but I want it to stop."

His father straightened, and their eyes clashed. Although Cal's posture remained relaxed, the hard glint in his eyes warned his father that he'd stepped over the line.

Jim obviously wasn't used to having anyone challenge his authority, but Cal didn't show the slightest inclination to back down. She remembered that only yesterday he'd denied that anything was wrong with his parents' marriage.

Ethan broke in with a request for a beer and a casual remark about a town council meeting. He must be the family peacemaker. Tensions eased, and Lynn asked Jane about her morning with Annie. Jane heard the coolness in her voice and knew she must be wondering why her new daughter-in-law had so much time to spend helping her mother put in a garden but refused to spare a few hours for sightseeing with her.

Jane glanced at Cal. She saw an expression of resignation in his face. He didn't expect her to keep her word.

She felt a moment of sadness, but it did no good wishing for the impossible when she knew she owed him this. "It's been a bother, but don't tell her that. She simply doesn't understand that every hour she pulls me away from my research is an hour I can never regain."

There was a moment of strained silence. Jane refused to look at Cal. She didn't want to see his relief as she embarrassed herself in front of his family. With a sense of dread, she turned the screw. "I know her garden is important to her, but, really, it hardly compares with the work I'm doing. I tried to explain that to her, but she's so . . . I don't mean to imply she's ignorant, but, let's be frank, her understanding of complex issues is limited."

"Why the hell does she even want you there?" Jim barked.

Jane pretended not to pick up on his belligerence, which was so like his son's. "Who can account for the whims of an old lady?"

Cal broke in. "I'll tell you what I think? Jane's got a cantankerous nature, just like Annie's, and I think that's why Annie loves having her around. The two of them have a lot in common."

"Lucky us," Ethan muttered.

Her cheeks burned, and Cal must have sensed that she'd

gone as far as she could because he turned the conversation to a discussion of Ethan's skiing trip. Before long they were all seated at the dinner table.

Jane did her best to look bored while she drank in every detail. She observed the easy affection between the two brothers and the unconditional love Jim and Lynn had for their sons. Despite the problems between her in-laws, she would have given anything to belong to this family instead of the distant father she'd grown up with.

Several times during the meal the conversation turned toward Jim's work: an interesting case he had, a new medical procedure. Jane found his descriptions too gory for the dinner table, but it didn't seem to bother anyone else, and she concluded they were all accustomed to it. Cal, in particular, kept pressing his father for details.

But Jane was most fascinated by Lynn. As the meal progressed, she spoke of art and music, as well as a reading group discussion she was leading on a new novel. She was also an excellent cook, and Jane found herself feeling increasingly intimidated. Was there anything this former mountain girl didn't do well?

Ethan nodded toward the table's centerpiece, a crystal vase holding an arrangement of lilies and dendrobium orchids. "Where'd you get the flowers, Mom? Since Joyce Belik closed her shop after Christmas, I haven't seen anything like that around here."

"I picked the arrangement up when I was in Asheville on Thursday. The lilies are getting a little limp, but I'm still enjoying them."

For the first time since they'd begun to eat, Jim addressed his wife directly. "Do you remember the way you used to decorate the table right after we got married?"

She was still for a moment. "It was so long ago I've forgotten."

"Well, I haven't." He turned toward his sons. "Your mother'd pick dandelions out of somebody's backyard, stick 'em in an old pickle jar, and show 'em off to me when I came in from class like they were some exotic flower I'd never seen before. She'd get as excited about a jar full of dandelions as other women get about roses.''

Jane wondered if Jim had intended to embarrass his wife with this reminder of her humble roots, but if so, his strategy backfired. Lynn didn't seem at all embarrassed, but his own voice had deepened with an emotion that surprised her. Maybe Jim Bonner wasn't as contemptuous of his wife's humble roots as he pretended to be.

''You used to get so annoyed with me,'' she said, ''and I can't blame you. Imagine. Dandelions on the dinner table.''

''It wasn't just flowers she used for centerpieces. I remember one time she scrubbed up a bunch of rocks she thought were pretty and set them in a bird's nest she found.''

''You very rightly pointed out that a bird's nest on the kitchen table was disgusting and refused to eat until I threw it out.''

''Yeah, I did, didn't I?'' He rubbed his fingers on the stem of his wineglass and frowned. ''It might have been unsanitary, but it sure was pretty.''

''Really, Jim, it was no such thing.'' She smiled, cool, serene, unaffected by the currents of old emotions that seemed to have claimed her husband.

For the first time since they'd sat down, he met Lynn's eyes straight on. ''You always liked pretty things.''

''I still do.''

''But now they have to have labels on them.''

''And you enjoy those labels much more than you ever enjoyed dandelions or birds' nests.''

Despite her promise to distance herself from the family, Jane couldn't bear the idea of witnessing any more unpleasantness.

"How did you manage in those first years after you were married? Cal said you had no money."

Cal and Ethan exchanged a glance that made Jane wonder if she'd stumbled on a forbidden topic. She realized her question was overly personal, but since she was supposed to be obnoxious, what difference did it make?

"Yeah, Dad, exactly how did you manage?" Ethan said.

Lynn dabbed at the corners of her lips with her napkin. "It's too depressing. Your father hated every minute of it, and I don't want his dinner spoiled."

"I didn't hate every minute of it." Jim seemed pensive as he leaned back in his chair. "We lived in this ugly two-room apartment in Chapel Hill that looked out over an alley where people'd throw rusted bedsprings and old couches. The place was hopeless, but your mother loved it. She tore pictures out of *National Geographic*s and hung them on the walls. We didn't have any curtains, just two window shades that had turned yellow, and she made tissue-paper flowers out of pink Kleenex to pin across the bottoms. Things like that. We were poor as church mice. I stocked grocery shelves when I wasn't in class or studying, but she had the worst of it. Right up until the day Cal was born, she got up at four in the morning to work all day in a bakery. But no matter how tired she was, she'd still find time to pick those dandelions on her way home."

Lynn shrugged. "Believe me, working in that bakery wasn't nearly as difficult as the farm chores I'd been doing on Heartache Mountain."

"But you were pregnant," Jane pointed out, trying to imagine it.

"I was young and strong. In love." For the first time, Lynn looked slightly ruffled. "After Cal was born, we had medical bills on top of everything else, and since I couldn't work in the bakery and still take care of him, I began experimenting with cookie recipes."

"She'd start baking as soon as she'd given him his two

o'clock feeding, work until four, then go back to sleep for an hour or so until he woke again. After she'd fed him, she'd wake me up for class. Then she'd wrap everything up, load Cal into an old buggy she'd found in a junk shop, pack the cookies around him, and walk to campus where she'd sell them to the students, two cookies for twenty-five cents. She didn't have a license, so whenever the campus cops came around, she'd cover up everything but Cal's head with this big blanket.''

She smiled at Cal. ''Poor thing. I knew nothing about babies, and I nearly suffocated you in the summer.''

Cal regarded her fondly. ''I still don't like a lot of covers on me.''

''The cops never caught on,'' Jim said. ''All they saw was a sixteen-year-old mountain girl in a pair of worn-out jeans pushing a dilapidated buggy with a baby everybody figured was her little brother.''

Ethan's expression grew thoughtful. ''We always knew you had it tough, but you'd never tell us any of the details. How come?''

And why now? Jane wondered.

Lynn rose. ''It's an old and boring story. Poverty's only charming in retrospect. Help me clear the table for dessert, will you, Ethan?''

To Jane's disappointment, the conversation shifted to the much less interesting topic of football, and if Jim Bonner's troubled gaze kept straying back to his wife, no one else seemed to notice.

As boorish as his behavior had been that afternoon, Jane was no longer quite so eager to pass judgment. There was something sad lurking in the depths of his eyes that touched her. When it came to Cal's parents, she had the feeling that nothing was quite what it seemed.

For her, the most interesting moment came when Ethan asked Cal how his meetings were going, and she learned what her husband was doing with his time. Cal had been enlisted by the local high-school principal, an old classmate of his, to visit county businessmen and persuade them to get involved with a new vocational program for high-risk students. He also seemed to be giving Ethan a considerable amount of money to expand a drug program for county teens, but when she pressed for more details, he changed the subject.

The evening dragged on. When Jim asked her a question about her work, she patronized him with her explanation. Lynn issued an invitation to join her book group, but Jane said she had no time for ladies' social gatherings. When Ethan said he hoped he'd see her at Sunday services, she told him she wasn't a believer.

I'm sorry, God, but I'm doing the best I can here. These are nice people, and they don't need any more heartache.

It was finally time to go. Everyone was rigidly courteous, but she didn't miss Jim's frown as he said good-bye or the deep concern in Lynn's eyes as she hugged her son.

Cal waited until he'd pulled out of the driveway before he looked over at her. "Thanks, Jane."

She stared straight ahead. "I can't go through that again. Keep them away from me."

"I will."

"I mean it."

"I know that wasn't easy for you," he said softly.

"They're wonderful people. It was horrible."

He didn't speak again until they reached the edge of town. "I've been thinking. What say the two of us go out on a date sometime soon?"

Was this to be her reward for humiliating herself tonight? The fact that he'd chosen this particular time to extend his invitation made her waspish. "Do I have to wear a paper bag over my head in case somebody might see me?"

"Now why d'you have to go and get all sarcastic on me? I asked you out, and all you have to say is yes or no."

"When?"

"I don't know. How about next Wednesday night?"

"Where are we going?"

"Don't you worry about that. Just wear the tightest pair of jeans you've got and maybe one of those slinky halter tops."

"I can barely button my tight jeans, and I don't have a slinky halter top. Even if I did, it's too cold."

"I imagine I can keep you pretty warm, and don't worry about buttons." The deep timbre of sexual promise she heard in his voice made her shiver. He glanced over, and she felt as if he were stroking her with his eyes. He couldn't have made his intentions any clearer. He wanted her, and he intended to have her.

But the question remained, was she ready for him? Life had always been serious business for her, and nothing could ever make her a casual sort of person. Could she deal with the pain that would await her in the future if she let down her guard with him?

Her head had begun to ache, and she turned to look out the window without answering him. She tried to distract herself from the sizzling undercurrents that vibrated between them by turning her thoughts to his parents, and as the Jeep passed through the silent streets of Salvation, she began sorting through what she'd learned about them.

Lynn hadn't always been the reserved, sophisticated woman who had entertained so graciously tonight. But what about Jim? Jane wanted to dislike him, but all evening she'd caught glimpses of yearning in his eyes when he'd looked at his wife, and she couldn't seem to work up a good solid dislike for a man who had feelings like that.

What had happened to the two high school kids who had once been in love? she wondered.

Jim wandered into the kitchen and poured himself the last cup of decaf. Lynn stood at the sink with her back to him. She always had her back to him, he thought, although it didn't make much difference because, even when she faced him, she never let him see anything more than the polite mask she wore for everyone except their sons.

It was during her pregnancy with Gabe that Lynn had begun transforming herself into the perfect doctor's wife. He remembered how he'd welcomed her increasing reserve and the fact that she no longer publicly embarrassed him with bad grammar and overexuberance. As the years passed, he'd grown to believe that Lynn's transformation had prevented their marriage from turning into the disaster everyone had predicted. He'd even thought he was happy.

Then he'd lost his only grandson and a daughter-in-law he'd adored. Afterward, as he'd witnessed his middle son's bottomless grief and been helpless to cure it, something inside him seemed to have snapped. When Cal had phoned him with the news that he'd married, he'd finally begun to feel hopeful again. But then he'd met his new daughter-in-law. How could Cal have married that cold, supercilious bitch? Didn't he realize she was going to make him miserable?

He cradled the coffee mug in his hands and looked over at his wife's slim, straight back. Lynn was shaken to the core by Cal's marriage, and both of them were trying to come up with a reason why he'd chosen so badly. The physicist had a subtle sex appeal that he'd seen right away, even if Lynn hadn't, but that didn't explain why Cal had married her. For years they'd both despaired over his preference for women who were too young and intellectually limited for him, but at least all of them had been sweet-natured.

He felt helpless to deal with Cal's problems, especially when he couldn't even deal with his own. The conversation at the dinner table had brought it all back to him, and now he felt the passage of time ticking away so loudly he wanted to shove his hands over his ears because he couldn't go back to fix all the places where he'd made the wrong choices.

"Why haven't you ever said anything about that day I bought the cookies from you? All this time, and you've never said a word."

Her head came up at his question, and he waited for her to pretend she didn't know what he was talking about, but he should have realized that wouldn't be her way. "Goodness, Jim, that was thirty-six years ago."

"I remember it like it was yesterday."

It had been a beautiful April day during his freshman year at UNC, five months after Cal was born, and he'd been coming out of a chem lab with some of his new friends, all of them upperclassmen. Now he didn't remember their names, but at the time he'd craved their acceptance, and when one of them had called out, "Hey, it's the cookie girl," he'd felt everything inside him turn cold.

Why did she have to be here now, where his new friends could see her? Anger and resentment turned to acid inside him. She was so damned hopeless. How could she embarrass him like this?

As she'd brought the buggy with the wobbly wheels to a stop, she'd looked thin and ragged, barely more than a child, a raw mountain girl. He forgot everything he loved about her: her laughter, the way she'd come so eagerly into his arms, the little spit hearts she'd draw on his belly before she'd settled beneath him so sweet and giving he couldn't think of anything but burying himself inside her.

Now as he watched her come closer, every poisonous word his parents had said shrieked in his ears. She was no good. A Glide. She'd trapped him and ruined his life. If he ever expected to see a penny of their money, he had to divorce her. He deserved something better than a roach-infested apartment and a too-young mountain girl, even one so tender and joyous she made him weep with love for her.

Panic welled inside him as his new friends called out to

her. "Hey, Cookie Girl, you got any peanut butter?"

"How much for two packs of chocolate chip?"

He wanted to run, but it was too late. His new friends were already examining the cookies she'd baked that morning while he slept. One of them leaned forward and tickled his son's belly. Another turned back to him.

"Hey, Jimbo, come on over here. You haven't tasted anything until you've tried this little girl's cookies."

Amber had looked up at him, laughter dancing in eyes as blue as a mountain sky. He could see her waiting for the moment he would tell them she was his wife, and he knew she was savoring the humor of the situation as she savored everything about their life together.

"Yeah, uh . . . okay."

Her smile remained bright as he walked toward her. He remembered that her light brown hair had been pulled into a ponytail with a blue rubber band, and that she'd had a wet spot on the shoulder of his old plaid shirt where Cal must have drooled.

"I'll take the chocolate chip."

Her head tilted quizzically to the side—*You goof, when are you gonna tell 'em?*—but she continued to smile, continued to enjoy the joke.

"Chocolate chip," he repeated.

Her faith in his honor was infinite. She waited patiently. Smiled. He slipped his hand in his pocket and drew out a quarter.

Only then, when he held out the money, did she understand. He wasn't going to acknowledge her. It was as if someone had turned out a light inside her, extinguishing her laughter and joy, her faith in him. Hurt and bewilderment clouded her features. For a moment she only stared at him, but, finally, she reached into the buggy for the cookies and held them out with a trembling hand.

He tossed her the quarter, one of four she'd given him that morning before he'd left for class. He tossed her the quarter as if she were nothing more than a street corner beggar, then he laughed at something one of the other guys said and turned away. He didn't look at her, just walked away while the cookies burned in his hand like pieces of silver.

It had happened more than three decades ago, but now his eyes were stinging. He set the coffee on the counter. "What I did was wrong. I've never forgotten it, never forgiven myself, and I'm sorry."

"Apology accepted." She flicked on the faucet, putting a deliberate end to the subject. When she turned off the water, she said, "Why did Cal have to marry her? Why couldn't they just have lived together long enough for him to see what kind of woman she is?"

But he didn't want to talk about Cal and his cold wife. "You should have spit in my face."

"I just wish we'd met Jane ahead of time."

He hated her easy dismissal of his wrong, especially when he suspected she hadn't dismissed it at all. "I want you back, Lynn."

"Maybe we could have changed his mind."

"Stop it! I don't want to talk about them! I want to talk about us, and I want you back."

She finally turned, and she gazed at him out of blue, mountain sky eyes that revealed nothing. "I never left."

"The way you were. That's what I want."

"You *are* in a mood tonight."

To his dismay, he could feel his throat closing up, but even so, he couldn't be silent. "I want it the way it was at the beginning. I want you silly and funny, imitating the landlady and teasing me for being too serious. I want dandelions back on the dinner table, and fatback and beans. I want you to start giggling so hard you wet your pants, and when I walk in the door, I want you to throw yourself at me like you used to."

Her forehead crinkled with concern. She walked over to

him and rested her hand on his arm in the same comfort-place she'd been touching for nearly four decades. "I can't make you young again, Jim. And I can't give you back Jamie and Cherry and everything the way it used to be."

"I know that, dammit!" He shook her off, rejecting her pity and her suffocating, never-ending kindness. "This isn't about them. What happened has made me realize I don't like the way things are. I don't like the way you've changed."

"You've had a hard day. I'll give you a back rub."

As always, her sweetness made him feel guilty, unwor-thy, and mean. It was the meanness that had been driving him lately and telling him to push her so far, to hurt her so badly, that he'd destroy the icy reserve and find the girl he'd thrown away.

Maybe if he gave her some evidence that he wasn't as bad as he knew himself to be, she'd soften. "I've never screwed around on you."

"I'm glad to know that."

He couldn't let it go at that, giving her only the part of the truth he wanted her to see. "I had chances, but I never went all the way. Once I got myself right to the motel door—"

"I don't want to hear this."

"But I backed off. God, I felt good about that for at least a week. Smug and self-righteous."

"Whatever you're doing to yourself, I want you to stop it right now."

"I want to start over. I thought maybe on our vacation . . . but we hardly talked to each other. Why can't we start over?"

"Because you'd hate it now just as much as you hated it then."

She was as unreachable as a distant star, but he still needed to touch her. "I loved you so much, you know that, don't you? Even when I let my parents talk me into agreeing to a divorce, I still loved you."

"It doesn't matter now, Jim. Gabe came along, and then Ethan, and there wasn't any divorce. It was all so long ago. There's no sense in stirring up the past. We have three wonderful sons and a comfortable life."

"I don't want to be comfortable!" Fury exploded inside him, fueled by frustration. "Goddammit! Don't you understand anything? Jesus, I hate you!" In all their time together, he had never once touched her in violence, but now he grabbed her arms and shook her. "I can't stand this any longer! Change back!"

"Stop it!" Her fingers dug into his upper arms. "Stop it! What's wrong with you?"

He saw the fear on her face, and he jerked away, appalled by what he'd done.

Her icy reserve had finally melted, leaving rage behind, an emotion he'd never until that moment seen on her face. "You've been torturing me for months!" she cried. "You belittle me in front of my own sons. You poke at me and jab me and draw blood in a thousand ways every day! I've given you everything, but it's still not enough. Well, I won't put up with it anymore! I'm leaving you! I'm finished!" She raced from the kitchen.

Panic welled inside him. He started to run after her, but then stopped just as he reached the door. What would he do when he caught her? Shake her again? Christ. What if he'd finally pushed her too far?

He drew a deep breath and told himself she was still his own Amber Lynn, sweet and gentle as a mountain afternoon. She wouldn't leave him no matter what she said. She just needed time to calm down, that was all.

As he heard her car peel out of the driveway, he kept repeating the same thing to himself.

She wouldn't leave him. She couldn't.

*   *   *

Lynn's chest was so tight that she had to gasp for breath as she raced along the narrow, winding road. It was a treacherous piece of highway, but she'd been driving it for years, and not even her tears made her slow down. She knew what he wanted from her. He wanted her to open her veins again and bleed with love for him the way she once had. Bleed with love that would never be returned.

She struggled for breath and remembered that she'd learned her lesson years ago when she'd been little more than a baby, naive and ignorant at sixteen, utterly convinced that love could conquer the enormous gap between them. But that naïveté hadn't lasted. Two weeks after she'd told him she was pregnant with Gabe—Cal had only been eleven months old—her innocence was shattered forever.

She should have seen it coming, but of course she hadn't. When she'd told him she was pregnant, she'd bubbled over with happiness even though Cal wasn't yet a year old, and they were barely managing as it was. He had sat frozen as she'd babbled on.

"Just think, Jim! Another sweet baby! Maybe it'll be a girl this time, and we can name her Rose of Sharon. Oh, I'd love to have me a girl! But a boy'd might be better so Cal'd have somebody to roughhouse with."

When his expression didn't change, she'd started to get scared. "I know it'll be a mite hard for a while, but my baking business is goin' real good, and just think how much we love Cal. And we'll be real careful from now on to make sure there ain't no more. Tell me you're happy about the baby, Jim. Tell me."

But he hadn't said anything; he'd just walked out the door of their little apartment, leaving her alone and frightened. She'd sat for hours in the dark until he'd returned. He hadn't said a word. Instead, he'd pulled her into bed and made love to her with a ferocity that had driven away her fear.

Two weeks later, while Jim was in class, her mother-in-law had come to see her. Mildred Bonner had told her that Jim didn't love her and wanted a divorce. She'd said he'd planned to break the news to her the same night Lynn had announced that she was pregnant again, but now he felt honor-bound to stick by her. If Lynn truly loved him, Mildred said, she would let him go.

Lynn hadn't believed her. Jim would never ask for a divorce. He loved her. Didn't she see the evidence every night in their bed?

When he came home from studying at the library, she told him about his mother's visit, expecting him to laugh it off. Only he didn't. "What's the use of talking about it now?" he said. "You got pregnant again, so I can't go anywhere."

The rose-colored world she'd built shattered at her feet. Everything had been an illusion. Just because he loved to have sex with her didn't mean he loved her. How could she ever have been so foolish? He was a Bonner and she was a Glide.

Two days later his mother came to the apartment again, a fire-breathing dragon demanding that Lynn set her son free. Lynn was ignorant, uneducated, a disgrace to him! She could only hold him back.

Everything Mildred said was true, but as much as Lynn loved Jim, she knew she wasn't going to let him go. On her own, she could have managed, but her children needed a father.

She found some hidden reservoir of strength that gave her the courage to defy his mother. "If I ain't good enough for him, then you'd better fix me up so's I am, because me and my babies ain't goin' nowhere."

It hadn't happened easily, but gradually the women had formed a fragile alliance. She'd accepted Mildred Bonner's guidance in everything: how to talk, how to walk, what food to fix. Mildred insisted that Amber sounded like a white trash name, and she must call herself Lynn.

While Cal played at her feet, she devoured the books on Jim's English reading lists and exchanged baby-sitting with another woman so she could sneak into some of the larger lecture halls and lose herself in history, literature, and art, subjects that fed her poet's soul.

Gabe was born, and his family loosened the purse strings enough to take over Jim's school expenses and her medical bills. Money was still tight, but they were no longer desperate. Mildred insisted they move into a better apartment, one she furnished with Bonner family pieces.

Lynn's transformation was so gradual that she was never certain when Jim grew aware of it. He continued to make love to her nearly every night, and if she no longer laughed and teased and whispered naughty words in his ear, he didn't seem to notice. She grew more restrained out of the bedroom as well, and his occasional approving glances rewarded her for her self-control. Gradually, she learned to keep her love for her husband locked away where it would embarrass no one.

He finished his undergraduate work and entered the grueling years of medical school, while her world was defined by the needs of her young sons and her continuous efforts at self-improvement. When he finished his residency, they returned to Salvation so he could join his father's practice.

The years passed, and she found contentment with her sons, her work in the community, and her passion for the arts. She and Jim had their separate lives, but he was unfailingly considerate of her, and they shared passion, if not intimacy, in the bedroom. Gradually the boys left home, and she found a new serenity. She loved her husband with all her heart and didn't blame him too much for not loving her back.

Then Jamie and Cherry had died, and Jim Bonner had fallen apart.

In the months that followed the deaths, he'd begun

wounding her in so many countless ways she sometimes felt as if she were slowly bleeding to death. The unfairness left her reeling. She'd become everything he'd wanted, only now he didn't want that. Instead, he seemed to want something that she no longer had within herself to give.

12

Annie called Jane shortly before eight o'clock on Monday morning and announced she wasn't up to doing any gardening for a few days, and she didn't want either of them bothering her until she asked. As far as she was concerned, she said, a pair of newlyweds should have something better to do anyway than pester an old lady to death.

Jane smiled as she hung up the phone and returned to the oatmeal she was cooking. When she was an old lady, she hoped she had the guts to be as good at it as Annie.

"Who was that?"

She jumped and dropped her spoon as Cal, all bedroom-rumpled and gorgeous, wandered into the kitchen. He wore jeans and an unbuttoned flannel shirt. His hair was tousled, and he was barefoot.

"Don't sneak up on me like that!" She told herself the unwelcome thudding in her heart was caused by fright and not the sight of him so disheveled and outrageously handsome.

"I wasn't sneaking. I'm just a quiet walker."

"Well, stop it."

"You are one grouchy fud."

"Fud?"

"P.H.D. Us dumb jocks call you guys fuds."

She snatched up a clean spoon and jabbed it back into the oatmeal. "Us fuds call you guys dumb jocks, which just goes to show how smart some of us fuds really are."

He chuckled. What was he doing here? He was usually gone by the time she came downstairs for breakfast. Even on the mornings last week when he'd stayed around to drive her to Annie's, they hadn't eaten together. He'd been in his study.

"Who was on the phone?" he repeated.

"Annie. She doesn't want us bothering her today."

"Good."

He walked over to the pantry and came out with one of the half dozen boxes of Lucky Charms he kept there, along with potato chips, cookies, and candy bars. She watched from the stove as he poured a mountain of the multicolored cereal into a serving bowl, then walked over to the refrigerator, where he got the milk.

"For a doctor's son, you have an abysmal diet."

"When I'm on vacation, I get to eat what I like." He grabbed a spoon, slung one leg over the counter stool, and sat with his knees splayed, bare heels hooked over the rungs.

She tore her eyes away from those long, narrow feet only to shudder at the sight of him digging in. "I'm making plenty of oatmeal. Why don't you eat some of it instead of that stuff?"

"For your information, this isn't stuff. It happens to be the culmination of years of scientific research."

"There's a *leprechaun* on the box."

"Cute little guy." He gestured toward her with his milky spoon. "You know what the best part is? The marshmallows."

"The marshmallows?"

"Whoever thought of adding all those little marshmallows was one smart guy. I've got it written in my contract that the Stars have to keep the training table stocked with Lucky Charms just for me.''

''This is fascinating. I'm talking with a man who graduated *summa cum laude*, and yet I could swear I'm in the presence of an idiot.''

''The thing I wonder about is this . . . As good as Lucky Charms are, maybe there's another cereal just waiting to be invented that's even better.'' He took another bite. ''That's what I'd do with myself if I had a brain as big as yours, Professor. Instead of messing around with that top quark, I'd come up with the best breakfast cereal in the world. Now, I know that'd be hard. They've already added chocolate and sprinkles and peanut butter, not to mention all these different-colored marshmallows, but answer me this— Has anybody thought about M&Ms? No, ma'am, they haven't. Nobody's been smart enough to figure out there's a big market for M&Ms in breakfast cereal.''

She absorbed this as she watched him eat. He sat there at the counter—bare feet, naked chest showing through his unbuttoned shirt, muscles rippling like liquid steel every time he moved. A gorgeous picture of dumbness. Except this gorgeous dummy was smart as a fox.

She filled her bowl and carried it over to the counter along with a spoon. ''Peanut or plain?''

He thought it over. ''It prob'ly wouldn't pay to get too fancy right off. I'd go with plain.''

''Wise decision.'' She added her own milk and sat down next to him.

He glanced over at her. ''You're really going to eat that?''

''Of course I am. This is cereal as God intended.''

He reached over without an invitation and scooped up a heaping spoonful that included all the brown sugar melting at the center.

''Not bad.''

''You took my brown sugar!''

"But you know what'd really be good on it?"

"Now let me think . . . M&Ms?"

"You are one smart lady." He picked up the Lucky Charms box and shook a few on top of her oatmeal. "This'll give you the crunch that's missing."

"Gee, thanks."

"I do like those marshmallows."

"So you've said." She pushed the Lucky Charms to the side, and took another bite. "You know, don't you, cereal like that is made for children?"

"Then I guess I'm a kid at heart."

The only thing about him that reminded her of a kid was his immature attitude toward women. Was that what had kept him out until three in the morning? Picking up younger women?

She saw no need to keep herself in suspense any longer. "Where were you last night?"

"Checking up on me?"

"No. I wasn't sleeping very well, and I heard you come in late, that's all."

"Where I was doesn't have anything to do with you."

"It does if you were with another woman."

"Is that what you think?" He let his gaze ramble down over her body in what she could only interpret as a gesture of psychological warfare. She was wearing a red T-shirt with Maxwell's Equations printed on it, although the final equation disappeared into the waistband of her slacks where she'd tucked it in. His eyes lingered on her hips, which certainly weren't as slim as the hips he was accustomed to seeing on his women. Still, she took heart from the fact that he didn't look all that critical.

"It's crossed my mind." She pushed away her oatmeal and studied him. "I just want to know what the rules are. We haven't talked about this, and I think we should. Are we free to sleep with other people while we're married or not?"

His eyebrows shot up. "*We?* What's this *we?*"

She kept her expression carefully blank. "I beg your pardon? I'm not following you."

He shoved his hand through his hair. It had grown a bit longer in the last few weeks, and a spike stuck up on one side. "We're married," he said gruffly. "That's it."

"That's what?"

"It!"

"Uhmm."

"You're a married woman, and a pregnant one, to boot, in case you forgot."

"And you're a married man." She paused. "In case you forgot."

"Exactly."

"So does that mean we're going to mess around with other people while we're married or we're not?"

"It means *we're* not!"

She concealed her relief as she rose from the stool. "Okay. No messing around, but we can carouse until all hours of the night with no explanation and no apologies, right?"

She watched him mull that one over and wondered how he'd work around it. She wasn't entirely surprised when he didn't try. "I get to carouse. You don't."

"I see." She picked up her oatmeal bowl and carried it to the sink. She could feel him waiting for her to rip into him, and she knew him well enough to suspect he was relishing the challenge of defending a position he knew very well was indefensible. "Well, I suppose from your point of view that's only logical."

"It is?"

"Of course." She gave him a silky smile. "How else can you possibly convince the world you're still twenty-one?"

*　　*　　*

On Wednesday night she took her time dressing for the mysterious date she'd finally agreed to go on, despite her misgivings. She showered, powdered, and perfumed. Then she was ashamed of herself for placing so much importance on the occasion. But she'd had such a good day, it was hard to be annoyed with herself for long. Her work had gone well, and she was enjoying the fact that Cal seemed to be hanging around the house a lot more this week. Today he'd even made an excuse to accompany her on her walk, saying he was afraid she'd get so preoccupied solving some damn formula that she'd get lost.

She didn't like admitting how much she enjoyed being around him. She'd never met anyone who made her laugh as he did, while his razor-sharp mind kept her on her toes. It was ironic that the intelligence that made him so attractive to her was also the source of her greatest concern.

She pushed the unhappy reminder of her baby's future aside and thought about the battered red Ford Escort that had been delivered a few hours ago and hidden away behind an old shed in the far corner of the estate. Buying a used car by telephone might defy conventional wisdom, but she was satisfied with her purchase. True, the car wasn't anything to look at with its dented door, broken front grill-work, and bad touch-up job, but it had fit comfortably into her budget, and all she needed was basic transportation to get her through the next few months until she returned to Chicago and the perfectly good Saturn waiting in her garage.

She also didn't intend to keep the car hidden, but she knew Cal was going to be furious, and she wanted to enjoy her evening before she broke the news to him that her imprisonment was at an end.

She smiled as she finished dressing. She'd followed his instructions about wearing jeans, but instead of the halter top, she'd chosen a mulberry silk blouse and a pair of semi-trashy gold hoop earrings that were more appropriate for one of Cal's baby dolls than a theoretical physicist. She couldn't figure out why she liked them so much.

She unbuttoned the top button of her silk blouse and watched it fall open to show the lacy top of her black bra. She studied herself, sighed, and rebuttoned the blouse. For now, trashy earrings were as far as she was prepared to go.

Cal came out into the foyer as she descended the stairs. He wore an old Stars' T-shirt that outlined all of those beautifully developed chest muscles and was tucked into a pair of jeans so tight, faded, and threadbare he might as well have been naked.

His gaze traveled over her like a lazy stream on a hot summer day. She flushed, then stumbled on the step and had to grab for the rail.

"Something wrong?" he inquired innocently.

Jerk. He knew very well what was wrong. He was a walking, talking sexual fantasy. "Sorry. I was contemplating Seiberg-Witten theory. Quite tricky."

"I'll bet." His eyes swept over her in a way that made her feel her primping time hadn't been wasted. "Couldn't find a halter top, huh?"

"They were all in the wash."

He smiled, and as she watched that unexpected dimple pop into the hard plane beneath his cheekbone, she wondered what she was doing with a man like this? He was so far out of her league, he might have come from another solar system.

She realized she'd forgotten her jacket and turned on the stairs to go back and fetch it.

"Runnin' scared already?"

"I need a jacket."

"Wear this." He went to the closet and pulled out his gray zippered sweatshirt. She came down to meet him, and as he set it around her shoulders, his hands lingered there for a moment. She caught the heady scent of pine, soap, and something that was unmistakably Cal Bonner, an intoxicating hint of danger.

The soft folds of the shirt settled over her hips. She glanced down at it and wished she were one of those women who looked cute in men's clothes, but she suspected she merely looked pudgy. He didn't appear to find anything wrong with her, however, so she took heart.

He'd left the Jeep in the motor-court, and, as always, he opened the door for her. As he started the car and headed down the drive toward the highway, she realized she was nervous, and she wished he'd say something to break the tension, but he seemed content to drive.

They passed through town, where the stores were closed for the night, along with the Petticoat Junction Cafe. Down one of the side streets, she saw a lighted building with a number of cars parked around it. She deduced that was the Mountaineer.

They reached the edge of town and drove around Heartache Mountain. Just as she'd decided he was taking her to Annie's, he slowed the Jeep and turned into a badly rutted gravel lane. The headlights picked out a ramshackle structure no bigger than a tollbooth sitting just beyond the heavy chain that stretched across the road.

"Where are we?"

"See for yourself." He stopped the car and pulled a flashlight from under the seat. After he'd lowered the window, he shone the beam outside.

She ducked her head and saw a starburst-shaped sign made up of broken lightbulbs, peeling purple paint, and the words, *Pride of Carolina*. "*This* is where you're taking me for our date?"

"You said you'd never gone on a drive-in date when you were a teenager. I'm making it up to you."

He grinned at her dumbfounded expression, flicked off the flashlight, and got out of the car to unfasten the chain that barred the road. When he returned, he drove forward, jarring her as the car hit the ruts.

"My first date with a multimillionaire," she grumbled, "and this is what I get."

"Don't hurt my feelings and tell me you've already seen the movie."

She smiled and grabbed the door handle to keep from banging against it. Despite her grumbling, she wasn't exactly displeased with the idea of being alone with him at this abandoned drive-in. It would benefit their baby, she told herself, if she and Cal got to know each other a little better.

The Jeep's headlights swept the deserted lot, which looked like an eerie science-fiction landscape with its concentric mounds of earth and row upon row of metal speaker poles. The car lurched as he headed toward the rear of the drive-in, and she grabbed the dashboard with one hand while she instinctively covered her abdomen with the other.

He glanced over. "Waking the little guy up?"

It was the first time he'd acknowledged her pregnancy with anything other than hostility. She felt as if a blossom had slowly unfurled inside her, and she smiled.

He turned into the back row. "He can go back to sleep in a minute. That is, if he's not too busy solving equations."

"You won't think it's so funny when she starts grouping her Cheerios in multiples of ten while the other kids are gumming away at them."

"I swear, you're the most worryin' woman I've ever met. You act like having a brain is the worst tragedy on earth. The boy'll be fine. Just look at me. Having a brain didn't bother me any."

"That's because you keep yours under lock and key."

"Well, lock yours up for a while so we can enjoy the damn movie."

There was nothing much she could say to that, so she didn't try.

He moved to the center of the last row, just in front of a sagging chain-link fence, and pulled into one of the spaces so that the front wheels were elevated by the dirt mound. He picked up the speaker, brought it into the car, hung it on top of the steering wheel, then closed the window to shut out the chilly night air. She refrained from mentioning that the speaker had no cord.

He turned off the headlights and the engine, plunging them into darkness relieved only by a sliver of quarter moon. She shifted her attention to the distant screen, which was bisected by a silvery shaft of moonlight. "We should have gotten here earlier so we could get better seats."

"The back row's the best."

"Why is that?"

"No little kids lookin' through the windows. I like my privacy when I'm makin' out."

She swallowed hard. "Did you bring me here to make out?"

"Pretty much."

"Oh."

"You got a problem with that?" The moon slipped beneath a bank of clouds, leaving them in darkness. He flicked on the overhead light, and she saw the corner of his mouth kick up, making him the very picture of a self-satisfied man. He twisted toward the backseat, reached down, and came up with a large bag of grocery-store popcorn.

Her brain was flashing out warning signals at the exact speed of light, but she was in no mood to listen. She'd wanted to be courted, and he was doing that, even if he'd chosen a peculiar way to go about it. And no matter what he said, she didn't think he still hated her because he smiled too much when they were together.

He was also wily as a fox, she reminded herself, and

he'd made no secret of the fact that he desired her. Since his moral code seemed to dictate fidelity, at least for the next few months, he either had to seduce her or go without. She wanted to believe he would be pursuing her even if they weren't caught in this impossible situation, but she couldn't quite make that leap of faith. Maybe she could strike a compromise.

"I don't have a problem with it as long as you understand that I won't go all the way on a first date."

He opened the bag and took out a handful of popcorn. "I respect you for that. 'Course, maybe we should discuss exactly how you're calculating when we had our first date. I seem to remember a surprise birthday—"

"Cal . . ."

He tossed the popcorn into his mouth. "There's some beer and juice in a cooler in the backseat. See if you can reach over there and get it."

She turned around and saw a small Styrofoam cooler resting on the seat. She knelt and reached back for it, only to find herself being gently, but forcibly, upended. As she awkwardly scrambled to balance herself on the rear seat, she heard a chuckle that had a faintly diabolical sound to it.

"Good idea, sweetheart. I'll just come right back there with you."

Before she could react, he had let himself out the driver's door, opened the back, and settled down next to her.

"Jeez . . ." She straightened her blouse. "Fathers must have locked up their daughters when they saw you coming."

"I didn't develop my best moves 'til I was in college."

"Why don't you just be quiet and watch the movie."

"Hand me one of those beers first."

She did as he asked, taking a can of apple juice for herself and refusing the popcorn. He sipped his beer; she sipped her juice. They both leaned their heads back against the seat in companionable silence, with the dome light glowing above them.

He stretched his arm across the seat behind her. "This movie's making me horny."

Her heart gave a queer thump in her chest. "Which part? Where Maria sings about the hills being alive with the sound of music? Or is it that *do re mi* thing the kids are doing?"

A grin flicked across that hard mouth. "It's Maria, all right. You've just got to wonder what's underneath that apron she's wearing."

The discussion was definitely getting dangerous. She couldn't remember feeling more at sea and less in touch with herself. She decided to buy a little time with a change of subject. "What have you been doing with your time when you're not meeting with the local business leaders?"

At first she didn't think he'd answer, but he shrugged. "I work out at the Y, visit friends, take care of some business. Today I spent a couple of hours at Dad's office. He likes it when I hang around." He frowned.

"Something wrong?"

"Not really. I don't know. I guess the problems he and Mom are having are more serious than I thought." The crease in his forehead deepened. "He said she's gone to stay with Annie for a while. I thought he meant overnight, but it seems she's been there since the weekend, and today he told me she doesn't have any plans to come back."

"Oh, dear."

"I can't understand her doing something like this. It really has him upset." He drained his beer and glared at her. "I don't want to talk about it anymore, so would you mind keeping your questions to yourself."

He was the one who'd volunteered the information, but she didn't call him on it.

He jabbed his empty can toward the distant screen. "With all your chattering, I can't keep my mind on the movie, and Maria's singing one of my favorite songs. Damn, but that woman looks good naked.''

"Maria does not sing naked in *The Sound of Music*!"

"I've got perfect eyesight, and that woman is naked as the day she was born. You can even see her—"

"You're mistaken. The person who's naked is Baron von Trapp. And he is certainly one impressive figure of a man."

"You call *that* impressive? That puny—"

"I do."

"Man-oh-man, if you think that's impressive, I could sure make you one happy woman."

"Braggart." Had she gone completely crazy? She was deliberately baiting him.

"You, on the other hand, might have warts on your belly for all I know."

"I do not have warts on my belly."

"Says you." He took her apple juice from her hand, and tossed it, along with his beer can, into the cooler, which he picked up and put in the front seat. "Okay, you can show me now."

"Show you what?"

"I'm being serious here. If you've got warts, my boy's gonna end up with them, and if that's true, I need time to prepare myself."

"You are a certifiable lunatic."

"Just unzip your jeans a little bit there. Enough for me to get a peek."

"No!"

"Okay, then. I'll have to go by feel."

She slapped his hands away as he reached for the snap. "I told you I'd make out with you! I didn't say I'd let you give me a medical exam."

By the time she realized what she'd said, he was grinning as if he'd just won the lottery. "That's right, you did say you'd make out. Well, come on now, honey. Show me your stuff."

"I will not."

"Coward."

"I won't be baited."

"You're scared to make out with me." In one motion, he pulled off her bulky sweatshirt and tossed it on top of the discarded cooler. "Scared you won't be able to handle me. You are one big scaredy-cat."

"I am not."

"Scared to show me what you've got. Scared you won't measure up to all those thousands of women in my past."

"There aren't *thousands* of women in your past."

His grin looked so much like a fox's that she could almost see the chicken feathers stuck to his mouth.

Her heart thudded against her ribs. She was frightened, aroused, and amused all at the same time, which made it difficult to frown and sound grouchy. "Oh, all right. I guess I'll make out with you. But keep your hands to yourself."

"That's not fair since I'm gonna let you put yours wherever you want."

A dozen locations sprang to mind. "I'm sure I won't want to."

"I seriously hope that's not true." He switched off the dome light and plunged them into darkness so thick she felt as if the stars had been turned off.

Her eyes gradually adjusted enough to make out his shape, if not his features. He cupped her shoulder, and she felt him come close. "Maybe you just need me to remind you where some of the best places are." His lips brushed past her trashy hoop earring and settled on the tender spot beneath. "This one, for example, is a nice warm-up spot."

She caught her breath and wondered how he knew she was sensitive there. "If you're going to talk through this, could you at least manage to say *ain't* a few times so I can fantasize?"

His lips tugged on her earlobe, right next to the gold

wire, and his elbow bumped against the door. "Who could you fantasize about that's better than me?"

"Well . . ." She struggled to speak as her skin turned to goose flesh. "There's this studmuffin physicist who used to be a top-quark hunter at Fermilabs . . ."

"I doubt he says *ain't*." He played at the corner of her mouth. "You're supposed to be showing me what you're made of. So far I'm doing all the work here."

She lost what remained of her restraint and tilted her head just far enough for her lips to meet his. The contact jolted her so that she forgot all about playing games, and as their kiss deepened, she abandoned herself to the pleasure of the erotic. She tasted beer and popcorn, along with a hint of toothpaste and something dangerous that reminded her of thunder.

"You are the damnedest woman," he whispered.

She kissed him again. He pulled her shirttail free, and his big hands, strong and possessive, settled on the skin beneath. His thumbs trailed up the small ridges of her spine 'til they came to her bra, then he whispered against her open mouth. "We have to get rid of this, Rosebud."

She didn't even consider arguing. As she enjoyed the sweet invasion of his tongue, he made short work of the buttons on her blouse, despite the fact that the darkness kept him from seeing exactly what he was doing, then he released the front hook on her bra. His movements were accompanied by bumps and thuds as he banged against one part of the car or another.

He bent to take her in his mouth. Her nipples were tender from her pregnancy, and when he began to suckle her, she bucked and dug her fingers into his hair. The exquisite pain of the gentle suction left her wanting both to cry out for him to stop and beg him not to.

She knew she had to touch him as he was touching her, and she dragged at his T-shirt. The interior of the car had grown hot and steamy, and the soft cotton felt damp beneath her hands. Her shoulder bumped against the window, and she felt the moisture that had congealed on it seep through her blouse.

He helped her free his T-shirt, then turned his attention to her jeans. He pitched her shoes into the front seat, then tugged at the denim while she explored the contours of his bare chest.

She gave an oof of surprise when he whipped off her jeans and her naked bottom came in contact with the cold upholstery. The shock jolted her and suddenly everything seemed to be happening too fast. She needed to think this over, weigh the facts, consider her options. "I didn't . . . I don't . . ."

"Hush." His husky whisper filled the steamy interior as he cupped her thigh and pushed it away from its mate. She heard a soft curse.

"It's too dark," he muttered. "I still can't see you."

She stroked the contours of his pectorals and trailed her thumb over the hard point of his nipple. "Go by feel," she whispered.

He did better than that. He went by taste, and she thought she would die from this pleasure she had dreamed of but never experienced.

"You don't—" She gasped. "You don't have to do that."

His chuckle wasn't altogether steady, and she moaned when his hot whispery breath fell on her. "Mind your own business."

Once again he dropped his head, and she felt as if all the parts of her were unraveling. She banged her elbow against the steamy window when she gripped his bare, damp shoulders. He swore and bumped against the seat as he shifted his weight, but none of it mattered.

It was too exquisite, too miraculous. She climbed and spiraled, but just as she felt herself beginning to slip over the edge, he drew back. "Oh, no, you don't. Not without me."

She lay open and vulnerable before him. His breathing came fast and heavy. "God, this was a stupid idea. We should be doing this in the bedroom where we can see each other, but I can't wait that long. I need you now."

She reached for the snap on his jeans and felt the hard, thick shape of him. His breath caught on a hiss as she took her time unzipping, exploring until his restraint broke with a hoarse exclamation. "No more, Rosebud. I can't take anymore."

"Wimp." She dropped her mouth to his chest and licked a special trail all her own.

He gave a sound that was part chuckle and part moan. At the same time, he leaned back and lifted her so she straddled him. She had lost all of her clothing except the blouse that hung open from her shoulders. He had only lost his T-shirt. Although she had freed him from his jeans, the space was too confined for her to remove them completely. His chest was bare, however, as bare as her bottom, and she nipped him with her teeth.

He uttered a strangled exclamation, but she loved her position of supremacy, and she had no pity. Even though her feet were wedged awkwardly against the back of the front seat, she didn't let that prevent her from kissing him how and where she would.

While darkness deprived her of sight, her other senses grew more acute, and she suspected from his touches, tastes, and deep, intimate caresses that it was the same for him.

The faintest thread of moonlight caught a glimmering rivulet rolling down the steamy windows, and the sweat from their bodies was slick on her palms. He cupped her bare bottom in his big hands and lifted her. "Now, sweetheart. Now."

She moaned as he guided her down upon him, but her

body accepted him without question. She gave a sob and pressed her breast to his mouth. He caressed her with lips, teeth, and tongue until she had to draw back and move on him before she went crazy.

Even as he grasped her hips, he didn't try to force her into his rhythm but let her find her own. She raised and lowered herself upon him, rubbing the tips of her breasts against the soft hair of his chest and returning his deep, devouring kisses. She felt strong and sure as she met his passion. Sensation built upon sensation until reality slipped away and she felt as if she were being hurled through a supercollider, flying past the speed of light through a narrow underground passage toward the place where everything came apart.

And then she cried out as all the molecules that made up who she was fragmented: atoms dissociated, nuclei detached, everything broke open, shattered, and, at the end, left her more complete than she had ever been.

He went rigid with her cry. His teeth sank into the side of her neck, not hurting her, but holding her as he spilled himself within her depths. For a fraction of time she felt his utter defenselessness, and she sagged forward, protecting him as he found his ease.

Their hearts thundered together, one pressed against the other. She turned her lips to his hair.

Finally he stirred beneath her, a shift of his hand, a movement in his leg. Only gradually did she grow aware of the strain in her splayed thighs and the cramp in her calf. The air inside the car was so thick with heat it was hard to draw breath, but she didn't want to move. This intimacy was too precious to her.

"What am I going to do with you?" he muttered against her breast.

You could try loving me.

The unspoken thought jarred her, then filled her with dismay. Was this the destructive path her subconscious was taking? She wanted him to fall in love with her? When had she lost touch with reality? What made her entertain, even in her fantasies, the notion that this man who wanted no attachments could love her, especially when no one else had ever been able to?

"You're going to take me home," she said briskly. "That was quite pleasant, but I have a great deal of work to do tomorrow, and I need my rest."

"Quite *pleasant*?"

It had been earth-shattering, but she could no more confess that to him than she could explain how their coming together had given her an entirely new understanding of high-speed subatomic particle collisions.

God. Why was she thinking of that now? Everything people believed about her was true! She was a complete geek.

She reached for her clothes. Her panties were lost somewhere in the dark, so she drew her jeans on without them, pulling them up over her wetness.

He threw open the door, and as the dome light flashed on, she drew her blouse across her breasts. He glanced down at her as he zipped his jeans. "You're not bad, Professor, for someone who isn't a big-time player."

His casual dismissal of what had been so important to her made her want to weep. Fool! But what did she expect? Did she think he was going to declare his undying love for her simply because she'd finally given him what he must have known he'd get all along?

They rode home in silence. He went into the house with her, and she felt his gaze as she climbed the stairs to her room.

She hesitated, then looked down at him watching her from the foyer below. "Thank you for a lovely evening."

She'd meant to sound brisk, but her words had a wistful quality. She didn't want the evening to end this way. What if she held out her hand and invited him into her bed? The idea chilled her. Was that the only way she could keep him at her side?

He slouched against the front door and looked bored. "Yeah, it was great."

He couldn't have found a clearer way to tell her he was finished with her. With a man like Cal Bonner, she realized, the game was everything, and once it was over, he lost interest. Heartsick and angry, she turned and headed for her room.

Moments later, she heard him drive away.

13

Pleasant! She'd said it was *pleasant!* Cal sat at his favorite table in the corner of the Mountaineer and brooded. Usually there weren't any empty seats around him, but tonight everybody'd seemed to realize he had a giant mean-on, and they'd given him wide berth.

No matter how easily she'd dismissed what had happened between them, he knew Professor Rosebud had never had a better lover than she'd had tonight. There'd been none of that nonsense they'd gone through before, with her pushing his hands away. No, sir. He'd had his hands all over her, and she hadn't uttered a single protest.

But what stuck in his craw—what really stuck like a big old chunk of hard-boiled egg—was the fact that he'd just had some of the best sex of his life, and he'd never felt more unsatisfied.

Maybe it was his fault for getting cute. Why hadn't he just grabbed her right there in the house, carried her upstairs, and romanced her in his bed with all the lights on and that big mirror overhead? He could have done his best work there, not that he hadn't been pretty damn good tonight, but if they'd been in his bed, he would have seen everything he wanted to see. In duplicate.

He reminded himself this was the third time the two of

them had gone at it, but he wasn't any closer to seeing her naked now than he'd been that first night. It was getting to be an obsession. If only he hadn't turned off the dome light, he could have looked his fill, but despite that sassy mouth of hers, he'd known she was skittish, and he'd wanted her so much he hadn't been thinking straight. Now he had to face the consequences.

He understood his nature well enough to know that the only reason he found himself thinking about her a few thousand times a day was because he still didn't feel as if he'd really made love to her. How could he when he didn't know what she looked like? Once he found out, it'd be over. Instead of growing stronger every day, this attraction he felt toward her would disappear, and he'd be his old self again, ready to roam the fertile fields of dewy young females with flawless faces and sweet temperaments, although he was giving serious consideration to raising his minimum age requirement to twenty-four, since he was getting tired of everybody baiting him.

His thoughts strayed back to the Professor. Damn, but she was one funny lady. Sharp as a tack, too. Over the years, he'd developed a certain smugness about the fact that he was smarter than most everybody else, but that razor-sharp brain of hers made it hard to sneak much past her. Instead, she marched right alongside him, her brain cells clicking away, matching him step for step and move for move. He could almost feel her peering into every dusty corner of his mind and making a generally accurate assessment of whatever it was she found there.

"Reliving those three interceptions you threw against the Chiefs last year?"

His head shot up, and he found himself looking into the face of his nightmares. *Son of a bitch.*

Kevin Tucker's lips curled in a cocky grin that reminded Cal the kid didn't have to spend thirty minutes standing under a hot shower every morning just to work the kinks out.

"What the hell are you doing here?"

"Heard this is a beautiful part of the country, and I decided to take a look. I rented one of those vacation villas north of town. Nice place."

"You just happened to choose Salvation?"

"Strangest thing. I'd already crossed the city limits before it even occurred to me that this was where you lived. Can't imagine how I forgot that."

"Yeah, I can't imagine."

"Maybe you could show me some of the local sights." Kevin turned toward the bartender. "Sam Adams for me. Get the Bomber here another of whatever he's having."

Cal was drinking club soda, but he hoped Shelby kept her mouth shut about that.

Kevin sat down without an invitation and leaned back in the chair. "I didn't get a chance to congratulate you on your marriage. It sure surprised everybody. You and your new wife must have had a good laugh over the way I took her for a groupie that night she came to your hotel room."

"Oh, yeah, we laughed real hard about that."

"A physicist. I can't get over it. She didn't exactly look like your standard groupie that night, but she sure as hell didn't look like a scientist, either."

"Just goes to show."

Shelby brought the drinks over herself and gave Kevin the eye. "I saw you play fourth quarter against the 49ers last year, Mr. Tucker. You looked real good."

"I'm Kevin to you, dollface. And thanks. The old man here taught me everything I know."

Cal bristled, but he could hardly punch Kevin out with Shelby watching. It took her forever to finish flirting with Pretty Boy, but she finally left them alone.

"How 'bout cutting the bullshit, Tucker, and tell me why you're really here."

"I already told you. Just a little vacation. Nothing more."

Cal swallowed his fury, knowing the more he pressed, the more satisfaction Tucker'd get out of it. Besides, he had a pretty good idea why Kevin had shown up in Salvation, and he didn't like it one bit. The kid was playing a psych-out game. *You can't get away from me, Bonner. Not even during the off-season. I'm here, I'm young, and I'm in your face.*

Cal made his way to the kitchen at eight the next morning. He was in no mood for the nine o'clock meeting Ethan had scheduled with their local state representative so the three of them could discuss the teen drug program, and he wasn't looking forward to the lunch he'd set up with his mother to try and talk some sense into her, but neither could be postponed. Maybe if he'd had more sleep he wouldn't be so out of sorts.

But he knew he couldn't blame his foul mood on either lack of sleep or the stiffness in his joints. It was that sex viper he'd married who was responsible. If she didn't have this compulsion for keeping her clothes on, he'd have slept like a baby last night.

As he walked into the kitchen, he saw Jane sitting at the counter munching some kind of nutritious-looking bagel with honey squeezed on top. For a moment the homeyness of the scene made it hard for him to breathe. This wasn't what he wanted! He didn't want a house and a wife and a kid on the way, especially not with Kevin Tucker holed up five miles away. He wasn't ready for this.

He noticed that the Professor looked as neat as always. Her gold turtleneck was tucked into a pair of khaki slacks that were neither too tight nor too loose, and she'd pulled her hair back with a narrow, tortoise-colored clip-on head-band. As usual, she hadn't bothered with much more makeup than a swipe of lipstick. There wasn't one thing sexy about her appearance, so why did she look so delectable to him?

He grabbed a fresh box of Lucky Charms from the pantry, then collected a bowl and spoon. He slapped the milk carton down on the counter with more force than necessary and waited for her to rip into him about the way he'd run off last night. He knew it hadn't exactly been gentlemanly, but she'd hurt his pride. Now he was going to have to pay the price, and the last thing he wanted to hear at eight in the morning was a screaming banshee.

She raised both of her eyebrows over the tops of her glasses. "Are you still drinking 2 percent milk?"

"Something wrong with that?" He ripped open the cereal box.

"Two percent isn't low-fat milk despite what millions of Americans think. For the sake of your arteries, you should really switch to skimmed, or at least 1 percent."

"And you should really mind your own damned business." The Lucky Charms clattered into his bowl. "When I want your—" He broke off in mid-sentence, unable to believe what he was seeing.

"What's wrong?"

"Will you look at this?"

"My goodness."

He stared incredulously into a mound of dry cereal. All the marshmallows were missing! He saw lots of beige-colored frosted oat cereal, but not a single marshmallow. No multicolored rainbows or green shamrocks, no blue moons or purple horseshoes, not a single yellow whatchamacallit. Not one solitary marshmallow.

"Maybe someone tampered with the box," she offered in that cool scientist's voice.

"Nobody could have tampered with it! It was sealed up tighter than a drum when I opened it. Something must have gone wrong at the factory."

He sprang up from his stool and headed back into the

pantry for another box. This was all he needed to make a lousy morning worse. He emptied his old cereal in the trash, ripped open the new box, and poured it in the bowl, but all he saw was frosted oat cereal. No marshmallows.

"I don't believe this! I'm going to write the president of General Mills! Don't they have any quality control?"

"I'm sure it's just a fluke."

"Doesn't make any difference whether it's a fluke or not. It shouldn't have happened. When a person buys a box of Lucky Charms, he's got expectations."

"Would you like me to fix you a nice wheat bran bagel with a little honey on it? And maybe a glass of skimmed milk to go along."

"I don't want a bagel, and I sure as hell don't want skimmed milk. I want my Lucky Charms!" He stalked into the pantry and pulled out the remaining three boxes. "I'll guaran-damn-tee you one of these is going to have marsh-mallows in it."

But none of them did. He opened all three boxes, and there wasn't a single marshmallow in any of them.

By now the Professor had finished her bagel, and her green eyes were as cool as the missing marshmallow sham-rocks. "Perhaps I could make you some oatmeal. Or Whea-tena. I believe I have Wheatena."

He was furious. Wasn't there anything in life he could count on these days? The Professor had him spinning men-tal cartwheels; Kevin Tucker had materialized out of no-where; his mom had moved out on his dad; and now the marshmallows were missing from five boxes of his favorite breakfast cereal. "I don't want anything!"

She took a sip of milk and regarded him with perfect serenity. "It really isn't healthy to start the day without a good breakfast."

"I'll risk it."

He wanted to whip her up off that stool, toss her over his shoulder, and carry her up to his bedroom so he could finish what he'd started last night. Instead, he yanked his keys from his pocket and stalked out to the garage.

He wouldn't just write the president of General Mills, he decided. He was going to sue the whole damned company! Everybody from the board of directors right down to the shipping clerks. By damn, he'd teach General Mills not to ship out inferior cereal. He jerked open the door of his Jeep, and that was when he saw them.

Marshmallows. Hundreds of tiny marshmallows covering the seats. Red balloons, pink hearts, blue moons. They were scattered everywhere. Across the dashboard, on the front seat, and all over the backseat.

A red veil descended over his eyes. He slammed the door shut and charged into the kitchen. He was going to kill her!

She sat at the counter sipping a cup of tea. "Forget something?"

"Yeah, I forgot something all right. I forgot to smack you silly!"

She didn't look the slightest bit intimidated. Damn it! No matter what he threatened, no matter how loud he yelled, she didn't even cringe, probably because she knew he wouldn't touch her. Now he had to satisfy himself by pumping up the volume. "*You* are going to pay for this!"

He grabbed one of the Lucky Charm boxes and turned it over, spilling the cereal everywhere. He yanked open the sealed flap on the bottom, and sure enough, a neat slit in the inner bag had been carefully resealed with Scotch tape.

He gritted his teeth. "Don't you think this was just a little childish?"

"It certainly was. And immensely satisfying." She took a sip of tea.

"If you were pissed off about the way I took off last night, why didn't you just say so?"

"I prefer docudrama."

"I can't believe anybody could be so damned immature!"

"I could have been a lot more immature—emptying the marshmallows in your underwear drawer, for example—but I believe revenge should be subtle."

"Subtle! You ruined five perfectly good boxes of Lucky Charms and spoiled my whole day in the process."

"What a pity."

"I ought to . . . I swear I'm . . ." Damned if he wasn't carrying her upstairs right now and making love to her until she begged his forgiveness.

"Don't mess with me, Calvin. You'll only get hurt."

Seriously. He was seriously going to kill her. He regarded her through narrowed eyes. "Maybe you'd better explain why you got upset enough to do this. It's not like anything really important happened last night, is it? You yourself said it was—How did you put it? Oh, yeah. You said it was *quite pleasant*. Now to my way of thinking, *pleasant* doesn't add up to *important*." He regarded her closely. "But maybe it was more than pleasant for you. Maybe it was more important than you want to let on."

Was it his imagination or did something flicker in the depths of those melted shamrock eyes. "Don't be ridiculous. It's your lack of courtesy I found offensive. It would merely have been good manners on your part to have stayed around instead of running off like a teenager hurrying to tell his buddies he'd scored."

"Manners? Is that what five boxes of mutilated Lucky Charms is all about?"

"Yes."

Just one good shot. He was already late for his meeting, but he couldn't leave until he got off one good shot. "You're about the lowest breed of human being there is."

"What?"

"Right up there with the Boston Strangler and the Son of Sam."

"Don't you think that's a little extreme?"

"Not hardly." He shook his head and regarded her with disgust. "I married a damned cereal killer."

14

Jane smiled as she headed toward Heartache Mountain in her battered Escort late that afternoon. She'd spent nearly four hours last night sorting through all that cereal, but it had been worth it to see the expression on Cal's face. One day soon he'd figure out that he couldn't walk all over her. She hoped the marshmallow exercise would point him in the right direction.

Why did he have to be so thoroughly intriguing? Of all the pitfalls she had imagined in this marriage, growing to care so much about him had not been one of them. As much as he irritated her, she loved the fact that her intelligence didn't intimidate him, as it did so many others. She felt alive when she was with him: her blood pumping, her brain at full alert, all senses engaged. Until now, she'd only felt that way when she was engrossed in her work.

Everything would have been so much easier if she could dismiss him as an egotistical, self-centered jock, but he was far more complex than that. Beneath that belligerent good ol' boy exterior lay, not only a keen mind, but a highly developed sense of humor. In light of the marshmallow incident and the fact that he would soon find out about her car, she rather hoped it kicked in soon.

She pulled up in front of Annie's house and turned off

the ignition. The Escort shuddered for several seconds before it finally shut down. As she'd hoped, Lynn's car was nowhere in sight, so she was still at lunch with Cal, which gave Jane a chance to check on Annie.

She climbed the front steps and let herself in without knocking, just as Annie had ordered her to do the last time she'd been here. *You're family now, missy, in case you forgot.*

"Annie?" She walked farther into the empty living room.

To her dismay, Lynn Bonner poked her head through the kitchen door, then came slowly forward as she saw her daughter-in-law.

Jane noted the pallor of Lynn's complexion beneath her makeup and the dark smudges under her eyes. Plainly dressed in jeans and an old pink pocket T-shirt, she bore little resemblance to the well-groomed, stylish hostess who had presided so graciously at the dinner table five days earlier. She wanted to express her concern, but realized even that small gesture would do more harm than good. She wasn't going to add to Lynn's troubles, and that meant playing the bitch. "I didn't know you were here. I thought you were having lunch with Cal."

"His morning meeting ran long, and he had to cancel." Lynn set the dish towel she'd been holding over the back of the wing chair. "Did you stop by for any particular reason?"

"I came to see Annie."

"She's napping."

"Tell her I was here, then."

"What did you want to see her about?"

Jane began to say she'd been concerned about Annie, but stopped herself just in time. "Cal told me I had to drive up today to check on her." Did lies count with God when they were uttered with good intentions?

"I see." Lynn's blue eyes grew frosty. "Well, I'm glad

duty forced you to stop by because I want to talk to you. Would you like a cup of coffee or tea?''

The last thing she needed was a private chat with Cal's mother. ''I really can't stay.''

''This won't take long. Have a seat.''

''Maybe another time. I have a dozen really important things to do.''

''Sit!''

If Jane hadn't been so anxious to get away, she would have been amused. Apparently Cal hadn't received all his leadership abilities from his father, but then, she supposed any woman who had raised three strong-willed sons knew something about exercising her authority. ''All right, but just for a few moments.'' She took a place at the end of the couch.

Lynn sat in Annie's upholstered rocker. ''I want to talk with you about Cal.''

''I'm not comfortable talking about him behind his back.''

''I'm his mother, and you're his wife. If that doesn't give us a right to talk about him, I don't know what does. After all, we both care about him?''

Jane heard the faint question mark at the end of that statement and understood that Lynn wanted her to confirm her feelings for Cal. Instead, she kept her face carefully expressionless. Cal was right. Lynn and Jim had endured enough grief without having to mourn the failure of his marriage. Let them celebrate, instead, the end of a disastrous alliance. Maybe it would give them something to share.

Lynn's posture grew more rigid, and Jane's heart went out to her. She regretted the pain she was causing her now, but knew that, in the end, it was kinder this way. Her in-laws seemed destined for heartbreak, but at least she could make it as short-lived as possible.

''In some ways Cal is like his father,'' Lynn said. ''They

both have a lot of bluster, but they're more easily hurt than people imagine.'' A shadow crossed Lynn's face.

Maybe a simple concession on her part would somehow ease her mother-in-law's mind enough to end this conversation. ''Cal is a special person. I knew that the moment I met him.''

She immediately realized her mistake because a spark of maternal hope ignited in her mother-in-law's eyes, and she could see Lynn nurturing the possibility that the frosty, snobbish bride her eldest son had brought home wasn't as bad as she appeared to be.

Jane's hands tightened in her lap. She hated causing this woman pain. There was something frail about Lynn, a sadness that lay just beneath that sophisticated veneer. No matter how bad Jane made herself look, she couldn't hold out false hopes. In the end that would be more cruel than anything else.

She forced her stiff lips into a thin smile. ''If anyone ever doubts that he's special, all they have to do is ask him. He does have an ego.''

Lynn's chin shot up at the same time her fingers gripped the arm of the chair. ''You don't seem to like him very much.''

''Of course I do, but no one's perfect.'' Jane felt as if she were suffocating. She had never been deliberately cruel in her life, and even though she knew she had to do this, it made her ill.

''I can't understand why you married him.''

Jane had to get out of here before she fell apart, and she lurched to her feet. ''He's rich, intelligent, and he doesn't interfere with my work. Is there anything else you want to know?''

''Yes.'' She released her hold on the arm of the chair and stood. ''Why in the hell did *he* marry *you*?''

Jane knew she had to drive the final nail into the coffin of Lynn's hopes. ''That's easy. I'm smart, I don't interfere with his work, and I'm good in bed. Look, Lynn, don't get yourself in a tangle over this. Neither Cal nor I have a big emotional investment in this marriage. We hope it works out, but if it doesn't, we'll both survive. Now if you'll excuse me, I need to get back to my computer. Tell Annie if she wants anything to call Cal.''

"I want him to finish paintin' my house."

Jane's head snapped around, and she was dismayed to see Annie standing in the doorway that led to the back bedroom. How long had she been there, and how much had she overheard? Annie was unpredictable. She obviously hadn't informed Lynn that Jane was pregnant, but what had she said? Beneath the wrinkles and blue eye makeup, the old woman regarded her with what could only be compassion.

"I'll tell him," Jane said.

"You do that." Annie gave a short nod and walked into the kitchen.

Jane hurried to her car, tears stinging her eyes. Damn Cal for making her come to Salvation! Damn him for forcing her into this marriage and believing it would be so easy to distance his parents!

But as she jabbed the key into the ignition, she knew the fault didn't lie with Cal. It was hers alone. She was to blame for everything, and the wrong she'd done had spread until it touched more people than she could ever have imagined.

She swiped at her eyes with the back of her hand and drove blindly down the lane, thoughts of the butterfly effect swirling through her mind. It was a concept that scientists who studied chaos theory talked about, the notion that something as simple as a butterfly's wings stirring the air in Singapore could cause a ripple effect that would eventually affect weather systems in Denver. The butterfly effect could also be a mini morality lesson, and she remembered talking to her third graders about it, telling them that any good deed, no matter how small, could keep multiplying until it had changed the whole world forever for the better.

Her deed had done the same thing, but in reverse. Her selfish act was causing pain to an increasing number of innocent people. And there was no end in sight. The harm kept spreading, the butterfly effect multiplying. She had hurt Cal, she was hurting his parents, and, worst of all, her bad judgment was going to hurt their baby.

She was too upset to work, so she drove into town and went to the drugstore. As she came out, she heard a familiar voice.

"Hey, beautiful. Did you pray for me?"

She whirled around and found herself looking into a pair of cocky green eyes. For absolutely no reason that she could think of, her flagging spirits lifted a few notches. "Hello, Mr. Tucker. I didn't expect to see you here."

"Why don't you call me Kevin? Even better, how about calling me *honey* and really pissing off the old man."

She smiled. He reminded her of a young golden retriever: attractive, overly eager, full of restless energy and unlimited self-confidence. "Now let me guess. You've shown up in Salvation to cause Cal as much trouble as possible."

"Me? Now why would I do something like that? I love the old guy."

"If someone doesn't put you in your place soon, there's no justice in the world."

"My place is sitting on the bench, and I don't like it one bit."

"I'm sure you don't."

"Let me buy you some lunch, Jane—I can call you Jane, can't I? Why are you driving that old heap around? I didn't know they still allowed cars like that on the road. Whose is it?"

She opened the door of the Escort and set her packages inside. "It's mine, and don't talk about it like that, or you'll hurt its feelings."

''That car's not yours. The Bomber'd never let you drive a junker like that in a million years. Come on, let's go have some lunch at the Mountaineer. It's the best meal in town.''

He grabbed her arm, and she found herself being swept around the corner toward a small, tidy-looking wooden house with a roughly carved sign on the porch indicating this was the bar she'd been hearing about. The entire time they walked, he talked.

''Did you know this is a dry county? There are no bars. The Mountaineer is what they call a bottle club. I even had to buy a membership card to get in. Don't you think that's bogus? You can still drink in this county, but you have to have a membership card to do it.''

He led her up the stairs, across a wooden porch, and into a small entryway where a young woman in jeans stood next to an old classroom lectern that held a reservation book. ''Hi there, sweetheart. We need a table for two. Someplace cozy.'' He flashed his membership card.

The hostess smiled at Kevin and directed them through a small, spartan dining room that looked as if it had originally served as the living room of the house, but was now furnished with half a dozen square wooden tables, all of which were empty. Two steps led down into an open area with a brick floor, mahogany bar, and large stone fireplace whose hearth held a rush basket full of old magazines. Country music played in the background, but the noise wasn't deafening, and an assortment of local people sat at the round tables and barstools enjoying their lunches. The hostess led them to a small table tucked near the fireplace.

Jane had never been a fan of bars, but she had to admit this one was cozy. The walls were hung with nostalgic advertising signs, yellowed newspaper stories, and football memorabilia including a blue-and-gold Stars' jersey emblazoned with the number eighteen. Next to the jersey hung an assortment of framed magazine covers, all of them picturing her husband.

Kevin glanced over at them as he held out a cane-backed chair for her. "As good as the food is, the view sure could spoil your appetite."

"If you didn't want that kind of view, you shouldn't have come to Salvation."

He snorted as he took his seat. "The whole town's brain-washed."

"Grow up, Kevin."

"I should have known you'd be on his side."

She laughed at the injured expression on his face. "I'm his wife! What did you expect?"

"So? You're supposed to be this genius or something, aren't you? Can't you be fair-minded?"

She was saved from replying by the arrival of the wait-ress, who regarded Kevin with rapacious eyes, but he was absorbed in the menu and didn't seem to notice. "We'll have a couple of burgers, fries, and beer. Make it Red Dog."

"Will do."

"And two side orders of coleslaw."

Jane could barely resist rolling her eyes at his high-handedness. "Make that a cobb salad for me, no bacon, light with the cheese, dressing on the side, and a glass of skimmed milk."

Kevin grimaced. "You serious?"

"Brain food."

"Whatever."

The waitress left. While they waited for their orders to arrive, Jane listened to a monologue whose central subject seemed to be Kevin Tucker. She bided her time until their food arrived, then she got down to business. "Exactly what are you up to?"

"What do you mean?"

"Why did you come to Salvation?"

"It's a nice place."

"There are a lot of nice places." She drilled him with

her schoolmarm eyes. "Kevin, put down those fries and tell me exactly what you're doing here." She realized she felt protective of Cal. How strange, especially considering how upset she was with him.

"Nothing." He shrugged and returned a handful of fries to their blue plastic basket. "Just having a little fun, that's all."

"What do you want from him, other than his job?"

"Why would I want anything from him?"

"You wouldn't be here otherwise." She rubbed her thumb along her milk glass. "Sooner or later he'll have to retire, and then the job'll be yours. Why can't you just wait?"

"Because I should have it now!"

"Apparently the coaches don't agree."

"They're fools!"

"You seem to go out of your way to give him a hard time. Why is that? Just because you're rivals doesn't mean you have to be enemies."

His expression grew sullen, making him look younger than his years. "Because I hate his guts."

"If I hated someone as much as you seem to hate Cal, I'd do my best to stay away from him."

"You don't understand."

"Explain it."

"I— He's a real prick, that's all."

"And?"

"He's— I don't know." He looked down. Nudged the edge of his plate. "He's a fairly decent coach."

"Ahh."

"What's that mean?"

"Nothing. Just *ahh*."

"You said it like it was supposed to mean something."

"Does it?"

"Do you seriously think I'd want him coaching me, having him on my ass all the time yelling at me that my arm's worthless because I don't have a football brain to go with it? Believe me, that's the last thing I need. I'm a damned good quarterback without his help.''

But an even better one with Cal's help, Jane imagined. So that's why Kevin was here. It wasn't just Cal's job he coveted; he also wanted Cal to coach him. But unless she missed her guess, he didn't have a clue how to ask him and still hold on to his pride. She tucked the information away.

For his part, Kevin was transparently anxious to change the subject.''I'm sorry about that night at the hotel. I thought you were another groupie; I didn't know the two of you were an item.''

''That's all right.''

''You sure kept your relationship a secret.''

Not for the first time, she wondered about Junior and the other players who had arranged her birthday night visit. What had they made of all this? And more important, had they kept their mouths shut?

She decided to probe a bit. ''A few people knew we were seeing each other.''

''Guys on the team?''

''A few.''

''They never told me.''

So Cal's friends hadn't talked.

''You sure don't seem like his type.''

''Maybe you don't know Cal as well as you think.''

''Maybe I don't want to.'' He sank his teeth into his burger, taking a bite too large to pass muster with any authority on etiquette. Still, his enthusiasm was contagious, and she realized she was hungry.

As she ate, he entertained her with funny stories, most of which were risqué. The fact that he was the central subject of each one should have put her off, but it didn't. She had the feeling that his self-centeredness resulted from a lack of confidence he was determined to conceal from the world. Although there were a lot of reasons why she shouldn't, she couldn't help liking Kevin Tucker.

He finished his beer and grinned at her. "Are you interested in cheating on the Bomber? Because if you are, I think you and me could have a good thing going."

"You're impossible."

He smiled, but his eyes were sober. "I know on the surface, we don't have too much in common, and you're a couple of years older than me, but I like being with you. You understand things. And you're a good listener."

"Thank you." She couldn't help smiling back. "I like being with you, too."

"But you probably wouldn't be interested in an affair, would you? I mean, you only got married a couple of weeks ago."

"There *is* that." She knew she shouldn't be enjoying this, but her confidence had been badly shattered last night, and Kevin Tucker was adorable. Still, she had enough sins on her conscience without pumping up her ego at the expense of his. "How old are you?"

"Twenty-five."

"I'm thirty-four. Nine years older than you."

"I don't believe it. You're nearly as old as the Bomber."

" 'Fraid so."

"I don't care." His lips tightened into a stubborn line. "The Bomber might care about all that age stuff, but it doesn't mean anything to me. The only thing is . . ." He looked vaguely chagrined. "As much as I hate the Bomber's guts, I've sort of made it a policy not to screw around with married women."

"Good for you."

"You like that?"

"It speaks well of you."

"Yeah, I guess it does." He looked pleased and reached across the table and took her hand. "Promise me something, Jane. If you and the Bomber split, promise that you'll give me a call."

"Oh, Kevin, I really don't think—"

"Well, now, isn't this cozy."

A deep, belligerent voice cut her off, and her head snapped up in time to watch Calvin James Bonner charging toward them looking like a blast furnace about to erupt. She half expected to see ribbons of smoke sliding from his nostrils, and she tried to pull her hand away from Kevin's grasp, but, naturally, he held her fast. She should have known he wouldn't miss such a golden opportunity to aggravate her husband.

"Hey, there, old man. Me and the missus was just havin' ourselves a little chat. Pull up a chair and join us."

Cal ignored him and gave Jane a visual blast with enough power to explode a mushroom cloud over the western half of North Carolina. "Let's go."

"I'm not quite finished with my lunch." She gestured toward her half-eaten salad.

"Oh, you're finished, all right." He snatched the salad out from under her and dumped what was left of it on Kevin's plate.

Her eyes widened. Was she wrong, or could she possibly be witnessing a major jealousy tantrum? Her spirits rose several more notches even as she tried to figure out how she wanted to handle this. Should she make a scene in public or in private?

Kevin took the decision out of her control by springing to his feet. "You son of a bitch!"

A fist flew, and the next thing she knew, Kevin was lying on the floor. With a hiss of alarm, she jumped up and rushed to him. "Kevin, are you all right?" She glared up at her husband. "You cretin!"

"He's a pansy. I barely touched him."

Kevin spouted a mouth-soaper of an obscenity, and as he scrambled to his feet, she reminded herself that she was dealing with two overgrown male children, both of whom were hot-tempered and intensely physical. "Stop it right now!'' she exclaimed as she rose. "This isn't going any farther.''

"You want to settle it outside?" Cal sneered at Kevin.

"No! I'm gonna kick your ass right here.''

Kevin shoved Cal in the chest. Cal stumbled backward, but didn't fall.

Jane's hands flew to her cheeks. They were starting a barroom brawl, and unless she was mistaken, one of the things they were fighting over was her! She pushed the enticing thought away by reminding herself that she abhorred violence, and she had to put a stop to it.

"There will be *no* ass kicking!" She used her sternest voice, the one that she occasionally employed with rowdy third-grade boys. But *these* boys paid no attention. Instead, Cal threw Kevin into a barstool, then Kevin dragged Cal against the wall. A framed *Sports Illustrated* cover showing her husband taking off his helmet came crashing down.

Jane knew she couldn't overpower them physically, so she tried another tactic. Reaching behind the bar, she snatched up one of the dispenser hoses, aimed it at the two brawlers, and pushed the trigger. It was either water or club soda, she couldn't tell which, but it lost too much of its power by the time it reached them to have any effect.

She spun toward the onlookers, who'd gotten up from their chairs to watch, and implored several of the men. "Do something, will you? Stop them!"

They ignored her.

For a moment she considered letting them beat each other's brains out, but they were too strong, and she didn't have the stomach for it. She swept up a full beer pitcher from the top of the bar, rushed over, and flung it at them.

They gasped, sputtered, and went right back to pulverizing each other as if nothing had happened. It was an unpleasant reminder of exactly how tough they were.

Kevin slammed his fist into Cal's stomach, then Cal delivered a solid punch to Kevin's chest. None of the businessmen or retirees watching showed any inclination to help, so she knew she was on her own, but the only other action she could think of went against her grain. Still, she couldn't come up with a better idea so she sat down on a barstool, dragged in a huge gulp of air, and began to scream at the top of her lungs.

The sound was annoying, even to her, but she kept at it. The onlookers immediately shifted their attention from the fight to the crazed blonde sitting on a barstool wailing like a banshee. Cal got so distracted that he allowed Kevin to catch him in the side of his head. Then Kevin lost his focus and ended up on the floor.

She sucked in more air and kept screaming.

"Will you stop it!" Cal bellowed, staggering away from the wall.

She was starting to get dizzy, but she forced herself to let loose a fresh stream of shrieks.

Kevin scrambled up from the floor, his chest heaving. "What's wrong with her?"

"She's hysterical." Cal wiped the beer from his eyes with the back of his hand, dragged in some air, and lurched toward her with a purposeful gleam in his eye. "I'm going to have to slap her."

"Don't you dare!" she yelped.

"Got to." The gleam in his eye now had a faintly diabolical cast to it.

"Touch me and I'll scream!"

"*Don't touch her!*" three people in the crowd called out at once.

She crossed her arms over her chest and glared at the onlookers. "You could have helped, you know, and then this wouldn't have been necessary."

"It's only a bar fight," Kevin grumbled. "No reason to make such a big deal out of it."

Cal took her arm and pulled her down off the barstool. "She's a little high-strung."

"I'll say." Kevin pulled up his shirttail to wipe the beer from his face. A cut on his cheekbone was bleeding, and one eye had puffed up.

A middle-aged man wearing a starched white shirt and black bow tie regarded her curiously. "Who is she, anyway?"

Cal pretended not to hear.

"Darlington," she said, holding out her hand to shake. "Jane Darlington."

"She's my wife," Cal muttered.

"Your wife?" The man looked faintly bewildered as he took her hand.

"The same," she replied.

"This is Harley Crisp. He runs the local hardware store." Jane had never heard a more begrudging introduction.

Harley dropped Jane's hand and turned to Cal. "How come when she finally showed up here, she was with Tucker and not you?"

Cal clenched his jaw. "They're old friends."

Jane realized everyone in the bar was now assessing her, and none of them looked particularly friendly.

"Nice you could finally spare the time to come meet the people who live here, Miz Bonner," Harley said.

She heard several other hostile murmurs, including one from the attractive bartender, and knew that the story of Cal's chilly scientist wife who thought she was more important than everyone else had spread.

Cal diverted the crowd's attention by directing the bartender to put the damages on Kevin's lunch tab. Kevin looked sulky, like a kid who'd been sent to his room. "You threw the first punch."

Cal ignored him. Instead, he grabbed Jane with a hand still damp from beer and headed toward the front door.

"Nice to have met you all," she tossed back over her

shoulder at the hostile crowd. "Although I would have appreciated a little more help."

"Will you shut up?" he growled.

He drew her across the porch and down the steps. She saw the Jeep parked at the curb, and it reminded her she had one more battle to fight. Being married to Cal Bonner was becoming an increasingly complicated business.

"I have my own car."

"Hell you do." His lip was bleeding and beginning to swell on one side.

"I do."

"You don't."

"It's parked in front of the drugstore even as we speak." She reached into her purse, withdrew a tissue, and held it out to him.

He paid no attention. "You bought a car?"

"I told you I was going to."

He braked to a stop. She dabbed the tissue gently against his lip, only to have him jerk away. "And I told you you weren't."

"Yes, well, I'm a bit too old and a lot too independent to pay attention to you."

"Show me." He spit out the words like bullets.

She remembered Kevin's unkind comments about her Escort and felt a moment of trepidation. "Why don't I just meet you at the house?"

"Show me!"

Resigned, she walked down the block to the town center, then turned toward the drugstore. He stalked silently at her side and his heels seemed to strike white-hot sparks as they hit the pavement.

Unfortunately, the Escort's appearance hadn't As she came to a stop next to it, he looked stu me this isn't it."

"All I needed was basic transportation. I ha good Saturn waiting for me at home."

He sounded as if he were strangling on a bone. "Has anybody seen you drive this?"

"Hardly anybody."

"Who?"

"Only Kevin."

"Shit!"

"Really, Cal, you need to watch your language, not to mention your blood pressure. A man of your age—" She saw her mistake and quickly changed direction. "It's perfectly fine for what I need."

"Give me those keys."

"I will not!"

"You win, Professor. I'll buy you a car. Now give me the damn keys."

"I have a car."

"A real car. A Mercedes, a BMW, whatever you want."

"I don't want a Mercedes or a BMW."

"That's what you think."

"Stop bullying me."

"I haven't even started."

They were beginning to attract a crowd, which wasn't surprising. How often had the people of Salvation, North Carolina, seen their local hero standing in the middle of town dripping beer and blood?

"Give me those keys," he hissed.

"In your dreams."

Luckily for her, the crowd made it impossible for him to snatch them away as he wanted. She took advantage of that to shove past him, open the door, and jump into the car.

He looked like a pressure cooker about to explode. "I'm warning you, Professor. This is the last drive you're taking in that junker, so enjoy every minute of it."

This time his high-handedness didn't amuse her. Obviously the marshmallows hadn't done the trick, and it was take stronger measures. Mr. Calvin Bonner needed to figure out for once and for all that he couldn't run a marriage like he ran a football play.

She gritted her teeth. "You know what you can do with your warnings, buster. You can take them and—"

"We'll talk about this when we get home." He hit her dead on with those nuclear winter eyes. "Now drive!"

Seething, she peeled out of the parking place. The car blessed her by backfiring. She set her jaw and headed for home.

She'd had it.

15

Jane used the small screwdriver she always carried in her purse to disable the automatic gates. Now they would remain shut and it had taken her less than two minutes. When she reached the house, she parked the Escort in the driveway, stomped inside, and fetched some twine that she secured in a tight figure eight around the twin knobs set side by side in the double front door. She fashioned a wedge from several cooking utensils and used it to secure the back door.

She was checking the bolts in the French doors that opened off the family room when the intercom began to buzz. She ignored it and headed for the garage, where she used the small ladder that was stored there to unplug the automatic door opener from its ceiling outlet.

The angry buzzing of the intercom assaulted her ears as she stalked back into the kitchen. She yanked all the first-floor draperies closed and pulled the phone off the hook. When that was done, she grabbed her screwdriver, made her way to the intercom, and punched the button.

"Cal?"

"Yeah, listen Jane, there's something wrong with the gate."

"There's something wrong, all right, buster, but it

doesn't have anything to do with the gate!'' With a twist
of her wrist, she loosened the connection, and the buzzer
fell silent. Afterward, she stalked upstairs, booted up her
computer, and set to work.

It wasn't long before she heard the rattling of doors accompanied by a determined pounding. When it grew so
loud it disturbed her concentration, she tore a tissue in two
and wadded the pieces in her ears.

Blessed quiet.

An *Escort!* Cal hauled himself up onto the lower section
of roof that jutted out over the first-floor study. First she'd
sabotaged his Lucky Charms, and now she'd embarrassed
him in front of the entire town by driving a ten-year-old
Escort! He couldn't explain why both offenses seemed a
lot worse than the fact that she'd managed to lock him out
of his own house. Maybe because he was enjoying the challenge of getting back in, not to mention the anticipation of
the fight they were going to have after he'd managed it.

He walked as lightly as he could across the roof because
he didn't want the damn thing to spring a leak the next
time it rained. As he glanced up at the dark clouds skidding
across the darkening sky, he figured that rain might not be
too far off.

He reached the end of the roof, where it met up with the
corner of the balcony that extended across the front of the
house, and experienced a moment of disappointment because there wasn't a bigger gap to make this more of a
contest. Still, the grillwork railing was too shaky to hold
his weight, so that made it a little more interesting.

Using the bottom edge of the balcony as a handhold, he
lowered himself over the side and, legs dangling,
his way along the balcony's edge until he came to
ner column. A clap of thunder reverberated, and
to pelt him, plastering his shirt to his back. He
legs around the column for support, then, braci

on the wobbly grillwork, shinnied up the slippery surface and lowered himself over the railing.

The lock in the French doors that led into his bedroom was flimsy, and it annoyed him that Miss Big Brain hadn't done anything to secure it. She probably thought he was too *old* to make it this far! The fact that his lip hurt, his ribs ached, and his bad shoulder throbbed like a sonovabitch fueled his irritation, and as he jimmied the doors open, his temper flared up again. She should at least have had enough respect for him to shove a chair in front of the knob!

He walked across his dark bedroom into the hallway and moved toward the light that spilled out from her room. She sat with her back to the door and all her formidable concentration focused on the columns of incomprehensible data scrolling past on her computer screen. Puffs of blue tissue stuck out of both ears, making her look like a cartoon rabbit. He thought about marching up behind her and giving her the fright of her life by pulling the tissues out. It was exactly what she deserved, but since she was pregnant, he modified his plan. Not that he believed Annie's dire warnings about marked babies and twisted cords, but still, he wasn't taking any chances.

The smell of beer clung to him like barroom smoke as he made his way downstairs. He was wet, sore, completely pissed off, and every bit of it was her fault! His blood pounded in anticipation as he reached the foyer. Throwing back his head, he bellowed out her name.

"*Jane Darlington Bonner!* You get down here right this minute!"

Jane's head shot up. His roar penetrated her homemade ear plugs. So, he'd managed to find a way inside. As she pulled out the wads of tissue and tossed them in the basket, she wondered how he'd done it. Some amazing feat of bravado, no doubt, since the great quarterback wouldn't dream ~eaning himself by anything as obvious as breaking a window. Despite her pique, she felt a certain amount of pride.

As she rose from her desk and discarded her glasses, she tried to figure out why she had no desire to lock herself in her room. She'd never liked conflict and never been all that good at it—witness her dismal skirmishes with Jerry Miles. Maybe she wasn't anxious to avoid this battle because it would be with Cal. All her life she'd been so polite, so dignified, so careful not to offend. But Cal was impatient with politeness, unimpressed by dignity, and impervious to offense. She didn't have to watch what she said or mind her manners. She could simply be herself. As she crossed the room, her pulses hummed, and her brain cells went on full alert. She felt completely and wondrously alive.

From the foyer below, Cal watched her approach the top of the stairs. Her trim little butt swayed from side to side inside her slacks, and her green knit top emphasized a pair of breasts so unimpressive in their size he couldn't figure out why he was so anxious to set eyes on them. Her hair, pulled away from her face with barrettes like an upper-crust schoolgirl's, swung back and forth, as saucy as her mouth.

She looked down at him, but instead of being scared as she should have been, he could swear he saw a spark of mischief in her eyes. "Somebody looks mad," she drawled, all spunk and sass.

"You—" He slammed his hands on his hips. "—are going to pay for this."

"What are you gonna do, big guy? Spank me?"

Just like that, he got hard. Damn it! How did she keep doing this to him? And what kind of kinky talk was that for a respectable college professor?

An unwilling vision of that sweet little butt curving 'neath his palm shot through him. He clenched his jaw rowed his eyes, and gave her a look so mean-assed ashamed of himself for using it on a poor, def pregnant female. "Maybe a bare-butt spanking is exactly what you need."

"Really?" Instead of fainting from fear the way any sensible woman would have done, she got this calculating look on her face. "Might be fun. I'll think about it."

Just like that she turned on her heel and swept back to her room, leaving him standing at the bottom of the stairs in her dust. He was stunned. How did she manage to keep turning the tables on him like that? And what did she mean, she'd think about it?

He remembered that mangled Escort sitting in the drive right where his kickass Jeep should have been and charged up the stairs after her. He wasn't half done with this fight!

Jane heard him coming and was ashamed of the thrill of anticipation the sound of those pounding feet gave her. Until these past few weeks, she hadn't realized how heavily the mantle of maintaining her dignity had weighed on her shoulders. But Cal had no more use for dignity than a dog for panty hose.

He flew through her bedroom door and jabbed his finger in the general direction of her forehead. "Starting right now, the two of us are going to get a few things straight. I'm the head of this household, and I expect respect! I don't want to hear another piece of sass out of you. Do you understand what I'm saying?"

His confrontation techniques undoubtedly worked very well with men, but she felt a flash of sympathy for those poor young girls he'd chosen as his past companions. He must have devastated those curvaceous little infants.

But for some reason the picture of him yelling at a defenseless twenty-year-old beauty queen wouldn't take shape in her mind, and it didn't take her long to understand why. He would never do it. Cal was incapable of unleashing the full force of his anger on someone he regarded as weaker than himself. The knowledge gave her a deep sense of pride.

"Your lip is bleeding again," she said. "Go in the bathroom, and I'll fix it."

"I'm not going anywhere until we settle this."

"Pretty please. I've always fantasized about tending a wounded warrior."

That gave him pause. He got this dangerous, squinty-eyed look that made her knees a little wobbly. He was 190 pounds of dynamite getting ready to detonate, so why wasn't she afraid?

He stuck a thumb in the pocket of his jeans. "I'll let you patch me up under one condition."

"What's that?"

"After you're done, you sit quietly—and I mean with your mouth shut—while I take you apart."

"Okay."

"Okay?" His roar nearly blew out her eardrums. "Is that it? Lady, you must not understand what I've got in mind because if you did, you wouldn't be standing there telling me 'okay'!"

She smiled just because she knew it would further irritate him. "I believe that open communication is important to a marriage."

"We're not talking about open communication. We're talking about me taking you apart limb by limb." He paused and thrust out his jaw. "Hand to bare butt."

"Whatever." She waved breezily as she set off toward the bathroom.

She almost felt sorry for him. He was an intensely physical man cursed with a strong moral conscience, which made it extremely difficult for him to have a truly satisfactory fight with a female. She finally understood why he loved football with its hard hits and thick rule book so much. To Cal, the combination of rough body contact and swift justice would be the best of all worlds.

This presented a definite problem in his relationship with women.

She crossed the cryptlike bathroom to the medicine cabinet and began a search of its contents. "I hope there's something in here that really stings."

When he made no comment, she turned, then gulped as she saw him pulling his shirt over his head. As he stretched, his scraped rib cage grew more prominent, and his navel formed a narrow oval. She saw the tufts of silky hair under his arms, the scar on his shoulder. "What are you doing?"

He tossed the shirt aside and popped the button on his jeans. "What do you think I'm doing? I'm taking a shower, or don't you remember you poured a pitcher of beer over my head, then locked me out of my own house in the middle of a savage thunderstorm? And that front gate you sabotaged had better be back in service first thing tomorrow morning or there's gonna be some big-time hell to pay." He pulled down his zipper.

She turned away, making the movement as casual as possible. Luckily the bathroom contained enough mirrors that by tilting her head she had a full view. Unfortunately, it was only of his back. Still that was pretty magnificent. Broad shoulders tapered to narrow hips and tight, flat buttocks. There was a red mark on one side of his spinal column from his fight with Kevin. She frowned at the collection of old scars and new scars and thought of all his aging warrior's body had endured.

He swung open the door of the cylindrical shower stall, which looked as if it belonged on the starship *Enterprise*, and stepped in. Unfortunately, the frosting on the bottom half of the glass kept her from seeing more.

"You're exaggerating about the savage thunderstorm," she called out above the sound of the water. "It just started raining."

"*Before* I made it over the top of the balcony."

"Is that how you got in?" Impressed, she turned toward the shower.

"Only because *you* didn't have enough confidence in me to secure those top doors."

She smiled to herself at the injured note in his voice. "I'm sorry. I wasn't thinking."

"Obviously not." He ducked his head under the spray. "Do you want to join me?"

She yearned to say yes, but his voice held a silky seductive note that reminded her of a snake slithering up the Tree of Knowledge, so she pretended not to hear. While he showered, she searched through the drawers of the vanity trying to locate some antibiotic ointment.

She found a tube of Crest Tartar Control squeezed up from the bottom and a column of neatly capped deodorant. His black comb was spanking clean and still had all its teeth. The drawer also held dental floss, a pair of shiny silver nail clippers, shaving cream and several razors, along with Extra Strength Tylenol, and a large tube of Ben Gay. And condoms. A whole box of them. The fact that he would be using these condoms with someone other than herself gave her a pang so sharp she ached.

Pushing the image aside, she knelt to look under the sink and found more Ben Gay, three cartons of Epsom salts, and a tube of antibiotic ointment. The water shut off and, moments later, the shower door clicked.

"Tucker's using you," he said. "You know that, don't you?"

"That's not true." She turned in time to watch him wrap a thick black towel around his waist. His chest was still wet, the dark hair matted.

"Sure it is. He's using you to get back at me."

The fact that he didn't believe Kevin could find her attractive stung enough that it forced her to retaliate. "That may be true, but there's also a subtle sexual chemistry between Kevin and me."

He'd been in the process of pulling a hand towel from the rack to dry his hair, but his arm stalled in mid-reach

"What are you talking about? What sexual chemistry?"

"Sit down so I can fix your lip. It's bleeding again."

Droplets from his wet hair flew as he took an abrupt step forward. "I won't sit down! I want to know what you mean."

"An older woman, a *very* attractive younger man. It's been happening since the beginning of time. But don't worry. He won't mess around with married women."

His eyes had narrowed into mean-street slits at her description of Kevin. "Is that supposed to be comforting?"

"Only if the idea of Kevin and me together is discomfiting."

He snatched the towel and vigorously rubbed his hair. "You know he's only interested in you because you're wearing my ring. If it weren't for that, he wouldn't pay any attention to you."

He'd found her most vulnerable spot, and, just like that, the fun went out of the game. His meaningless threats of violence hadn't bothered her, but the fact that he believed she was too geeky for another man to find attractive stung to the quick. "No, I don't know that." She headed toward her bedroom.

"Where are you going?" he called after her. "I thought you were going to patch me up?"

"The antibiotic is on the vanity. Do it yourself."

He followed her into her bedroom, coming to a stop just inside the door. "Does Kevin— Does he mean something to you?" He flung down the hand towel. "How the hell could he mean anything to you? You don't even know him!"

"Our discussion is over."

"I thought you believed in open communication?"

She said nothing, but gazed out the window, wishing he'd go away.

He came up behind her, and she heard a curious gruffness in his voice. "I hurt your feelings, didn't I?"

She slowly nodded.

"I didn't mean to. I just— I don't want you to get hurt, that's all. You don't have a lot of experience with jocks. They can be—I don't know—hard on women, I guess."

"I know." She turned back to him in time to watch a crooked rivulet of water slide toward a flat brown nipple. "I think I've had enough high drama for today. You'd better go."

He came closer instead, and when he spoke, his voice held a surprising note of tenderness. "We didn't even get to the bare-butt spanking."

"Maybe some other time."

"How 'bout we just do the bare-butt part?"

"I don't think it's a good idea for us to bare anything to each other for a while."

"Now why do you say that?"

"Because it makes everything too complicated."

"Last night wasn't complicated. At least not 'til you got all snooty."

"Me!" Her head shot up. "I've never been snooty in my life!"

"Oh, yeah?" Her renewed feistiness must have been what he was waiting for because the glimmer of battle once again flared in his eyes. "Well, I happen to have been at that drive-in with you, and, believe me, you were snooty."

"When?"

"You know very well."

"I don't."

"That *quite pleasant* crap."

"I don't know what— Oh, that." She regarded him more closely. "Did what I said bother you?"

"Hell, no, it didn't bother me. You think I don't know how good I am? And if you don't realize it, well, I guess that's your problem and not mine."

He looked sulky, and she realized she had hurt his feelings last night. The knowledge touched her. Despite his seemingly boundless self-confidence, he had insecurities like everyone else. "It was more than pleasant," she admitted.

"Damn right."

"I'd say it was— It was—" She regarded him out of the corner of her eye. "What word am I looking for?"

"Why don't you start out with pretty damn terrific?"

Her spirits made a quantum leap upward. "Terrific? Yes, that's a good start. It was definitely terrific. It was also . . ." She waited.

"Exciting, and sexy as hell."

"That, too, but . . ."

"Frustrating."

"Frustrating?"

"Yeah." A combative thrust to that square jaw. "I want to see you naked."

"You do? Why?"

"Because I do."

"Is this a guy thing?"

His truculence faded, and one corner of his mouth—the uninjured corner—curled. "You could say that."

"Believe me when I tell you that you're not missing much."

"I'm probably a better judge of that than you are."

"Oh, I'm sure that's not true. You know those endlessly long legs you see on models? Those legs that go all the way up to their armpits?"

"Uh-huh."

"I don't have them."

"Is that a fact."

"My legs aren't short, but they're not exceptionally long, either. Just average. And as for breasts— Do you consider yourself a breast man?"

"They've been known to catch my attention."

"Mine won't. Now my hips are a different matter. They're huge."

"Your hips are not huge."

"I look like a pear."

"You do not look like a pear."

"Thank you for the vote of confidence, but since you haven't seen me naked, you're not exactly a competent judge."

"We can take care of that right now."

He was at his most enticing: gray eyes glinting, that unexpected dimple on display just beneath his cheekbone, funny, warm, sexy. And she was at her most vulnerable. In a flash of insight that nearly knocked her from her feet, she realized that she was in love with him. Deeply and forever in love. She loved his masculinity, his intelligence, his complexity. She loved his sense of humor and his loyalty to his family, as well as that old-fashioned moral code that dictated he watch out for a child. Even one he didn't want.

There was no time to think about it, no place to run so she could ponder the enormity of what had happened. She watched him lift his arm and trace the curve of her jaw with his thumb. "I like you, Rosebud. I like you a lot."

"You do?"

He nodded.

She noted that he'd said he liked her, not loved her, and swallowed the lump in her throat. "You're just saying that to get me naked."

The creases of amusement deepened at the corners of his eyes. "It's tempting, but this is too important to lie about."

"I thought you hated me."

"I did. But it's hard to hold on to a good—and entirely *justifiable*—hatred with you."

Hope sprang inside her. "You forgive me?"

He hesitated. "Not exactly. It's a pretty big thing to forgive."

Once again, she felt a great wave of guilt sweeping through her. "You know I'm sorry, don't you?"

"Are you?"

"I—I can't be sorry about the baby, but I am sorry about the way I used you. I didn't think of you as a real person, just a dehumanized object that could give me what I wanted. If anyone treated me that way, I'd never forgive them, and if it's any consolation, you should know that I'll never forgive myself."

"Maybe you could do what I've been doing and work on separating the sin from the sinner."

She gazed into his eyes, trying to see through them to his heart. "Do you really not hate me anymore?"

"I already told you that I like you."

"I don't see how you could."

"I guess it just happened."

"When?"

"When did I decide I liked you? That day at Annie's when you found out I was smart."

"And you found out I was old."

"Don't remind me. I still haven't recovered from that. Maybe we could say the DMV made a mistake on your license."

She ignored the hopeful glimmer in his eyes. "How could you have decided you liked me that day? We had a terrible fight."

"Beats me. It just happened."

She considered what he was revealing. Nothing could be farther from a declaration of love, but his words did show a certain warmth of feeling. "I'll need to think about it."

"About what?"

"Whether or not I'm going to get naked."

"All right."

That was another thing she liked about him. For all his bullying and bluster, he knew how to distinguish what was important from the trivial, and he seemed to understand he couldn't hurry her on this.

"There's one more thing we have to settle."

She regarded him warily, then sighed. "I like my car. It has personality."

"So do a lot of psychopaths, but that doesn't mean you want one in your house. Now here's the way it's going to be—"

"Cal, please don't waste your breath giving me one of your high-handed lectures because I'll only end up locking you out of the house again. I asked you to help me find a car, you refused, so I did it myself. The car stays. And it won't even hurt your reputation. Think about it. When people see me driving around in it, they'll take it as one more sign of how unworthy I am to be your wife."

"You've got a point there. Everybody who knows me knows I wouldn't be keeping any woman around for very long who drove a heap like that."

"I won't even comment on what that says about your sense of values." He had a wonderful sense of values. It was his taste in women that needed an overhaul.

He grinned, but she refused to let it effect her. She wouldn't be so easily won over. "I want your word of honor that you won't touch my car. No driving it away or sending a tow truck when I'm not looking. The car is mine, and it stays. And just so we understand each other, I'm telling you right now that if you lay a finger on my Escort, you'll never enjoy another box of Lucky Charms in this house."

"More marshmallow sabotage?"

"I never repeat myself. Think rat poison."

"You are the most bloodthirsty woman I've ever met."

"It's a slow and painful death. I don't recommend it."

He laughed and headed back into the bathroom, where he shut the door only to pop his head back out. "All this arguing has stirred up my appetite. How 'bout we scrounge up something to eat as soon as I get dressed?"

"All right."

As the rain continued to fall outside, they dined on soup, salad, and sandwiches, with a side order of taco chips.

While they ate, she managed to wheedle a few more details out of him about his work with teenagers and discovered he'd been devoting his time to disadvantaged kids for years. He'd help fund rec centers, made speeches to recruit volunteers for after-school tutoring programs, set up intramural leagues, and lobbied the Illinois state legislature to improve their drug- and sex-education programs.

He shrugged off her comment that not all celebrities would be willing to give up so much time with no obvious reward to themselves. It was just something to do, he growled.

The hallway clock struck midnight and, gradually, their conversation dwindled. An awkwardness settled between them that hadn't been there before. She toyed with an uneaten bread crust. He shifted his weight in the kitchen chair. She'd been so comfortable all evening, but now she felt awkward and self-conscious.

"It's late," she finally said. "I think I'll head up to bed." She picked up her plate as she stood.

He rose, too, and removed it from her hand. "You cooked. I'll clean up."

But he didn't head toward the sink. Instead, he stayed where he was and gazed at her with hungry eyes. She could hear his unspoken question. *Tonight, Rosebud? Are you ready to cut through all this pretense and do what we both want?*

If he had reached out for her, she would have been lost, but he didn't do that, and she understood that this time she would have to make the first move. His eyebrows rose in a silent dare.

Wings of a panic beat at her breastbone. The new knowledge that she had fallen in love with him made all the difference. She wanted sex between them to matter.

The powerful brain that had guided her throughout her life refused to function, and confusion gripped her. She felt paralyzed, and the most she could manage was a polite, social smile. "I've enjoyed tonight, Cal. I'll fix the gate first thing tomorrow."

He said nothing; he merely watched her.

She tried to think of some casual comment to defuse the tension, but nothing came to mind. He stood there watching her. She knew he was aware of her uneasiness, but he didn't seem to share it. Why should he when he didn't share her feelings? Unlike her, he hadn't fallen in love.

She turned away, enveloped by a sense of loss. As she left the kitchen, her brain told her she was doing the right thing, but her heart told her she was a coward.

Cal watched her disappear through the doorway, and disappointment filled him. She was running away, and he wasn't sure why. He hadn't pushed her tonight. He'd given her space, made certain the conversation stayed on safe topics. As a matter of fact, he'd been enjoying himself so much he'd nearly forgotten about sex. Nearly, but never entirely. He wanted her too much to put it out of his mind. She'd enjoyed their lovemaking last night—he knew she had—so why was she denying both of them one of life's most basic pleasures?

He carried the dishes from their dinner to the sink and rinsed them off. His disappointment turned into irritation. Why did he let her bother him so much?

Disgusted with himself, he stalked upstairs, but entering his bordello bedroom only made his mood grow bleaker. A crack of thunder rattled the windows, and he realized the storm had intensified. Good. It matched his mood. He sat down on the side of the bed and yanked off one shoe.

"Cal?"

He looked up to see the bathroom door swing open, but just then a blinding flash of lightning shook the walls, and the house was plunged into darkness.

Several seconds ticked by, and then he heard a soft giggle.

He flung down his other shoe. "We just lost our electricity. You want to tell me what's so funny about that?''

"It's not exactly funny. It's more of a good news/bad news situation.''

"In that case, hit me with the good news first.''

"They're both sort of rolled up into one.''

"Stop stalling.''

"All right. Now don't get mad, but . . .'' Smothered laughter drifted toward him. "Cal . . . I'm naked.''

16

One month later

Cal poked his head into her bedroom through the connecting bathroom door. A glint shone in his eyes. "I'm taking a shower. You want to get in with me?"

She slid her gaze over his deliciously naked body, so beautifully delineated in the morning light, and had to resist the urge to lick her lips. "Maybe another time."

"You don't know what you're missing."

"I think I do."

The inadvertently wistful note in her voice seemed to amuse him. "Poor little Rosebud. You've really boxed yourself into a corner, haven't you?" With a cocky smile, he disappeared into the bathroom.

She stuck out her tongue at the empty doorway, propped her cheek on her bent elbow, and thought about that April night one month ago when she'd made her impulsive decision to take off her clothes and go to him. The unexpected electrical failure just as she'd walked into his bedroom had marked the beginning of a night of pleasure and passion that she would never forget. She smiled to herself. In the month that had passed since then, Cal had gotten very good at making love by touch.

She'd gotten rather good at it herself, she thought with

a certain amount of pride. Maybe his lusty nature and lack of inhibition had freed her from her own inhibitions. She would do anything . . . everything . . . except let him see her naked.

It had become a game. She would only make love with him at night with the lights out, and she always awakened sometime before dawn so she could return to her own room or slip into his if they'd fallen asleep in her bed. He could have changed the rules. He could have overpowered her, or left her so breathless at high noon with his kisses that she relented, but he never did. He was a competitor, and he didn't want to win by guile, only by her total surrender.

Her insistence on making love in the dark had begun as a gentle form of sexual teasing, but as one week faded into another and she realized how deeply she had fallen in love with him, something changed. She began to worry about how he would react when he finally saw her. She was now four months pregnant, and although she bloomed with health, her waist had thickened to the point where she couldn't come close to fastening her slacks and her days wearing tucked-in blouses were a thing of the past. With her expanding belly and unimpressive breasts, she could never compete with all those beauties in his past.

But it was more than the shortcomings of her body that made her hesitant. What if mystery was the lure that drew him to her bed each night? Mystery and the enticement of the unknown? Once his curiosity was satisfied, would he lose interest?

She wanted to believe it wouldn't matter, but she knew how much Cal loved a challenge. Would he enjoy her company as much if she bent to his will? She seemed to be the only woman in his life, with the exception of his mother and grandmother, who stood up to him.

He was an intelligent, decent man with a generous heart. But he was also domineering and competitive. Was it only the novelty of her rebellion that made him seek her company, both in and out of bed?

She faced the fact that her time for playing games had run out. She needed to stop being a coward, take off her clothes so he could see her, and face the truth. If he didn't want her for who she was, but only for the challenge of conquering her, then what they had together was worthless. She had to do it soon, she decided. It was crazy to keep this going on any longer.

She got out of bed and made her way to her bathroom. After she'd taken her morning vitamins and brushed her teeth, she returned to her room, and, with one hand on her growing belly, wandered over to the window so she could gaze out at the May morning. The mountainside was alive with blooms: dogwood, rhododendron, flame azaleas, along with budding mountain laurel. Her first Appalachian spring was more beautiful than she could ever have imagined. Violets, trillium, and lady slippers had unfolded in the woods where she walked, and wisteria bloomed at the side of the house along with a white shower of blackberry blossoms. She had never experienced such a breathtaking, joyous May.

But, then, she'd never been in love, either.

She understood how vulnerable she'd made herself, but as the guarded look Cal had carried in his eyes for so long was replaced by laughter and tenderness, she began to believe that he might be falling in love with her. Two months ago the idea would have been absurd, but now it didn't seem so impossible.

For people who should have nothing in common, they never ran out of subjects to talk about or things to do. While she spent her mornings at the computer, Cal worked out and took care of his local commitments, but they spent most afternoons and many evenings together.

Cal had finished painting Annie's house while she'd put in the garden. They'd visited Asheville several times together, where they'd dined at some of the city's best restaurants and walked the grounds of the Biltmore Estate with busloads of tourists. They'd hiked some of the easier trails in the Great Smoky Mountain National Park, and he'd taken her to see Connemara, Carl Sandberg's home, where she'd been enchanted by the beautiful setting and he'd taken pictures of her playing with the goats that were kept there.

By unspoken agreement, they didn't go into Salvation together. When Jane had shopping to do, she went alone. Sometimes she ran into Kevin, and the two of them lunched together at the Petticoat Junction Cafe, where she ignored the hostile stares of the locals. Luckily, she could still conceal her pregnancy with loose-fitting dresses.

She and Cal continued to fight when he got high-handed, but it was generally a good kind of fighting, and he never displayed any of the cold hatred that had been so much a part of him in those early weeks. Instead, he roared away to his heart's content, and she refused to ruin his pleasure by not fighting back. The truth was, she enjoyed their battles as much as he.

She heard the shower cut off. Since there was no sense exposing herself to additional temptation, she gave him a few minutes to dry off and wrap a towel around himself before she rapped softly on the partially open bathroom door, then let herself in.

He stood at the sink with the black bath towel looped so low on his hips she was surprised it didn't drop off. As he spread shaving cream across his jaw, he took in her cherry red Snoopy nightshirt.

"When are you gonna show a little mercy, Professor, and stop encitin' me with those sexy negligees?"

"Tomorrow night I'm wearing Winnie-the-Pooh."

"Be still my heart."

She smiled, lowered the lid on the toilet, and took a seat. For a while she contented herself with watching him shave, but then she returned to the subject of yesterday's argument.

"Cal, explain to me once more why you won't spend a little time with Kevin?"

"Are we back to this again?"

"I still don't understand why you won't coach him. He really respects you."

"He hates my guts."

"That's only because he wants to move up in the world. He's young and talented, and you're standing in his way."

His muscles tensed. He didn't like the fact that she spent time with Kevin, but since she'd made it clear that she regarded him as a friend, and since Cal had apparently told Kevin he'd break both his arms if he so much as touched her, they'd settled into an uneasy truce.

He tilted his head and shaved under his chin. "He's not as talented as he thinks. He's got a great arm—no doubt about that. He's quick and aggressive, but he has a lot to learn about reading defenses."

"Why don't you teach him?"

"It's like I said, I don't see the logic in training my competition, and I also happen to be the last person in the world he'd take advice from."

"That's not true. Why do you think he's still hanging around Salvation?"

"Because he's sleeping with Sally Terryman."

Jane had seen the curvaceous Sally in town several times, and she decided Cal had a point, but since it wasn't the one she wanted to make, she ignored it. "He'd be a lot better player if you worked with him, and you'd be leaving something important behind when you retire."

"Which won't be for a long time." He ducked his head and rinsed off the shaving cream.

She knew she was treading on dangerous ground and stepped carefully. "You're thirty-six, Cal. It can't be much longer."

"Which just goes to show what you know." He grabbed a hand towel and dried his face. "I'm at the top of my game. There's no reason for me to retire."

"Maybe not right away, but certainly in the foreseeable future."

"I've got a lot of good years left."

She thought of the shoulder he rubbed when he thought no one was looking, the whirlpool he'd had installed in the bathroom, and knew he was fooling himself.

"What are you going to do when you retire? Do you have some business ventures lined up? Are you going into coaching?"

His back muscles tensed ever so slightly. "Why don't you just stick to those top quarks, Professor, and leave my future to me?" He headed into his bedroom, whipping off his towel as he walked over to his bureau and pulled out a pair of briefs. "You remember, don't you, that I'm taking off for Texas later this afternoon."

He'd changed the subject. "Some kind of golf tournament, I think you said."

"The Bobby Tom Denton Invitational."

"He's a friend of yours?" She got up from the toilet and leaned against the doorframe that led into his bedroom.

"Honey, don't tell me you've never heard of Bobby Tom Denton. He's only the most famous wide-out to ever play football."

"Wide-out?"

"Wide receiver. They're the ones quarterbacks throw to. I want to tell you, the day he blew out his knee and had to retire was one of the worst days in the history of pro ball."

"What's he doing now?"

He yanked on a pair of khakis. "Mostly putting up a good front. He lives in Telarosa, Texas, with his wife Gracie and their new baby. He acts like his family and the charity foundation he runs are all he needs in life."

"Maybe they are."

"You don't know Bobby Tom. From the time he was a little kid, he lived to play ball."

"It sounds as if he's doing some important work."

"The Denton Foundation?" He pulled a dark brown polo shirt over his head. "It does a lot of good, don't get me wrong. This golf tournament alone brings in a couple hundred thousand for a whole bunch of good causes, but I guess the way I look at it, there are lots of people in this country who could run something like that, but there's only one guy in the world who can catch a football like B.T."

In Jane's opinion, running a charitable foundation seemed a lot more important than catching a football, but she knew when to hold her tongue. "Retirement could be exciting. Think about yourself, for example. You'll have the chance to start a whole new life while you're still young."

"I like the life I have."

Before she could say anything else, he closed the distance between them and pulled her into his arms, where he proceeded to kiss her until she was breathless. She felt him harden through his slacks, but it was daytime, and he drew back with obvious reluctance to gaze down at her through heated eyes. "You ready to cry 'uncle' yet?"

Her eyes drifted to his mouth, and she sighed. "Just about."

"You know, don't you, that I won't make it easy on you. I'm not going to be satisfied with anything less than stripping you naked in broad daylight."

"I know."

"I might even make you walk around outside."

She regarded him glumly. "I wouldn't be surprised."

" 'Course I wouldn't make you do something like that stark naked."

"You're all heart."

"I'd prob'ly let you wear one of those nice pairs of high heels you've got."

"A man in a million."

He started to kiss her again. Then he was cupping her breasts, and they were both breathing so hard she didn't ever want to stop. Just that morning she'd told herself she was going to stop playing games with him, and now was the time. With one hand she reached for the hem of her nightshirt.

The telephone rang. She inched her nightshirt higher and continued kissing Cal, but the phone's persistence ruined the mood.

He groaned. "Why isn't the answering machine picking up?"

She let go of the nightshirt. "The cleaning women were here yesterday afternoon. They must have turned it off by mistake."

"I'll bet it's Dad. He was going to call me this morning." He relinquished her with reluctance, rested his forehead against hers for a few moments, then kissed the tip of her nose.

She couldn't believe it. She'd finally worked up the nerve to let him see her pudgy body, and the stupid phone had to ring! Giving him his privacy, she headed for her bathroom, where she showered, then dressed. Afterward, she made her way to the kitchen.

Cal was slipping his wallet into the pocket of his khakis. "That was Dad on the phone. He and Mom are meeting for lunch in Asheville today. I hope he can convince her to put an end to this craziness and move back home. I can't believe she's being so stubborn."

"There are two people involved in that marriage."

"And one of them is bullheaded."

She'd given up arguing with him about this. He was convinced that his mother was at fault in his parents' separation because she was the one who'd moved out, and nothing Jane said could persuade him that there might be another side to the story.

"Do you know what Mom told Ethan when he offered her some pastoral counseling? She told him to mind his own business."

She lifted an eyebrow at him. "Ethan might not be the best person to offer counsel."

"He's her pastor!"

She barely resisted rolling her eyes. Instead, she patiently pointed out the obvious. "You and Ethan are both too involved personally to be counseling either one of them."

"Yeah, I guess." As he picked up his car keys from the counter, he frowned. "I just don't understand how something like this could happen."

She gazed at Cal's troubled face and found herself wishing Lynn and Jim could settle their differences, not only for themselves but for their sons. Cal and Ethan loved their parents, and this estrangement was painful for them.

Once again she wondered what had happened to Lynn and Jim Bonner. For years they seemed to have managed to live together very well. Why had they separated now?

Jim Bonner strode into the Blue Ridge dining room at the Grove Park Inn, Asheville's most famous hotel and resort. It had always been one of Lynn's favorite places, and he'd asked her to meet him here for lunch. Perhaps its pleasant associations would soften his stubborn wife's heart.

The Grove Park Inn had been constructed at the turn of the century to serve as a luxurious refuge from the summer heat for the nation's wealthy. Built into the side of Sunset Mountain from rough-hewn granite, the massive structure was either ugly or splendid, depending on your viewpoint.

The Blue Ridge dining room, like the rest of the hotel, was furnished in the rustic charm of the Arts and Crafts movement. He walked down several steps that led to a lower dining area and spotted Lynn sitting at a small table positioned by the tall windows that overlooked the mountains. He drank in the sight of her.

Since he refused to visit her on Heartache Mountain, he either had to telephone or watch for her when he knew she'd be coming to town. He made excuses to drop by church on Wednesday evenings when she met with the worship committee and kept his eyes peeled for her car in the Ingles grocery store lot.

For her part, she seemed to do her best to avoid him. She always chose times when she knew she wouldn't run into him to stop at the house, either when he had office hours or was making his hospital rounds. He'd been relieved when she'd agreed to meet him today.

His pleasure at the sight of her faded into irritation. This past month didn't seem to have changed her, while he felt bruised and old. She wore a loosely woven lavender-and-cream jacket that he'd always liked, along with silver earrings and a silky top and skirt. As he pulled out the heavy wooden chair across from her, he tried to convince himself those were marks of sleeplessness he saw under her eyes, but they were probably only shadows cast by the light coming in through the windows.

She gave him the same cordial nod she used to greet strangers. What had happened to the enchanting young mountain girl who'd giggled uncontrollably and decorated his dinner table with dandelions?

The waiter approached, and Jim ordered two glasses of their favorite wine, only to have Lynn request a Diet Pepsi instead. After the waiter left, he regarded her inquisitively.

"I've gained five pounds," she explained.

"You're on hormone replacement therapy. You have to expect some weight gain."

"It's not the pills that are doing it to me; it's Annie's cooking. If something doesn't have a stick of butter in it, she doesn't think it's edible."

"Sounds to me as if the best way to get those five pounds off would be to come home."

She paused for a moment before she spoke. "Heartache Mountain has always been my home."

He felt as if a cold draft had blown across the back of his neck. "I'm talking about your real home. Our home."

Instead of responding, she picked up the menu and began to study it. The waiter delivered their drinks and took their order. While they waited for their food, Lynn spoke of the weather and a concert she had attended the week before. She reminded him to have the air conditioner checked and talked about some new road construction. It made him ache inside. This beautiful woman who used to speak only from her heart now never did.

She seemed determined to avoid anything personal, but he knew she wouldn't be able to avoid talking about their sons. "Gabe called from Mexico last night. Apparently neither of his brothers has seen fit to tell him you've moved out."

Concern furrowed her brow. "You didn't say anything, did you? He's got enough to deal with as it is. I don't want him worrying."

"No, I didn't say anything."

Her relief was visible. "I'm so worried about him. I wish he'd come home."

"Maybe someday."

"I'm worried about Cal, too. Have you noticed?"

"He looks fine to me."

"Better than fine. I saw him in town yesterday, and I've never seen him look happier. I don't understand it, Jim. He's always been a good judge of character, and that woman's going to break his heart. Why can't he see her for what she is?"

Jim grew grim at the thought of his new daughter-in-law. He'd seen her on the street a few days earlier, and she'd walked right past him, just as if he didn't exist. She'd refused to show up at church, declined social invitations from some of the nicest women in town, and even failed to attend a testimonial dinner for Cal the Jaycees had given. The only person she'd give the time of day to seemed to be Kevin Tucker. None of it boded well for his son.

"I don't understand it," Lynn went on. "How can he be so happy when he's married to such a . . . a . . ."

"Cold-hearted bitch."

"I hate her. I can't help it. She's going to hurt him badly, and he doesn't deserve it." Her brow furrowed, and her voice developed a huskiness that indicated the depth of her upset. "All these years we've waited for him to settle down and marry someone nice, someone who loved him, but look who he's picked—a woman who doesn't care about anyone but herself." She regarded him with troubled eyes. "I wish there was something we could do."

"We can't even straighten out our own troubles, Lynn. How could we expect to solve Cal's?"

"It's not the same thing. He's— He's vulnerable."

"And we're not?"

For the first time, she sounded vaguely defensive. "I didn't say that."

Bitterness tightened his chest and rose like bile in his throat. "I've just about had it with this cat and mouse game you're playing. I'm warning you, Lynn; I'm not going to put up with it much longer."

He realized right away that he'd made a mistake. Lynn didn't like being backed into a corner, and she always met aggression with her own brand of quiet stubbornness. Now she regarded him levelly. "Annie told me to tell you she doesn't want you calling the house."

"Well, that's just too bad."

"She's really angry with you."

"Annie's been angry with me since I was eight years old."

"That's not true. Her health is making her cranky."

"If she'd stop putting a stick of butter in everything, she might start feeling better." He leaned back in the chair. "You know why she doesn't want us talking. It's because she's got a good thing going having you on Heartache Mountain full-time to take care of her. She won't give that up easily."

"Is that what you think?"

"You bet it is."

"You're wrong. She's trying to protect me."

"From me? Yeah, right." His voice softened. "Damn it, Lynn, I've been a good husband to you. I don't deserve to be treated like this."

She looked down at her plate, and then up at him, her eyes full of pain. "It's always about you, isn't it, Jim? From the very beginning everything has revolved around you. What you deserve. How you felt. What kind of mood you were in. I've built my life around trying to please you, and it hasn't worked."

"That's ridiculous. You're blowing this whole thing out of proportion. Look, forget everything I said that night. I didn't mean any of it. I was just—I don't know—having some kind of mid-life crisis or something. I like you the way you are. You've been the best wife a man could ever have. Let's just forget all of this happened and go back to the way things were."

"I can't do that because *you* can't do it."

"You don't know what you're talking about."

• "Someplace inside you there's this knot of resentment that formed the day we got married and has never gone away. If you want me back, it's only out of habit. I don't think you like me very much, Jim. Maybe you never have."

"That's absurd. You're overdramatizing this whole thing. Just tell me what you want, and I'll give it to you."

"Right now I want to please myself."

"Fine! Please yourself. I'm not standing in your way, and you don't have to run away to do it."

"Yes, I do."

"You're going to blame me for everything, aren't you? Go ahead! You explain to your sons what a bad guy I am, then. And while you explain it, remind them that *you're* the one who's walking out on a thirty-seven-year marriage, not me."

She regarded him levelly. "You know what I think? I think you walked out on our marriage the day we said our vows."

"I knew you'd start throwing up the past at me. Now you're going to blame me for the sins of an eighteen-year-old boy."

"That's not what I'm doing. I'm just tired of living with the part of you that's still eighteen, the part of you that still hasn't dealt with the fact that you knocked up Amber Lynn Glide and had to take the consequences. The boy who thinks he deserves something better has never gone away." Her voice grew soft and weary. "I'm tired of living with the guilt, Jim. I'm tired of always feeling as if I have to prove myself."

"Then stop doing it! I haven't made you live that way. You've done it to yourself."

"And now I have to figure out how to undo it."

"I can't believe how selfish you're being. Do you want a divorce, Lynn? Is that what all this is leading up to? Because if you want a divorce, you just tell me now. I'm not living in this limbo forever. Just tell me right now."

He waited to see her shock. What he had suggested was unthinkable. But there was no shock, and he began to panic. Why didn't she tell him to stop talking so crazy, that their situation wasn't nearly bad enough to even think about divorce? But once again, he'd miscalculated.

"Maybe that would be for the best."

He went numb.

She got a faraway look on her face, almost dreamy. "You know what I wish? I wish we could start all over. I wish we could meet each other again with no past history, just two strangers getting acquainted. Then, if we didn't like what we found, we could walk away. And if we did like what we found . . .'' Her voice grew thick with emotion. ''The playing field would be level. There'd be a—a balance of power.''

''Power?'' Fear churned inside him. ''I don't know what you're talking about.''

She regarded him with a look of pity that cut right through him. ''You really don't, do you? For thirty-seven years you've had all the power in our relationship, and I've had none. For thirty-seven years I've had to live with the fact that I was a second-class citizen in our marriage. But I can't live that way anymore.''

She spoke so patiently, like an adult explaining something to a child, and it enraged him.

''Fine!'' He lost his ability to think clearly and acted on raw emotion. ''You can have your divorce. And I hope you choke on it.''

He threw down a wad of bills he didn't bother to count, shot up from his chair, and stalked from the dining room without a backward look. As he hit the hallway, he realized he was sweating. She'd turned his life upside down from the day he'd met her.

She wanted to talk about *power*! From the time she was fifteen years old, she'd had the power to twist his life out of shape. If he hadn't met her, everything might have been different. He wouldn't have come back to Salvation and been a family doctor, that's for sure. He'd have gone into research, or maybe he'd have hooked up with one of the big international outfits and traveled around the world to do the work on infectious diseases he'd always dreamed about. A million possibilities would have been open to him if he hadn't been forced to marry her, but because of her, he hadn't explored any of them. He'd had a wife and children to support, so he'd gone back to his hometown with his tail between his legs and taken over his father's practice.

Resentment seethed inside him. He'd had the course of his life irrevocably changed when he was still too young to understand what was happening. She'd done that to him, the same woman who'd sat in that dining room and told him she had no power. She'd fucked up his life forever, and now she blamed him.

He stopped in his track as all the blood rushed from his head. Jesus. She was right.

He sagged down on one of the couches that sat along the wall and dropped his head into his hands. Seconds lapsed, turning into minutes as all the mental barriers he'd erected against the truth grew transparent.

She'd been right when she'd said he'd always resented her, but his bitterness had become such an old, familiar companion he hadn't recognized it for what it was. She was right. After all this time, he still blamed her.

The many ways he'd punished her over the years came flying back in his face: the fault-finding and subtle put-downs, his blind stubbornness and refusal to acknowledge her needs. All those little punishments he'd inflicted against this woman who was the closest thing he had to a soul.

He pushed his fingertips into his eye sockets and shook his head. She was right about everything.

17

Jane's hands trembled as she stroked almond-scented lotion over every inch of her thirty-four-year-old body, including her rounding belly. Sunlight streamed through her bedroom window, and in the next room Cal's suitcase lay open on his bed, ready for his late afternoon flight to Austin. She'd made up her mind this morning, and now she wanted to do it before she lost her nerve.

She brushed her hair until it shone, then stared at her naked body in the mirrored wall behind the whirlpool. She tried to imagine how it would look to Cal, but all she could think about was how it wouldn't look. It wouldn't look like it belonged to a twenty-year-old centerfold.

With an exclamation of disgust, she stalked back into her bedroom, snatched up her prettiest robe, an apricot silk with a border of deep green laurel leaves at the hem and sleeves, and jabbed her arms into it. She was a physicist, for goodness sakes! A successful professional woman! Since when did she decide to measure her self-worth in terms of her hip size?

And since when could she respect a man who viewed her as only a body? If her measurements didn't meet Cal's standards, then it was long past time she found that out. They couldn't have a lasting relationship if the only thing that kept him interested in her was the mystery of what she looked like naked.

She wanted a real relationship more than she'd ever wanted anything. It hurt too much to be afraid all the caring was one-sided. She needed to stop procrastinating and find out if anything lasting existed between them, or if she were merely another touchdown for Cal Bonner to score.

She heard the faint whir of the garage door sliding open, and her heart jumped into her throat. He was home. Misgivings shot through her. She should have picked a more convenient time, a day when he wasn't getting ready to fly halfway across the country to a golf tournament. She should have waited until she was calmer, more sure of herself. She should have—

Her cowardice disgusted her and she resisted a nearly irresistible urge to grab every article of clothing in her closet and stuff herself into all of them until she was the size of a polar bear. Today she would begin the process of discovering whether she'd given her heart away in vain.

Taking a deep breath, she secured the robe's sash in a bow and padded barefoot into the hallway.

"Jane?"

"I'm up here." As she stopped at the top of the stairs, the thudding of her heart made her feel light-headed.

He appeared in the foyer below. "Guess who I—" He broke off as he looked up and saw her standing above him at one o'clock in the afternoon wearing nothing but a slinky silk robe.

He smiled and tucked the fingers of one hand in the pocket of his jeans. "You sure do know how to welcome a guy home."

She couldn't have spoken if she wanted to. Heart pounding, she lifted her hands to the robe's sash while her heart whispered a silent prayer. *Please let him want me for myself and not just because I'm a challenge. Please let him love me just a little bit.* Her clumsy fingers tugged on the robe's sash, and her gaze locked with his as the frail garment parted. With a shrug of her shoulders, she let it slide down her body and fall in a puddle at her feet.

Warm sunlight washed her body, revealing everything: her small breasts and rounding belly, her *huge* hips and very ordinary legs.

Cal looked dazed. She rested one hand lightly on the banister and moved slowly down the steps, wearing nothing but a fragile veil of almond-scented lotion.

Cal's lips parted. His eyes glazed.

Her foot touched the bottom step, and she smiled.

He licked his lips as if they had gone very dry and spoke in a voice that held a slight croak. "Turn around, Eth."

"Not on your life."

Jane's head shot up. With a gasp of dismay, she saw the Reverend Ethan Bonner standing in the archway just behind Cal.

He studied her with undisguised interest. "I hope I didn't show up at a bad time."

With a strangled moan, she spun around and dashed back up the stairs, all too aware of the view she presented them from behind. She scrambled for her robe and, crumpling it in front of herself, fled to her bedroom, where she slammed the door and sagged against it, more mortified than she had ever been in her life.

It seemed as if only a few seconds passed before she heard a soft rapping. "Honey?" Cal's voice held the tentative note of a man who knew he only had a few minutes to disarm a ticking bomb.

"I'm not here. Go away." To her dismay, tears stung her eyes. She had thought about this for so long, placed so much importance on it, and now it had ended in disaster.

The door bumped against her. "Step back now, sweetheart, and let me in."

She moved away, too dispirited to argue. With the silk

robe still crumpled in front of her, she pressed her bare back to the adjacent wall.

He entered gingerly, like a soldier expecting land mines. "You all right, sweetheart?"

"Stop calling me that! I've never been so embarrassed."

"Don't be, honey. You made poor Eth's day. Hell, you probably made his whole year, not to mention mine."

"Your brother saw me *naked*! I stood there on the stairs, naked as the day I was born, making a complete fool of myself."

"Now that's where you're wrong. There was nothing foolish about the sight of you naked. Why don't you let me hang that robe up for you before it gets ruined."

She clutched it more tightly to her midriff. "He was *looking* at me the whole time, and you didn't say a word. Why didn't you warn me we weren't alone?"

"You sort of took me by surprise, sweetheart. I wasn't thinking straight. And Eth couldn't help looking. It's been years since he's seen a beautiful naked woman in the flesh. I'd be worried about him if he hadn't looked."

"He's a minister!"

"It was a blessed event. You sure you don't want me to hang that robe up?"

"You're making a joke out of this."

"Absolutely not. Only an insensitive jerk would think something this traumatic was funny. Tell you what. I'll go downstairs right this minute and kill him before he gets away."

She refused to smile. Instead, she decided to pout. It was something she'd always wanted to do, but until that moment, she'd never quite been able to figure out how to. Now it seemed to come naturally. "I've just received the shock of my life, and you're treating it as a big joke."

"I'm a pig." He drew her a few inches away from the wall and rubbed his hands along her bare spine. "If I were you, I'd tell me to get lost because I don't even deserve to breathe the same air as you."

"That's so true."

"Honey, I'm really getting worried about that pretty robe. Squashed up between us, it's getting ruined. Don't you think you should let me have it?"

She pressed her cheek to his chest, enjoying the warm stroking of his hands along her back, but still not quite done with her pout. "I won't ever be able to look him in the eye again. He already thinks I'm a heathen. This will prove it."

"True, but Ethan's had a lifelong attraction to women with sin in their blood. It's sort of his tragic flaw."

"He can't have missed the fact that I'm pregnant."

"He'll keep his mouth shut if I ask him to."

She sighed, giving up her pout. "I'm going to have to go through with this, aren't I?"

He cupped her cheek and gently stroked his thumb along her jaw. "I'm pretty sure you passed the point of no return when you hit that top step."

"I suppose."

"But if you don't mind, since you've waited this long, hold out for just a few seconds more so I can open those curtains the rest of the way and get more light in here."

She sighed as he made his way to the window. "You're not going to make this easy, are you?"

"Nope." He tugged on the cord, letting the bright early-afternoon sunlight flood into the room.

"What about Ethan?"

"My brother's no fool. He's long gone by now."

"You take off your clothes first."

"No way. You've seen me naked dozens of times. It's my turn."

"If you think I'm going to be undressed while you lie there fully clothed . . ."

"That's exactly what I think." He walked over to her bed and stacked the pillows against the headboard. Then he kicked off his shoes and stretched out, crossing his arms behind his head like someone about to enjoy a good movie.

She was torn between amusement and irritation. "What if I've changed my mind?"

"We both know you've got too much pride to back off now. Tell me if you want me to close my eyes."

"As if you would." Why had she made such a big deal out of this? For a brilliant woman, she was a complete idiot. Damn him anyway. Why hadn't he just pulled that robe out of her hands and put an end to all this? But, no. That was too easy. Instead, he lay there with the glint of challenge in those gray eyes, and she knew he was testing her mettle. Her irritation grew. This was *his* test, not hers. He was the one who had something to prove, and it was time to give him his chance.

She shut her eyes and dropped the robe.

Dead silence.

A dozen thoughts ran through her mind, all of them horrible: he hated her body, he'd fainted from the sight of her hips, her pregnant belly repulsed him.

The last thought lit the fuse to her temper. He was a *worm*! Lower than a worm! What kind of man was repulsed by the body of the woman carrying his child? He was the lowest form of life on earth.

Her eyes flew open. "I knew it! I knew you'd hate my body!" She slammed her hands on her hips, marched over to the bed, and glared down at him. "Well, for your information, mister, all those cute little sex kittens in your past might have had perfect bodies, but they don't know a lepton from a proton, and if you think that I'm going to stand here and let you judge me by the size of my hips and because my belly's not flat, then you're in for a rude awakening." She jabbed her finger at him. "This is the way a grown woman looks, buster! This body was designed by God to be functional, not to be stared at by some hormonally imbalanced jock who can only get aroused by women who still own Barbie dolls!''

''Damn. Now I've got to gag you.'' With one swift motion, he pulled her down on the bed, rolled on top of her, and covered her lips with his own.

His kiss was deep and fierce. It started at her mouth, then traveled on to her breasts, her belly, the backs of her knees, with several thrilling stops in between. Her irritation faded as need took its place.

She wasn't certain when he got rid of his own clothes because she quickly lost herself in the pleasures of feeling that strong, solid body beneath her hands and lips. For a man of action, he'd always been a leisurely lover, and today was no exception. As the bright sunlight pooled over their bodies, he satisfied his curiosity by exploring every inch of her, turning her this way and that, across the light, toward the light until she begged him.

''Please . . . I can't take any more.''

He nuzzled her breast with his lips and his husky breath fell hot over her damp skin. ''You're going to have to take a lot more before we're through.''

She punished him for his teasing with a torment of her own, using her mouth on him in the way she knew he loved, but the deep, moist taking also served to inflame her own need, so that when he finally reached his limit, she had also reached hers. He covered her with his body and entered her. She immediately climaxed.

''Now see what you've done,'' she complained when she came back to earth.

His eyes were the deep gray of a spring thunderstorm, his voice smoky with the most delicious sort of menace as he pushed himself deep inside her. ''Poor honey. I guess I'll have to start all over again with you.''

''I'm not interested anymore,'' she lied.

''Then close your eyes and think about something else 'til I'm done.''

She laughed and he kissed her, and in no time at all they were lost in each other. She had never felt so free. In shedding her clothes, she had also shed the last of her defenses.

"I love you," she whispered, as he entered her. "I love you so much."

He kissed her lips as if he were sipping her words. "Sweet . . . My sweet. So beautiful . . ."

Their bodies found a rhythm as ancient as time, and they climbed together through every barrier that separated them. As he loved her with his body, she knew with a fierce certainty that he also loved her with his heart. It could be no other way, and the knowledge catapulted her over the top. Together, they touched creation.

They spent the next few hours in various states of undress. He allowed her to wear a pair of powder blue sandals, but nothing else. She allowed him to wear his black bath towel, but insisted he keep it draped around his neck.

They ate a late lunch in bed, where they played sexual games with the juicy slices of an orange. Afterward, as they showered together, she knelt before him with the water pouring over them and loved him until they both lost control.

They were insatiable. She felt as if she'd been created only to please this man and, in turn, take pleasure only from him. She had never been so well loved, so certain of her powers as a woman. She felt brilliant and strong, soft and giving, utterly fulfilled, and although he hadn't spoken the words, she knew in the very center of her being that he loved her. Such intensity of emotion couldn't be coming only from her.

He postponed leaving until he had barely enough time to get to the airport. As the Jeep flew down the driveway, she smiled and hugged herself.

Everything was going to be all right.

*   *   *

The best country western band in Telarosa, Texas, played a lively two-step, but Cal turned down invitations to dance from a Dallas Cowboy cheerleader and a knockout Austin socialite. He was a pretty good dancer, but tonight he wasn't in the mood, and not just because he'd played a semilousy round of golf in the tournament that day. Depression had settled on him as thick and dark as mountain midnight.

Part of the reason for his depression sidled up next to him, looking a lot more cheerful than a man who'd given up football should ever look. A blond-haired baby girl, who showed every sign of being a future mankiller, snuggled in the crook of his arm, occupying the same space all those game balls used to take up. As far as Cal could tell, the only times Wendy Susan Denton hadn't been glued in her daddy's arm were when Bobby Tom had been swinging a golf club or letting her mother nurse her.

"Did Gracie show you the new addition we put on the house?" Bobby Tom Denton said. "With the baby and everything, we decided we wanted more room. Plus, ever since Gracie was elected mayor of Telarosa, she's needed a home office."

"Gracie showed me, B.T." Cal glanced around him, looking for an escape route, but he couldn't find one. It occurred to him that having spent a few minutes alone with B.T.'s wife, Gracie Snow Denton, had been one of the few pleasures of this weekend. At the time, Bobby Tom had been charming sports' reporters and carrying Wendy around, so Cal hadn't been forced to look at that delicate wiggling bundle and see his own future.

To his surprise, Cal liked Wendy's mom a lot, even though Mayor Gracie wasn't the type of woman anybody ever figured a legend like Bobby Tom would marry. He'd always hung around with gorgeous bombshells, while Gracie was pretty much a cute BB. She sure was nice, though. Straightforward and genuinely caring about people. Sort of like the Professor, although she didn't have the Professor's habit of fading out in the middle of a conversation to ponder some theory only she and a dozen other people on the planet could possibly understand.

"Gracie and I sure had ourselves some fun designing the new addition on the house." Bobby Tom grinned and pushed his Stetson back on his head. Cal decided Bobby Tom could give Ethan a few lessons when it came to being movie-star handsome, although B.T. had more character lines in his face than the reverend. Still, he was a good-looking son of a gun.

"And did she tell you about the brick street I bought from that town in West Texas? Gracie found out they were tearing it up to put in asphalt, so I went over there and made a deal with them for it. Nothin' like used brick for beauty. Be sure you take a look at the back of the house and see what we did with it."

Bobby Tom went on about antique brick and wide-plank flooring as if they were the most important things in the world, while the baby nestled blissfully in the crook of his arm sucking her fists and making goo-goo eyes at her adoring papa. Cal felt as if he were suffocating to death.

Just two hours earlier, Cal had overheard a conversation the great wide receiver was having with Phoebe Calebow, the Stars' owner, about *breast-feeding*! It seemed B.T. wasn't sure Gracie was *doing it* right. He didn't think she was taking it *seriously* enough. Bobby Tom, who'd never taken anything but football seriously, had acted as if breast-feeding a baby was the most important topic in the world!

Even now, the memory made Cal start to sweat. All this time Cal had figured Bobby Tom was just putting on a front, pretending everything was wonderful in his life, but now he knew Bobby Tom *believed* it. He didn't seem to realize anything was wrong. The fact that the greatest wide-out in the history of pro ball had turned into a man who was centering his life around a wife and a baby and wide-plank flooring was horrifying! Never in a million years would Cal have thought that the legendary Bobby Tom Denton could have forgotten who he was, but that's exactly what had happened.

To his relief, Gracie came up and drew Bobby Tom away. Just before they walked off, Cal saw the look of utter contentment on his face as he gazed down at his wife, and it felt like a kick delivered to his very own stomach.

He finished off his beer and tried to tell himself he'd never once looked at the Professor like that, but the thing was, he couldn't be sure. The Professor'd been turning him inside out lately, and who knew what kind of goofy expression he had on his face when he was near her.

If only she hadn't told him she loved him, he might not feel so panicky. Why did she have to say those words? At first when she'd said them, he'd felt kind of good about it. There was something satisfying about winning the approval of a woman as smart and funny and sweet as the Professor. But that insanity had vanished when he'd hit Telarosa and run head-on into Bobby Tom Denton's life after football.

Bobby Tom might be happy with all this permanency crap, but Cal knew he couldn't ever be. There was nothing waiting for him on the other side of playing ball, no charity foundation to run, no honest work he could care about, nothing that would let him hold up his head like a man should. And that, he admitted to himself, was the crux of it.

How could a man be a man without honest work? Bobby Tom had the Denton Foundation, but Cal didn't have B.T.'s talent for making money multiply. Instead, he pretty much let it sit around in a few accounts here and there and pick up interest. Cal didn't have any worthy life waiting for him on the other side of the goal line. All the other side of the goal line held for him was exactly nothing.

It also held Jane, and yesterday afternoon when he'd said good-bye to her, he'd known she was no longer thinking about the short term like he was. She was thinking about wide-plank flooring and monogrammed bath towels and where they should settle down when they were old. But he wasn't even close to being ready for that, and he didn't want her telling him she loved him! Next thing, she'd be asking him to look at paint chips and pick out wall-to-wall carpeting. Now that she'd said the words, she was going to expect him to do something about it, and he wasn't ready for that. Not yet. Not when the only worthy work he knew how to do was throw a football. Not now when he was facing the toughest season of his life.

While Cal was playing golf in Texas, Jane took long walks up the mountain and daydreamed about the future. She considered places they might live and ways she could rearrange her schedule so she could occasionally go on road trips with him. On Sunday afternoon she pulled the ugly rose metallic wallpaper from the walls of the breakfast nook and made a pot of homemade chicken noodle soup.

When she awakened on Monday morning to the sound of the shower, she realized Cal had returned some time after she'd fallen asleep last night and was disappointed that he hadn't slipped into bed with her. In the past few weeks she'd gotten into the habit of keeping him company while he shaved, but the bathroom door remained firmly shut, and it wasn't until she made her way to the kitchen for breakfast that she finally met up with him.

"Welcome home." She spoke softly and waited for that moment he would take her in his arms. Instead, he muttered something unintelligible.

"How was your golf game?" she asked.

"Crap."

That explained his bad mood.

He carried his cereal bowl over to the sink and splashed it full of water. As he turned, he stabbed one finger toward the bare walls of the breakfast nook where she'd stripped off the wallpaper. "I don't like coming home and finding my house torn apart."

"You can't have liked those awful roses."

"It doesn't matter whether I liked them or not. You should have talked to me before you took it on yourself to start redecorating my house."

The tender lover she'd spent the weekend daydreaming about had disappeared, and uneasiness crept through her. She'd begun to think of this awful place as her house, too, but obviously he didn't regard it the same way. She drew a deep breath and repressed her hurt as she struggled to speak reasonably. "I didn't think you'd mind."

"Well, I do."

"All right. We can pick out some new paper. I'll be happy to put it up for you."

A look of abject horror crossed his face. "I don't pick out wallpaper, Professor! Not ever! And neither do you, so just leave it alone." He snatched up his car keys from the counter.

"You want to leave the wall like that?"

"You bet I do."

She debated whether she was going to tell him to go to hell or cut him some slack. Despite her hurt, she decided on the later. She could always tell him to go to hell later. "I made some homemade chicken noodle soup. Will you be back in time for dinner?"

"I don't know. You'll see me when you see me. Don't try to tie me down, Professor. I won't have it." With that, he disappeared into the garage.

She sat down on one of the kitchen chairs and told herself not to overdramatize what had just happened. He was jet-lagged, upset about performing badly in the golf tournament in front of his friends, and that had made him surly. There was no reason to believe his withdrawal had anything to do with what had happened between them the day he'd left. Despite this morning's churlish display, Cal was a decent man. He wasn't going to turn against her just because she'd taken off her clothes in broad daylight and told him she loved him.

She made herself eat half a piece of toast while memories of all the reasons she'd been reluctant to let him see her naked came back to her. What if her fears had proved correct? What if she'd stopped being a challenge to him, and he was no longer interested in having her in his life? Two days ago, she'd been so certain he loved her, but now she wasn't sure. About anything.

She realized she was brooding and got up, but instead of going to work, she found herself wandering through the house. The telephone rang, two quick tones that indicated a call was coming in on Cal's business line, which she never answered.

As she passed the door of his study, the machine clicked on, and she heard a voice she remembered all too well. "Cal, it's Brian. Look, I have to talk to you right away. While I was on vacation, I figured out how we can do this. Nothing like a white sand beach to unlock the brain cells; I'm just sorry it took so long. Anyway, I met with someone over the weekend to make sure it was possible, and it looks like we have a winner. But if we're going to act on it, we should do it now." He paused and his voice dropped. "I didn't want to use your fax for obvious reasons, so I sent a report to you express mail on Saturday that explains everything. You should get it this morning. Call me as soon as you read it." He chuckled. "Happy anniversary."

She remembered Cal's attorney, Brian Delgado, all too well: greedy eyes, arrogant carriage, disdainful manner. Something about the call disturbed her, probably that gloating note she'd heard in his voice. What an unpleasant man.

She glanced at her watch and saw that it was nine o'clock. She'd already wasted too much time this morning brooding, and she wasn't going to add Brian Delgado's call to her worry list. Returning to the kitchen, she poured herself a mug of coffee and carried it to her room, where she turned on her computer and logged in.

The date flashed, and the hair on the back of her neck prickled. For a moment she didn't understand why, but then she finally took in what she was seeing, and it came to her. *May 5.* She and Cal had been married two months ago today. *Happy anniversary.*

She pressed her fingertips to her lips. Was it a coincidence? She remembered Delgado's gloating. *I didn't want to use your fax for obvious reasons* ... What obvious reason? The fact that she might read this mysterious report before Cal saw it? She jumped up from her chair and went down to the study, where she sat behind the desk replaying the message and thinking.

Shortly before ten, the FedEx carrier arrived. She signed for the package, then carried it into Cal's study. Without a moment's hesitation, she ripped it open.

The report was several pages long and contained numerous typos, indicating that Delgado had probably prepared it himself. No wonder. Heartsick, she read every damning detail of Delgado's proposal and tried to absorb the fact that all the time Cal had been making love to her, he'd also been plotting revenge.

Over an hour passed before she could bring herself to go upstairs and pack. She called Kevin and asked him to come over. When he saw her packed suitcases, he immediately began to protest, but she refused to listen. Only after she threatened to carry the computer downstairs herself did he finally do as she wanted and load it into her car. Afterward, she made him leave, then she settled down to wait for Cal to come home. The old Jane would have slipped away, but the new one needed to face him down for the last time.

18

Jane hadn't left!

Cal spotted her through the sliding doors in the family room as she stood in the backyard looking up at Heartache Mountain. Muscles he hadn't even realized were tense began to ease. She was still here.

He'd been working out at the Y when Kevin had burst into the weight room with the news that his wife had packed up her computer and was getting ready to head back to Chicago. It had taken Kevin a couple of hours to track him down, and as Cal had sped home, still dressed in his sweat-soaked T-shirt and gray athletic shorts, he'd been terrified she might already have gone.

He still didn't understand why she wanted to do something so drastic. Granted, he'd been surly and rude this morning. He'd regretted it ever since, and he'd already made up his mind to get back in plenty of time to eat her homemade chicken noodle soup. But Jane wasn't one to run from a fight. He could easily imagine her taking a cast-iron skillet to his head, but he couldn't imagine her just packing up and leaving.

Now she stood below him, all buttoned up and battened down, and it occurred to him that the only person he knew whose clothes were as neat as hers were his younger brother's. She'd chosen one of those high-waisted cotton dresses to travel in, a creamy buttery color, with big tan buttons going all the way up the front. It fit her so loosely no one could tell she was pregnant, but she somehow still managed to look tidy and trim. The dress's full skirt covered most of her legs, but not those slender little ankles or the narrow feet tucked in a pair of simple leather sandals.

A tortoiseshell headband held her hair neatly back from her face. He watched the sunlight play in the golden strands and thought how pretty she looked. She was a classic, his wife, and as he watched her, he felt a jumble of emotions: tenderness and lust, confusion and resentment, anger and longing. Why did she have to go and get all temperamental on him now? One bad disposition was more than enough for any family, and that bad disposition belonged to him.

But his disposition wasn't the real problem. A couple of hours in the bedroom, and he could make her forget all about what a prick he'd been this morning, let alone any asinine ideas she had about going back to Chicago. No, the real problem lay deeper. Why did she have to tell him she loved him? Didn't she understand that once those three words were spoken, nothing could ever be the same?

If only she'd come into his life ten years earlier, before he'd had to deal with getting older and the fact that he couldn't see anything but a blank space waiting for him after he stopped playing ball. It was easy for the Professor to think about settling down. She had worthwhile work to do that would keep her busy for the rest of her life. He didn't, and now he couldn't get past the feeling that his life was careening in a direction he wasn't ready for it to take, a direction that might suit Bobby Tom Denton, but sure as hell wasn't right for him.

As he reached for the handle on the sliding glass door, he felt certain of only one thing. Jane had worked herself into a serious snit, and the best place to coax her out of it was under the sheets. But before he could get her there, he had some serious making up to do.

"Hey, Professor."

Jane turned toward Cal's voice and shaded her eyes with her hand. He was rumpled, sweat-stained, and gorgeous as he walked out on the deck. Something caught in her throat, something large and painful that made her feel as if she were choking.

He leaned on the rail and gave her a wolfish grin. "I've been working out, and I haven't had time to shower, so unless you're in the mood for some really raunchy sex, you'd better run upstairs right now and turn that water on for me."

She pushed her hands in the pockets of her dress and slowly mounted the wooden stairs. How could he behave like this when he had done something so unforgivable?

"Brian Delgado called this morning." She stepped onto the deck.

"Uh-huh. What say you get right in the shower with me so you can scrub my back?"

"Delgado sent you a report. I read it."

That finally got his attention, although he didn't look particularly alarmed. "Since when did you get interested in reading about my contracts?"

"The report's about me."

His grin vanished. "Where is it?"

"On your desk." She looked him square in the eye and tried to swallow the bubble of pain that choked her voice. "You need to make a decision about me right away because you only have two days before the Preeze board of directors meets. Luckily, your attorney's already done the initial work. He's met with Jerry Miles, and the two of them have most of the sordid details sketched out. All you need to do is sign a check with lots of zeros."

"I don't know what you're talking about."

"Don't you dare lie to me!" She balled her hands into fists. "You told Delgado to ruin me!"

"I'm going to call him right now and straighten this out. It's a misunderstanding." He turned toward the sliding doors, but she moved forward before he could open them.

"A misunderstanding?" She couldn't hide her bitterness. "You give your attorney orders to destroy my career, and you call that a misunderstanding?"

"I never told him that. Just give me an hour, and then I'll explain everything."

"Explain it now."

He seemed to realize she deserved something more, and he moved away from the door toward the deck railing. "Tell me what was in that report."

"Delgado set it up with Jerry Miles, the director of Preeze, that you'll give the labs a grant on the condition that they get rid of me." She took a deep, unsteady breath. "Jerry's waiting to hear from you before he fires me, then he's planning to announce your generosity to the board of directors when they meet on Wednesday."

Cal cursed softly under his breath. "Wait till I get hold of that son of a bitch. This isn't the first time Delgado's gone off half-cocked."

"You're saying this whole thing is his idea?"

"Damn right it is."

Emotion stuck in her throat. "Don't do this, Cal. Don't play games with me."

Outrage flashed in his eyes. "You know I wouldn't do something like this!"

"Then you didn't have him investigate me? You didn't tell him to find out where I was most vulnerable and use it against me?"

He rubbed his chin with the back of his knuckles, looking more ill at ease than she'd ever seen him. "That was a long time ago. It's complicated."

"I'm very bright. Explain it."

He wandered back toward the sliding doors, and her heart sank as she noticed he couldn't meet her eyes. "You have to remember how things were between us when all this started. I've never been a man to let anyone get the best of me, and I wanted you punished." He tucked one thumb in the waistband of his shorts, then pulled it back out again. "I did tell Brian I intended to get even, and I ordered him to have you investigated so I could strike back at you."

"And what did your investigation turn up?"

"That you don't have any dark secrets." He finally looked at her. "That you're brilliant and dedicated. And that your work means everything to you."

"You hardly needed a team of detectives to figure that out."

"I didn't know that at the time."

"So you decided to take my work away from me," she said quietly.

No!" He gripped the door handle. "After the first few weeks, I cooled off and dropped the whole thing. I let it go!"

"I don't believe you. No lawyer would put something like this into motion without authorization."

"He had my authorization. Not for this, but . . ." He pushed the door open and moved into the house. "I just never got around to telling him to back off, that's all!"

"Why is that?" she asked as she followed him.

"We just didn't talk about it." He stopped next to the fireplace. "There were a bunch of other things going on. One of my endorsements got screwed up. The whole thing was a mess, and it took a while to get straightened out. Then he went on vacation, and I ducked a couple of his calls."

"Why?"

"I wasn't in the mood to deal with contracts."

"I wasn't a contract."

"No. But I just didn't think what was happening between us was any of his damned business!" He looked frustrated. "It never occurred to me that he'd try to take action against you without my go-ahead."

"But it sounds as if you'd already given him that."

"Yes, but—" He opened his hand in a gesture that was oddly vulnerable. "Jane, I'm sorry. I didn't think for a minute he'd do anything without talking to me."

She should have felt better. After all, he hadn't been actively plotting against her this past month, but she still felt awful. "This wouldn't have happened if you'd picked up the phone and told him to call off his dogs. Why didn't you do it, Cal? Were you afraid you were going to lose your macho by backing off?"

"It just wasn't important, that's all. Things had settled down between us, and revenge was the last thing on my mind."

"Too bad you didn't let your bloodsucker know that."

He plowed his hand through his already rumpled hair. "Look, no harm's been done. I have no intention of giving Preeze a penny, and if anybody there tries to get rid of you, I'll slap them with a discrimination lawsuit so fast they won't know what hit them."

"It's my business, Cal, not yours."

"Just give me a couple of hours. I'll straighten it all out, I promise."

"And then what?" she asked quietly.

"Then you won't have to worry about anything like this again."

"That's not what I mean. After you straighten it out, what happens between us?"

"Nothing happens. Everything will be the way it was." He moved toward his study. "I'm going to make my phone calls, then I'll unload your car and we can go out to eat. I can't believe you even considered running away."

She followed him to his study, then stopped in the doorway. She rubbed her arms, but the chill she felt came from inside instead of outside. "I don't think we're going to be able to go back to the way things were."

"Sure we can." He moved toward his desk. "I swear to God, I'm going to fire Delgado."

"Don't blame him for what you started," she said softly.

He spun back toward her, his body rigid. "Don't you dare say that! *You're* the one who started this, and don't you forget it!"

"How can I when you throw it in my face every chance you get?"

He glared at her, and she glared back at him. Then she looked away. This game of assigning blame accomplished nothing.

She pushed her hands into the pockets of her dress and reminded herself that her worst fear had been groundless. He hadn't been plotting against her at the same time they were making love. But the awful knot in her stomach wouldn't go away. What had happened was merely a symbol of all the problems that lurked between them, problems she'd ignored or glossed over as if they didn't exist.

She remembered how hopeful she'd been only a few days earlier that he loved her. She remembered all the dream castles she'd built in her head. It was ironic that a person who'd been trained in the scientific method could be so swift to abandon logic for wishful thinking.

She withdrew her hands from her pockets and clasped them in front of her. "I need to know where we're headed, Cal, and what your feelings are toward me."

"What do you mean?"

The discomfort in his voice indicated that he knew exactly what she meant. "How do you feel about me?"

"You know how I feel."

"Actually, I don't."

"Then, you must not have been paying attention."

He was going to make this even more difficult than it

already was, but she wouldn't back away. The time for daydreaming had passed. She needed to know exactly where she stood. "The only direct remark I can ever remember you making is that you like me."

"Of course, I like you. You know that."

She met his eyes squarely and forced herself to speak the words that wanted to remain stuck in the back of her throat. "I told you I loved you."

His gaze dropped, and she realized he couldn't look her in the eye. "I'm— I guess I'm flattered."

She dug her fingernails into her palms. "I don't think so. I think my honesty has scared you to death. And I also think you don't love me back."

"What the hell does something like that mean anyway?" He stalked to his desk. "We've gotten along together better than either of us ever could have imagined, and we're going to have a baby. Why do we have to stick a label on it? I care about you, and in my mind that counts for a lot." He dropped down into his chair as if the discussion had come to an end.

She wouldn't leave it there. Perhaps she'd gained a bit of wisdom in the last few months, or maybe it was simply stubbornness, but it was time he added something more to this relationship than sex and a few laughs. "I'm afraid caring isn't enough for me when I think about our future."

He gestured toward her with an impatient hand. "The future will take care of itself. Neither of us wants to be boxed in right now."

"The last time we talked about it, the idea was that we'd get a divorce as soon as the baby is born. Do you still want that?"

"It's way ahead. How do I know what's going to happen?"

"But that's still your plan?"

"That was the original plan."

"And now?"

"I don't know. How can either of us know? One day at a time."

"I don't want to measure time in days any longer."

"Well, that's the way it has to be for now."

He wouldn't commit, and she could no longer accept anything less. Tears pushed at her eyes, but she refused to let them fall. She had to bail out now, while she still retained her dignity, and she intended to do it honestly.

"I'm afraid I can't handle this anymore, Cal. I didn't mean to fall in love with you—I know you didn't ask me to—but that's what happened. I seemed destined to screw up where you're concerned." She licked her dry lips. "I'm going back to Chicago."

He shot up from the desk. "Like hell you are!"

"I'll contact you after the baby's born, but until then, I'd appreciate it if you'd communicate with me through my lawyer. I promise I won't make things tough for you when it comes to visitation."

"You're running away." He glared down at her, clearly on the attack. "You don't have the guts to stay and work this out, so you want to run away."

She struggled to speak calmly. "What is there to work out? You're still going to want a divorce."

"I'm not in any hurry."

"But you're still planning on it."

"So what? We're friends, and there's no reason for it to turn nasty."

Pain swelled in her chest as he confirmed what she already knew. He didn't view their marriage as permanent. He was merely marking time. She turned away from him and walked out into the foyer.

He was beside her in an instant. A vein throbbed at his temple, and his expression was stark. She wasn't surprised. A man like Cal didn't take well to ultimatums.

"If you think I'm going to come running after you, you're wrong! Once you go out that door, our marriage is over for sure. You're out of my life, do you hear me?''

She nodded stiffly and blinked away the tears.

"I mean it, Jane!''

Without a word, she turned and walked from his house.

Cal didn't stand around to watch her drive away. Instead, he kicked the door shut and stalked into the kitchen, where he grabbed a bottle of scotch from the pantry. For a moment he couldn't make up his mind whether to drink it or smash it against the wall. He'd be damned before he let her push him into something he wasn't ready for.

He wrenched off the cap and tilted the bottle to his lips. The scotch burned all the way down. If this was the way she wanted things, then fine. He dashed the back of his hand across his lips. It was about time his life got back to normal.

But instead of feeling better, he wanted to throw back his head and howl. He took another swallow and nursed his grievances against her.

He'd offered her more than he'd ever offered any woman—he'd offered her his damned friendship!—and what did she do? She threw it right back in his face just because he didn't feel like getting down on one knee and volunteering for a life sentence picking out fucking *wall-paper*!

His hand clenched around the bottle. He wouldn't give in. There were lots of women out there who were younger and prettier, women who didn't see the need to pick fights with him over every little thing, who'd do what he said and then leave him alone. That's what he wanted. Someone young and beautiful who'd leave him alone.

He took another swig then went into his study where he set about the business of getting seriously drunk.

Jane knew she couldn't leave until she'd said good-bye to Annie. Neither could she give in to her grief right now, so she blinked her eyes and took big, shuddering gulps of air as she drove to the top of Heartache Mountain. Lynn's car wasn't in sight, and she was grateful she could say good-bye to Annie without a hostile witness.

The house looked so different from when she'd first seen it. Cal had painted it white. He'd fixed the crooked shutters and the broken step. As she entered and called out Annie's name, she pushed away the memory of the laughter they'd shared while they'd worked.

When she reached the kitchen, she saw Annie through the screen door. She was sitting outside in the sun snapping green beans from a pottery bowl on her lap. As Jane watched the rhythmic motion of Annie's gnarled fingers, she wanted to take the bowl from her and snap the beans herself. Bean snapping was one task that hadn't been influenced by technology. It was performed exactly the same way now that it had hundreds of years ago. It suddenly seemed to her that snapping those beans would bring something solid into her life, a link with all the women who had come before her, all the women throughout history who'd snapped beans and survived the heartache of men who didn't love them back.

She bit her lip, then stepped outside. Annie turned her head. " 'Bout time you decided to stop by.''

She sat down in the tubular lawn chair next to Annie and regarded the bowl that rested in her lap on top of a piece of newspaper to collect scraps. At that moment, its contents seemed precious and utterly necessary to her well-being. "Can I do those?''

"I don't like waste.''

"All right." Her hands trembled as she took the bowl. With utmost concentration, she bent her head, pulled out a bean, and carefully snapped off the ends. Apparently she didn't take off too much because Annie didn't criticize. She let the ends drop into her lap and focused on breaking the beans into bite-sized lengths.

"Those is store-bought beans. The ones from my garden'll be a lot better."

"I wish I were going to be here long enough to see them come in." Her voice sounded almost normal. A little toneless, maybe. A shade tight. But almost normal.

"They'll be ready long before Cal has to leave for trainin' camp and the two of you head back to Chicago."

Jane didn't say anything. Instead, she picked up another bean, pushed her thumbnail into the end, and tore it off.

For the next few minutes she applied herself only to the beans, while Annie watched a bluebird hop from one branch to another in her magnolia tree. But instead of bringing her peace, Annie's quiet and the warmth of the sun on her skin, along with the peaceful repetition of this woman's task, made her defenses too complicated to keep in place, and they slowly crumbled.

A tear slipped over her bottom lid, trailed down her cheek, and splashed onto the bodice of her cotton dress. Another fell and then another. A shuddering little hiccup slipped out. She continued to break the beans and stopped fighting her grief.

Annie watched the bluebird fly away and then followed the path of a squirrel in the same tree. One of Jane's tears dripped into the beans.

Annie began to hum softly under her breath. Jane finished the last bean, then searched frantically through the bowl for one she might have overlooked.

Annie reached into the pocket of her old apron, drew out a pink tissue, and handed it over. Jane blew her nose and began to speak. "I—I'm going to miss you s-so much, Annie, but I can't stand it anymore. I have to go away. H-he doesn't love me."

Annie pursed her lips with disapproval. "Calvin, he don't know what he feels."

"He's old enough to have figured it out by now." She gave her nose an angry blow.

"Never knew a man who hated getting older so much. Usually, it's women who'll fight the years."

"I couldn't leave without saying good-bye." She had to get away, and she nearly dropped the beans as she stood.

"Set those right down before you spill 'em all over the ground."

Jane did as she said. Annie struggled out of her chair. "You're a good girl, Janie Bonner. He'll come to his senses soon."

"I don't think so."

"Sometimes a wife needs a little patience."

"I'm afraid I'm fresh out." More tears rolled down her cheeks. "Besides, I'm not a real wife."

"Now that's plain nonsense."

She didn't have any words left to argue, so she wrapped the small, frail-boned woman in her arms. "Thanks for everything, Annie, but I've got to go." After a gentle hug, she pulled away and turned toward the house.

That was when she saw Lynn Bonner standing on the back step.

19

"**Y**ou're leaving my son?"

Lynn looked angry and confused as she stared at Jane. She moved down into the yard, and Jane's heart sank. Why had she stayed so long? Why hadn't she simply said her good-byes to Annie and left? She quickly turned away and dashed her hand across her damp cheek.

Annie stepped into the breach. "I got snap beans for dinner, Amber Lynn, and I'm makin' 'em with fatback whether you like it or not."

Lynn ignored her and walked toward Jane. "Tell me why you're leaving Cal."

As Jane turned to face her, she tried to slip back into the cool persona Lynn expected. "Be grateful," she managed. "I've been a terrible wife."

But those dishonest words threatened to unleash a fresh flood of tears. She'd been the best wife he'd ever have, damn it! The best wife she'd known how to be! She turned away.

"Have you?" Lynn sounded deeply troubled.

Jane had to get out of here before she completely shattered. "I have a plane to catch. It would be best if you'd talk to Cal. He can explain better."

She began moving toward the side of the house, but

she'd barely taken two steps before Lynn's astonished exclamation brought her to a halt.

"My God, you're pregnant!"

She whipped around and saw Lynn staring at her midsection. Automatically, her gaze dropped, and only then did she notice the protective hand she'd unconsciously placed there. The gesture had pressed her dress against her body and outlined her gently rounded abdomen. She snatched it away, but she was too late.

Lynn looked bewildered. "Is it Cal's?"

"Amber Lynn Glide!" Annie snapped. "Where are your manners?"

Lynn seemed more shaken than accusatory. "But how am I supposed to know if it's his or not when I don't understand anything about this marriage? I don't know what they see in each other or how they got together. I don't even know why she was crying." Her voice caught. "Something's very wrong here."

The final threads of Jane's badly frayed emotions unraveled, and as she saw the lines of suffering etched into Lynn's face, she knew she had to tell her the truth. Cal's desire to protect his parents had been well-meaning, but now it had grown destructive. If she'd learned anything in these past four months, she'd learned that deception only led to hurt.

"It's Cal's baby," she said quietly. "I'm sorry you had to find out like this."

Lynn's hurt was obvious. "But, he never— He didn't say anything. Why didn't he tell me?"

"Because he was trying to protect me."

"From what?"

"From you and Dr. Bonner. Cal didn't want either of you to find out what I'd done to him."

"Tell me!" Her expression grew as fierce as a mother lion whose cub had been threatened, never mind that her cub was now king of the jungle. "Tell me everything!"

Annie picked up the pottery bowl. "I'm goin' inside and fix my beans the way I like. Janie Bonner, you stay right here till you get this settled with Amber Lynn, you hear me?" She shuffled toward the back porch.

Jane's legs wouldn't hold her any longer, and she sank down into the lawn chair. Lynn took the other chair and sat facing Jane. Her jaw was set, her manner confrontational. Jane found herself remembering the scrappy young girl who'd baked cookies at two in the morning so she could support her husband and her baby. The expensive yellow linen dress and chunky amber jewelry didn't hide the fact that this woman knew how to fight for her own.

Jane clasped her hands in her lap. "Cal wanted to spare you and his father pain. You've been through so much this past year. He thought—" She dropped her gaze. "The bald truth is that I desperately wanted a child, and I tricked him into getting me pregnant."

"You did what?"

Jane forced her head back up. "It was wrong. Unconscionable. I didn't intend for him ever to find out."

"But he did."

She nodded.

Lynn's lips had grown thin and taut. "Whose decision was it to get married?"

"His. He threatened to take me to court and sue for custody if I didn't do what he wanted. Now that I know him better, I doubt that he'd have carried out his threat, but I believed him at the time."

Taking a deep breath, she described the morning she'd opened the door to Jodie Pulanski, then told Lynn about the men's plan for his birthday. She explained her own yearning for a child as well as her concern about finding someone to father it. She spoke without embellishment, refusing to justify her behavior in any way.

When she described her reaction to seeing Cal on television and her subsequent decision to use him, Lynn pressed her fingers to her lips, and a gasp of horror mingled with a strangled laugh that held an edge of hysteria. "Are you saying you chose Cal because you thought he was *stupid*?"

She thought about trying to explain to Lynn how he'd used *ain't* and looked so dumb and gorgeous but gave it up. There were some things a doting mother would never understand. "Obviously I misjudged him, although I didn't figure that out until several weeks after we were married."

"Everybody knows Cal is smart as a whip. How could you have believed anything else?"

"I guess some of us aren't as smart as we think we are." She continued with her story, ending with the exposure of their marriage in the media and her decision to come with him to Salvation.

Lynn's face showed a flash of anger, but to Jane's surprise, it wasn't directed at her. "Cal should have told me the truth from the beginning."

"He didn't want anyone in the family to know. He said none of you were good liars, and the story would come out if he told you."

"He didn't even take Ethan into his confidence?"

Jane shook her head. "Last Friday Ethan saw me . . . Well, he figured out that I was pregnant, but Cal swore him to secrecy until he could tell you himself."

Lynn's eyes narrowed. "There's more. This doesn't explain your hostility to us."

Jane's clasped hands cramped in her lap, and once again she had to force herself to meet Lynn's gaze. "I told you that I'd already agreed to a divorce as soon as the baby was born. You'd recently lost one daughter-in-law you cared about, and it seemed cruel to let you get attached to another. Not that you necessarily would have," she said hastily. "I know I'm not what you had in mind for Cal. But, still, it wouldn't have been right for me to barge into your family when I wasn't planning on staying."

"So you decided to behave as badly as possible."

"It—it seemed like the kindest thing to do."

"I see." Her expression gave away little, and Jane realized she was once again confronting the self-possessed woman she'd first met. She regarded Jane through steady blue eyes. "What were your feelings toward Cal?"

Jane hesitated, then skittered around the truth. "Guilt. I've done him a terrible wrong."

"People said I tricked Jim into getting me pregnant, but it wasn't true."

"You were fifteen, Lynn. I'm thirty-four. I knew exactly what I was doing."

"And now you're compounding that wrong by running out on him."

After everything she'd revealed, she would have expected her mother-in-law to be glad to be rid of her. "He's not . . . He's not ready for a permanent marriage, so it doesn't make much difference when I leave. Something came up, and I have to get back to my job. It's better this way."

"If it's better, why were you crying your eyes out?"

She felt her nostrils quiver and knew she was once again on the verge of losing control. "Don't push this, Lynn. Please."

"You've fallen in love with him, haven't you?"

She lurched to her feet. "I have to go. I promise you can have as much contact with this child as you want. I'd never try to keep your grandchild away from you."

"Do you mean that?"

"Of course."

"You won't try to keep the baby from us?"

"No."

"All right, I'm going to hold you to it." She stood. "Starting now."

"I don't understand."

"I'd like my contact with my grandchild to start now."

Her softly pitched voice belied the stubborn set of her mouth. "I don't want you to leave Salvation."

"I have to."

"So you're already breaking your word?"

Her agitation grew. "The baby's not born yet? What do you want from me?"

"I want to know who you are. Since the day we met, you've thrown up so many smoke screens I have no idea."

"You already know I tricked your son in the most underhanded, dishonest way possible. Isn't that enough?"

"It should be, but somehow it's not. I have no idea what Cal's feelings are toward you except that he's been happier than I can remember in a long time. And I also have to ask myself why Annie's so taken with you. My mother's difficult, but she's no fool. So what has she seen that I haven't?"

Jane rubbed her arms. "What you want is impossible. I won't go back to Cal."

"Then you can stay here with Annie and me."

"Here?"

"Isn't this house good enough for you?"

"It's not that." She started to say something about her job, but she couldn't muster the energy. There had been too much drama that day, and she was exhausted. The thought of driving to Asheville and getting on a plane was overwhelming.

Another bluebird lighted on the magnolia tree, and she realized that what she really wanted was to stay on Heartache Mountain. Just for a little while. Lynn was going to be her baby's grandmother, and she already knew the truth. Would it be so terrible to stay here just long enough to show her that she wasn't a bad person, simply a weak one?

Her legs felt shaky. She yearned for a cup of tea and a cookie. She wanted to watch the bluebirds in the magnolia tree and let Annie boss her around. She needed to sit in the sun and snap beans.

Lynn's eyes held both dignity and silent supplication, and Jane found herself responding to it. "All right, I'll stay. But only for a few days, and you have to promise me you won't let Cal come up here. I don't want to see him again. I can't."

"Fair enough."

"Promise me, Lynn."

"I promise."

Lynn helped her unload her suitcase and showed her into the small spare room at the back of the house that held a narrow iron bed and an old black Singer sewing machine. The walls were covered in faded yellow paper printed with blue cornflowers. Lynn left her alone to unpack, but Jane was so tired that she fell asleep, fully dressed, and didn't awaken until Lynn called her for dinner.

The meal proved to be surprisingly peaceful, despite Annie's complaints that Lynn hadn't mixed any butter in the mashed potatoes. Just as they finishing cleaning up, the telephone on the kitchen wall jangled. Lynn answered, and it didn't take Jane long to figure out who was calling.

"How was your golf trip?" Lynn twisted the phone cord around her finger. "That's too bad." She glanced at Jane and her forehead puckered. "Yes, you heard right. She's here. Yes . . . Talk to her?"

Jane shook her head and regarded her pleadingly. Annie stood up from the table where she'd been supervising the cleanup and, with a grunt of disapproval, made her way into the living room.

"I don't think Jane wants to talk right now . . . No, I can't make her come to the phone . . . I'm sorry, Cal, but I really don't know what her plans are, except that she doesn't want to see you." She scowled. "You watch your tone of voice with me, young man, and you can just pass on your own messages!"

There was a long pause, but whatever Cal said didn't seem to satisfy her because her expression grew more fierce. "That's all well and good, but you and I have a lot to talk about, including the fact that you have a wife who's four months pregnant, and you neglected to mention it!"

Time ticked by. Lynn's frown gradually eased and puzzlement took its place. "I see . . . Is that so?"

Jane was beginning to feel like an eavesdropper, so she joined Annie in the family room, where the old woman dozed on the couch while one of the evening news magazines played on television. She had just taken a seat in the rocker when Lynn came in from the kitchen.

She stopped just inside the doorway and crossed her arms over her chest. "Cal told me a different story from the one you told, Jane."

"Oh?"

"He didn't mention anything about you tricking him."

"What did he say?"

"That the two of you had a brief affair, and you got pregnant."

Jane smiled, feeling a little better for the first time all day. "That was nice of him." She looked over at Lynn. "You do know he's lying, don't you?"

Lynn gave a noncommittal shrug. "I guess for right now I'm reserving judgment about everything."

Annie's head popped up from the couch, and she scowled. "Unless either one of you's got somethin' to say that's more important than Mr. Stone Phillips, I suggest you both hush up."

They hushed up.

Later that evening after Jane had fallen asleep, Lynn sat on the couch trying to sort out her thoughts while her mother watched VH-1 with the volume muted, undoubtedly hoping one of Harry Connick, Jr.'s videos would come on. She missed Jim so much: the noises he made as he banged through the house, the soothing murmur of his voice in the middle of the night as he calmed a frantic parent on the telephone.

She missed the solid feel of that big warm body curled around her at night, even the way he always left the newspaper folded wrong side out. She missed living in her own house and being the boss of her own kitchen, but she also felt a strange kind of peace she hadn't experienced in years.

Jim was right. He'd lost the girl he'd married long ago, but she was wiser than to think he wanted that girl back. It was himself he wanted back, the way he'd been in high school, when all of life's possibilities still lay ahead of him.

As for herself, she knew there had been too many changes for her ever to be that happy, free-spirited person again. But neither was she the cool and controlled Mrs. Doctor Bonner, who had been well trained by her mother-in-law to repress all vulgar excesses of emotion.

So who was she? A woman who loved her family, that was certain. She took joy in the arts and needed these mountains around her as surely as she needed air to breathe. She was also a woman who could no longer accept second best from the man she'd loved since she was fifteen.

But Jim was proud and stubborn. By not capitulating when he'd mentioned divorce, she'd waved a red flag in his face. He never made idle threats, and if she didn't move back into the house and resume their marriage, he would get his divorce. That's the way he was, stubborn to a fault, just like his son. Both of them would break before they'd bend.

Her problems with Jim went back more than three decades, but what about Cal? She could read between the lines of what Jane had told her well enough to understand that Jane wanted a lifelong commitment, but Cal wouldn't give it to her.

What was it about her son that made him fight marriage and commitment so ferociously? He'd been raised in a loving family. Why was he so resistant to having one of his own?

Even as a very young child, competition had been everything to him. She remembered teaching him hopscotch when he was so small he'd barely been able to walk, let alone hop on one leg. She'd been little more than a child herself, and he'd been her play companion as well as her son. She'd drawn a chalk outline on the old sidewalk outside the apartment where they'd been living, and she'd never forget the sight of that bottom lip caught between his teeth, all his toddler's concentration focused on beating her. Now she suspected that the permanent ties of a wife and family had become one more symbol of the fact that the most important part of his life was coming to an end, and he had nothing to take its place.

Cal would undoubtedly have called his father right after he'd talked with her and told him about the baby. She'd been married to Jim long enough to know he'd be overjoyed at the idea of having new life in their family, and like her, he'd be concerned about Cal's happiness. Unlike her, however, he wouldn't be at all concerned about the feelings of the young woman sleeping in the spare room.

Lynn gazed over at her mother. "Cal must care about Jane, or he wouldn't have lied to me the way he did."

"Calvin loves her. He just don't know it yet."

"Neither do you. Not for a fact." Even though she'd asked for it, her mother's know-it-all attitude irritated her. Or maybe she wasn't yet ready to let go of her hurt that Annie knew Jane better than she did.

"You can believe what you want." Annie sniffed. "I know some things."

"Like what?"

"She don't put up with any of his nonsense for one. He likes that about her. She's a fighter, too, and she ain't afraid to go after him. Janie Bonner's as good as they come."

"If she's such a fighter, why is she leaving him?"

"I guess her feelin's got too much for her. She has a powerful love for that son of yours. You should see the way the two of 'em look at each other when they don't think nobody's watchin'. 'Bout set your eyeballs on fire.''

She remembered Cal's recent happiness, along with the tears in her daughter-in-law's eyes, and thought there was a good chance her mother was right.

Annie regarded her with shrewd eyes. "That baby of theirs is gonna be a smart little cuss."

"It seems inevitable."

"You ask me, it ain't good for a special child like that to grow up all by itself. Look how bein' an only child traum'tized Janie Bonner into gettin' in this predicament in the first place."

"You have a point."

"She told me she felt like a freak growin' up."

"I can see how she would."

"A child like that needs brothers and sisters."

"But the parents would have to be living under the same roof for that to happen."

"You're sure 'nough right about that." Annie leaned back in her rocker and sighed. "Seems me and you don't have much choice, Amber Lynn. Looks like we're gonna have to catch ourselves another Bonner."

Lynn smiled to herself as she walked out on the porch after her mother had gone to bed. Annie enjoyed believing the two of them had single-mindedly laid a trap for Jim. It wasn't so, but Lynn had given up trying to tell her mother that. Annie believed what she wanted to believe.

It was nearly midnight and chilly enough that she zipped the front of an ancient Wolverine sweatshirt from Cal's college playing days. She stared up at the stars and thought how much better she could see them from the top of Heartache Mountain than from their house in town.

The sound of an approaching car broke her concentration. All the men in her family were night owls, so it could only be Cal or Ethan. She hoped it was her oldest son come to claim his wife. Then she remembered her promise to

Jane that she would keep him away and frowned.

As it turned out, the car that appeared at the top of the lane didn't belong to either Cal or Ethan, but to her husband. She couldn't believe it. Not once since the night she'd left had Jim driven up here to see her.

She remembered the bitterness of their parting on Friday and wondered if he'd come to dangle the business card of his divorce lawyer in front of her. She had no idea how anybody got a divorce, beyond making an appointment with a lawyer. Was that how it happened? A person made an appointment with a lawyer, and, before they knew it, their marriage was over?

Jim got out of the car and moved toward her with that long graceful stride that had set her heart to beating for as long as she could remember. She should have expected him. Cal would have talked to him by now, and the prospect of a new grandchild would give him another excuse to browbeat her. She braced herself against one of the freshly painted posts that held up the tin roof of the porch and wished he hadn't found her so unworthy.

He came to a stop below the bottom step and gazed up at her. For a long time he said nothing—he merely studied her—but when he finally spoke, there was an odd formality in his voice. "I hope I didn't scare you showing up here so late."

"It's all right. As you can see, I'm still awake."

He dropped his gaze and for a moment she had the curious feeling he wanted to bolt, but that couldn't be so. Jim never ran from anything.

He looked up at her, and his eyes held that stubborn glint she knew so well. "I'm Jim Bonner."

She stared at him.

"I'm a doctor in town."

Had he lost his mind? "Jim, what's wrong?"

He shifted his weight as if he were nervous, but the only

time she had ever seen his confidence shaken was when
Jamie and Cherry had died.

He clasped his hands together and then immediately
dropped them to his sides. "Well, to be honest, I've got a
thirty-seven-year marriage that's on the rocks. I've been
pretty depressed about it, and instead of taking to the bottle,
I thought it might help me if I found a little female companionship." He drew a deep breath. "I heard in town there
was a nice lady living up here with her old battle-ax of a
mother, and I thought maybe I'd stop by and see if that
lady'd like to go out to dinner with me some time. Or
maybe catch a movie." A flicker of amusement caught at
the corner of his mouth. "That is if you don't have any
qualms about dating a married man."

"You're asking me out on a date?"

"Yes, ma'am. I'm kind of rusty at this sort of thing, so
I hope I'm going about it right."

She pressed her fingers to her lips, and her heart swelled.
During lunch on Friday she'd told him she wished they
could meet as strangers so they could start all over to see
if they liked each other, but he'd been so angry at the time,
she hadn't thought he'd even heard her. After all these
years, she had never imagined he could surprise her, but he
just had.

She resisted the urge to throw herself in his arms and tell
him all was forgiven. She didn't hold herself so cheaply
that this small bit of effort on his part, as much as she
appreciated it, could erase decades of not being good
enough. She wondered how far he was willing to take this.

"We may not be compatible," she replied, testing the
waters.

"Maybe not. I guess we won't be able to decide unless
we give it a try."

"I don't know. My mother might not like it."

"Now you leave your mother to me. I'm real good with
old ladies, even mean and crazy ones."

She nearly laughed. Imagine stubborn, hardheaded Jim Bonner doing something this romantic. She was charmed and touched, but not completely. Something saddened her, and it took a moment to figure out what. She'd spent most of her life feeling like a beggar for Jim's affection—always agreeable, always the one to make concessions and appease. He'd never had to put himself out for her because she'd never made any demands. She had never put a single road-block in his way, and now she was getting ready to run back to him just because he'd made one small effort to please her.

She could still remember the feel of his randy teenager's hands on her. Those first few times they'd had sex, she hadn't liked it very much, but it had never occurred to her to say no, even though she would rather have been sitting in the back booth at the drugstore sharing a Coke and gossiping about their classmates. Suddenly that made her angry. He'd hurt her when he'd taken her virginity. Not deliberately, but it had hurt nonetheless.

"I'll think about it," she said quietly. Then she gathered the sweatshirt tighter around her and went back inside.

A moment later, a spray of gravel hit the house as he peeled away, driving for all the world like an angry eighteen-year-old.

20

For two weeks, Cal stayed away from Heartache Mountain. During the first week, he got drunk three times and took a swing at Kevin, who'd refused his demand to get the hell out of Dodge. During the second week, he started to go after her half a dozen times, but his pride wouldn't let him. He wasn't the one who'd run away! He wasn't the one who'd screwed everything up with unreasonable demands.

He also had to face the fact that he wasn't absolutely sure any of those stubborn women would let him in the house. Apparently the only men welcome there were Ethan, who didn't count because he was Ethan, and Kevin Tucker, who sure as hell *did* count. Cal seethed as he thought of Tucker driving up to Heartache Mountain whenever he pleased, getting fed and fussed over, of Tucker, who somehow or another seemed to have moved into Cal's own house!

The first night Cal had gotten drunk at the Mountaineer, Tucker had swiped his keys, as if Cal weren't smart enough to have already figured out he wasn't in any condition to drive. It was the same night Cal had swung at him, but his heart hadn't been in it, and he'd missed. Next thing he knew, he was slumped in the passenger seat of Tucker's seventy-thousand-dollar Mitsubishi Spyder while Kevin drove him home, and he hadn't been able to get rid of the kid since.

He was pretty sure he hadn't told Kevin he could stay. As a matter of fact, he distinctly remembered ordering him out of his house. But Kevin had stuck around like a damned watchdog, even though he had a perfectly good rental house, not to mention Sally Terryman. The next thing Cal knew, the two of them were watching game films and he was showing Kevin how he always went to his first option instead of being patient, reading the defense, and finding the open man.

At least watching films with Kevin kept his mind off the fact that he missed the Professor so bad his teeth ached, which didn't mean he was any closer to figuring out what to do about it. He wasn't ready to be married forever and ever, not when he needed all his energy focused on playing ball, and not when he had no other life's work waiting for him. But he also wasn't nearly ready to lose Jane. Why couldn't she have left things as they were instead of making demands?

Crawling on his hands and knees up Heartache Mountain so he could beg her to come back was unthinkable. He didn't crawl for anybody. What he needed was a reason to go up there, but he couldn't think of a single one he wanted to admit out loud.

He still didn't understand why she'd stayed around instead of flying back to Chicago, but he was glad it had happened, since it was giving her time to come to her senses. She'd said she loved him, and she wouldn't have said those words if she didn't mean them. Maybe today was the day she'd be woman enough to admit her mistake and come back to him.

The door chimes sounded, but he wasn't in the mood for company, and he ignored them. He hadn't been sleeping too well or eating much more than an occasional bologna sandwich. Even Lucky Charms had lost their appeal—they held too many painful memories—so he'd been substituting coffee for breakfast. He rubbed a hand over his stubbly jaw and tried to remember how long it had been since he'd shaved; but he didn't feel like shaving. He didn't feel like doing anything except watching game films and yelling at Kevin.

The door chimes rang again, and he frowned. It couldn't be Tucker because somehow the sonovabitch had gotten a house key of his own. Maybe it was—

His heart made a queer jolt in his chest, and he banged his elbow on the doorframe as he made a dash for the foyer. But when he yanked the door open, he saw his father standing on the other side instead of the Professor.

Jim stormed in waving a supermarket tabloid folded open to an article. "Have you seen this? Maggie Lowell shoved it at me, right after I gave her a Pap. By God, if I were you, I'd sue that wife of yours for every penny she has, and if you don't do it, I will! I don't care what you say about her. I had that woman's number from the beginning, and you're too blind to see the truth." His tirade abruptly ended as he took in Cal's appearance. "What the hell have you done with yourself? You look terrible."

Cal snatched the tabloid out of his father's hand. The first thing he saw was a photograph of himself and the Professor that had been snapped at O'Hare the morning they'd left for North Carolina. He looked grim; she, dazed. But it wasn't the photograph that made his stomach drop to the bottom of his feet. It was the headline below it.

I Trapped the NFL's Best (And Dumbest) Quarterback into Marriage by Dr. Jane Darlington Bonner.

"Shit."

"You'll have a lot more to say than that when you read this piece of crap!" Jim exclaimed. "I don't care if she's pregnant or not—the woman's a compulsive liar! She says in here that she posed as a hooker and pretended to be your *birthday present* so she could get herself pregnant. How did you ever get tangled up with her?''

''It's like I told you, Dad. We had a fling, and she got pregnant. It was just one of those things.''

''Well, apparently the truth wasn't exciting enough, so she had to go and invent this outlandish story. And you know what? The people who read this rag are going to believe it's the truth. They're actually going to believe that's the way it happened.''

Cal crumpled the tabloid in his fist. He'd wanted a good excuse to go see his wife, and now he had it.

It was blissful, this life without men, or so they told themselves. Jane and Lynn lazed like cats in the sun and didn't comb their hair until noon. In the evening, they fed Annie her meat and potatoes, then smeared cottage cheese on ripe pears for themselves and called it supper. They stopped answering the phone, stopped wearing bras, and Lynn tacked a poster of a muscular young man in a Speedo to the kitchen wall. When Rod Stewart came on the radio, they danced with each other. Jane forgot her inhibitions, and her feet flew like dove's wings over the carpet.

To Jane, the rickety old house was everything a home should be. She snapped beans and filled the rooms with wildflowers. She put them in carnival glass tumblers, china bud vases, and a Bagels 2 Go commuter mug Lynn found on the top shelf. She didn't know exactly how she and Lynn had developed such an attachment to each other; maybe it was because their husbands were so much alike, and they didn't need any words of explanation to understand the other's pain.

They allowed Kevin into their women's house because he entertained them. He made them laugh and feel desirable even with pear juice trickling down their chins and seedpods caught in their hair. They let Ethan in, too, because they didn't have the heart to turn him away; but they were glad when he left since he couldn't hide his worry.

Lynn gave up her women's club meetings and coordinated outfits. She forgot to color her hair or do her nails, which grew ragged at the cuticle. Jane's computer stayed in the trunk of her Escort. Instead of trying to unlock the Theory of Everything, she spent most of her hours lying on an old wicker chaise that sat in the corner of the front porch, where she did nothing but let her baby grow.

They were blissfully happy. They told each other so every day. But then the sun would set and their conversation would begin to lag. One of them would sigh while the other stared out at the gathering dusk.

Along with the night, loneliness settled over the rickety old house on Heartache Mountain. They found themselves yearning for a heavier tread, a deeper voice. During the day, they remembered that they had been betrayed by the men they'd loved too well, but at night their house of women no longer seemed quite so blissful. They got into the habit of going to bed early to make the nights shorter and then rising at dawn.

Their days developed a pattern, and there was nothing to separate that particular morning two weeks after Jane had come to stay on Heartache Mountain from any of the others. She fed Annie her breakfast, did some chores, and took a walk. Just after she got back, a particularly bouncy tune from Mariah Carey came on VH-1, and she made Lynn stop ironing the curtains she'd washed so they could dance. Then she relaxed on the porch. By the time the lunch dishes were put away, she was ready to work in the garden.

The muscles in her arms ached as she tilled the soil between the garden rows, using a hoe to uproot the weeds that threatened her precious bean plants. The day was warm, and it would have been smarter to do this in the morning, but schedules had lost their allure for her. In the morning she had been too busy lying on the chaise growing her baby.

She straightened to rest her back and propped her palm on the handle of the hoe. The breeze caught the skirt of the old-fashioned calico print housedress she wore and whipped it against her knees. It was soft and threadbare from many washings. Annie said it had once been her favorite.

Maybe she'd get Ethan or Kevin to unload her computer if either came to visit today. Or maybe she wouldn't. What if she started to work and Rod Stewart came on the radio? She might miss a chance to dance. Or what if, while she lost herself in equations, a new crop of weeds grew up near her bean plants and threatened them with suffocation?

No. Work was not a good idea, even though Jerry Miles was almost certainly plotting behind the scenes to finish off her career. Work was definitely not a good idea when she had beans to weed, a baby to grow. Although the Theory of Everything beckoned her, she'd lost the stomach for bureaucracy. Instead, she gazed at the mountain sky and pretended it marked the boundary of her life.

That was how Cal found her. In the garden, with her palm curled over the handle of a hoe and her face lifted to the sky.

His breath caught in his throat at the sight of her standing against the sun in a faded calico housedress. Her French braid was coming undone so that blond wisps formed a corona about her head. She looked as if she were part of the sky and the earth, a joining of the elements.

Sweat and the breeze had molded the dress to her body, displaying, as clearly as if she were naked, the shape of her breasts and the hard round belly where his baby grew. She'd unfastened two of the buttons at the top of the dress's scoopy neck, and the sides fell apart in a V over a damp, dusty chest.

She was brown as a berry: her arms and legs, her dirt-smudged face, that moist V of skin that pointed to her breasts. She looked like a mountain woman, one of those strong, stoic creatures who had eked a living out of this unforgiving soil during the depression.

With her face still lifted to the sky, she wiped the back of her arm across her forehead, leaving a dirty streak in its place. His mouth went dry as the fabric stretched tight over those small high breasts and caught just beneath her rounding belly. She had never been so beautiful to him as she was at that moment, standing without any cosmetics in his grandmother's garden and looking every one of her thirty-four years.

The tabloid newspaper rustled against his thigh, and Annie's voice rang out from behind him. "You get off my land, Calvin. Nobody invited you here!"

Jane's eyes flew open, and she dropped the hoe.

He turned in time to see his father charging around the side of the house. "Put that shotgun down, you crazy old coot!"

His mother appeared on the back porch and stopped behind Annie. "Well, now, aren't we just a picture of *Psychology Today*'s Family of the Year."

His mother. Although he'd spoken to her over the phone, she'd ducked his dinner invitations, and he hadn't seen her in weeks. What had happened to her? She never used sarcasm, but her voice fairly dripped with it. Shocked, he took in the other changes.

Instead of one of her expensive casual outfits, she wore a pair of black jeans unevenly cut off at mid-thigh, along with a green knit top that he seemed to remember having last seen on his wife, although there hadn't been a dirt smudge on it at the time. Like Jane, she wore no makeup. Her hair was longer than he'd ever seen it, and untidy, with threads of gray showing up that he hadn't known were there.

He felt a flash of panic. She looked like an earth mother, not like *his* mother.

Jane, in the meantime, had dropped the hoe and marched

across the yard toward the steps. Her bare feet were tucked into dirty white Keds with slits in the sides and no shoe-laces. As he watched, she silently took her place on the porch with the other women.

Annie remained in the middle with the shotgun still aimed at his gut, his mother stood on one side of her, Jane on the other. Despite the fact that none of them were exceptionally large, he felt as if he were staring at a trio of Amazons.

Annie had drawn her eyebrows on crooked that morning, giving her a decidedly malevolent look. "You want this girl back, Calvin, you're gonna have to set yourself to a serious courtship."

"He doesn't want her back," Jim snapped. "Look what she's done." He snatched the newspaper from Cal's hand and shoved it toward the women.

Jane moved down onto the top step, took it from him, and bent her head to study the page.

Cal had never heard his father sound so bitter. "I hope you're proud of yourself," he snarled at Jane. "You set out to ruin his life, and you've done a damn good job of it."

Jane had taken in the gist of the article, and her gaze flew up to meet Cal's. He felt the impact in his chest and had to tear his eyes away. "Jane didn't have anything to do with that newspaper story, Dad."

"Her name's on the damn by-line! When are you going to stop protecting her?"

"Jane's capable of a lot of things, including being stubborn and unreasonable"—he shot her a hard-eyed look—"but she wouldn't do that."

He saw that she wasn't surprised by the way he'd come to her defense, and that pleased him. At least she trusted him a little. He watched her clutch the tabloid to her chest as if she could hide its words from the world, and he made up his mind Jodie Pulanski would pay for the pain she was causing her.

His father continued to look thunderous, and he realized he was going to have to give him at least part of the truth. He'd never tell him what Jane had done—that was nobody's business but his—but he could at least explain her behavior toward his family.

He took a protective step forward as his father closed in on her. "Are you getting regular prenatal care, or have you been too busy with your damn career to see a doctor?"

She met the old man square in the eye. "I've been seeing a doctor named Vogler."

His father gave a begrudging nod. "She's good. You just make sure you do what she tells you."

Annie's arm was starting to shake, and Cal could see the shotgun was getting too heavy for her. He caught his mother's eye. She reached out and took it away. "If anybody's going to shoot either one of them, Annie, I'll do it."

Great! His mother had turned crazy, too.

"If you don't mind," he said tightly, "I'd like to speak with my wife alone."

"That's up to her." His mother looked at Jane, who shook her head. That really pissed him off.

"Anybody home?"

The female triumvirate turned in one body, and all of them began to smile like sunbeams as his backup quarterback came strolling around the corner of the house like he owned the place.

Just when he'd thought things couldn't get worse . . .

Kevin took in the women on the porch, the two Bonner men standing below, and the shotgun. He arched his eyebrow at Cal, nodded at Jim, then moved up on the porch to join the women.

"You beautiful ladies told me I could stop by for some of that fried chicken, so I took you at your word." He leaned against the post Cal had painted only a month earlier. "How's the little guy doing today?" With a familiarity that indicated he'd done it before, he reached out and patted Jane's belly.

Cal had him off the porch and flat on the ground within seconds.

The shotgun blast nearly knocked out his eardrums. Bits of dirt flew into his face and stung his bare arms. Between the noise and the fact that the dirt had temporarily blinded him, he didn't have time to land his punch, and Kevin managed to roll out from beneath him.

"Damn, Bomber, you've done more damage to me this spring than happened all last season."

Cal swabbed the dirt from his eyes and lurched to his feet. "Keep your hands off her."

Kevin looked peeved and turned to Jane. "If he acted this way to you, it's no wonder you left him."

Cal gritted his teeth. "Jane, I'd like to talk to you. Now!"

His mother—his sweet, reasonable mother—stepped in front of her as if Jane were her kid instead of him! And his old man wasn't helping any. He just stood there looking at his mom as if he didn't understand anything.

"What are your intentions toward Jane, Cal?"

"That's between the two of us."

"Not exactly. Jane has family now to look after her."

"You're damn right she does! I'm her family."

"You didn't want her, so right now Annie and I are her family. That means we're the ones looking out for her best interests."

He saw that Jane's eyes were glued to his mother's face, and he took in her stunned, happy expression. He remembered the cold sonovabitch who'd raised her, and in spite of everything—the shotgun, his mother's desertion, even Kevin Tucker—he couldn't help but feel glad that she'd finally found herself a decent parent. If only she hadn't found *his* decent parent.

But his warmth cooled as his mother gave him the same I-mean-business look that, twenty years earlier, had meant turning over his car keys.

"Are you going to honor those wedding vows you made to Jane, or are you still planning to get rid of her after the baby's born?"

"Stop making it sound like I've got a contract out on her!" He jabbed his thumb at Tucker. "And could we discuss this in private, without Bozo here listening in?"

"He stays," Annie interjected. "I like him. And he cares about you, Calvin. Don't you, Kevin?"

"I sure do, Mrs. Glide. I care a lot." Tucker shot him a Jack Nicholson smirk, then turned to Lynn. "Besides, if he doesn't want Jane, I do."

Jane had the gall to smile.

But his mother had always been single-minded when she needed to be. "You can't have it both ways, Cal. Either Jane's your wife, or she's not. What's it going to be?"

He'd reached the end of his rope, and his temper snapped. "All right! No divorce. We'll stay goddamned married!" He glared at the three women. "There! Are you finally satisfied? Now I want to talk to my wife!"

His mother flinched. Annie shook her head and clucked her tongue. Jane gave him a look of utter contempt and swept into the house, taking the tabloid newspaper with her.

The screen door slammed, and Kevin let out a low whistle. "Damn, Bomber, maybe instead of watching all those game films, you should have been reading a few books on female psychology."

He knew he'd blown it, but he also knew he'd been pushed past the point of reason. They'd publicly humiliated him, making him look like a clown in front of his wife. With a furious glare at all of them, he spun on his heel and stalked away.

Lynn wanted to cry as she watched him disappear. Her heart went out to him, this stubborn oldest son who'd also been her play companion. He was furious with her, and she could only hope she was doing the right thing and that someday he would understand.

She expected Jim to rush after Cal. Instead, he walked the rest of the way to the porch, but he turned to Annie instead of her. Knowing his feelings about her mother, she waited for his customary display of belligerence, only to be surprised.

"Mrs. Glide, I'd like permission to take your daughter for a walk."

She caught her breath. This was the first time Jim had come to the house since that night two weeks ago when she'd turned him down. In the days that followed, she'd known she'd done the right thing, but at night when her defenses were down, she'd wished it could have been different. Never had she expected him to swallow his pride enough to repeat his performance as the polite suitor.

Annie, however, didn't seem to find anything odd about it. "You stay in sight of the house," she warned him.

A muscle ticked in his jaw, but he gave her a stiff nod.

"All right, then." Her mother's bony knuckles dug into the small of her back. "You go on now, Amber Lynn; Jim asked you nice and proper. And you be polite, not snippy like you've been with me lately."

"Yes, ma'am." Lynn moved down off the step, wanting to laugh even as she felt her eyes tear.

Jim's hand curled around her own. He gazed down at her, and the warm golden flecks in his hazel eyes suddenly reminded her how tender he'd been through her three pregnancies. When she was at her fattest, he'd kissed her belly and told her she was the most beautiful woman in the world. As her hand nestled like a small bird in his larger one, she thought how quick she was to forget the good and remember the bad.

He led her toward the path that curved into the woods.

Despite her mother's words, they were soon out of sight of the house.

"Pretty day," he said. "A little warm for May."

"Yes."

"It's quiet up here."

It astonished her that he was still willing to address her as if they'd just met. She rushed to join him in this new place where neither had ever hurt the other. "It's quiet, but I love it."

"You ever get lonely?"

"There's a lot to do."

"What?"

He turned to gaze at her, and she was struck by the intensity in his expression. He wanted to know how she spent her day! He wanted to listen to her! With a sense of delight, she told him.

"All of us get up early. I like to walk in the woods as soon as the sun's up, and when I get back, my daughter-in-law—" She faltered, then glanced at him from the corner of her eye. "Her name is Jane."

He frowned, but said nothing. They moved deeper into the woods where rhododendron and mountain laurel stretched on each side of the path, along with clusters of violets, trillium, and a burgundy carpet of galax. A pair of dogwood celebrated with a splash of white blossoms their escape from the fungus that had destroyed so many of the species in the Carolina mountains. Lynn inhaled the rich, moist scent of earth that smelled new.

"Jane has breakfast ready when I'm done walking," she went on. "My mother wants bacon and eggs, but Jane fixes whole grain pancakes or oatmeal with a little fresh fruit, so Annie is generally trying to pick a fight with her as I'm coming into the kitchen. Jane's wily, though, and she does a better job of getting her way with Annie than anyone else in my family. When breakfast is over, I listen to music and clean up the kitchen."

"What kind of music?"

He knew exactly what kind. Over the years he'd switched their various car radios from her classical stations to his country and western hundreds of times. "I love Mozart and Vivaldi, Chopin, Rachmaninoff. My daughter-in-law likes classic rock. Sometimes we dance."

"You and . . . Jane?"

"She's developed a passion for Rod Stewart." Lynn laughed. "If he comes on the radio, she makes me stop whatever I'm doing and dance with her. She's like that with some of the newer groups, too—ones you've never even heard of. Sometimes she has to dance. I don't think she did much of it when she was growing up."

"But she— I heard she's a scientist," he said cautiously.

"She is. But mostly now she says she just wants to grow her baby."

Time ticked by as he took that in. "She sounds like an unusual person."

"She's wonderful." And then, impulsively, "Would you like to come back for supper tonight so you can get to know her better?"

"Are you inviting me?" His face registered both surprise and pleasure.

"Yes. Yes, I think I am."

"All right, then. I'd like that."

They walked for a while without speaking. The path narrowed, and she moved off it, leading him toward the creek. They'd come here dozens of times when they were kids and sat side by side on an old log that had long since rotted away. Sometimes they'd simply watched the water rush over the mossy rocks, but most of the time, they'd made out. Cal had been conceived not far from here.

He cleared his throat and lowered himself onto the trunk of a yellow buckeye that had fallen along the edge of the creek bed in some forgotten storm. "You were pretty tough on my son back there."

"I know." She sat next to him, but not quite touching. "I have a grandchild to protect."

"I see."

But she could tell he didn't see at all. Just weeks ago, his uncertainty might have made him snap at her, but now he seemed more contemplative than irritated. Was he beginning to trust her?

"Do you remember that I told you my marriage was breaking up?"

She felt herself tensing. "I remember."

"It's my fault. I just want you to know that if you're thinking about . . . seeing me."

"All your fault?"

"Ninety-nine percent. I blamed her for my own short-comings and didn't even realize it." He braced his forearms on his knees and gazed at the rushing water. "For years I let myself believe I'd have become a world-famous epidemiologist if I hadn't been forced to marry so young, but it wasn't until after she left me that I figured out I was kidding myself." He clasped his hands together, those strong, healing hands that had served as the gateway for both birth and death in this county. "I would never have been happy away from these mountains. I like being a country doctor."

She was touched by the depth of emotion she heard in his voice and thought he might finally have rediscovered a part of himself that he'd lost. "What about her one percent?"

"What?" He turned his head.

"You said you were 99 percent to blame. What about her one percent?"

"Even that wasn't really her fault." She didn't know if it were a trick of the light or a reflection from the water, but his eyes seemed full of compassion. "She didn't have many advantages when she was growing up, and she never had much formal education. She says I always looked down on her because of it, and she's probably right—she is about most things—but I think now she might have made it easy for me to look down on her because, even though she's accomplished more than most people could in two lifetimes, she's never thought much of herself.''

Her mouth snapped open, but then she shut it. How could she refute what was so patently true?

For a moment she let herself contemplate how far she had come in her life. She saw all the hard work and self-discipline that had been necessary for her to become the woman she'd wanted to be. As if from a distance, she viewed who she was and found she liked what she saw. Why had it taken her so long to accept herself? Jim was right. How could she have expected him to respect her when she didn't? In her mind that accounted for more than one percent of the blame, and she told Jim so.

He shrugged. ''I guess I don't much care what the number is.'' He picked up her hand, which rested on her thigh, and ran his thumb along the ragged edge of one of her fingernails, then up over the ridge of her wedding band. He didn't look at her, and his voice held a soft, gravelly note that was filled with emotion. ''My wife is so much a part of me, she's like the breath coming into my body. I love her very much.''

His simple, emotion-filled statement shook her, and her words snagged in her throat. ''She's very lucky.''

He lifted his head and gazed at her. She recognized the moisture gathering in the corners of his eyes as tears. In thirty-seven years, she had never once seen her husband cry, not even the day they'd buried Cherry and Jamie.

''Jim . . .'' She slipped into his arms and found that old familiar place that God had created just for her out of Jim's bone and muscle and flesh. Feelings she couldn't express choked her, making her brain fuzzy, so that the next words she spoke weren't what she'd intended at all. ''You should know I don't sleep with men on the first date.''

"Is that so?" His voice was husky.

"It's because I started having sex when I was too young." She drew away from him, looked down into her lap. "I didn't want to, but I loved him so much that I didn't know how to say no."

She glanced up to see how he'd taken her statement. She didn't want to throw more guilt in his face; she merely needed him to understand how it had been.

His smile held a hint of sadness, and he brushed the corner of her mouth with his thumb. "Did it turn you against sex for life?"

"Oh, no. I was blessed with a wonderful lover. Maybe a little clumsy when he got started, but it didn't take him long to get it right." She smiled.

"I'm glad to hear that." His thumb trailed over her bottom lip. "You should know right now that I don't have a lot of sexual experience. I've only been with one woman."

"That's nice."

He pushed her hair back from her face on one side with his fingers. "Did anybody ever tell you you're beautiful? A lot messier than my wife but still a traffic-stopper."

She laughed. "I couldn't stop traffic if I had a red light in the middle of my forehead."

"That just goes to show what you know." He took her hand and drew her to her feet. As his head dipped, she realized he was going to kiss her.

The brush of his lips was gentle and familiar. He kept his body away from hers so only their mouths touched, along with their hands, which were linked at their sides. Their kiss quickly lost its gentleness and grew urgent with passion. It had been so long for them, and there was so much they needed to express that lay beyond words. But she loved his courtship and wanted more time.

He drew back as if he understood and regarded her with glazed eyes. "I—I have to get back to my office. I'm already going to be late for my afternoon appointments. And when we make love, I don't want to be rushed.''

She felt heavy-limbed and wobbly with anticipation. She tucked her hand in his as they moved back to the path.

"When you come over for dinner, maybe we'll have some time to talk, and you can tell me about your work."

A smile of pure pleasure lit his face. "I'd like that."

She realized that she couldn't remember the last time she'd asked him anything beyond a cursory, "How was your day?" This business of listening to each other was going to have to go both ways.

His smile faded, and his forehead creased. "I don't suppose I could bring my son along when I come to dinner?"

She hesitated for only a moment before she shook her head. "I'm sorry. My mother wouldn't allow it."

"Aren't you a little old to be taking orders from your mother?"

"Sometimes she has a feeling about how things should go. Right now, she has feelings about who should come to the house and who shouldn't."

"And my son isn't welcome?"

She regarded him unhappily. "I'm afraid not. I hope . . . soon. It's really in his hands, not Annie's."

His jaw set in its familiar stubborn line. "It's hard to believe you're letting an old woman who's half-crazy make decisions about something so important."

She drew him to a stop and pressed a kiss to the corner of that stubborn jaw. "Maybe she's not as crazy as you think. After all, she was the one who told me I had to take this walk with you."

"You wouldn't have done it otherwise?"

"I don't know. I have a lot at stake in my life right now, and I don't want to make a mistake. Sometimes mothers know what's best for their daughters." She regarded him levelly. "And their sons."

He shook his head, and his shoulders slumped in resignation. ''All right. I guess I know when I'm in over my head.''

She smiled and had to restrain herself from kissing him again. ''We eat early. Six o'clock.''

''I'll be there.''

21

Lynn showed Jane off to Jim that night as if she were a beloved child brought before a stranger to display her tricks. She sang Jane's praises until he began to look dazed, then shooed the two of them into the living room so they could patch up whatever differences remained between them.

As Jane took a seat in Annie's chair, the resemblance between father and son made her ache, and she wanted to move next to him on the couch and fold herself into those sturdy Cal-like arms. Instead, she drew a deep breath and told him how she had met Cal and what she had done.

"I didn't write the tabloid article," she said, when she reached the end of her story, "but nearly every word of it was true."

She expected his censure.

"I guess Ethan would have a few things to say here about divine providence being responsible for getting you and Cal together," he said.

He surprised her. "I don't know about that."

"You love Cal, don't you?"

"With all my heart." She dropped her gaze. "But that doesn't mean I'm going to be an afterthought in his life."

"I'm sorry he's giving you such a hard time. I don't

332

think he can help it. The men in our family are pretty hard-headed.'' He looked uncomfortable. ''I guess I have a confession of my own.''

''Oh?''

''I called Sherry Vogler this afternoon.''

''You called my doctor?''

''I couldn't relax about your pregnancy until I made sure everything was all right. She gave you a clean bill of health, but I couldn't bully her into telling me whether I have a grandson or a granddaughter on the way. She said you'd decided to wait, and I had to wait, too.'' He looked sheepish. ''I know I was out of line talking to her behind your back, but I don't want anything to happen to you. Are you angry?''

She thought of Cherry and Jamie and then of her own father, who'd never seemed to care at all. The next thing she knew, she was smiling. ''I'm not angry. Thanks.''

He shook his head and grinned. ''You're a nice lady, Janie Bonner. The old bat was right about you, after all.''

''I heard that!'' the old bat called from the next room.

Later that night as Jane lay sleepless in her narrow iron bed, she smiled at the memory of Annie's indignation. But her smile faded as she thought of all she would be losing when she left here: Jim and Lynn and Annie, these mountains that seemed to be more a part of her every day, and Cal. Except how could she lose something she'd never had?

She wanted to close her eyes and cry her heart out, but she punched the pillow instead and pretended it was Cal. Her anger faded, and she lay back to stare at the ceiling. What was she doing here? Was she subconsciously waiting for him to change his mind and realize he loved her? Today had shown her that wasn't going to happen.

She remembered the humiliating moment this afternoon when he'd shouted out that he would stay married. His offer had cut her to the quick. The words she'd longed to hear had been uttered on the cusp of his anger, and there hadn't been an ounce of true meaning behind them.

She made herself face the truth. He might very well come around, but it would be out of duty instead of love because he didn't feel the same way about her that she felt about him. She had to accept that and start living her life again. It was time for her to leave Heartache Mountain.

The wind had whipped up outside, and the room had grown chilly. Although it was warm under the covers, the cold seemed to have settled into her bones. She curled deeper into the bedclothes and accepted the fact that she had to leave. She'd always be thankful that she'd taken these two weeks for herself, but now she had to stop hiding and resume her life.

Miserable, she finally fell asleep, only to be jolted awake by a crash of thunder and a cold, wet hand settling over her mouth. She sucked in her breath to scream, but the hand clamped down tighter, and a deep, familiar voice whispered in her ear. "Shhh . . . It's me."

Her eyes shot open. A dark shape loomed over her. Wind and rain blew in through the window next to her bed and whipped the curtains against the wall. He eased his hand from her mouth and reached out to close the window just as a boom of thunder shook the house.

Rubber-limbed from the fright he'd given her, she struggled to sit up. "Get out!"

"Lower your voice before Medea shows up with her handmaiden."

"Don't you dare say anything bad about either one of them."

"They'd eat their own children for dinner."

This was too cruel. Why couldn't he just leave her alone? "What are you doing here?"

He planted his hands on his hips and scowled down at her. "I came to kidnap you, but it's wet and cold out there, so I'll have to do it some other time."

He lowered himself onto the straight chair that sat at the

sewing machine next to her bed. Beads of water glistened in his hair and on his nylon parka. As another flash of lightning lit the room, she saw that he was still just as unshaven and haggard-looking as he'd been this afternoon.

"You planned to kidnap me?"

"You don't seriously think I'm going to let you stay here much longer with these crazy women, do you?"

"It's none of your business what I do."

He ignored that. "I had to talk to you without those vampires listening in. For one thing, you need to stay away from town for the next few days. A couple of reporters have shown up anxious to check out that tabloid article."

So that was why he'd shown up tonight. Not to bring her a declaration of undying love, but a warning about the press. She struggled to swallow her disappointment.

"They're a bunch of bloodsuckers," he growled.

She sat higher in the pillows and met his gaze straight on. "Don't do anything to Jodie."

"Fat chance."

"I mean it."

He glared at her, and a flash of lightning picked out the hard glitter of her eyes. "You know damn well she's the one who sold that story to the tabloid."

"The damage is done, and there's nothing more she can do, so what's the point?" She pulled the quilt to her chin. "It'd be like squashing an ant. She's pitiful, and I want you to leave her alone."

"It's not in my nature to let somebody hit me without hitting them back."

She stiffened. "I know."

"All right." He sighed. "I'll leave her alone. I guess we don't have to worry too much about it anyway. Kevin held a press conference this evening, and he says he's holding another one tomorrow for the next batch of reporters who show up. Believe it or not, he's pretty much defused the whole thing."

"Kevin?"

"Your knight in shining armor." She didn't miss the bite of sarcasm in his tone. "I walked into the Mountaineer to get a beer and found him holding court with a bunch of reporters. He told them that the story was true."

"What?"

"But only up to a point. He said the two of us had been dating for months before that fateful night. According to him, the birthday thing was a surprise you'd arranged. Middle-age kinkiness, I believe he called it. I've got to say, the kid was pretty convincing. By the time he was done, even I believed that's the way it happened."

"I told you he was a sweetie."

"Oh, yeah? Well, your sweetie also made it clear that the only reason you and I started to date was because *he'd* just dumped you, and you were so upset about it he passed you on to me as a consolation prize."

"That jerk."

"My sentiments exactly."

Despite his words, he didn't sound all that upset with Kevin. He rose and pushed the chair aside. She stiffened as he sat on the edge of the bed.

"Come on home, sweetheart. You know I'm sorry about what happened before, don't you?" He closed his hand over her arm, where it lay beneath the covers. "I should have called Brian as soon as my feelings toward you changed, but I guess I wasn't ready to face what was happening. We can work it out. We just need to be alone for a while to do it."

He was breaking her heart. "There's nothing to work out."

"There's the fact that we're married, and we have a baby coming. Be reasonable, Jane. We just need a little time."

She hardened herself against the frailty inside her that made her want to agree. She refused to be another weak-willed woman victimized by her emotions. "My home is in Chicago."

"Don't say that." Once again, the edge of anger was back in his voice. "You've got a perfectly good home on the other side of this mountain."

"That place is yours, not mine."

"That's not so."

A rap sounded on the door, startling them both. Cal shot up from the edge of the bed.

"Jane?" Lynn called out. "Jane, I heard something. Are you all right?"

"I'm fine."

"I heard voices. Do you have a man in there?"

"Yes."

"Why'd you have to go and tell her that?" Cal hissed.

"Do you want him there?" Lynn asked.

Jane fought the tide of misery rising in her chest. "No."

There was a long pause. "All right, then. Come in my room. You can sleep with me."

Jane pushed back the covers.

Cal caught her arm. "Don't do this, Jane. We need to talk."

"The time's past for talking. I'm going back to Chicago tomorrow."

"You can't do that! I've been doing a lot of thinking, and I have things to tell you."

"Go tell them to somebody who cares." She jerked free and rushed from the room.

Jane was going to bolt, and Cal couldn't let it happen. Not in a million years. He loved her!

He'd learned from his father that the women got up early, so he arrived at Heartache Mountain right at dawn. He hadn't slept at all since he'd climbed back out into the rain from Jane's bedroom window last night. Now that it was too late, he saw the mistake in his strategy.

He should have told her he loved her the minute he came into her room, while he still had his hand over her mouth. Instead, he'd gone on about kidnaping and reporters, jabbering away instead of getting to the heart of the matter, the only part of what he had to say that meant anything. Maybe he'd been ashamed that it had taken him so long to figure out what should have been obvious to him for a long time.

The reality of his feelings had hit him like a lightning bolt. Yesterday afternoon he'd been struck by the truth as he'd driven hell-for-leather off the mountain right after he'd made a fool of himself by yelling out that he'd stay married. The expression on her face—the look of absolute contempt—had devastated him. Her good opinion meant more to him than any sportswriter's. She was everything to him.

Now he understood that loving her wasn't a new feeling, only his acceptance was new. Looking back, he figured he'd probably fallen in love with her when he'd tackled her in Annie's backyard that day he'd found out how old she was.

More than anything in his life, he knew he couldn't let this marriage break up. As much as the idea of ending his career scared him, it didn't scare him half as much as losing her. That meant he had to get her to listen to him, but first, he had to make certain she stayed put.

The front door of Annie's house was locked with the new dead bolt he'd installed not two weeks earlier. He figured there wasn't a chance in hell they'd open it for him, so he kicked it in and made his way to the kitchen.

Jane stood at the sink in her Goofy nightshirt with her hair all rumpled and her mouth open in an oval of surprise. As she took in his appearance, her eyes widened with alarm.

He'd caught a glimpse of himself in the mirror as he'd come through the living room, and he wasn't surprised by her reaction. With his outlaw's stubble, red eyes, and trigger-happy temper, he looked like the meanest hombre this side of the Pecos. Which was just fine with him. Let all of them know right from the beginning that he meant business.

Annie sat at the table with an old flannel shirt pulled on over pink satin pj's. She hadn't put on her makeup yet, and she looked every one of her eighty years. As he stalked across her kitchen floor, she started to sputter and struggle to her feet. He walked right past her and snatched the shotgun from its resting place in the corner.

"Consider yourselves disarmed, ladies. And nobody leaves here without my permission."

Taking the shotgun with him, he stalked back out through the front of the house to the porch, where he leaned the antique weapon against the house and slouched down into the old wooden rocker that sat near the front door. He propped his heels on the red-and-white Igloo cooler he'd brought with him. It held a six-pack of beer, a package of bologna, some frozen Milky Ways, and a loaf of Wonder bread, so they could just forget about starving him out. Then he leaned back and closed his eyes. Nobody threatened his family. Not even his own family.

Ethan showed up around eleven o'clock. Cal hadn't heard much noise from inside: some muted conversation, water running, Annie coughing. At least she wasn't smoking these days. No way would his mother and Jane let her get away with that.

Ethan stopped on the bottom step. Cal noted with disgust that he'd ironed his T-shirt again.

"What's going on here, Cal? And why's your Jeep blocking the road?" He walked up onto the porch. "I thought they wouldn't let you in the house."

"They won't. Hand over your car keys if you plan to go inside."

"My car keys?" He eyed the shotgun propped against the house.

"Jane thinks she's leaving today, but since she can't get

that rattletrap she drives out of here with my car in the way, she'll try to convince you to drive her. I'm just making sure you don't get tempted."

"I wouldn't do that to you. I hope you know that you look like a Wanted poster."

"You might not mean to give her your keys, but the Professor's nearly as smart as God. She'll figure out something."

"Don't you think you're getting just a little paranoid?"

"I know her. You don't. Hand 'em over."

With a great deal of reluctance, Ethan withdrew his car keys and passed them to Cal. "Have you thought about just sending her a couple dozen roses? It works for most men."

Cal gave a snort of disgust, got up from the rocker, and walked over to open the broken door. He stuck his head inside just long enough to call out, "Hey, Professor. The Reverend's come to visit. The same one who saw you naked as a jaybird."

Pulling back, he held the door open for Ethan to enter, then resumed his seat in the rocker. As he extracted a frozen Milky Way from the cooler, he decided his lack of principles were a match for her brains any day.

Kevin showed up an hour later. Cal knew he should thank him for the press conferences, but old habits died hard. He scowled at him instead.

"What the hell's going on, Bomber? Why are there two cars blocking the road?"

He was getting more than a little tired of explaining himself. "You don't go inside unless you hand over your keys."

Unlike Ethan, the kid didn't give him any argument. He shrugged, pitched them over, and stuck his head in the front door. "Don't shoot, ladies. It's the good guy."

With a snort, Cal crossed his arms over his chest, tucked his chin, and shut his eyes. Sooner or later she was going to have to come out and talk to him. All he had to do was wait.

At one o'clock, the old man arrived. Damn people kept coming, but nobody was leaving.

Jim jerked his head toward the road. "It looks like a parking lot."

Cal held out his hand. "Give me your keys if you want to go inside."

"Cal, this has to stop."

"I'm doing my best."

"Can't you just tell her you love her?"

"She won't give me a chance."

"I hope you know what you're doing." Jim tossed over his keys and went inside.

Cal hoped so, too, and he wasn't going to admit he had doubts. Especially not to his old man.

Cal's feelings for Jane were so clear to him now, he couldn't believe he'd ever been confused. The thought of living his life without her left him with an emptiness nothing would ever fill, not even football. If only he could forget the way he'd thrown her love back at her that day she'd left him. It was the most precious gift he'd ever received, and he'd tossed it away like week-old garbage. Now she was doing the same to him.

Despite her brief flirtation with the dark side to get herself pregnant, she had more integrity than anybody he knew, and he had to put his trust in the belief that, once she loved somebody, it would last forever. Still, when he looked the truth straight on, he knew he deserved what was happening to him because he hadn't possessed the good sense to value what God had given him. He also knew he'd sit out here for the rest of his life if that's what it took to get her back.

The afternoon dragged on. The blare of rock music coming from the backyard signaled that an impromptu party had broken out, but still Jane didn't appear to talk to him.

He smelled charcoal and heard Ethan calling out, "Gin!" At one point Kevin ran around the side of the house to catch a Frisbee somebody had thrown. Everybody seemed to be having a great time except him. He was a stranger in his own family, and they were dancing on his grave.

He straightened as he saw two figures moving through the woods on the east side of the house. For a moment he thought Jane had convinced someone to help her sneak away on foot, but just as he got ready to bolt out of the chair, he recognized his father and mother.

They stopped near an old white ash he'd climbed when he was a kid. His father pressed his mother against the trunk. She wrapped her arms around his neck, and the next thing he knew, they were going at it like a couple of teenagers.

His parents' estrangement was finally over, and he smiled for the first time in days. But his smile faded as he saw the direction his father's hands were taking and realized he was getting ready to feel up his mother!

With a shudder, he turned the rocker around. There were some things he didn't want to witness, and that was right at the top of his list.

For the next couple of hours he dozed on and off between brief visits from Kevin and Ethan, neither of whom seemed to have any idea what to talk about. Ethan settled on politics, while Kevin rather predictably picked football. His father was noticeably missing, but he didn't let himself dwell on what the old man and his mother might be doing. He heard nothing from Jane.

It was close to dusk when his mother appeared. She was badly mussed, and the redness on her neck looked suspiciously like beard burn. A bit of dried leaf clung to her hair, just behind her ear, giving further evidence that she and the old man had been doing something more than collecting wildflowers out in those woods.

She gazed down at him, and her forehead creased with

worry. "Are you hungry? Would you like me to bring you a plate of food?"

"Don't do me any favors." He knew he sounded surly, but he felt as if she had betrayed him.

"I'd invite you inside, but Annie won't allow it."

"You mean Jane won't allow it."

"You've hurt her, Cal. What do you expect her to do?"

"I expect her to come out here so we can talk."

"So you can yell at her, you mean?"

Yelling was the last thing on his mind, and he started to tell her that only to find himself once again alone on the front porch. For someone who'd set out to protect his parents from his personal life, he'd made an unholy mess of it.

Night settled over the mountain, and failure twisted at his belly. He leaned forward and dropped his head into his hands. She wasn't going to come out. How had he screwed things up so badly?

The screen door creaked on its hinges, and he looked up to see her. His boots dropped to the floor, and he straightened in the chair.

She had on the same thing she'd worn the day she'd left him: that buttery cotton dress with the big tan buttons down the front. This evening there was no headband in her hair. It fell helter-skelter around her beautiful face and looked just as it did when they'd finished making love.

She slipped her hands into the pockets. "Why are you doing this?"

He wanted to sweep her right off the porch and into the woods where he'd love her until she was the one with beard burn and dry leaves in her hair. "You're not leaving, Jane. Not without giving us a chance to work this out."

"We've had lots of chances, and we've blown every one."

"You mean *I* have. I promise you I won't blow the next one."

He rose from the rocker and moved toward her. She took an instinctive step back against the railing. He forced himself not to go any closer. He wasn't the only one who didn't like being backed into a corner.

"I love you, Jane."

If he'd expected his announcement to sweep her off her feet, he'd badly miscalculated. Instead of showing pleasure, her big, sad eyes seemed to swallow her face.

"You don't love me, Cal. Don't you see? This has turned into another game for you. Last night you finally realized that you were going to lose, but you're a champion, and losing isn't acceptable. Champions do whatever it takes to win, even saying things they don't really mean."

He stared at her, flabbergasted. She didn't believe him! How could she think this was just about winning? "You're wrong. That's not it at all. I mean what I said."

"Maybe right this second you do, but remember what happened after you saw me naked. The game was over, Cal, and you lost interest. This is the same way. If I agreed to take you back, you'd lose interest."

"I didn't lose interest after I saw you naked! Where did you get that crazy idea?" He realized he was yelling, and frustration made him want to yell even louder. Why was it so impossible for him to communicate like a normal person?

He swallowed hard and ignored the film of sweat that was breaking out on his forehead. "I love you, Jane, and once I make up my mind about something, it's made up for good. We're alike that way. Call off your watchdogs."

"They're not my watchdogs, they're yours!" Agitation showed in her expression. "I've tried to get them to leave, but they won't do it. They've got this idea that you need them. *You!* Ethan's told me all the sentimental stories from your childhood, and Kevin has described every touchdown you've ever made or even thought about making. As if I care! Your father's narrowed in on your academic accomplishments, which is the last thing I want to hear about!''

"I'll bet my mother hasn't been singing my praises."

"For a while she concentrated on the good causes you support. Then she began to explain how she used to play hopscotch with you, but she started to cry and had to walk away, so I'm not sure what she was trying to tell me."

"And Annie? What did she say?"

"That you're a spawn of Satan, and I'm better off without you."

"She did not."

"Close enough."

"Jane, I love you. I don't want you to go."

Her face twisted with pain. "Right now you love the challenge of me, but that's not enough to build a life on." She hugged herself and rubbed her arms. "These past few weeks have finally cleared the cobwebs from my brain. I don't know what I was thinking of to believe we could have a lasting relationship. It can't always be raging fights and knockdown arguments. You feed on that, but I need someone who's going to be there for me after the challenge is gone."

"For all your brains, you don't understand anything!" God, he was yelling again. He took a deep breath and lowered his voice. "Can't you just take a chance that I mean exactly what I say?"

"It's too important to take chances."

"Listen to me, Jane. This isn't about fights and challenges. I love you, and I want to stay married for the rest of our lives."

She shook her head.

Pain cut through him. He was spilling his guts, but she wasn't buying any of it. He couldn't think of a single thing that would convince her.

She spoke softly. "I'm leaving tomorrow, even if I have to use the police to get me out. Good-bye, Cal." She turned away and walked inside.

He squeezed his eyes shut as despair washed through him. He was weak-kneed and aching, just as if he'd taken a career-ending hit. Except he wasn't going to give up. Not ever.

As much as the idea of public declarations upset his sense of privacy, he couldn't think of anything else to do but take his case to the people. Clenching his jaw, he followed her inside.

22

Annie had her eyes glued to VH-1, where a Whitney Houston video mutely flickered. His parents sat on the couch holding hands and gazing at each other as if they were posing for a DeBeers anniversary ad. Ethan and Kevin had pulled kitchen chairs up to the gateleg table in the corner and were playing cards. All of them looked up at Cal as he walked in. Jane had already disappeared.

He felt foolish, but he knew that reaction came from pride, an emotion he couldn't afford right now when he needed the entire team behind him. He struggled to compose himself. "Jane doesn't think I'm serious about loving her."

Ethan and Kevin regarded him over the top of their cards. His mother's forehead creased. "Do you know that she likes to dance? Not those country and western line dances, but rock and roll."

He didn't exactly see how that was going to help him right now, but he filed it away.

"I'm sick of all this commotion!" Annie slapped the remote on the arm of her chair. "Jim Bonner, you go get Janie right this minute and make her come out. It's time things got settled around here, so I can have some peace and quiet."

"Yes, ma'am." With a flicker of a smile at his wife, Jim rose from the couch and headed toward the spare bedroom.

Jane looked up from the suitcase she'd been packing and saw Jim standing in the doorway. "What's wrong?"

"You have to come out in the living room now and face Cal."

"I already faced him, and I don't want to do it again."

"You have to. Annie says."

"No."

One eyebrow shot up. "What did you say?"

"I said no?" Unfortunately, it came out as a question instead of a statement, but there was definitely something intimidating about this man and his raised eyebrow.

"Right now I'm the closest thing you've got to a father, and I'm telling you to get yourself out there!"

Bemused, she watched as he jabbed his hand in the general direction of the living room. She couldn't help comparing the authoritarian look in his eyes with the way her own father had always regarded her, as if he were vaguely repulsed.

"No arguments. March!"

She thought about asking him if he intended to ground her if she disobeyed, but decided that wasn't a good idea. "Jim, this isn't going to work."

He walked over and pulled her into his arms for a reassuring squeeze. "He needs to have his say. He deserves that."

She rested her cheek against his shirt front. "He already had his say on the front porch a few minutes ago."

"Apparently he didn't finish." He gently pushed her away and gave her a nudge toward the door. "Go on now. I'm right behind you."

Cal looked even more dangerous in the living room than he'd looked on the porch, where the light had been dimmer. She noted his narrowed gunslinger's eyes and cattle rustler's expression. She wanted to believe that the three other men present would come to her rescue if he proved to be completely unreasonable, but she suspected that they were on his side.

Cal ignored her as she made her way to stand near the television, the farthest point in the room from the place he occupied near the kitchen door. As if she were invisible, he addressed the room's other occupants.

"Here are the facts . . . I love Jane, and she loves me. I want to stay married, and she wants to stay married. All of you are standing in the way." He fell silent.

Seconds ticked by. One after the other.

"That's it?" Ethan finally asked.

Cal nodded.

Kevin tilted his head toward her. "Hey, Jane, he says we're in the way. If we weren't here, would you go off with him?"

"No."

"Sorry, Bomber. You'll have to think of something else."

Cal glared at Kevin. "Will you get the hell out of here? This doesn't have anything to do with you. I mean it, Tucker. I want you out of here. Now!"

Jane saw that Kevin was only prepared to defy Cal so far, and he'd reached his limit. But as he began to rise, Annie's words forced him back in his seat. "He's part of this, and he stays!"

Cal turned on her. "He's not family!"

"He's the future, Calvin, the same future that you don't want to look at."

Her words seemed to infuriate him. He reached into his pocket, drew out a set of keys, and fired them at Kevin, who came slowly to his feet as he caught them.

"Sorry, Mrs. Glide, but I just remembered a previous engagement."

Jane rushed toward him, finally seeing a way out of this mess. "I'll go with you."

Everyone in the room seemed to stiffen.

"That," Kevin said, ". . . is a really bad idea."

"Sit down, Jane." Jim spoke in his firm paternal voice. "It's too late for you to get a plane out tonight, anyway, so you might as well hear Cal out. Kevin, thanks for your concern."

Kevin nodded, shot Jane a sympathetic smile, gave Cal a worried look, and left.

She sank down into a chair near Annie's. Cal stuck his hands in his pockets and cleared his throat, still addressing his family instead of her. "She thinks I only want her because she's playing hard to get, and that once the challenge is gone, I won't be interested. I told her that's not true, but she doesn't believe it."

"You do like a challenge," Lynn pointed out.

"Trust me . . . living with somebody who's trying to discover the Theory of Everything is more than enough challenge. Do you have any idea what it's like to see mathematical formulas scrawled on the front page of your newspaper first thing in the morning, or on the bottom of a grocery list when all you want to do is remember to buy beer? Or how about all over the lid of your cereal box before you even have your eyes open?"

"I never wrote on your cereal box!" Jane bolted out of the chair.

"You sure as heck did! Right across the lid of my Lucky Charms."

"You're making this up. He's making it up! I admit I sometimes doodle a bit, but—" She broke off as she remembered a morning several weeks ago when a cereal box had been the only thing available. Resuming her seat, she spoke stiffly. "That sort of thing constitutes an irritation, not a challenge."

"For your information, Professor, sometimes I can be talking right to you, and without any warning, you're gone." He splayed his hands on his hips and stalked toward her. "Physically you're standing right there in front of me, but your brain has taken off into hyperspace."

She shot up her chin. "An irritation, not a challenge."

"I'm going to kill her." Gritting his teeth, he slumped down onto the couch next to his parents and glanced over at his brother. "You see what I'm up against?"

"On the other hand," Ethan said, "she looks real good naked."

"Ethan!" Mortified, Jane turned to Lynn. "It's not the way it sounds. It was an accident."

Lynn's eyes widened. "A strange accident."

"You're getting off the subject," Annie said. "Personally, I believe Calvin. If he says he loves you, Janie Bonner, he means it."

"I believe him, too," Lynn said.

"Me, too," Jim offered.

Ethan remained silent.

Jane looked toward him as if he were her lifeline.

He regarded her with a hint of apology. "I'm sorry, Jane, but there isn't even any question about this."

She had let herself entertain the fantasy that they were her family, looking out for her best interests, but now that the chips were down, blood called out only to blood. They weren't the ones who'd wake up every morning wondering if this would be the day her husband was going to lose interest in her.

"You're all wasting your breath." Cal leaned forward, resting his lower arms on his knees and speaking in a hard flat voice. "Bottom line is, she's a scientist, and scientists require proof. That's what you want, isn't it, Jane? You want me to prove my feelings to you, just like you prove those equations you scribble all over the house."

"Love doesn't work that way," Lynn pointed out.

"She won't accept that, Mom. Jane needs something tangible to stick in her equations. And you know why that is?

Because nobody's ever really loved her before, and she doesn't believe it can happen now.''

She drew back in the chair as if he'd struck her. There was a ringing in her ears, a searing sensation inside her head.

Cal shot to his feet. ''You want proof of the way I feel? Okay, I'm going to give it to you.'' In three quick steps he was looming over her. Without warning, he swept her into his arms and carried her toward the door.

''Stop it, Cal! Put me down.''

Lynn jumped to her feet. ''Cal, this isn't a good idea.''

''I've done it your way,'' he shot back. ''Now I'm doing it mine.'' He kicked the front door open and carried her outside.

''You can't settle this with sex,'' Jane hissed. She gathered her anger around her as a shield to protect her broken heart. Why didn't he understand he couldn't use strong-arm tactics to solve something this complex? He was ripping her apart, and he didn't even seem to be aware of it.

''Who said anything about sex? Or is that wishful thinking?''

She sputtered with outrage as he bore her off the front porch and began walking toward the road. Although she wasn't close to being petite, he acted as if she weighed hardly anything. His breathing remained normal, his arms steady, even as he carried her down the road toward three cars that blocked the way.

He lowered her to the ground in front of his Jeep, pulled a batch of keys from his pocket, and threw several sets on the hood. Then he steered her toward his father's Blazer, which blocked the other two cars. ''Get in.''

''Cal, this is just postponing the inevitable.''

He pushed her inside and shut the door.

She turned her head to the window. If she wasn't careful, he would wear her down, and she would agree to stay with him. That would be disastrous. Better to endure the pain now than have to go through it again when he realized he'd made a mistake.

The Professor needs something tangible to stick in her equations. And you know why that is? Because nobody's ever really loved her before, and she doesn't believe it can happen now.

She rejected Cal's words. This was his problem, not hers. She wasn't so lacking in self-esteem that she would throw away love that was honestly offered. Maybe it was true that no one had ever really loved her, but that didn't mean she wasn't ready to grab it when the real thing came along.

Did it?

Cal turned out onto the highway, interrupting the painful path of her thoughts. "I appreciate the fact that you didn't air all our dirty linen in front of my family."

"I can't imagine there's even a piece of underwear elastic they haven't seen."

"It's okay, Jane. I won't snap your head off if you bring up the subject. I know I've done that before, but it won't happen again. It doesn't take a lot of insight to know that you see me as pretty aimless right now, and I appreciate the fact that you didn't hit me with that in front of my family."

"Aimless?"

"Just because I don't know what I'm going to do when I stop playing ball doesn't mean I'm not worthy of you. I know you might think that, but everything will change as soon as I get things figured out. I just need a little more time to sort through my options, that's all."

She stared at him, flabbergasted. This was the first time he'd acknowledged that he wouldn't be playing football forever. But what did that have to do with her feelings toward him? Not for a moment had she regarded his lack of plans for the future as a roadblock.

"I've never said I don't believe you're worthy."

"You don't have to say it. I know what you're thinking. Worthy people work."

"You work."

It was as if she hadn't spoken. "You're a physicist. That's worthy work. My father's a doctor; Ethan's a minister. The guys down at the Mountaineer are teachers, plumbers, backhoe operators. They tend bar or build houses. They work. But what am I?"

"You're a football player."

"And then what?"

She caught her breath, still unable to believe he was willing to admit his professional career was coming to an end. "Only you know the answer to that."

"But, you see, I don't know the answer. I don't have any idea what I'm going to do with the rest of my life. God knows, I've got enough money tucked away for three lifetimes, but I've never seen money as the mark of anybody's worth."

She finally understood. All along, Cal's refusal to acknowledge either his age or the fact that he'd soon be forced to retire hadn't been rooted in pigheadedness, but despair over finding work that would satisfy him.

She didn't know why she was so surprised. This was the same man who'd insisted on marrying a woman he hated just so his child would be legitimate. Beneath all that macho strut, Cal had a strong set of old-fashioned values. Those values dictated that a man without worthy work didn't deserve respect.

"Cal, there are so many things you could do. You could coach, for example."

"I'd be a terrible coach. You might not have noticed, but I don't have a lot of patience with stupidity. If I told somebody something once and he didn't get it, I wouldn't have the patience to tell him a second time. That's not the way to build a successful football team."

"What about Kevin? He says he's learned more about football from you than anyone."

"That's because he catches on the first time."

"You're very good on television. Why don't you think about broadcasting?"

"I can't work up any enthusiasm for it. Once in a while it's okay, but not for a life's work. Not for me."

"You have a degree in biology. You could use that."

"My degree is fifteen years old. I don't remember a darned thing. I only got it because I like science and the outdoors."

"You have a lot of experience in business. Maybe you could start a company."

"Business bores me. Always has. Always will." He glanced over at her, but didn't quite meet her eyes. "I've been thinking that maybe I could work on my golf game. In a couple of years, I might be able to qualify for the pro tour."

"I thought you were a mediocre golfer."

"Not exactly mediocre," he said defensively. "A little better than that." He sighed. "Never mind. Stupid idea."

"You'll think of something."

"Darn right I will, so if that's what's holding you back, put it right out of your mind. I've got no intention of spending the rest of my life lazing around and living off my money. I couldn't dishonor you like that."

He meant that he couldn't dishonor himself. She wondered how long this had been twisting away inside him? "Your future job prospects aren't what's between us, Cal. You still don't understand. I can't stand having my love tossed back in my face again. It's too painful."

He flinched. "You'll never know how sorry I am about that. I had a panic reaction. Some people take a lot longer to grow up than others, and I guess I'm one of them." He reached over and covered her hand with his. "You're the most important thing in the world to me. I know you don't believe it, but I'm going to prove it to you.''

Releasing her, he swung the Blazer into a parking place in front of the hardware store, then cursed softly under his breath. "It's closed for the night. I didn't even think about that."

"You're bringing me to the hardware store to prove you love me?"

"I promise I'll take you dancing soon. Rock and roll, not country and western." He got out of the car, came around to open the door for her, and drew her out to stand next to him. "Come on."

Completely mystified, she let him lead her into the narrow alley that ran between the pharmacy and hardware store. When they reached the back door, he tested the knob, but the door was locked. The next thing she knew, he'd kicked it in.

A security alarm shrieked.

"Cal! Have you gone crazy?"

"Pretty much." Grabbing her arm, he pulled her inside. What was he doing?

He manacled her wrist with his fingers and drew her past lawn chairs and lighting fixtures to the paint section. The alarm continued its disconcerting wail. "The police are going to come!" she exclaimed.

"Don't you worry about the police; Odell Hatcher and I have been friends for years. You just worry about whether or not we can find the right wallpaper for that kitchen of ours."

"*Wallpaper?* You brought me here to pick out *wallpaper*?"

He looked at her as if she were dull-witted. "How else am I supposed to prove my feelings for you?"

"But . . ."

"Here we are." He settled her, not ungently, onto one of the stools that lined the counter in the wallpaper department, then turned to regard the shelves, which were stocked with dozens of wallpaper books. "Damn, I didn't know it was going to be this complicated." He began reading off the shelf labels. "*Bathrooms. Dining rooms. Vinyls. Flocks.* What the hell is a flock? Don't they have something with— I don't know—horses or something? Do you see a horse category?"

"Horses?"

For the first time, a shadow of a smile tugged at the corner of his mouth, as if he were beginning to realize just how ridiculous this was. "You could help out a little bit here instead of just saying things back to me."

The wail of a police siren joined the security alarm, and tires screeched in front of the store. "Stay right here," he ordered. "I'll take care of this. On second thought, maybe you'd better crouch down behind the counter just in case Odell has his gun out."

"Gun! I swear, Calvin Bonner . . . when this is over, I'm going to—"

Her threat died on her lips as he pulled her from the stool and pushed her to her knees on the carpet behind the counter.

"Odell, it's me!" he called out. "Cal Bonner."

"Get out of the way, Cal!" a rough voice replied. "We got a robbery goin' on here. Don't tell me they took you hostage!"

"There's no robbery. I kicked in the door because I have to pick out some wallpaper. My wife's here, too, so if you've got any ideas about firing that gun you've got in your hand, forget it. Tell Harley I'll settle up with him tomorrow. And help me turn off this damned alarm."

It took Cal a good fifteen minutes, along with the appearance of Harley Crisp, the hardware store owner, before the alarm was turned off and things set straight.

While Cal was talking his way out of a breaking and entering charge, Jane got up from behind the counter and sat on the stool so she could ponder how, in Cal's mind, picking out wallpaper constituted proof of his love. She couldn't see even the smallest link. He'd been angry with her for stripping off the wallpaper, but what did replacing it have to do with love? There was certainly a link in his mind, however, and if she forced him to explain his logic, he'd give her that incredulous look that called into question the results of all the IQ tests she'd ever taken.

As confusing as this was, she did understand one thing. To Cal's way of thinking, this late-night shopping expedition proved his love, and that was that. A traitorous warmth began to sneak through her.

Harley Crisp finally closed the door behind him, taking along a sizable chunk of Cal's cash. They were left alone in the store.

Cal looked down at her with an expression that was suddenly uncertain. "You don't think all this is stupid, do you? You do understand about the wallpaper?"

She didn't have a clue, but nothing would make her admit it, not while he was gazing at her with his heart in his eyes and a forever kind of love softening his voice.

"What I really wanted to do for you, sweetheart, was win a football game," he said huskily. "Dan Calebow did that for Phoebe once, and I wanted to do it for you, except the season hasn't started yet, and winning a game wouldn't count with you. Besides, compared to this, that'd be so easy it wouldn't prove anything. I wanted to do something hard. Really hard." He waited, an expectant look on his face.

"Pick out wallpaper?" she offered tentatively.

His eyes came alive, as if she'd just given him the keys to the universe. "You do understand." With a groan, he pulled her off the stool and into his arms. "I was scared to death you wouldn't. I promise I'll figure out the work thing just as soon as I can."

"Oh, Cal . . ." Her words caught on a happy sob. She didn't have the faintest idea how he'd sorted all this out in his mind. She didn't understand about breaking into the hardware store or picking out wallpaper, but she knew this was real. Cal's feelings for her weren't about the challenge she presented to him. He was giving her his warrior's heart, and she wouldn't let those old wounds from her childhood keep her from taking it.

They gazed deeply into each other's eyes and saw a pathway into their own souls.

"It's a real marriage now, sweetheart," he whispered. "Forever and ever."

And then, right there in the hardware store, he pulled her down onto the carpet behind the counter and began making love to her. Naturally, he didn't want her wearing even a single stitch of clothes, and she felt the same about him.

When they were naked, he surprised her by reaching for his jeans. She propped herself up on one elbow and watched him withdraw a bedraggled pink bow from the pocket, its pom pom loops flattened almost, but not quite, beyond recognition.

"You kept it," she said.

He leaned forward to nuzzle her breast. "At first I had the idea of making you eat it, then I was going to tie you up with it while I let those rats nibble on you."

"Uhmm." She lay back and did some nibbling of her own. "What are you going to do with it now?"

He muttered something that sounded like, "You'll think it's stupid."

"I will not."

He drew back and gazed at her. "Promise you won't laugh."

She nodded solemnly.

"You were the best birthday present I ever got."

"Thank you."

"I wanted to give you something back, but I've got to

warn you that it's not half as good as my present. Even so, you have to keep it."

"All right."

He draped the pink bow around his neck and grinned. "Happy birthday, Rosebud."

23

"I swear, Jane, this is the craziest thing I ever let you talk me into. I don't know why I listened."

Cal had listened because he'd been jumping through hoops this past month trying to please her as she grew bigger than a house and grouchier than a bear. Even now, she wanted to bash him over the head, just on general principles. But she loved him too much. So she settled for snuggling into his big arms instead.

They sat in the back of a black stretch limousine heading for Heartache Mountain. The trees that lined the road were splashed with October's colors: yellows, oranges, and reds. This would be her first mountain autumn, and she'd been aching to see it, as well as get reacquainted with the friends she'd made before they'd had to leave Salvation. Cal and his family had dragged her to every important function, and it hadn't been long before the townspeople's resentment toward her had disappeared.

As the limo neared Salvation her anticipation grew. Cal had ordered the car because the hamstring injury that had him sidelined for the next few weeks also kept him from driving, and he wouldn't let her behind the wheel until after the baby was born. It was probably just as well. Her back was killing her from those awful airline seats, and she felt too crummy to concentrate on the mountain roads. She'd been having Braxton-Hicks contractions for several weeks, those practice contractions that lead up to the real thing, but they'd been worse than normal this afternoon.

He kissed the top of her head. She sighed and snuggled closer. If she'd needed anything more to convince her of Cal's love, these past few weeks had done it. As her pregnancy had advanced to its final week, she'd become demanding, moody, and generally bitchy. In response, he'd been unendingly affectionate and obnoxiously good-humored. Several times she'd tried to prick his temper just for the challenge of it, but instead of rising to the bait, he'd laughed at her.

Easy for him to be so happy, she thought sourly. He wasn't the one carrying around a thousand pounds of future Olympic athlete and Nobel laureate. He wasn't stuck in this oversize tent of a dress with a stupid Peter Pan collar; an aching back; nagging, unproductive contractions; and a pair of feet she hadn't seen in weeks! On the other hand, he was sidelined for the next few games, so he wasn't exactly on top of the world. Still, his injury was the reason they were able to fly home to Salvation in the middle of the season.

She reached down to rub his thigh. It wasn't his hamstring, but it was the closest thing she could comfort. Her eyes filled with ever-ready tears as she thought of the pain he'd been in on Sunday when that ignorant cretin who played for the Bears had sacked him on fourth and two. Cal had been playing a glorious game up until then, and if Jane could have gotten her hands on that Neanderthal after the game, she would have taken him apart.

Kevin had pretended to be sympathetic when Cal had been helped off the field, but Jane wasn't fooled. Kevin reveled in every moment of playing time he could get, and she knew he would make the most of the next two weeks while Cal was out. If she weren't so annoyed with him, she'd be proud of his progress this season. Even Cal was proud of him, although he'd never admit it.

Sometimes she thought Kevin spent more time at their house than he spent at his own. They had sold her home in Glen Ellyn and settled in Cal's condo until they decided where they were going to live permanently. For some reason, Cal had insisted on participating in every decision about paint color and furniture purchases, right down to throw pillows. He and Kevin had assembled the baby's crib together, and put up bright yellow shutters in the sunny second-story bedroom that was to be the nursery.

Even Kevin didn't know that Cal was going to announce his retirement at the end of the season. Cal wasn't entirely happy about it, since he still didn't know what he would do with himself, but he was tired of fighting his injuries. He also said he'd learned there were more important things in life than playing football.

"Women are not supposed to fly when they're nine months pregnant," he growled. "It's a wonder they didn't arrest me for bringing you on that plane."

"They wouldn't have dared. You celebrities can get away with anything." She gave him the pouty lip that made her feel so deliciously like a bimbo. "Yesterday I realized I couldn't stand the idea of having our baby in Chicago. I want to be near family."

He was a sucker for the pouty lip, and he nipped it between his own before he went on with his complaint. "You could have decided that a month ago, and I'd have sent you out here while it was still safe to travel."

"Then we'd have been split up, and neither of us could have stood that."

It was true. They needed each other in more ways than they could ever have imagined. Not only had they found passion together, but they'd found contentment, as well as an energy that had spilled over into their jobs. Cal was well on his way to breaking his all-time passing record, and her work had never gone better.

Just after they'd returned to Chicago, she'd been awarded the Coates' Prize in Physics for a paper she'd done on duality. Unbeknownst to her, the rumors about the prize had been circulating for weeks, making Jerry Miles's vendetta against her look foolish. In August, he'd been dismissed and replaced with one of the most respected physicists in the country, a man who had convinced Jane to take a permanent position at Preeze. He'd even gone so far as to bribe her with several eager young physicists to serve as her staff.

At that moment, however, Cal didn't have his wife's blossoming professional career on his mind, but her physical well-being, and she tried to ease his worries. "Be logical, Cal. I talked to Dr. Vogler this morning. She knows my medical history, and she's perfectly capable of delivering this baby."

"I still say you could have made up your mind about this a long time ago."

Her desire to have their baby here had grown stronger as her pregnancy advanced, but she wouldn't even consider leaving Cal behind in Chicago. His injury over the weekend had given her the chance she needed.

The baby twisted, and her spine felt as if it were being clamped by a giant fist. He'd go ballistic if he realized she was in this much pain, and she barely bit back a gasp.

It was gradually occurring to her that Cal was right, and getting on that plane had been a stupid thing to do. Still, first-time labor took forever, and Jim and Lynn would be waiting for her. Her father-in-law would tell her if he thought she should call Vogler.

Luckily, Cal was distracted and didn't notice anything wrong. "What's that on the inside of your wrist?" He picked up her hand.

She could barely catch her breath. "Uh . . . It's nothing."

She tried to snatch it away, but he held fast. "It's just a little pen mark. I must have marked myself accidentally."

"Now that's real strange. This looks a lot more like an equation than an accidental squiggle."

"We were coming in for landing," she sniffed, "and I couldn't get to my notebook." She caught her breath as the baby scored a 9.7 with a triple axel double toe loop. This time her back pain hit along with a fierce contraction that seemed to last forever, but might still only be a Braxton-Hicks. She swallowed a groan, which would really upset him, and distracted herself from the pain by trying to start a quarrel.

"You don't fight with me anymore."

"That's not true, sweetheart. We've been fighting ever since you told me we had to go on this trip."

"We've been arguing, not fighting. You haven't yelled once. You never yell anymore."

"I'm sorry, but I just can't seem to work up a good mad at you."

"Why not? Even *I* can't stand myself!"

"Crazy, isn't it. I can't explain."

She glared at him. "You're doing it again."

"What?"

"That thing that irritates me."

"Smiling?"

"Yes. That."

"Sorry." His hand settled over her drum-tight abdomen. "I'm so happy, I can't seem to stop."

"Try harder!"

She suppressed her own smile. Who would ever have thought a warrior like Cal Bonner would put up with this much nonsense? But he didn't seem to mind. Maybe he understood how wonderful it felt to be completely unreasonable and still see all that unqualified love shining back. How could she ever have doubted his feelings for her?

When Cal Bonner made up his mind he was in love, he stuck to it.

Cal had talked her out of her fear of having a brilliant child by making her understand that most of the misery in her childhood came, not from her intelligence, but from being raised by a distant, unfeeling parent. That was something their child would never have to worry about.

He leaned forward and peered out the window. "Damn!"

"What's wrong?"

"Can't you see? It's starting to rain!" His voice grew agitated. "What if we're up on that mountain and you decide to go into labor, but the road gets washed out so we can't get back down? What are we going to do then?"

"That only happens in books."

"I was crazy to let you talk me into this."

"We had to come. I told you. I want to have the baby here. And I dreamed Annie was on her deathbed."

"You called her as soon as you woke up this morning. You know she's all right."

"She sounded tired."

"She probably stayed up all night planning a new hate crime against our father."

She smiled. He always did that now. He referred to his mother and father as if they belonged to her as well. Not only had he given her his love, he'd given her his parents, too.

Emotions she couldn't control bubbled up inside her. Her smiled faded, and she started to cry. "You're the most wonderful husband in the world, and I don't deserve you."

She thought she heard a long-suffering sigh, but it could have been the hiss of tires on wet pavement.

"Would it make you feel better if I told you that I'm writing down every unreasonable thing you've done this past month, and I promise to take it out of your hide as soon as you're back to normal?"

She nodded.

He laughed and kissed her again as the limousine began to climb Heartache Mountain. "I love you, Janie Bonner. I really do. The night you barged into my house with that pink bow tied around your neck was the luckiest night of my life."

"Mine, too," she sniffed.

All the lights were on at Annie's, and Jim's red Blazer was parked in front. She'd seen her in-laws two weeks earlier when they'd flown to Chicago to watch Cal play and behaved like newlyweds the whole time. That night, Cal had thrown a pillow over his head and announced that they were buying a new guest room bed. One that didn't squeak!

She was anxious to see Jim and Lynn, and she didn't wait for the driver to open the door for her.

"Hold on, Jane! It's raining, and—"

She was already waddling toward the porch. Even though Cal was limping on his bandaged leg, he caught her elbow before she reached the steps and steadied her. The door burst open, and Lynn flew out.

"Cal, what were you thinking of? How could you have let her do this?"

Jane burst into tears. "I want to have my baby here!"

Lynn exchanged a look with Cal over the top of her head.

"The smarter they are," he murmured, "the harder those hormones hit 'em."

Jim appeared behind Lynn and hugged Jane as he drew her inside. Another spasm hit her. She groaned and sagged against him.

He caught her shoulders and pushed back far enough so he could look down at her. "Are you having contractions?"

"Some back pain, that's all. A few Braxton-Hicks."

Annie cackled from her rocker by the TV. Jane lumbered over, intending to give her a hug, but found she couldn't lean down that far. Annie squeezed her hand instead. "'Bout time you come back to see me."

"How often are you having these back pains?" Jim asked from behind her.

"Every couple of minutes, I guess." She gasped and pressed her hand to her back. *"Bugger!"*

Cal limped across the carpet. "Are you trying to tell me she's in labor now?"

"I wouldn't be surprised." Jim steered her away from Annie and sat her on the couch, where he put his hand on her abdomen and glanced at his watch.

Cal looked wild-eyed. "The county hospital's a good ten miles from here! Ten miles on these roads'll take us at least twenty minutes! Why didn't you say something, honey? Why didn't you tell me you were having contractions?"

"Because you'd rush me off to the hospital, and they'd send me home. Most of this back pain is from that airline seat, anyway. *Owww!*"

Jim checked his watch. Cal's expression was frantic. "Dad, we've got to get her off the mountain before the road washes out in the rain!"

"It's barely sprinkling, Cal," his mother pointed out, "and that road hasn't washed out in ten years. Besides, first babies take their time."

He paid no attention, darting to the door instead. "The limo's already left! We'll put her in the Blazer. You drive, Dad. I'll get in the backseat with her."

"No! I want to have our baby *here*!" Jane wailed.

Cal shot her a horrified glance. "Here!"

She sniffed and nodded.

"Wait just a minute." His voice grew dangerously low, giving her a small thrill of pleasure that penetrated her misery. "When you kept saying you wanted to have our baby *here*, I thought you meant this area in general and, more specifically, the county hospital!"

"No! I meant *here*! Annie's house." She hadn't meant any such thing until just this moment, but now she knew she couldn't find a more perfect birthing nest.

Cal's eyes reflected a weird combination of frenzy and fear as he twisted toward his father. "My God! She's on her way to becoming the most famous physicist in the country, and she's *dumb as a post*! You are *not* having your baby in this house! You're having it at the county hospital!"

"Okay." She smiled at him through her tears. "You're yelling at me."

He groaned.

Jim patted her hand. "Just to be safe, why don't you let me check you first, honey? Is that all right? Do you mind going into the bedroom so I can see how far along you are?"

"Can Cal come, too?"

"Of course."

"And Lynn? I want Lynn there."

"Lynn, too."

"And Annie."

Jim sighed. "Let's go, everybody."

Cal put his arm around her and led her toward Lynn's old room. Just as they passed through the door, a spasm hit her that was so strong she gasped and grabbed the doorframe. This one lasted forever, and only after it was over did she notice what else had happened.

"Cal?"

"What, sweetheart?"

"Look down. Are my feet wet?"

"Your feet? Are your—" He made a queer, strangled sound. "Your water broke. *Dad! Jane's water broke!*"

Jim had gone into the bathroom to wash, but Cal had yelled so loudly he had no difficulty hearing him. "All right, Cal. I'll be there in a minute. I'm sure there'll be plenty of time to get her to the hospital."

"If you're so damn sure, why do you have to check her first?"

"Just to be safe. The contractions are fairly close."

Cal's muscles went rigid. He steered her toward the double bed, while Lynn fetched a stack of towels, and Annie pulled back the wedding ring quilt. Jane refused to sit until Lynn had the bed protected, so Cal reached under her dress and pulled down the sodden brown maternity tights he'd helped her into that morning. By the time he had them off, along with her shoes and panties, Lynn had spread a piece of plastic sheeting and some towels over the bed. Cal eased her down on it.

Annie chose a whitewashed wooden chair at the side of the room and settled in to watch the proceedings. As Jim came back into the room, Jane finally absorbed the fact that he intended to give her a pelvic and began to feel embarrassed. He might be a doctor, but he was also her father-in-law.

Before she could think too much, another contraction hit, this one with double the intensity of the last. A scream slipped past her lips, and through the wrenching pain, it occurred to her that something didn't seem right. It wasn't supposed to happen this way.

Jim delivered a few softly uttered instructions to his son. Cal held her knees open during the examination. Lynn clasped her hand and hummed ''Maggie May.''

''Damn, I've got a foot,'' Jim said. ''It's a breech.''

She gave a hiss of alarm, and then another pain hit.

''Cal, get under her,'' Jim ordered. ''Hold her in your lap and keep her legs open; you're going to get wet. Jane, don't push! Lynn, run out to the car and get my bag.''

Pain and fear encompassed her. She didn't understand. What did Jim mean, he had a foot? What did her foot have to do with it? She gazed frantically at Jim as Cal leaped into the bed. ''What's happening? I can't be having the baby now. It's too fast. Something's wrong, isn't it?''

''The baby's breech,'' he replied.

She uttered a deep groan, then cried out in pain. Breech births were high-risk, and the babies were delivered by C-section in well-equipped operating rooms, not in mountain cabins. Why hadn't she insisted they drive right to the hospital. She had endangered their precious baby by coming here first.

"The head was down when she went to the doctor on Wednesday," Cal said. Ignoring his injured leg, he slid behind her.

"Sometimes they turn," Jim answered. "It's rare, but it happens."

Cal lifted her onto his lap. With her back pressed to his chest, and his legs straddling her, he clasped her knees to keep them separated.

Her baby was in trouble, and all thoughts of modesty fled. Sitting in his lap with his powerful warrior's body encircling her, she knew he would fight the world to keep their baby safe.

Jim gave Jane's knee a gentle squeeze. "This is going to go very fast, honey. Not anything like you expected. Right now I'm going to get the other foot down, and you can't push. Cal, we have to be careful of the cord in this position. Keep her from pushing."

"Breathe, sweetheart. Breathe! That's it. Just like we practiced. You're doing great."

Pain consumed her. She felt as if she were being devoured by an animal, but Cal made her breathe with him, all the time murmuring words of love and encouragement. Funny words. Tender words.

The urge to push grew stronger, impossible to resist, and horrible sounds came from her throat. She had to push!

But Cal, the leader of men, refused to let her give in. He threatened and cajoled, and she did as he said because he gave her no other choice. She panted as he ordered, then blew out great puffs of air that ended in a scream as she fought the natural instincts of her body.

"That's it!" Jim exclaimed. "That's it, honey! You're doing great."

She could no longer distinguish one pain from another. It wasn't at all like the childbirth films they'd seen, where the couple played cards and walked in the hallways, and where there was resting time between contractions.

Minutes ticked by and her world was reduced to a thick fog of pain and Cal's voice. She followed him blindly.

"Breathe! That's it! That's it, sweetheart! You're doing great." It was as if she could feel his strength passing into her body, and she drew on it.

His voice grew hoarse. "Keep breathing, honey. And open your eyes so you can see what's happening."

She looked down and saw Jim guiding the baby feetfirst from the birth canal. She and Cal cried out together as the head appeared. Ecstasy flooded through her, a sense of absolute bliss, at the sight of their child in his grandfather's strong, capable hands. Jim quickly suctioned the mouth and nose with an ear syringe Lynn handed him, then gently laid the infant on Jane's belly.

"A girl!"

The baby made a mewing sound. They reached down to touch the wet, squirming, bloody infant. Jim cut the cord.

"Cal!"

"She's ours, sweetheart."

"Oh, Cal . . ."

"God . . . She's beautiful. You're beautiful. I love you."

"I love you! Oh, I love you!"

They murmured nonsense, kissed each other, and cried. Tears streamed down Lynn's face, too, as she picked up the baby and wrapped her in a towel. Jane was so intent on the baby and her husband that she barely noticed either the fact that Jim had delivered the placenta or the broad grin on his face.

Lynn laughed and murmured nonsense of her own as she used a soft, damp washcloth to do a quick cleanup where Annie could see.

Annie Glide regarded her great-granddaughter with satisfaction. "This one's going to be a crackerjack. A real crackerjack. Just you wait and see. Glide blood runs true."

Lynn gave a watery laugh, then brought the baby back to Jane, but Cal's capable, quarterback's hands scooped her up first. "Come here, sweetheart. Let's get a good look at you."

He held the baby in front of Jane so they could drink in the sight of her tiny, wizened face together, then he dropped his lips to the miniature forehead. "Welcome to the world, sweetheart. We're so glad you're here."

Bemused and utterly at peace, Jane watched father and daughter get acquainted. She found herself remembering that moment so long ago when she'd cried out to Cal, *This is my baby! Nobody's baby but mine!* As she gazed around the room at two grandparents who looked as if they'd been handed the stars, a cantankerous great-grandmother, and a father who was falling head over heels in love even as Jane watched, she realized how wrong she had been.

Right then, she knew she'd found it. The ultimate Theory of Everything.

Cal's head shot up. "I just figured it out!" His hoot of laughter startled his newborn daughter's eyes open, but she didn't cry because she already had his number. Big, loud, softhearted. A pushover.

"Jane! Mom! Dad! I know what I'm going to do with my life!"

Jane stared at him. "What? Tell me?"

"I can't believe it!" he exclaimed. "After all this worry, it's been staring me in the face the whole time."

"Why didn't you tell me you was worried, Calvin?" a querulous voice piped up from the corner. "I could of told you what you needed to know years ago."

They turned to stare at her.

She scowled at them. "Anybody with half a brain could have figured out Calvin was destined to be a mountain doctor, just like his daddy and granddaddy afore him. Bonner blood runs true.''

"A doctor?'' Jane twisted her head and gazed at him in astonishment. "Is she right? You're going to be a doctor?''

Cal glared at his grandmother. "Don't you think you could have said something a long time ago?!''

She sniffed. "Nobody asked me.''

Jane laughed. "You're going to be a doctor? That's perfect!''

"By the time I'm done, I'm going to be an *old* doctor. You think you can handle having your husband go back to school?''

"I can't think of anything I'd enjoy more.''

At that moment Rosie Darlington Bonner decided she'd been ignored long enough. This was her big moment, darn it, and she wanted some attention! After all, she had lots to do. There were pesky little brothers to welcome into the world, friends to make, trees to climb, parents to appease, and, most of all, great novels to write.

There were also *lots* of math tests to flunk along the way, not to mention an unfortunate experience in chem lab with a cretin of a science teacher who didn't appreciate good literature. But maybe it was better the two people looking down at her with those goofy expressions on their faces didn't know about the chem lab yet . . .

Rosie Darlington Bonner opened her mouth and howled. *Here I am, world! Ready or not!*

Author's Note

It's said we're attracted to what we fear the most, and I'm beginning to believe that's true, since this is my second book that involves science and technology, an area in which I am—let's be honest—a complete doofus.

A number of books were extremely helpful in my research, even though I only understood a fraction of them, and I'd like to acknowledge the following: Paul Davies, *God and the New Physics*; James Gleick, *Chaos: Making a New Science*; Leon Lederman (with Dick Teresi), *The God Particle*. Also Mudhusree Mukerjee's article, "Explaining Everything," in *Scientific American*, January 1996, proved to be extremely useful.

Thanks to my husband, Bill, for being my viewing companion as I watched superstar Professor Richard Wolfson's sixteen-part videotaped lecture series on "Einstein's Relativity and the Quantum Revolution," produced by The Teaching Company. Professor Wolfson and Bill—God bless them both!—had a wonderful time.

A big thank you to everyone at Avon Books for their support, especially my editor, Carrie Feron, and her wonderfully competent assistant, Ann McKay Thoroman. Continued appreciation to my agent, Steven Axelrod.

A number of people were especially helpful in the preparation of this book. I'd like to acknowledge Dr. Robert Miller, Pat Hagan, Lisa Libman, my buddy Diane, and all the Phillips family cereal eaters. Speaking of cereal... Thanks Bryan, Jason, and Ty, even though you should have been studying instead. Go Boilers!

And to my readers—You'll never know how much your letters mean. Thank you.

Susan Elizabeth Phillips

Susan Elizabeth Phillips
www.susanephillips.com